Michael Slade's bestselling team of investigators return for a thrilling tale of modern horror steeped in ancient legend. Detectives Robert DeClerq and Zinc Chandler find themselves not the hunters, but the hunted, as a vicious killer plots to bring down the famed "Special X" unit.

P9-DEM-750

MICHAEL SLADE

EVIL EYE

A SIGNET BOOK

SIGNET
Published by New American Library, a division of
Penguin Putnam Inc., 375 Hudson Street,
New York, New York 10014, U.S.A.
Penguin Books Ltd, 27 Wrights Lane,
London W8 5TZ, England
Penguin Books Australia Ltd, Ringwood,
Victoria, Australia
Penguin Books Canada Ltd, 10 Alcorn Avenue,
Toronto, Ontario, Canada M4V 3B2
Penguin Books (N.Z.) Ltd, 182–190 Wairau Road,
Auckland 10, New Zealand

Penguin Books Ltd, Registered Offices:
Harmondsworth, Middlesex, England

Published by Signet, an imprint of New American Library, a division of Penguin
Putnam Inc.
Previously published in Great Britain by Hodder and Stoughton.

First Signet Printing, July 1997
15 14 13 12 11 10 9 8 7 6 5

REGISTERED TRADEMARK—MARCA REGISTRADA

PUBLISHER'S NOTE
This is a work of fiction. Names, characters, places, and incidents either are the
product of the author's imagination or are used fictitiously, and any resemblance
to actual persons, living or dead, business establishments, events, or locales is
entirely coincidental.

for the
Royal Canadian Mounted Police
the thin red line

and for
Les Wiseman,
who passed on the twist

PART I

BLACK GHOST

We're foot-slog-slog-slog-sloggin' over Africa—
Foot-foot-foot-foot-sloggin' over Africa—
(Boots-boots-boots-boots-movin' up an' down again!)
There's no discharge in the war!

—KIPLING

RORKE'S DRIFT

"Here they come!" the sentry yelled down from his outlook on the storehouse roof.

"Stand to!" the color-sergeant ordered in the yard.

A jolt of fear and tension ran through the 152 men in the makeshift army post. Around the wall of mealie bags piled waist-high to fortify the storehouse, hospital, and open yard between, click met click as Redcoats in single-breasted tunics and tropical helmets fixed twenty-two-inch bayonets to their Martini-Henry rifles. The phalanx of razor-sharp "lungers" glittered under a scorching sun. Here and there, the slouch hat and dark corduroy uniform of a Colonial volunteer broke the thin red line. Behind the perimeter, noncombatants worked feverishly to build a biscuit-box barricade across the yard as a second line of defense should the first line fail. With the sentry's warning, all eyes turned toward the Oskarberg.

The heights of Shiyane Hill—dubbed the Oskarberg in honor of Sweden's king by Reverend Otto Witt, whose mission the British had commandeered—loomed over the barricades 400 yards to the rear. Around its right flank the first Zulus appeared, a vanguard of unmarried warriors from the *iNdluyengwe* regiment who quickly took up the "beast's horns" of *impi* attack formation. Stripped to the skin for hand-to-hand combat, most wore little more than a leopard skin headband and *umutsha* loincloth. Their three-foot *umbhumbhulozu* shields were black with white patches on the lower half. Some carried rifles. Some carried knobkerrie clubs. Most carried the deadly assegai stabbing spear, called an *iklwa* from the sucking noise made when it was yanked from an enemy's body.

"How many?" Lieutenant Bromhead shouted up to the roof.

"Four thousand . . . or more, sir," the sentry yelled down.

"Nothing remains but to fight," someone said at the wall.

Eleven days earlier, Lord Chelmsford had invaded Zululand with 3,500 men, fording the Mzinyathi River here at Rorke's Drift. "Drift" is the African term for a river crossing, and this land was settled by trader James Rorke in 1849. The homestead was purchased by Reverend Witt in 1878. Rorke's store became his church, and Rorke's house his own. When Chelmsford arrived to conquer Zululand, he converted the mission into his supply depot, using the church for storage and the house as a hospital. The chapel was crammed floor to ceiling with sacks of tea, coffee, sugar, flour, and "mealie" maize, and with heavy crates of biscuits and tinned meat. The hospital had thirty patients, of whom nine couldn't move. The Zulu War had commenced the day the British forded the river, so "B" Company of the 2nd Battalion, 24th Regiment of Foot, had stayed behind to garrison the drift.

Lieutenant John Chard of the Royal Engineers was in command. Thirty-two years old, he had yet to face enemy action. Despite a noon eclipse of the sun, it was a scorching 100 degrees Fahrenheit in the shade. Sheltered in his tent down by the river, Chard was writing a letter home when two galloping horsemen thundered across the drift ninety minutes ago with shocking news. "The camp has fallen to Zulus!" they reported.

The depot ran rife with the news by the time Chard arrived. In command of "B" Company, Lieutenant Bromhead was having the yard fortified with 200-pound sacks of mealies dragged from the storehouse. Near as they could tell, the facts were: Lord Chelmsford rode out of camp with half his men to hunt for the enemy in the Mangeni Valley, and while gone the main Zulu *impi* 20,000 strong attacked those camped at the base of Isandlwana, a flat mountain resembling a lion in repose. The worst defeat suffered in any Colonial war, 1,500 British Redcoats and local troops were slaughtered ruthlessly. And now Zulus were nearing Rorke's Drift.

Laboring against the clock under a brutal sun, the 24th secured the rear of the depot facing the hill by running two ox-wagons into the gap between the storehouse and the hospital, completing the barrier with biscuit boxes and mealie bags. The only way to barricade the front of the yard was to build a rampart along the rocky incline from the hospital veranda across to the stone corral just left of the storehouse. Mealie bags piled three feet high on top of this natural ledge presented a seven-foot wall to Zulus on foot, except in front of the hospital where the slope didn't step down. The rampart was incomplete when the Zulus attacked, so nothing but a plank secured the barricade at one point. British Redcoats defending the mission were outnumbered forty to one.

Advancing at a fast run backed by the *impi* snaking around the hill, 600 *iNdluyengwe* dashed toward the rear wall. Stooped low to keep their heads down, they made the most of scant cover afforded by grass and bush, ducking behind anthills and boulders dotting the dusty slope. At several hundred yards, Redcoat marksmen crouched behind the wagons and lining the rear of both buildings opened fire, wreaths of black smoke swirling from their rifles. The Zulus were so thick it was hard to miss. The .45 slugs exacted a devastating toll, the force of impact lifting the front men off their feet to hurl them tumbling, rolling, or sprawling into the rank behind. Undaunted, those warriors leaped over the dead, charging forward. Chamber levers clicked down to eject spent casings, brass glinting as they tinkled about army boots. Volley upon riproaring volley blasted from the post. *Whizz zip,* closer came the hail of throwing spears, reinforced by shots from Brown Bess muskets on the hill. The swarming black onrush now fifty paces away, the entrenched white line braced to meet it at bayonet point. A burst of crossfire mowed the vanguard down. Rifles blazed from the storehouse to the Zulus' right. Rifles barked from the barricade dead ahead. Rifles roared from the rear of the hospital. And as if by magic, the onslaught stopped.

One of those shooting from inside the hospital was Lance-Sergeant Rex Craven of the 24th. For generations, Craven had served king and queen. John Craven helped Wolfe take Quebec from France, William Craven

fought at Waterloo, and young Rex—before his posting
here—had earned the queen's shilling in the 9th Frontier
War. Dark haired, dark eyed, with dark muttonchops
meeting his bushy dark mustache, the Lance-Sergeant
had hurt his knee during the recent invasion when a
horse crossing the Mzinyathi slipped and pinned his leg
against a rock. Invalided to the hospital, Craven cursed
fate for denying him glory in this Colonial war, unaware
the Zulus would bring the war to him. Zulus take no
prisoners and dismember the dead, so nothing truly remained for Craven but to fight and die.

Unable to reach the rear wall in the teeth of such
crossfire, the *iNdluyengwe* circled the hospital in a wide
sweep with senior men of the *uThulwana, uDloko,* and
iNdlondlo regiments close on their heels. Those with rifles stayed out back and went to ground, taking cover
behind the cookhouse and ovens, or wriggling through
the bloody grass to gain a shallow ditch. Leaning against
the door frame to favor his hurt knee, Craven sniped
these skirmishers.

The defenders' Achilles' heel was the front of the hospital. Fearless of the point-blank fire, the Zulus stormed
the incomplete barricade to engage the whites hand-to-
hand. Bromhead's men met the charge with their bayonets. Spikes rattled on shields, assegais clattered with
gun barrels, as blacks threw themselves against the mealie bags. Stabbing and slashing the defenders, some
scaled the waist-high wall while others clawed the barricade in an attempt to pull it down. Redcoats parried,
jabbed, and thrust with bloody lungers. They rammed
rifle butts and threw left hooks to drive back blacks. The
24th was a Welsh regiment, so Cymric voices shouted
warnings and encouragement as African voices returned
the battle cry "*uSuthu*!"

The sentry slid off the storehouse roof to reinforce
the barricade. He shot an attacker rushing the porch.
Dropping his spear, a six-foot Zulu grabbed the private's
empty rifle, left hand gripping the muzzle and right the
bayonet, yanking and pushing alternatively to wrench
away the gun. The Redcoat clung to the small of the
butt while his other hand fed the chamber a live round,
enabling him to blow a point-blank hole through the
warrior.

Now the senior *uDloko* and *uThulwana* charged the front. Against this tide of red shields with white spots and white shields with black patches Bromhead massed a counterattack. Zulus clashed their spears against their shields, then rushed the wall in an all-out assault. One behind the other, the Redcoats formed two firing lines. At Bromhead's order, the front rank fired and reloaded, the back rank stepping through them to fire in turn. Step after step the relentless phalanx drove forward, forcing the Zulus back to the bushes where they regrouped and charged again. Back and forth, the fight for the hospital raged, the veranda drenched in blood and littered with corpses.

The post was soon surrounded on all sides by Zulus. Though armed with antiquated guns spitting musket balls blown by powder horns, African snipers on Shiyane Hill picked the Redcoats off. The Oskarberg overlooked the yard between the buildings, so those manning the front rampart had their backs exposed. Smoky air above hummed as shots zipped in. Birds flitted through the haze with vultures hovering higher up, waiting to pick the bones. Lieutenant Chard was constantly on the move, eyes along the perimeter so he could shift men to quell developing trouble.

The yard between the two buildings was proving too dangerous to hold. Chard gave orders to fall back to the inner line, the biscuit-box barricade bisecting the yard. Shoulder to shoulder, here the Redcoats could concentrate their fire, backed by the storehouse to protect them from the hill.

No sooner did the British withdraw from the veranda than the Africans overran the hospital. They banged their spears against the wooden doors, and grabbed the rifles of defenders shooting at them through loopholes. Thick smoke billowed from the far side of the building, where the Zulus set fire to the thatch roof. Abandoned to battle the besiegers on their own, Lance-Sergeant Craven and the other patients were trapped within the burning infirmary.

SKINHEAD

New Westminster, British Columbia
Tuesday, December 7, 1993

Sheriff's deputies on the third floor of the Law Courts removed a skinhead from the cells for transport to FPI on a psychiatric remand. The German's blond hair was shaved to the scalp, his blue eyes pinpoints of paranoid psychosis. Rings from his ears and nose were sealed in the envelope of personal effects that would accompany him to the Forensic Psychiatric Institute. Pierce holes marred pale Aryan flesh stretched over Teutonic bones with angles as sharp as if chipped by a chisel. Black swastikas were tattooed down one arm, and a Celtic Cross on the other shoulder trailed the runic symbol of Viking Youth. The skinhead wore a black leather jacket with silver studs, fatigue pants, and steel-toed boots. Only half a dozen teeth remained in his mouth, exposed each time he snarled "*Knochenpolizei!*"

Police handcuff behind and sheriffs cuff in front. The DS who snapped steel around the skinhead's wrists was double-cursed with the name Ernie Costello. Both he and his partner Bert Polk wore dark brown pants, light brown shirts, dark brown windbreakers, and brown peaked caps. Not only did the uniform attract "Brownies," but teamed with Bert, Ernie was half of the "*Sesame Street* Boys." As if that wasn't bad enough, Deputy Doug Abbott was a Brownie, too. The team was either Bert & Ernie or Abbott & Costello.

"*Knochenpolizei!*" the skinhead sneered as he was caged in back of the brown Chevy Caprice with sheriff's decals on the doors.

"What's that mean?" Bert asked over the roof from the driver's side.

"Bone Police," Ernie said, opening the passenger's door.

Both deputies thought the M (short for mental) was more a danger to himself than them. Yes, he'd assaulted the arresting officers, kicking and screaming "*Knochen-polizei!*" like a nut, but after a "hold doc" shot in the arm, drugs had calmed him down. Obviously the M was one sick fuck, lost in a weird world of Bone Police, so Bert & Ernie didn't "suitcase" him with wrists and ankles joined. The regular jail-run deputies packed guns, but not those on special FPI trips. And so on this misty day at twilight, the car left the Law Courts loading bay.

Mike in hand, Ernie broadcast to home base. "Ten-eight, ten-seventeen," he said. "New West to FPI, with one male mental patient."

Bert watched the skinhead in the rearview mirror. "Spooky guy. Kraut, huh? What kinda beef?"

"B and E," Ernie said, replacing the mike. "Sporting goods. Caught in the act. Tripped the silent alarm. New West cops found him gathering loot. Thermal coat, polar tent, Arctic stuff. Second he saw the uniforms, he went berserk."

"Name?"

"Don't know. Wouldn't give it. No ID. Won't speak English. Fingerprints wired to Germany. Till they call, he's John Doe, mystery man."

"How'd he get into the country?"

Ernie shrugged. "Had a passport? Smuggled in? The coast leaks like a sieve."

"Arctic stuff?" Bert wondered. "Why would he steal that?"

The haze off the water was more Scotch mist than fog. The route took them along the Fraser River. The oncoming headlights were haloed beams whitening drop-lets suspended in the gloom. River boats moaned their foghorns while rumbling trains idled in Burlington Station. Smokestacks by the river belched white fumes, polluting under cover of dark to fool the populace.

The Trans-Canada Highway was clogged with traffic creeping east from Vancouver to Fraser Valley bedroom towns. They crossed on the overpass, then turned right on the Lougheed Highway, driving parallel to the rush-hour jam. Wedged between the highways was Colony Farm.

Bert drove down Colony Farm Road overhung by tow-

ering elm trees, the eeriest and loneliest mile in Coquitlam. The encircling hills were carpeted with monster
houses, but here on the flatlands between the Fraser and
Coquitlam rivers time had stood still since 1905, when
the province acquired 1,000 acres to establish a colony
for mental outcasts. Covered by a mat of grass, thistle,
and bramble, the fields on both sides of the road had
not been plowed for decades.

A mile ahead stood FPI, the Riverside unit for the
criminally insane, a dual-winged brick building brown-
gray and cream, with blue bars on the windows and
crows cawing from the eaves. Involuntary home of those
judges think too sick to be thrown into jail, men confined
by the grills have butchered, raped, mutilated, and eaten
victims. Bert thought it odd a black-on-white sign read
CAUTION, PATIENTS ON ROAD & GROUNDS.

The car passed from one lamp pool to the next, the
posted speed 25 kph, dim bulbs far apart since the road
was rarely used after dark, nothing else down here but
FPI with its back to dikes along the water. Winter runs
to Riverside gave Bert the creeps.

Again he eyed the skinhead in the rearview mirror.
"What earned the Kraut a psych remand, Ern?"

"Clicked his heels and gave Doddering Dodd a *Sieg
heil.*"

"No shit?"

"Judge asked how he intended to plead to the B and
E and assaults. He replied '*Knochenpolizei!*' and '*Endlö-
sung!*' Interpreter translated that as 'Bone Police' and
'Final Solution.' That was enough for Old Man Dodd.
Did you know he fought Rommel at El Alamein?"

"The Desert Fox and Doddering Dodd? The judge's
so feeble he can barely climb to the bench. What's all
the fuss about Bone Police?"

"Beats me," Ernie said, twisting in his seat. "The
guy's a neo-Nazi nut who should be . . . Christ, Bert!
The M's having a fit!"

The skinhead had vanished from the rearview mirror.
As Bert craned around to peer through the plastic
shield, Ernie grabbed the mike to alert home base. "New
West from Ninety-One. We got a ten-eighteen medical
problem. Male M's having a seizure in back. Advise FPI
our ETA is two or three minutes."

Bert scrambled out and opened the rear door of the car. The skinhead was thrashing on the seat and mewling like an epileptic. "Drag him out," Ernie cried, rushing around the back to the driver's side. "Could be the M's swallowed his tongue."

"Right," Bert said, trying to get a grip on either jerking leg.

Schreck means terror in German, and this German was terrified. Mind throbbing insanely from the squeezing of his brain, Schreck sat in back of the sheriff's car with handcuffs biting his wrists, fearing the skeletons plotting his death. The Bone Police beyond the plastic shield wore brown caps and windbreakers with crests on both shoulders. Several times the driver watched him in the mirror, the eye sockets of his skull baleful black holes. When they turned to conspire, Schreck faced the zigzag seams of their cranial bones. As they conversed, he heard the squeak of fleshless hinged jaws. Skeletal fingers on the steering wheel, the driver drove the car down a long deserted road.

Sweat trickling from his brow made Günter Schreck blink.

Every time he closed his eyes his mind screened a memory on his shut lids. The memory was from East Germany before the Wall came down, when he was arrested by People's Police for Nazi Thought Crimes. Ravenscrag was the cold stone asylum where they sleep-deprived him for days, then dragged him to the Red Room and strapped him naked to a tilted table. A doctor in a white lab coat smeared something greasy on his temples before affixing electrodes to both offending sites. Thirty times more juice than normal electroshock therapy, the jolt was so strong he jumped like a live fish in a frying pan, eyes bugging out of his head as flesh burned from the faces of the watching cops.

Opening his eyes, Schreck gazed ahead down Colony Farm Road.

Closing his eyes, he relived the jolts of the Red Room, and saw the flesh burn off the cops to expose the Bone Police.

Opening his eyes, he watched the skeleton driving

speak, reading lipless teeth that mouthed the word
"*Elektroschock*."

Closing his eyes, Schreck began to convulse. Electric
jolts surged through his psychotic mind. Falling sideways
on the seat in back of the sheriff's car, he thrashed until
his leg was grabbed and one of the skeletons dragged
him out. They were going to kill him here. That's why
they drove down this deserted road. Left foot held by
the Bone cop and right foot free, he kicked the skull in
the nose and drove splintered bones back into the black
holes of its eyes.

Blood gushing from his nose, Bert dropped to the
tarmac.

Schreck's steel-toed boot kicked again, walloping
Ernie between the legs, crumpling him by his partner as
the skinhead got out of the car.

Bone Police could only be killed by crushing their
skulls, so Schreck stomped his boot up and down on
both heads, collapsing the bones in on themselves until
each face was one black hole instead of two hollow eyes,
the blood of both men mingling to stream fingers across
the road.

The skinhead tugged the handcuff key from Ernie's
Pro Carry belt. He unlocked the shackles and threw
them away. A coyote skulking nearby howled. Free,
Schreck tossed back his head and werewolf howled, too.
Then he ran east across the misty fields, toward the Co-
quitlam River dividing Colony Farm, beyond which
Mary Hill rose to Dora Craven's home.

RED SERGE

Coquitlam

Corporal Nick Craven was telling a speeding ticket
joke. The five-minute warning had summoned the
Mounties to their tables, and now they stood behind
their chairs in ranks across the room, parallel lines of

Red Serge like in a barracks mess, ready for the head table to be piped in, the Regimental Dinner about to start. As they waited, the Horsemen joshed.

"So there I am," Nick said, "fresh out of Depot, a day or two at my first post in southern Alberta, idling by a speed trap just north of the border, Interstate Fifteen crossing the line from Montana, when *whoosh!* this Caddy streaks by at 160 klicks an hour. Sign by the road says the speed's 100."

"I see what's coming," the Mad Dog said.

"This is *my* story. You'll get your turn, Ed. So on goes the siren and on goes the lights, and pedal to the metal I creep up on his ass. We're both barreling from Coutts to Milk River, and damn if the guy isn't waving at me in the rearview mirror. Finally, I inch alongside and thumb him over. It takes about half a mile for both cars to stop.

"Ticket book out, I approach the driver's door and note the plate's from Texas. Big blue Caddy convertible from the gas-guzzling years. Grinning behind the wheel is Lyndon Johnson. Not the real Johnson, but his lookalike. Ten-gallon hat, string tie, steer horn clasp, the works. Beside him's a Dale Evans clone, flowery cowgirl shirt and jeans tucked into boots, heavy makeup caking her eyes. 'Sir,' I say, 'any idea how fast you were going?'

" 'Sure do,' he says. 'Ah love yer country, son. We ain't had freedom like this Down South fer too many years.' "

"That's a Texas accent?" the Mad Dog scoffed. "You sound like Foghorn Leghorn, that rooster cartoon. Give 'm the blue?"

"Didn't have the heart. He was disillusioned when I explained our speed was in kilometers, not miles per hour. I warned him and suggested he drive German autobahns."

"That's a traffic joke?" the Mad Dog sniggered. "I saw the punch line a mile . . . a *klick* away. Me, I'm on the Lougheed a few years back, driving up-Valley for an ERT conference, when I spot this car ahead weaving down the road. First it crosses the centerline, then veers onto the shoulder, back and forth, got to be one of the best impaireds I've snagged, so on goes the wail and wigwags to pull the drunk over."

The Mad Dog scanned the table to see if any female Members were in earshot.

"Sitting behind the wheel is a naked broad, poking the best set of tits you ever did see, not a stitch to hide the buff before my eyes, except a flimsy G-string around one ankle."

"Don't tell me," Craven said, "you asked her to blow?" The Mounties chuckled at the breathalyzer double entendre.

"No, she told me to give her the ticket fast. Said she had a job stripping in a local bar, and having been late three times that week, she'd been warned once more and the boss would kick her out the door. Due onstage in five minutes, that's why she was changing costume in the car. Told me to try swapping undies for a G-string with my foot on the gas."

"Give 'er the blue?"

"Didn't have the heart. I drove her to work Code three while she changed in my car."

The Mounties this end of the table guffawed.

"Her name?" Nick asked.

"Brittany Starr."

"Why do I get the feeling there's more to the tale than—"

The wheeze of bagpipes filling cut Craven short as all eyes turned to face the entrance hall. The droning noise became tunes of glory to pipe the head table into the banquet room. The Royal Canadian Mounted Police has its roots in the British Colonial Army. As with so much Canadian history, the origin of the Force lies in fear of the States. Canada as a country was two years old when Yankee whiskey traders crossed the border to build Fort Whoop-Up in Alberta. From Winnipeg to the Rockies, the plains were unsettled, so after the British Colonial Army crushed the Manitoba Rebellion of 1870, Lieutenant Blake mushed west by dog sled to report on conditions. To keep Americans south of the 49th Parallel, he recommended forming the North-West Mounted Police. The Force was recruited in 1873 and dispatched on the Great March West to wipe out Fort Whoop-Up. Because the trek was through Indian land, the Mounties were issued the scarlet tunic, since both the Cree and Blackfoot respected Queen Victoria's Redcoats. Whoop-Up traders hightailed it before the Force arrived, and Fort Macleod was hewed to raise the Union Jack. After a war campaign, Scottish regiments hold a dinner at which commanders are piped in to show they survived. The North-West (Royal Canadian) Mounted Police maintains that kilted tradition.

Inspector Jack MacDougall was the officer blowing the bag. He wore the red-and-black tartan of his Highland clan. Because Coquitlam Detachment was hosting this Regimental Dinner to honor the new deputy commissioner of "E" Division, the OIC of the local Mounties should have followed the piper. The officer in charge, however, had been called out to Colony Farm where two sheriff's deputies were stomped to death two hours ago, so following MacDougall were Deputy Commissioner Eric Chan, Chief Superintendent Robert DeClercq, and Inspector Zinc Chandler.

Special X—the Special External Section of the RCMP—had grown to become the elite unit in the Force. Special X cops investigated crimes with links outside Canada, so cases took its Members around the world. Chief Superintendent Robert DeClercq was in command. Before his promotion to commanding officer of all Mounties in B.C., Inspector Eric Chan was head of Special X Administration. Inspector Jack MacDougall was head of Special X Operations. Inspector Zinc Chandler had just returned from sick leave, having been stabbed in the back during the Ripper case.

The stirring shrill of the Scottish march filled the vaulted lodge, rising from the banquet tables lined with Red Serge, up beyond both balconies on the second floor, through cedar beams and arched trusses to echo down from the peak. The procession wound by a red brick fireplace surmounted by the huge, stuffed bison head of the Force, flanked by RCMP flags and red-and-blue banners. Up and down the standing ranks they snaked, past the Mad Dog and Corporal Craven, until they reached the head table along one side of the room. The music wailed through Dutch doors across from the fireplace, over the stone veranda outside and the turquoise swimming pool, down the rocky knoll to Oliver Road where Evil Eye sat listening in a parked car.

Listening to the bagpipes and the African voice in the box.

The box on the passenger's seat of the Ford.

When Harry L. Jenkins left the United States in 1904 to make his fortune as a lumber baron in B.C., he named his 1650-acre Coquitlam farm "Minnekhada" for the Minikahda Golf Club in Minneapolis. The Sioux Indian term means "beside running waters." In 1932, another lumber magnate bought the farm and nearby knolls to build a Tudor-style Scottish hunting lodge. He became lieutenant governor in 1936, so royalty—including the queen—graced the banquet room of tonight's Regimental Dinner, back when a pet monkey fetched bananas from a fruit bowl on the table. Nestled between the broad reaches of the Pitt River and the sweeping slopes of Burke Mountain, Minnekhada was the perfect marsh shoot. In 1958, a second lieutenant governor bought the lodge. Guests supplied with walkie-talkies blasted waterfowl, while drinks mixed in a cabin extended bar service into the great outdoors. Donning black ties or fancy gowns after dark, the hunters dined in style on game prepared by starched cooks and maids. The province acquired this retreat in 1975, so except for dress-ups like tonight's Red Serge Dinner, Minnekhada, tucked away in northeast Coquitlam, was now the sanctuary of beaver, bear, deer, fox, bullfrog, and eagle.

A low-slung sliver of moon smiled a reflection off the misty Pitt River.

Evil Eye scanned binoculars across Addington Marsh to Minnekhada Lodge.

The black hump of Burke Mountain loomed behind the knoll.

Under the Jacobean roof and wall dormers, Mounties stood inside the Dutch doors and veranda windows, Chan and MacDougall having locked arms to snap back drams of Scotch, the traditional way the Mounted's CO "pays the piper."

The muffled voice from the box on the passenger's seat grew more insistent.

REX LANCELOT CRAVEN was carved into the ebony lid.

Engraved on the plaque below was RORKE'S DRIFT.

The African voice from the box urged Evil Eye to club and gut a Redcoat.

KU KLUX KLAN

Every Mountie has a reason why he or she became a cop.

Rachel Kidd's reason was the Ku Klux Klan.

Born in Birmingham, Alabama, Rachel was a fetus in her mother's womb that horrible night in 1957 when her father was abducted by four racists in ghostlike sheets and pointed hoods. They drove him to a deserted waste and lit a burning cross. The Klansmen castrated her dad with a razor blade, then passed his severed testicles around in a paper cup so each could raise half his hood ashed gray by the burning cross to spit on the emasculated black's manhood. They staked him to the ground to pour kerosene on his wound, and left her dad screaming at the foot of the cross.

The cops who investigated were Klansmen, too.

Soon as her dad could travel, the Kidds moved to Seattle.

Rachel's mom was from a nine-kid family. To have a similar brood was her maternal instinct. Within a year she left her eunuch husband for a Boeing technician who played baritone sax. Rachel spent every Sunday with her deserted dad.

In July 1970, father and daughter picnicked at Peace Arch Park on the weekend after both Independence and Dominion days. Marking the border between the States and Canada was a towering white arch etched CHILDREN OF A COMMON MOTHER flying both flags. North and South were on parade for a joint celebration with all the hoopla, color, and folderol each nation could muster. The honor guard on her side was blue, and looked like those shown on the evening news about My Lai, Kent State, and the gassing and clubbing of blacks demanding civil rights. The mounted guard on their side was red, dressed in the snazziest uniform Kidd had ever seen: brown felt flat-brim Stetson hat, high-neck scarlet tunic with a white lanyard and cross-chest Sam Browne belt, blue breeches with a yellow stripe, brown riding gauntlets and boots with spurs, gleaming buttons, badges, and insignia with all the glamour and dash of the high noon of Empire and dominance of the British over "lesser breeds without the Law."

"What's over there?" Rachel asked, pointing across the border.

"That," said her father, disgust in his voice, "is where those against establishing the American Colony of Vietnam are going. That was the end of the Underground Railway for fugitive slaves."

Rachel was twelve and searching for something true to believe in.

Dazzled by the Redcoats, she thought, *I'll become one of them.*

The grass is always greener . . .

The first problem she encountered was females were barred from the Force. But by the time she came of age that had changed. The next problem she encountered was recruiting standards favored a college degree. So Kidd applied to Simon Fraser University and enrolled in the School of Criminology. The last problem she encountered was citizenship: to keep Yankee traitors out, only Canadians may recruit. The Force has its roots in the British Colonial Army.

Attending SFU on the outskirts of Vancouver, Kidd shared a basement suite with two undergrads, a Jamaican woman majoring in English, and a Caucasian gay studying Biology. A *Canadian* Caucasian gay.

"Tony," she said, one day while they were cooking spaghetti. "Ever thought of marriage?"

Tony blinked. "No," he replied.

"I've been thinking of a marriage of convenience, so I can join the Mounted Police. Know any countrymen whose marriage prospects wouldn't be ruined by marrying me?"

"Uh-oh," Tony said.

The marriage was a sham to get her citizenship, so it was ironic the marriage became a moral union in fact when Tony contracted a virus on an Amazon trek, disease turning him into a living skeleton as doctors scratched their heads and friends shunned the plague, only Rachel—"in sickness and health"—to see him to the end. A month after she scattered Tony's ashes on his favorite mountain, the Force—on a "visible minority" recruitment drive—selected her for the next troop into Depot Division.

Kidd was in the Mounted.

"So what's the occasion?" her father asked, dining with Rachel last night at the Oyster Bar on Chuckanut Drive in Washington State, halfway between Seattle and Vancouver.

"You're shucking oysters with *Corporal* Kidd of the Mounted Police."

"Sounds like you're in the army, not a cop."

"Dad, I'm the first black to get this rank."

"But are you happy?"

"It was rough when I first joined, but the Force is changing fast. The white prairie boy recruit days are history. Women made it into the commissioned ranks last year."

"What's that?"

"Inspector and above."

"Ranks between you and them?"

"Sergeant and Staff Sergeant."

"Sounds more like the army every second." A wry smile curled his lips. "All that effort whuppin' Redcoat butts so my only child could join and climb their ranks."

Corporal Rachel Kidd's first shift on duty in her new rank began at seven P.M. With Coquitlam Detachment hosting tonight's dinner at Minnekhada Lodge, only a skeleton crew manned the office on Christmas Way. Every available Member called out to the killings of Bert and Ernie on Colony Farm Road, Kidd arrived at work to find GIS deserted.

The sign on the door read 247 GENERAL INVEST. SEC- TION. A box with items from her desk in Burglary Detail under one arm, Kidd paused in the corridor outside to savor the moment, then walked into the short entrance hall of the bull pen. To punks, the cops in GIS were "the bulls," and for a moment she wondered if that made her a "cow"? The bull pen's shape was a lopsided T: the entrance hall the stem, the stubby arm to the left the glassed-in office of Staff Sergeant Tipple, the man in charge of all Plainclothes Members. The main room oc-

cupied the fat arm of the T angling right, with desks and
chairs for nine GIS bulls. Rachel approached her new
post beside the staff's overlooking window, and dropped
the box on the desk to stake her claim.

As Kidd sat filling the drawers with personal odds and
ends, along the corridor outside in the Operations Communications Center, a call came in.

"Coquitlam RCMP, GRC," the switchboard answered.

"Something is wrong at my neighbor's," the caller
said.

The line was transferred to a complaint taker at the
next post.

"Name?" the c.t. asked.

"Winifred Parker."

"Address?"

A number on Mary Hill Road.

"Problem?"

"I'm the local Block Watch rep. My neighbor's home
and won't answer the phone. Her house backs on Colony Farm. With this nut on the loose, I'm afraid to
check."

"Neighbor's name and address?"

The caller gave both.

The c.t. passed the complaint to the dispatcher at the
next post, and the dispatcher sent a patrol car to Mary
Hill Road.

Alone in GIS, Kidd surveyed her new digs. Her back
toward the staff's window, she faced the far end of the
right T-arm. Two paired partners' desks lined each side,
with a ninth desk in the entrance hall. Above the bulle-
tin board beside the face-to-face corporals' posts, a
round clock ticked time over her head.

Tick tock . . .

Tick tock . . .

Traitor, she thought.

Of all Canadian institutions, the Mounted is most sacred. With lineups from East to West jostling to get in,
Canadians want it reserved for *true* Canadians, not a
Southern buttinsky like her. The undercurrent *traitor*
would always flow from them. Hard to know which was
the biggest albatross: being a woman, being black, or
being American. Dad, on the other hand, thought her a
traitor, too. American whites had taken his balls, but

love-it-or-leave-it remained, and she had left it for a foreign frontier. Dad was flummoxed by her belief a politician should never be head of state, because every politician ends up spattered with shit. The Queen had seen Truman, Eisenhower, Kennedy, Johnson, Nixon, Ford, Carter, Reagan, Bush, and Clinton through, and *still* had her good name. Charles had dropped the Ming vase. Charles had fumbled the ball. So hopefully Charles would stand aside for his unsullied son. But meanwhile, there was the constant Queen, and the unbending ethic of her Mounted Police: Do anything to damage the honor of this Force, and we won't close ranks around you, we'll throw you to the wolves. *Sorry, Dad, but if my frontier makes me a traitor to both countries, then a double traitor I will be.*

Now all she needed was a good murder case.

Commissioner Kidd.

It had a nice ring.

At 7:25 P.M., in the OCC along the corridor, the dispatcher got a call from the patrol car. He conveyed the report to the radio room constable, who briefed the watch commander, then called GIS.

A phone in the bull pen rang.

Rachel picked it up.

"Consta . . . Corporal Kidd," she said. "GIS."

Coquitlam is the Indian word for "smelling of fish slime." Tourist brochures say it means "river of little red fish." When Hanging Judge Begbie arrived in 1858 to found the Mainland Colony of B.C., he was followed by Colonel Moody and 400 Royal Engineers charged with selecting a site for construction of the Imperial capital. Vying with New Westminster for the Royal City location was a hill farther upstream where the muddy Fraser joined the Coquitlam River. Moody chose "the first high ground on the north" bank instead of the second, then as a consolation named the rejected heights after his wife. Thus Mary's (later Mary) Hill.

West of the Coquitlam River is the City of Coquitlam. East of the Coquitlam River is the City of Port Coquitlam. The flatlands on both banks are Colony Farm. Colony Farm climbs the slope to Mary Hill Road, the upper side of which was recently denuded of trees when it was ravished by gang housing known as Citadel Heights. Hugging the Colony Farm curb was an old peaked pioneer home, in front of which Rachel Kidd parked by two patrol cars with red-and-blue wigwags flashing.

A female constable left the porch to brief Kidd by the driver's door.

"The house is locked, Corporal. Front and back. No sign of forced entry we can find."

"Did you break in?"

"No. Looked in the kitchen window. You can see the body on the floor by the sink. Her skull's crushed. No way she isn't dead."

"Possible the killer's still inside?"

"Maybe. The porch angles around three sides of the house. I've been at this corner watching two walls. Constable Stekl's kitty-corner, eyeing the other two. No sounds from within."

"Ident's coming," Kidd said. "Stay where you were and let's keep it sealed. Who responded first? You or Stekl?"

"Stekl," the patrol cop replied.

From Mary Hill Road to the front porch was perhaps fifty feet. The green-and-white house was single-story with an attic peak, built on a stone foundation with no cellar. The windows flanking the front door were dark, but light glowed from the kitchen at back. The porch rounded the left side of the house, where the constable stopped while Kidd pressed on. Her view ahead was down the hill across the Coquitlam River bisecting Colony Farm, the Lougheed Highway off to the right by Riverview Hospital, FPI off to the left by the junction of the rivers, and connecting them Colony Farm Road lined with flashing police cars like those parked here. Between this house and the crime scene where Bert and Ernie were murdered stretched a mile of misty murky muddy marsh.

"Don't shoot," Kidd said, rounding the rear, where another constable stood by the far shadowed corner. "No sign of anyone inside?"

"Nothing," said Stekl.

The back door was solid wood, cat scratched below but with no jimmy marks. The window to the right threw light onto the porch, and looked into a kitchen as cozy as could be. A cast-iron stove squatted beside a modern range, with a basket of wood ready to feed the firebox. Against the far wall separating the kitchen from the front parlor stood a Formica table under a fading photo of a girl feeding pigs. Crumpled between this table and the sink beneath the window through which Kidd peered, the body of a woman lay blood-pooled on the floor, face twisted sideways to expose the back of her head smashed in like a soft-boiled egg.

"You first on the scene?"

"Yeah," Stekl replied.

"Anyone hanging about?"

"Not a soul."

"Who called it in?"

"Woman named Parker. Lives in the house across the road."

"Speak to her?"

"Yeah. She knows the victim well. Says Dora Craven lived here thirty-five years."

"By herself?"

"Seventeen years. Before that, eighteen years with her son."

"One kid?"

"Yep."

"Better check him out."

"I doubt he'll be a suspect," the constable said. "Dora Craven's son is Corporal Nick Craven of Special X."

BLACK & WHITE

Jack MacDougall viewed the Mounted as his Canadian clan. Just as the tartan he donned to pipe in Chan symbolized his Highland heritage, so Red Serge proclaimed his allegiance here. For him the camaraderie in this room was as good as it gets. The cheerful copper glow of the fire burnished the rustic wood decor as Members flushed by spirits and wine swapped tales of skirmishes along the thin red line. Once the DC and MacDougall had "paid the piper" by downing a dram, "Grace Before Meat" was said by Inspector Zinc Chandler, followed by roast beef and Yorkshire pudding from the two large gas ovens with bread warmers in the lodge kitchen. Tradition held the commanding officer personally serve the most junior Member, so Chan carried a plate from the head table and placed it before a constable just weeks out of training at Regina's Depot Division. The lights were dimmed when dessert was brought in, mincemeat haloed by blue brandy flames, and cooled with custard or vanilla ice cream. A bottle of port was served to De-Clercq as impromptu host for his okay on potability, a ritual he performed with flourish and a nod of his head. The bottle sent to each table was passed to the left, hand to hand for custom was it must not touch down. Glasses filled, six bars of "God Save the Queen" were played, then Jack MacDougall gave the Loyal Toast.

"The Queen!" replied the Force, glasses high.

Jack took advantage of the coffee and cigars break to change his tartan for Red Serge. Having piped Chan in as a Scot, he'd pipe him out as a Redcoat. Spindled oak staircases bordered the room, climbing to balconies on either side, off which were the former bedrooms. The second lieutenant governor's second wife had a yen for pink, so she had redone the royal and master suites in that shade, using the same color scheme in the dog's room.

Poor pup.

Shaking his head at this damage done to the masculine character of the lodge, Jack changed in one of the upstairs rooms and was ready to descend when his beeper buzzed.

The message was to call Coquitlam OCC.

Nick Craven was razzing the Mad Dog about Brittany Starr, probing what happened *after* they Code three'd to the strip bar, when MacDougall tapped him on the back and said, "Got a moment?"

"Sir?"

"Follow me."

The inspector led the corporal to a side room and shut the door. "Brace yourself," he warned. "I have bad news. There's no easy way to break this. Your mother is dead."

Nick flinched as if he'd been jabbed in the heart. At first his throat was so dry he couldn't get out the word. "How?" he asked.

"Murder," said Jack. "A blow to the back of her head. She didn't see it coming and died instantly. Get your coat and we'll drive there."

Suddenly the confines of the room closed in, as if somehow the space had shrunk to half its size, shoving details at Nick's face. The picture of Lord Tweedsmuir playing polo on the manicured grass near Minnekhada's stables. The eagle-feathered headdress in a glass case, given to the second lieutenant governor when he became honorary Chief "Red Cloud" of the Kootenay Indians. The decoys, dog and horse figurines, antique shotguns, and prints of hunting scenes . . .

"Nick," Jack said. "Get your coat."

"Don't have one," he replied, coming around. "Left it at Mom's so she could work on the stain. Spilled tea at my birthday party."

"Today's your birthday?"

"Right," he said bitterly. "Surprise present, huh? Some asshole bludgeons my mom."

"When was the party?"

"Late this afternoon. Tea for two, Mom and me, for her to give me my present. Dutiful son. Big obligation. Rushing to party here. So focused on leaving, I didn't remove my coat. Sip sip. Thanks, Mom. Quick in and out. More haste, less speed, I dropped my teacup. Afraid the tea soaking through would stain my Red Serge. Clean it, Mom. Bye bye. Jesus Christ!"

"Beating yourself up won't help her. What time did you leave?" MacDougall asked, switching from friend to cop.

"Close to five. I was here for cocktails at five-thirty."

"How close?"

"Five, ten minutes after."

"Have you met Rachel Kidd?"

"Coquitlam Burglary? No, but I hear she's dynamite in looks."

"Kidd's promoted corporal, Coquitlam GIS. She took the call. Her case. Better speak to her. Except for the killer, you may be the last to see your mom alive. Come on."

They exited from the side room to six bars of the RCMP Regimental March, leading to the junior Member who Chan served giving the Corps Toast to the Force. While waiting in the entrance hall for Jack to inform the DC and DeClercq of the crime, Nick counted black-and-white-checkered tiles on the floor.

Chessboard, he thought.

The main door of Minnekhada Lodge faced north. The paved courtyard outside was hemmed in on the right by a rocky outcrop and graced on the left by a fountain with a statue of Pan playing the flute. A path curved by the carriage house to the parking lot, hidden by cedars and dark with shadows. They drove north out of the lot, then looped south, descending the knoll past the lodge and swimming pool to the driveway gate with thirteen-foot Celtic towers beside Oliver Road. On a clear day there would be a panoramic vista across the Pitt River and Fraser Valley to Mount Baker seventy miles south in Washington state.

Out the gate, Jack turned right along bumpy Oliver Road. Buck brush and a ditch edged the lodge side, with cars unable to find space in the lot parked single file along the marsh shoulder. The Mounties passed the black Ford, but neither cop saw Evil Eye duck out of view, or heard the African voice from the box crying for Redcoat blood.

From Minnekhada, they angled southwest across the rural stretch between the Pitt and Coquitlam rivers, en route to the corner where the latter joined the Fraser by Mary Hill.

"My mother died in May," Jack said. He glanced at Nick, lost in thought on the passenger's side. "Anything is better than slow, painful cancer. Your dad was a Member who died young, I recall from your file."

"Shot himself with his service revolver the night I was born."

"Your mom dying removes the buffer of immortality. Same with me."

"I don't understand," Nick said as they approached Lincoln Park.

"As long as one parent remains alive, we're secure in the belief a generation stands between us and death.

When we lose that buffer, the loss is immense. Not only do we snap the anchor to our youth, and suffer in most cases the end of undying love, but now we're facing the Reaper sharpening his scythe."

"Did you bury or cremate your mom?"

"Buried her in the heather and played the pipes by her grave."

"What'd you play?"

" 'Amazing Grace.' My favorite tune. Only song that comes close is 'Danny Boy.' "

"Ask a favor?"

"Sure."

"Play the pipes for my mom?"

"Name the place. Name the time. In sunshine or in shadow, I'll be there."

Mary Hill Road was sealed at both ends by flashing police cars. The cop blocking the Pitt River Road junction waved them through. Clustered by the curb in front of Dora Craven's home were several patrol vehicles with an Ident Section van summoned from the crime scene down on Colony Farm Road. Corporal Kidd approached when Jack and Nick parked behind. The Mounties shook hands by the front fender.

"Where is she?" Craven asked.

"In the kitchen."

As Nick moved toward the porch, Rachel touched his arm. "I sympathize with you," she said, "and don't mean to be cruel, but this is my case and it will be done by the book. No one but me enters the house until Ident is through, and that may take until tomorrow morning. You don't want to see her like this."

"How do you know it's her?"

"White female. Late fifties. Washing dishes in the kitchen. Your mom lived alone in the house, so that's a start. The victim has two moles on the back of her left hand and a cameo ring."

"It's her." Nick sighed.

"What happened?" Jack asked. "Got a theory?"

"About ten after five, two sheriff's deputies had their skulls crushed by a psych escapee down on Colony Farm. This house backs on that murder scene. John Doe—we don't know who he is—fled this way, but Dog Services lost his trail at the Coquitlam River. Near the time he escaped, this victim on his flight path was bludgeoned in her home. The time, location, MO, and psych profile match."

"Fill in the time frame, Nick," MacDougall said.

"I came by at four-thirty so Mom could give me my birthday present. I left sometime between five P.M. and ten after."

"Front or back?"

"Let myself out the front. The door locked behind me when it shut. Mom worked up at Riverview for thirty-five years. She spooked me with warnings about nuts on the run. As a kid, I imagined them skulking in the bush outside my room. I sure she was locked in whenever I left."

"Both doors were locked but not bolted when I got here," said Kidd. "Ident used a skeleton key to let us in. There's no sign of forced entry anywhere. If it was John Doe, how'd he get in?"

"Mom would *never* open the door to a stranger after dark," Nick emphasized.

"No sign of sexual assault and her purse has money in it. Easily fenced valuables weren't stolen. Was she expecting someone?"

"No. She'd mention it."

"What was she doing when you arrived?"

"Dicing vegetables for supper."

"And when you left?"

"Removing a tea stain from my overcoat."

"You ate with her?"

"Just a cup of tea. She baked a pumpkin pie as my birthday cake. I never liked cake. I promised I'd come by tomorrow for a piece." Nick glanced away. "All that effort and I left her with an untouched pie. I didn't want to spoil my appetite."

"Perhaps someone unexpected dropped by?"

"Like who?" asked Nick.

"A relative?"

"My dad shot himself the day I was born. Mom and I left Alberta for B.C. the following month. Her parents died in a car crash when she was sixteen and Mom was an only child. She took a job in the Riverview laundry and leased this house. To make ends meet, she sewed dresses on consignment at night. The laundry quickly killed her looks and Mom never remarried. Eventually she purchased this house. Our last relative died last month. My dad's younger sister—my Aunt Eleanor—fell down the stairs in the house where I was born. Now Mom's dead, so I'm the only 'relative' alive."

"What about friends?"

"Mom wasn't the drop-in-unannounced kind. Enjoyed her own company and privacy. Her friends would know she was having tea for two with me."

"Any problems? Enemies?"

"None," Nick said. "Mom was the best mother a boy ever had. Since she retired in June, she's been sewing teddy bears for Somali kids."

"Thanks for being so frank," Kidd said. "I've got the picture. The focus will be on John Doe, not wasting time. But rest assured I'll follow up every promising lead."

"Let's leave her to do her job, Nick," MacDougall suggested. "We all have a second family in the Force. The camaraderie at Minnekhada Lodge will take your mind off this."

"I'm okay, Inspector. I need some space to grieve. I think I'll go down and help the searchers on Colony Farm."

"Here," Kidd said. "Take my flashlight."

MacDougall left the corporals face to face on the curb. As he opened the driver's door to get in, he eyed them together over the car roof. Black and white were the same age. Black and white were the same height. The sardonic moon grinned down from above and behind Nick's head. Face-on, the pallid glow lightened Kidd's African features. Turned away, Nick's British face was darkened by shadow. Though races apart, under this wan moon they might be twins.

Jack did a U-turn and vanished up the road.

"I hear you just got your hooks. Congratulations," said Nick.

"Thanks. But don't worry. I'll bounce the case off Staff Sergeant Tipple."

"American, aren't you?"

"Once upon a time." Rachel frowned. "Is that cause for concern?"

"Indirectly. When'd you leave?"

"At eighteen. For SFU."

"Remember this is Canada, not the States. 'Fruit of the Poisoned Tree' is much weaker here."

"Spit it out, Nick. What's bothering you?"

"I hope you're not tainted by the American Bill of Rights? Promise me, whatever it takes, you'll nail who killed my mom. *Whatever it takes*. Understand? Use your brain. No candy-assed Charter of Rights and Freedoms bullshit."

In the shadow of the moon, Rachel saw black tears well from his eyes.

"Promise," Nick said.

"I promise," she replied.

COP KILLER

When Jack MacDougall returned alone to Minnekhada Lodge, the Ford was still parked on Oliver Road and the Rorke's Drift box remained on the passenger's seat, but Evil Eye no longer lurked inside the car. Turning left between the high Celtic towers of the driveway gate, he drove the police car up the moonlit knoll, Scotch mist from Addington Marsh now creeping up the hill, Scottish hunting lodge crowning the slope, reminding him of the Western Isles and misty lochs of his youth. Here could be Dunollie Castle, thirteenth-century seat of the Mac-Dougall Lords of Lorn, who once owned a third of Scotland. Here could be the wild Pass of Brander, where Robert Bruce routed the Clan MacDougall in 1308. Here could be the MacDougall Isles of Coll, Tiree, and Mull, the "Mull of Kintyre" of McCartney's tune and David Balfour's voyage in Stevenson's *Kidnapped*. Ahead could be the MacDougall hearth calling him home, home to the pipes and heather of a Scottish grave.

Looping around behind the lodge, MacDougall parked the car in the isolated lot, then stepped out into the chilly embrace of night. A robust man forced to endure the elements in public school, a Scottish keep of sooty stone, cold showers, thick porridge, and welts from the cane, he paused by the car, shut his eyes, and inhaled a deep breath, slowly sucking winter mist into his barrel chest, a bracer to whet his palate for the peaty burn of single malt drams waiting in the lodge. A hardy man whose first posting was north of the Arctic Circle, the inspector wore no coat over his Red Serge, now dyed the color of clotting blood by tall cedars masking the thin lunar grin.

From the tree shadows, a phantom emerged to stalk the Mountie across the dark lot.

Jack heard a Steller's jay take flight from one of the cedars.

Jack heard hearty laughter from the lodge down the path.

Behind him, Jack heard footsteps closing fast, but before he could turn to see who was there, a Zulu knobkerrie smashed the back of his head, driving bone splinters into his brain.

Moonlight silvered the steel in Evil Eye's other hand.

HORSEMEN

"A Member is down!"

The cry sparked like electricity around the lodge, short-circuiting merriment in a blackout of anger and shock. "A Member is down!" is Force jargon for "One of our own is dead." The subtext is "This one's personal." Hear those words and Mounties drop everything else. Kill a Horseman and you take on the entire 16,000-Member Force.

The cop who threw the verbal bomb into the banquet room stood at the door, sweat trickling down his cheeks from an all-out sprint, hands shaking from overexertion or something else. DeClercq leaned over the podium for closing remarks, the last item on the agenda before the head table was piped out, hoping Jack would be back in

time to play Pied Piper, when his joke about Chan and
Princess Di was cut off.

"A Member is down!" the shaking cop repeated.

"Where?" DeClercq shouted to project across the
room.

"The parking lot. Between two cars. I spotted the trail
of blood."

"How?" DeClercq barked.

"Head smashed in. His guts are ripped out."

"Jesus Christ!" someone cursed among the chorus of
gasps.

"Who?" DeClercq snapped.

"Inspector MacDougall."

The tension in the lodge was a bowstring at full draw.
A deep emotional connection bound them together. Policing is a fraternity of brothers and sisters, and no fraternity is tighter than the Mounted Police. They are the
Mounted. They are the Force. They are Members, capital M. They are the Thin Red Line. Canada is the only
country with a police force as its global national symbol,
and those in this room were that icon. The loss they felt
was the loss of a family member. The last time a cop
was killed, they prayed collectively it would never happen again, while deep down knowing it would—and now
it had.

Each felt rage and the urge for revenge.

Each felt more vulnerable than a moment ago.

Nothing spooked cops more than a cop killer on the
loose.

There would be fallout.

And the devil to pay.

"Stop!" DeClercq ordered as several cops made for
the door. "We keep our heads. We hold the line. We're
trained for this. Corporal Rabidowski, secure the area.
Teams on Quarry and Oliver roads. No one gets out.
Only Members in."

"ERT Members follow me," the Mad Dog growled.
The Emergency Response Team fell in. The sergeant
grabbed a duffel bag from near his chair, unzipped it,
and passed out semiautomatic weapons. He was ready
for anything around the clock.

"Zinc," DeClercq said, turning to Chandler. "Every
dog team and a chopper on the double. Get a boat up the

Pitt River, too. Not only Ident, but specialists from the Lab. Strip HQ and detachments from Vancouver to the border. You're field-promoted head of Operations. Take Jack's job, bless his soul."

Chandler was on a cell phone to Coquitlam OCC when DeClercq turned back to the room. "Someone bring me a map of Minnekhada Park. Corporals divide constables into flying patrols. Sergeants gather here for orders to dispatch. Two thoughts, everyone. Don't mix them up. The parking lot is off-bounds to preserve forensics. The killer, on the other hand, may still be around. Search for him as best you can without ruining his trail. Dogs are coming."

A constable rushed from one of the side rooms with a map pulled off the wall. DeClercq slanted it on the podium as sergeants grouped behind.

"Sergeant"—DeClercq turned to Katherine Spann—"you and a flying patrol come with me. The rest of you pick a trail and be ready to move. Eric"—he turned to Chan—"get on the phone and—"

He stopped.

Realization dawned.

So caught up in the battle was he, DeClercq relied on Chan as his right-hand man, not his new superior in the chain of command.

"Dog's here," Chandler said as he swapped the cell phone for a portable radio, switching to dispatch channel. "Handler's by the parking lot."

"Your command," Chan said to DeClercq, no bullshit between friends.

"Cast the dog," DeClercq ordered. Then to Spann: "Grab the man who raised the cry and have him lead us back. Same route as he came."

Past the fountain with the statue of Pan playing his flute, the Mounties reached the parking lot by the same path MacDougall and Craven had taken earlier. As they neared the clearing of cedars and shadows, a German shepherd came at the cop in the lead.

"Wrong scent," DeClercq told the dog's master. "He found the body. Is there another track?"

The master called the shepherd back and snapped on a line, then led him to fingers of blood reaching out from between two cars. He reapplied the dog to key on a

different scent, casting him across the exit from the
source of blood. The dog made an abrupt perpendicular
turn, indicating he'd hit a track. The handler read the
sign and loosed the shepherd with the command "Find
'm out." Off and bounding down the drive to the road,
the dog blitzed past the ERT cops' scent mingled with
the killer's, leading his handler, Spann, and the flying
patrol toward the Celtic towers of the driveway gate.

DeClercq, Chan, and Chandler stayed behind.

Careful not to approach the corpse till Ident had
combed the scene, they stood in the lot facing the path
leaking blood between the cars, as Zinc shone a flashlight at MacDougall's remains. . . .

An only child, DeClercq was nine when his father died.
DeClercq was a Belgian form of the French *Leclerc* and,
way back on his father's side, DeClercqs in Antwerp
were noted architects during the Flemish Renaissance.
His dad was an artist before the war and a bomber pilot
during it. Ironically, after fifty ops over Germany and in
North Africa, he was killed by a drunk driver while
crossing a Montreal street. When peace lifted rationing
after the war, people spent their money on cars and
washing machines, so all the struggling artist left his son
was a set of lead soldiers, his pilot's flying log, and a
series of paintings—*Battles That Changed the World*—
planned for a book.

Withdrawn, Robert spent months alone in his room,
rearranging the soldiers and memorizing the log, holding
on to his father through the words he left behind . . .
*1942, May 30. 10/ Ops to Cologne. Over 1,000 A/C on
Tgt—Beautiful Blaze . . . 1942, June 5. 13/ Ops to Essen.
P.O.U/S. Reached Dutch Coast. Home on 3 Engines.
Bombs in Sea . . . 1942, Sept 13. 30/ Ops Tobruk—Raided
Flak Posns Using 2 x 500 & 11 x 250 lb. Fragmentation
Bombs. "Commandos" Raiding. Accurate Flak. Holes
in Fuselage. . . .*

That Christmas, he received a medieval fort and a
miniature cannon that shot tiny shells. This was back
when imagination, not lawsuits, designed toys. The lead
soldiers depicted the Norman Conquest of Britain. For
hours, days, weeks, he holed up in his room, knocking
the figurines off the battlements. One by one he gunned

them down with the cannon, readjusting the trajectory after each shot. A single, well-placed soldier took two weeks to hit.

Two days before his tenth birthday, cancer claimed his mom. His aunt gave Robert her present: *Battles That Changed the World.* Who fought whom, where, why, and how the victor triumphed, illustrated with the paintings by his dad. His aunt providing money for a copy to cut up, Robert pinned tactic maps around his new room: Marathon, Hastings, Blenheim, Quebec, Saratoga, Waterloo, Gettysburg . . . moving lead soldiers about the floor to re-create each battle. Models of Spits, Stukas, Flying Tigers, and Sopwith Camels hung above. The Red Knight of Vienna, the Silver Knight of Augsburg, and a pair of Roman gladiators fought on his desk. The boy slept in a war museum.

Doting on the orphan as if he were her son, the maiden aunt in Quebec became his guardian. When he was fourteen, she took him to Britain and France. Locked in a psychological danse macabre with death, his interest in fiction centered on Bradbury, Lovecraft, and Poe, so Jack the Ripper's East End, Madame Tussaud's Chamber of Horrors, and the Bloody Tower drew him like a moth to flame, until he discovered the second floor of Foyle's Books. Haunt of Walt Disney and George Bernard Shaw, Foyle's is a hodgepodge maze of forgotten tomes tracked by a cash system out of Dickens. It remained DeClercq's favorite London oddity.

"Yes?" said the clerk in Military History, raising eyes behind Coke-bottle glasses from a giant biography of Montgomery of El Alamein.

"Colonial battles? Where are they?"

"Ah," said the clerk. "French, are we?"

"French Canadian," Robert said, disappointed his English accent required work.

"Colonial Wars are shelved in two divisions," the clerk joshed, deadpan. "Glory and Blunders. Where does your interest lie?"

"Glory," Robert said.

"Over there. Under Flags and Bunting."

Sucked into a seducing hell of Redcoats, bagpipes, and singing swords, blood red spilling around the globe to Africa, India, Burma, Malaya, China, Australia, New

Zealand, Canada, Caribbean Islands, and other conquered lands, staining maps royal red for the Empire on
which the sun never set, Robert was entranced by tales
of the Iron Duke and Nelson Touch; Lords Raglan,
Lucan, and Cardigan's Charge of the Light Brigade into
the Valley of Death; the Siege of Delhi, Well at Cawn-
pore, and Relief of Lucknow during the Sepoy Mutiny;
the Opium War with China and storming the Heights of
Laloo; Wilfred Blake and the Ashanti War; Isandlwana,
Rorke's Drift, and Ulundi; Gordon of Khartoum and the
Road to Mandalay. . . .

"Thin Red Line, is it?"

The clerk snooped over his shoulder.

"Strange, when all the color you need is in your
own backyard."

Tactics had served DeClercq well in the Royal Canadian Mounted Police, where his campaigns were
launched against psychos and predators, not foreign folk
defending their homes. As in every war, there were battle casualties, but the *last* thing he became a Mountie
for was this. . . .

When Eric Chan was ten years old, his father sat him
down for a man-to-man talk. They were on the porch of
their Strathcona home, less than a block from Chinatown. The family next door was painting a dragon for
the New Year's parade.

"Son," the elder Chan said, an abacus in his hand, "four
secrets lead to success in Gold Mountain. One"—he
flicked across a bead—"be pragmatic. If you wish to prosper, you adapt. Two"—he flicked another bead—"be self-
reliant. Earn your own way. Don't expect handouts.
Three"—a third bead clicked—"be industrious. To succeed,
you must work hard. Four"—he pushed the beads back—
"be discreet. The ghosts despise a wealthy Chinese."

The antique calculator of wood and brass passed from
father to son.

"Your great-great-grandfather worked the Cariboo
mines. He was a British Columbian at the start. Not
once in five generations have we left this land, surviving
through hard work and the long view. The time has
come, youngest son, for you to join the business, so
where in our grocery does your future lie?"

"I want to be a Mounted Policeman," Eric said.

His father choked.

Only through "the long view" did Chan survive. The Chinese consider police work "the dishonorable profession," so Eric's nose was bloodied weekly at school. Finally, when he rapped on the door, the Force didn't want him either, for traditionally Red Serge enhanced a *white* face. If not for burgeoning heroin traffic from Asia, his application would have been denied. Eric Chan was the Mounted's first nonwhite.

While training at Depot Division in 1961, he was nicknamed "Charlie" by the ghost recruits. Ostracized, one afternoon he bussed to the library, where he read Earl Derr Biggers's *The House Without a Key.* Charlie Chan was the hero of the book, a great detective fond of prophetic proverbs. *Fresh weeds are better than withered roses,* Chan thought.

Eric's most embarrassing date was his first Red Serge Ball. Sally Fan, now his wife, flew in for the dance. As they entered the banquet hall, conversation hushed. Chan wondered why until he found their table: sixteen chairs and only two name tags. "It doesn't matter," Sally whispered. "Pretend it's a restaurant." A few minutes later, a couple approached from the head table with their plates and cutlery. "Mind if we join you? We're Kate and Robert DeClercq."

Chan worked hard to become the Force expert on Triads and heroin. Forming the Asian Gang Squad was his idea, after he drove the Five Dragons from the West Coast. When HQ began selecting Members for college degrees, he studied random processes and probability at UBC. Graduating with honors, he computerized the Force, programming the Headhunter dragnet in 1982. The Violent Crimes Analysis Section was also his idea. Corporal, to sergeant, to inspector, his foresight paid off, and now "the long view" had launched him to one of the six top positions in the RCMP.

As deputy commissioner, his next formal duty would be a Red Serge funeral. . . .

Chandlers had worked their Saskatchewan farm for a century. Zinc's dad had raised two boys to inherit the land, and never forgave his elder son for abandoning it to join the Force. Pop's last gasp on his deathbed was "At least one turned out a man."

Zinc and his brother Tom were dressed for bed. Pop sat at the kitchen table with his drinking buddies, and slopped a round of Canadian Club from the bottle in his hand. Fixing his rheumic eyes on the ten-year-old he slurred:

> "Take up the White Man's burden—
>   And reap his old reward:
> The blame of those ye better,
>   The hate of those ye guard.

"Think lively, son. Name the bard."

"Kipling, Pop," Zinc replied.

Her workday far from over while Pop held court, Zinc's mom sighed and turned from the sink. "Run along, boys. And say your prayers."

For hours he heard them carousing through the bedroom wall, betting who could identify the most obscure poem, thumbing the thick anthology that arbitrated the game. When the Plowmen Poets were so sloshed they could barely speak, Pop began to rant at life. The speech was a standard. The same each time.

First Pop quoted from Wordsworth's *The Fountain:*

> "The wiser mind
> Mourns less for what age takes away
> Than what it leaves behind."

Then he launched into a wild tirade on the tyranny of time: how life was so unfair because we peaked at twenty-one when we didn't know sweet-fuck-all, spending the wise years of our lives watching our flesh decline, sliding downhill slowly at first, but gaining speed rapidly as middle age took hold. "What's the use?" Pop shouted. "Why struggle on?" Then he turned his vitriol on Zinc's mom.

Oh, how he hated Pop for that. Lying in the bunk beds he shared with Tom, listening to the old man berate his wife.

"Would you believe it, boys. Look at her. Prettiest girl in Saskatchewan the day we wed. See what cruel time has done? Left me with a crinkled, gray-haired hag."

Shivering in the dark, Zinc's heart bled for her. Why did she put up with such abuse? For the sake of her sons? Because she was afraid? Crying himself to sleep, he promised one day he'd make the hurt up to her.

Come morning, Zinc knew what to expect. Hungover and sleep-deprived, Pop would make him run the gauntlet of the bards, hitting him with quote on quote to bring him to his knees, flaring at his mother if she tried to intervene.

"Stand back, woman," Pop would growl. "I'll not raise an illiterate lout.

> "For he who fights and runs away
>   May live to fight another day;
> But he who is in battle slain
>   Can never rise and fight again.

"Think lively, son. Name the bard."

"Goldsmith, Pop."

Then one day he'd stood up to the old man. Told him to his face he didn't deserve a wife like her, someone who saw him through drought, famine, near bankruptcy, and his boozing bouts, someone who made him a good home and defended him against gossip no matter how big an ass he was. Told Pop eye to eye he was a pisstank bully, but the beating he'd taken in return was so severe it made his mother scream, so Zinc never mouthed off like that again to save her distress.

Got the old man back, though, by becoming a cop.

Pop had hated cops since the Depression, when he was clubbed unconscious in the Regina Riot.

What Zinc hadn't joined the Force for was to shine a light on this . . .

The beam of the flashlight lit the aisle like a spotlight onstage. Jack's head was toward them with his legs in the far bushes. He lay faceup while a stream of blood flowed their way. A red smear on the ground showed he had been dragged, the back of his head concave where his skull was smashed in. Both his shirt and Red Serge waistcoat were slashed from sternum to groin, spilling pinkish-brown coils from his abdomen. The sliced bowels discharged yellowish-brown intestinal fluid into a pool of blood.

"Kill the torch," Chan said in disgust.

When the beam died, the sole light was the grin of the moon.

"Jack was clubbed from behind near the driver's door," said DeClercq, "then dragged by the feet half into the woods to shadow the body from sight."

"The bludgeoning killed him," Chandler said. "So why the disemboweling?"

The question hung pregnant in the night.

Finally, Chan said vehemently, "I want this prick. Jurisdiction or not, the case is ours." The "ours" registered with DeClercq as head of Special X—horror had psychologically pulled Eric back to the squad—and the rancor made him turn. By the anemic glow of the moon he saw muscles jump along the jaw of Chan's balding, foxlike face. Today DeClercq had lost both his right- and left-hand men: Eric to promotion and Jack to death. He was unaware the inspectors were that close, then their bond struck like a clock.

Prejudice, he thought.

Eric was Chinese.

Jack was gay.

The portable in Chandler's fist squawked to life. "Mad Dog"—Spann's voice—"we're looking for a car. Anything suspect?"

"Negative here. I'm at the junction of Oliver Road and Gilleys Trail."

"The dog?" Chandler said. "Where'd he lead?"

"Out the gate"—Spann again—"turning right past the cars lining Oliver Road. Nose up, he stopped by an empty space and worked in a circle. Handler read him as 'Off the track. This is the end.' The killer escaped in the missing car."

"Echo Five?" The Mad Dog.

"Copy, Bravo Three."

"Anything your end?"

"Negative," reported the roadblock north on Quarry Road.

"End of the trail," Chandler said. "General alert Coquitlam."

ACCUSED

Three months later . . .

The statue of the Hanging Judge in Begbie Square looks
south across the plaza of the New Westminster Courts,
over the roofs of the buildings along Columbia Street at
the muddy Fraser River flowing left to right toward the
sea. This blustery March morning without a cloud to mar
the sky, Morgan Hatchett left her home on 1st Street
near Queen's Park, a fine Victorian mansion marking its
centenary, with turrets, gables, balconies, and lots of
stone, to walk west down Agnes Street to the Law
Courts. Descending fifty-seven hillside steps to the fore-
court plaza, which used to have cobblestones until the
cracks between broke too many high-heel shoes, Hatchett paused at the bottom to pay her respects to the
Hanging Judge.

Sir Matthew Baillie Begbie was Morgan Hatchett's
idol.

In the 1840s and '50s, America was in an expansive
mood. Fresh from Mexican conquests and annexing Oregon in 1846, the Manifest Destiny was moving north,
driven by Polk's election cry of "Fifty-four-forty' or
Fight!" That number was the parallel where the eleventh
President of the United States hoped to redraw the border with British North America. A line up near where
the Alaska Panhandle ends today.

In 1857, gold was discovered in the Fraser Canyon, so
30,000 American miners swarmed north from California,
which was almost panned out, to make their fortune in
a land of Indians and Hudson's Bay fur traders. With
them came gamblers, claim jumpers, and gunmen re-
strained by no law but the lynching rope. Britain's army

was months away around Cape Horn (the Panama Canal opened in 1914); so what if the miners undermined the Queen's Realm and summoned the States like Oregon?

To stop that London sent a single man.

With royal proclamations to establish the Mainland Colony of British Columbia in his bag, Begbie docked on the West Coast on November 16, 1858. Three days later, beside the Fraser River, he swore James Douglas in as first governor, while Douglas swore him in as first and only judge.

The Royal City of New Westminster, named by Queen Victoria to be the capital, was literally carved out of the bush on the "first high ground after entering the Fraser River." Stern-wheeled steamboats carried miners upstream to the gold fields from here. On drafting the Gold Fields Act in 1859, Begbie trudged up the Fraser Canyon through Hell's Gate to hand it around the mining camps clinging to the precipitous drop. The rough-and-rowdy miners thought the judge a joke until he returned with the lash and the rope.

Bedecked in the robes and wig of a British judge, Begbie held court from astride his horse, a huge man of stern gaze with a waxed mustache and goatee, who quoted Greek and Latin poets in sentencing, then tacked whip strokes on the end. "My idea is," he maintained, "that if a man insists on behaving like a brute, after fair warning, and won't quit the Colony, treat him like a brute and flog him." The rope helped the Hanging Judge make his name.

A traveler named Cheadle reported in 1863, "Passed Judge Begbie on horseback. Everybody praises his just severity as the salvation of the Cariboo and the terror of rowdies." In 1865 alone, Begbie rode 3,500 miles, sleeping under canvas and living off the land. Juries that crossed him felt the lash of his tongue. Those who threatened to kill him were mocked in court with the admonition to get on with the shooting. Sitting on the balcony of a hotel, he overheard a plot to plug him as he rode out of town. Begbie found a pail of slops and dumped it over the heads below to express his contempt. Soon word the judge was coming would clear a mining camp.

On a rare vacation to Salt Lake City, Begbie met a

man who accosted him with "How do you do, Judge. I was one of your jurymen up in the Cariboo. You certainly did some hanging." Begbie replied with dry wit, "Excuse me, my friend, I never hanged any man. I simply swore in good American citizens like yourself as jurymen, and it was you that hanged your own countrymen."

Begbie kept the "British" in British Columbia.

In 1871, the colony became part of Canada, which then consisted of the Eastern Provinces. As first Chief Justice of British Columbia, by 1894—the year he died—Begbie's Court had four more judges. One, Sir Eustace Hatchett, was Morgan's granddad.

Morgan Hatchett firmly believed what modern times required was a return to the lash, the rope, and judges with Begbie's backbone.

Judges like herself.

Turning from the statue, she cut diagonally across Begbie Square to reach the high wooden doors of the Law Courts, so heavy they took both hands to tug open. Sunbeams slanting through the glass roof of the Great Hall within spotlit the Registry on the ground floor and two tiers of courts stacked above. Most judges snuck in the back door off their private parking lot. Hatchett used the main doors, so, as with Begbie, scum and outlaws would know trouble was in town.

An L-shaped staircase rose to the second floor, by the largest portrait of the queen in the world, so big you had to view it from across the hall. While Hatchett climbed, two laughing lawyers came down, mirth gone the instant they spotted her. Both straightened collar tabs and realigned their robes. Rumor was The Hatchet noted the rumpled in a book and gave them hell in court as a consequence.

Morgan rode the elevator up to the chambers of the Chief Justice of the Supreme Court on the fourth floor. There she robed in front of a full-length mirror: black silk robe with scarlet trim, matching vest over a plain black skirt, white wing collar with upside-down v tabs, and sensible black shoes. The wig had been retired in 1905, a desecration she rued. Iron gray hair chopped in a butch cut, eyes hard to drill into minds harboring guilt, mouth permanently pursed from decades of accusation . . . Maggie Thatcher was soft and fluffy compared to her.

At five to ten, Hatchett rode the judges' elevator down to the second floor, then walked the back corridor to Court 2–8.

"Order in Court! All rise!" the sheriff barked as she climbed four steps to the bench.

From every point of view, the Heritage Courtroom was a stage. When the new Law Courts replaced the Old Courthouse in 1980, Begbie's trial rooms were carefully dismantled and reassembled here, such Victorian craftsmanship a treasure from the past. The judge's bench was a stage indeed, with sashed red velvet curtains to both sides and a carved oak canopy, the high-backed throne flanked by two lesser chairs, oak paneling behind and tall brass lamps on the wide oak desk. From high in her private theater box, Hatchett gazed down on the rabble: robed barristers facing her at the counsel table, the accused raised beyond in the prisoner's dock, then the great unwashed filling the public gallery of her court, a murmuring mass of commoners summoned to this assize for jury duty.

A portly man rose from the counsel table. "Lyndon Wilde appearing for the Crown, My Lady. With me is John Crook."

The junior counsel bowed.

A tall gaunt man rose from the counsel table. "Vic Knight for the defense."

Hatchett's scowl deepened. She had an ax to grind. Before this trial was over he'd face the Knightmare of his career.

"Read the indictment," she ordered.

The court clerk read the count of murder to the accused. "Having heard the charge, how do you plead, guilty or not guilty?"

"Not guilty," said the man standing in the dock.

The clerk turned to the judge. "The accused pleads not guilty."

"Proceed," Hatchett ordered.

A wooden box of names in hand, the clerk addressed the dock. "These good persons who shall now be called are the jurors who are to pass between Our Sovereign Lady the Queen and you at your trial. If therefore you would challenge them or any of them, you must challenge them as they come to the book to be sworn, and before they are sworn you shall be heard."

The clerk addressed the gallery. "Members of the jury panel, answer to your names when called and come forward please."

It took half an hour to select twelve jurors. In Canada, both Crown and defense can challenge twelve times. The jury list provides names, addresses, and occupations. That and the silent face in court are what you get to decide. Those who survived challenging took a seat in the jury box. During selection, Morgan assessed the accused: blond hair short in a military cut, blue eyes firmly meeting hers. The Hatchet's glower said, *My friend, you're going down.*

After a brief coffee break while the jury chose a foreman, the court—now packed with Mounties—reconvened. "Mr. Wilde," Hatchett said, "please open for the Crown."

The portly prosecutor rose from the counsel table. He, too, locked eyes with the accused, then turned to the triers of fact. "Members of the jury," Wilde began, "this man stands charged that on the seventh of December, 1993, in the City of Port Coquitlam, in this Province, he did commit the second-degree murder of Dora Craven. The evidence for the Crown will take you back to that day. . . .

BIRTHDAY PARTY

Port Coquitlam
Tuesday, December 7, 1993

After conversing with Craven and MacDougall by the car, Kidd rounded Dora's house to check on Ident's progress collecting forensic clues. "Ten minutes will see the kitchen once-over done," said the senior tech. "If you keep to the path of contamination, you can come in then. Go for a coffee."

Rachel used the "coffee break" to cross Mary Hill Road to Winifred Parker's house, intent on questioning the woman who had called OCC. As she reached out to rap on the door, it opened by itself as in a schlock horror film.

"Saw you coming," said a disembodied voice.

The face that peered around the door was that of a human weasel, long pointed nose jutting inches from her cheeks, receding chin and forehead accentuating it, the beady eyes either side close-set and suspicious. "Nosy" Parker was seventy, eighty, ninety years old if she was a day, with tight white curls, Grand Canyon wrinkles, and glasses on a chain. Though she wore an Indian sweater and a knitted shawl, the temperature in her house was still eighty degrees.

Kidd knew Nosy well from having worked Burglary, and couldn't understand why she was *proud* of the name, putting the fact down to eccentricity. "Nothing gets by you, Winnie. Bull's-eye this time."

"He that eats the Queen's goose shall be choked by the feathers. I'm the feathers, Corporal."

Kidd smiled. Trust Winnie to know of her promotion today.

Nosy Parker's parlor looked out on Mary Hill Road, across from Dora Craven's front yard, porch, and door. Beyond her neighbor's house was Colony Farm. From here, FPI was visible to the left down where the Fraser met the Coquitlam River, but the site of the attack on Bert and Ernie was hidden by Dora's home and the wooded rise to the right. On top of the TV backed by the window sat binoculars.

"She's dead, isn't she?"

"Yes," replied Kidd.

"Poor Dora," Winnie said, crossing herself. "Think the nut killed her, like I feared?"

"We don't know. The doors were locked, so how'd he get in?"

"Saw you talking to Nick. Is he a suspect?"

Kidd was about to state no, but stopped herself. "Should he be?"

"It's easier to raise the devil than to lay him."

"Okay, Winnie. What'd you see?"

Kidd sat, notebook in hand, like a secretary. She glanced out the window now and then to picture events described.

"It was getting dark when Dora's son arrived. He pulled in off the road and parked in the yard. As *Oprah* was half over, the time was four-thirty. A street lamp shines on Dora's drive. His overcoat was open as he got out of the car, so I could see Red Serge underneath. He went around back where I lost sight of him at the far porch corner."

"Eyesight?"

"Binoculars sight," she corrected. "Twilight's the best time to watch barn owls and coyotes down on the farm."

"Of course," said Kidd.

"After *Oprah* finished, maybe ten minutes, the son came out the front door in a big hurry. He was dressed in Red Serge without the overcoat, and carrying a large plastic bag."

Tea stain and birthday gift, thought Kidd.

"Soon I heard sirens on the Lougheed, eh? Didn't pay much attention since there's sirens all the time. I watched the early news at five, and near the end caught a flash about the nut's escape. When I looked out the window, I saw the glow of red-and-blue lights from down on the farm behind Dora's house. No way was I going out with a nut on the run, so I phoned Dora to ask what was going on."

"Time?" Kidd asked.

"About six. I thought maybe she was in the bath or had unplugged the phone—sometimes she does that to be left alone—so I waited awhile, then called back. When she didn't answer by seven I got worried. She could see the action out her kitchen window. I figured she'd plug in the phone so Nick could check she was safe. That's when I rang you."

"From when Nick left just after five until Constable Stekl arrived, did anyone else approach the house across the street?"

"No," Winnie said.

"How long were you at the window?"

"The whole time. A crazy on the loose, no way I'll let down my guard."

"The bathroom?"

"Nope."

"The kitchen to make dinner?"

"All the excitement, I haven't eaten yet. Even if I watch TV, one eye's out the window."

"You asked if Corporal Craven was a suspect. What prompted that?"

"He who speaks of others burns his tongue."

Rachel was armed for Nosy's game. Parker was dying to tell her, but had to be coaxed. She closed her notebook as a sign her lips were sealed. "Better to ask the way than go astray," she countered. "A clear conscience is like a coat of mail. Life without a friend is death without a witness. It's not as thy mother says, but as thy neighbors say."

Nosy twitched her nose. "Yo mama taught you well."

"We Mounties are lucky to have you on guard. What you say stays between us. If it's crucial, I'll find a backup source. I wouldn't be true to my job if I didn't check every angle. You were Dora's friend in life. Now you're her witness."

"What sort of cop is he?"

"Good as far as I know."

"All I meant is there's a wild streak in Nick. His mother had an accident when he was in his teens. There used to be a paper shack next to their home. A squatter used it to sell drugs."

Nosy pointed to a scrapbook on a table spread with newspaper clippings. Rachel knew Winnie was a mainstay of Coquitlam Archives, tracking municipal affairs since troglodytes walked the earth. RETAIN COLONY FARM AS 'A PARK FOREVER' TO PRESERVE AREA'S WILDLIFE, NATURALIST SAYS trumpeted one headline. COQUITLAM MOUNTIES DEPLORE CRUMBLING BUILDING blared another. *Damn right,* thought Kidd. The scrapbook lay open— *Trust Nosy!*—at a 1975 clipping from *The Vancouver Sun.*

Jekyll to Hyde? Rachel wondered, staring at Nick's photo.

"Tell me, Winnie," she said.

The summer Nick got his driver's license, his mom was badly injured, hospitalized comatose from a head-on collision. Up to then he had walked the straight and narrow, avoiding teenage pitfalls for her sake. But now alone at home with a drug trafficker next door, Nick's repressed anger and guilt about his father's death blew like a volcano. From pot, to booze, to LSD, that school year was a blur. With money earned from selling lids of Maui Wowee, he purchased a 1200 cc. Harley-Davidson Low Rider. Cruising a personal highway to hell, he soon fell afoul of the cops. Nothing serious, but it was a start.

The tattoo on Nick's biceps dated from his school daze. Stoned and drunk, he remembered little of the procedure, except the artist was topless with piercings through her nipples. The tattoo depicted an hourglass almost out of sand, with the words HERE COMES above and THE NIGHT below. In his state, it probably seemed deep at the time.

Two months before graduation, the Harley got him expelled. Mr. Clayton, the vice principal, looked like Spiro Agnew but was less liberal in thought. Clayton viewed Nick as a long-haired punk to be knocked down a notch. Nick viewed Clayton as a blockhead and fascist old fart. Both itched like dogs with fleas to take the other on.

It was a warm April day and the girls' track team was running the oval. Clayton stood outside the school enjoying a little voyeuristic T&A. As he ogled the team in jiggly T-shirts and skimpy shorts, the throaty roar of a motorcycle shook the field. Like an Indy pace car, Nick fell in behind the team. "Get off the track, bum!" Clayton bellowed.

Reining the hog in a wheelie, Nick gunned by his nemesis. He flipped the bird at Clayton as the v.p. ate his dust, then shot up the loading ramp used to stock the woodwork room. Thundering down the main hall of the industrial wing, the Harley exited airborne out the opposite door. Evel Knievel might have approved . . . but Clayton gave him the boot.

As luck would have it, the principal was a levelheaded woman, so she softened Nick's expulsion with a fighting chance. He was suspended from classes for the rest of the year, but could write the government exams at the end. Pass them through independent study and he would graduate.

The thought of Clayton's balls for bookends made
Nick hit the books. By burning the midnight oil he
scored 84 percent. Graduation day saw Nick absent from
school. Absent until his name was called over the PA.
"Nicholas Craven," the voice repeated, pausing for ten
seconds, then the Harley kicked in and Nick wheeled
into the hall. Hair in a ponytail and dressed in bike
leathers, he climbed to the stage, boot chains jangling,
to accept his grad diploma from Clayton's shaking hand.
As you'd expect, his classmates gave him a standing
ovation.

Ironically, it was the Harley that saved Nick's soul.

That summer of graduation, his favorite thrill was racing the CPR through Maple Ridge, hell-bent to beat the
train to Fool's Crossing. Armed with warning lights but
no barrier, the crossing had claimed lives over the years.
Hair streaming behind him free from any helmet, pave-
ment zipping beneath him in a tarmac blur, muffler rapping like a werewolf's growl, Nick would veer the bike
uphill and descend toward the tracks. Crosscutting the
nose of the train, he'd split-second cheat death. Nothing
like it to jolt an adrenaline high.

Then came the tyke.

The tyke was on a trike plummeting out of control.
She had escaped from a hillside yard where her mother
stood screaming at the gate. The sidewalk slope was too
steep for the muscles of her legs, gravity spinning the
pedals so fast her feet were thrown off. The tricycle had
jumped the curb from sidewalk to road, hurtling the
child toward the flashing railway lights below.

As Nick swerved up the loop above Fool's Crossing,
he glimpsed the train and trike on a collision course.
Gearing down, he wrenched the fuel throttle and
plunged down the grade. The Harley roared by traffic
stopped at the crossing as an Idaho tourist snapped a
photograph. Five feet from the tracks, Nick passed the
trike, which was crushed a moment later under the train.
It was no heroic, he was going that way, but as the hog
zoomed by Nick hooked the child, tearing her from the
seat while leaving a shoe behind. Once the train passed,
tyke now on his hip, he rode her home as the tourist
snapped another photograph.

"I'm proud of you," his mom said when she arrived

home from the hospital. She pinned the newspaper photos by her bed: one of the rescue, the other the aftermath. Encircling the kid like a boa was Nick's tattooed arm, bared to where his jean jacket frayed at the shoulder. Nick's hair was tangled like the roots of a tree, and bugs were squashed on his stubbled cheeks and jaw. The caption under the photos read *Here comes the fright.* Nick—as with Kidd, studying Nosy's scrapbook eighteen years later—wondered if that referred to the incident or him.

A week later, his mom left a pamphlet in his room. With it was an RCMP recruitment form, and a note: *I can get you in.*

What the hell? Nick thought. *Fame is better than notoriety.*

Leaving Nosy Parker's home to cross Mary Hill Road to the murder scene, Rachel sensed binoculars following her. Though the street was still blocked at both ends, that hadn't stopped gawkers from assembling, or media crews from lugging in cameras and mikes. Running their gauntlet of insistent questions, Kidd parried with "The investigation is progressing." Strung tree to tree like a boxing ring, yellow tape with black words CAUTION POLICE DO NOT CROSS cordoned off Dora's house. As Stekl arrested a youth for violating the warning, Kidd angled around the porch to the back door, where she cinched plastic bags over her shoes and tugged latex gloves onto both hands.

Rachel was about to enter when a black cat crossed her path, hindering her by scratching the scratch marks lower on the door. Allergic to cats, Kidd shooed Dora's pet away.

The Identification techs inside were sheathed in "monkey suits," white overalls with attached hoods and boots, their hands double-gloved to ensure they didn't leave prints through the thin latex. Moving about the house, they looked like ghosts. One videotaped the crime scene in VHS. Another photographed it in 35mm color, except dusted prints, which were shot in black and white. Hairs and fibers, blood spatter analysis, tool marks, footprints, measurements: each Ident tech had a job. Outlined in tape across the floor from the door to the body was a "path of contamination" for Rachel to use, the route already cleaned of clues so it could be "tainted."

Kidd gazed down at the corpse.

"Bludgeoned with a blunt object," said the senior tech. "Standing at the sink when she was clubbed from behind. Blow caved in the back of her skull. Her body bounced off the sink to fall back faceup on the floor. Head twisted sideways and blood poured out. Careful you don't track through the pool."

"Find the weapon?"

"Missing from the house. Killer took it with him when he fled."

"Break-in?"

"No. Every entrance is secure with no tampering. No jimmy marks, dust scuff, glove smudge, fingerprints, or nothing."

"She let the killer in?"

"Near as we can tell."

"And was washing dishes when she was clubbed?"

"Apron and rubber gloves make that a safe bet. And blood pattern backs it up."

"Someone she knew," Kidd said, "who took her by surprise. Blows about the face often indicate a killer related to the victim. The more severe the beating, the closer the relationship. The window above the sink reflects the room behind. The image of a stranger would cause her to turn in fright. She knew the face behind her and didn't see the club."

"Whoever it was, my guess is she fed him pumpkin pie."

Kidd flinched. "Why?"

"There's a casserole in the oven uncooked. Must be dinner. The dishes in the sink were used to prepare but not eat a meal. Except for *two* small plates and dessert forks."

He led Kidd along the path of contamination to the fridge on the other side of the kitchen. A pumpkin pie sat on the lower shelf within, cut into six wedges with two Vs missing. Letters were gone from the words "Happy Birthday" in whipped cream.

"You cut a birthday pie for the person having the birthday," said Kidd. "Is there a man's overcoat drying in the house?"

"No. Should there be?"

"Casserole completed, she's washing dishes at the sink when Birthday Boy drops by. They have pie together for afternoon tea. Cups in the sink?"

"Two," said the tech.

"Finished, she adds the dishes to the others. When her back is turned, she's clubbed from behind. Perhaps she thought the killer was going to dry. Anything found to dispel that theory?"

"The opposite," said the tech.

A counter lined the rear wall of the kitchen, serving the cast-iron stove and modern cooking range. The tech pulled open one of four drawers beneath to withdraw a large brown envelope. *December 1993* was written on front. Inside were three bills stamped *Paid,* several early Christmas cards, and a typed but unsigned letter.

Careful of prints, the tech held up the letter for Kidd to read:

December 2, 1993
  Mother—
  It's taken my lifetime to uncover your whitewashed secret. Discussing it face to face on my birthday seems fitting. I'll call on the 7th.

GUILT

"Nicholas Craven, you have a Smartie stuck up your nose."

How the candy got there, he had no recall, for the childhood recollection didn't go back that far, but as Nick trudged down the Hill to Colony Farm, the torch offered by Kidd sweeping the misty path, a vivid memory of Mom stabbed him.

"Silly boy," she scolded him, *tilting back his chin, him seated on the table with her kneeling on the floor, as she tried to hook the candy-coated chocolate with her nail.*

Though he was only four, it seemed just yesterday, steam from the kettle wafting up his nose, Mom employing hot air to melt the stubborn blockage, until something sticky ran down his lip.

"Look," she said, holding up her hand-mirror.

The Smartie was red. "Blood!" sobbed Nick. Then he began to wail.

The memory faded with Mom cuddling him. . . .

If only he had stayed for pie and a second cup of tea, he'd have been here to protect her when the psycho chanced by, but no—*Sip sip. Thanks, Mom. Quick in and out*—he didn't want to miss the opening of the bar, so he left her to celebrate his birthday alone by falling victim to a nut.

As Nick tromped down Mary Hill, tears streaked his cheeks.

Only now when Mom lay dead in his childhood home did he fully appreciate all she'd done for him, toiling dawn to dusk to keep his early life secure, but taking the time to create "adventures" on her days off. No, he couldn't run to her now and say "You're the best, Mom." Opportunity lost.

"Close your eyes and sniff, Nicholas. Finest smell in the world. Mmm," she said. This was their "Adventure in Bakeryland," standing by the huge ovens in McGavin's on Broadway, smelling the loaves of brown and white and Danish pastries baking, Mom having marched into the manager's office to confide her son hoped to be a baker, so could they look around?

"Close your eyes and listen to the bottles clink," she said. This was their "Adventure in Coca-Colaland," Mom having marched into the bottling plant at Cornwall and Burrard to say her son hoped to be a beverage dispenser, so could they look around? The guy whose job it was to sit staring at passing bottles all day to ensure they were clean for filling had fallen asleep. As they went by, Nick snapped his fingers like he imagined hypnotist Reveen would do.

Then came "Adventure in Lumberland," a mill on the Fraser, "Adventure in Dairyland," when dairies were still in town, "Adventure in Frontierland," a drive to Fort Langley, "Adventure in Smellyland," a trek to the Steves-

*ton docks, and, best of all, "Adventure in Newspa-
perland."*

*The Sun Tower at Pender and Beatty is a Vancouver
landmark. "Skip" O'Rourke, a Luddite who retired when
computers spoiled the action, and the man to whom the
Headhunter sent photos of cutoff heads on stakes, was
news editor in the early sixties. "So you want to be a
reporter?" he said to Nick, puffing cigar smoke down
at the boy the height of his Guinness belly eyeing his
Popeye tattoo.*

Nick nodded.

*They were touring the editorial room, a collection of
reporters' desks supplying the rim, a U-shaped table
around the slot. Manning the slot till page proofs came
down, a copyboy scowled at this possible usurpation of
his future job.*

*"It's quiet now," the Skipper said, "because we've put
the three-star to bed. If you'd come on deadline, this
would be a madhouse."*

*Plunk! A cylinder dropped from the pneumatic tube.
Withdrawing the proofs, the copyboy flattened them on
O'Rourke's desk.*

*The Skipper grabbed a sheet of yellow copy from a
basket. "That suction tube sucked this story up to the
linotype room where it went into print." He gave Nick a
moment to read:*

SALMON DERBY IN PICTURES, PAGE *17*

*A sleepy chinook, fat, sassy, and happy with life,
yawned and hastily gulped his breakfast Sunday.*

Too hastily.

*With one munch, there in the cold, clear, predawn
waters off Seal Rock, that fat fish, all 28 pounds 12
ounces of him, had become Exhibit A in* The Sun's
25th annual Salmon Derby . . .

*"These proofs that just came down are what will go to
your home."*

"Why do we see errors in the paper?" asked Nick.

*"They're typos, son. We don't have time to catch
them all."*

*"Is that a typo?" Nick said, pointing to the proof of
the front page:*

SALMON DERBY IN PICTURES, PAGE *17*
A sleepy chink, fat, sassy, and happy with life, yawned and hastily gulped his breakfast Sunday . . .

Some typos you can live with—and some typos you can't. The cigar dropped from O'Rourke's mouth, spewing sparks. "Holy shit! Stop the presses!" he yelled. Till his teens Nick planned to be a newspaperman. All that excitement. What a job!

Memories of Mom kept pace with his tears as Craven lugged his burden of guilt across Colony Farm, down the path from Mary Hill Road and along the top of the dike, the Cheshire cat moon—a grin but no face—and Kidd's torch the only light, the outline of an old silo beyond the ditch to his left, a corrugated sewer pouring water into the trough, the route just two ruts underneath his feet, with old fencing of crooked posts and rusty wires right. On both sides, invisible wings flapped over the fields of marsh.

Midway in, the route was blocked by the Coquitlam River, dike meeting dike to form a T. The tributary was twenty feet across and shallow enough for a fugitive to wade. Along the back of the field on the opposite bank, Colony Farm Road stretched from FPI to the scene of the deputies' murders, then on to the Lougheed Highway. Nick followed the river dike left.

If only he'd asked certain questions at Minnekhada Lodge, like where the absent Coquitlam Members had been called out to, he might have rushed here to ensure Mom was protected.

But no, instead he'd swapped traffic ticket tales with Rabidowski.

Some son.

Ahead, the pale moonlight sheened a spooky bridge, like the relic in Irving's *The Legend of Sleepy Hollow*. Made of crisscross timbers, the skeletal span was weak, and minus both on-ramps, hadn't felt traffic for years. The only way to traverse the river without getting wet, Nick scaled the supports bracing this end to wobble his way across, then climbed down the buttresses on the far side, cutting his right palm on a nail in the awkward descent.

Sucking the wound, he floundered up the opposite dike.

A short hike downstream brought him to Riverside. Behind the grilled windows of the FPI facility for the criminally insane, human monsters glared at him. Now as the Mountie turned back along Colony Farm Road, heading upstream to glean everything known about the psycho who clubbed his mom from the cops investigating the earlier murders, Nick faintly heard gibbering laughter escaping from the asylum.

He who laughs last laughs loudest.

West Vancouver

Who says you can't have it all?

Twelve miles as the crow flies west from Coquitlam and Colony Farm, in her home atop Sentinel Hill, Gillian Macbeth stood naked before the living-room mirror. *Good-bye fair figure,* she thought.

Inherited from her father, Gill owned a string of Caribbean hotels, from which she split the profits with onsite managers, earning money to burn without having to work. Like her mother, the first female pathologist in the Commonwealth, who died from hepatitis, a risk of the job, Gill was perhaps the best forensic sawbones in town. Unmarried and forty, she'd worked out a relationship with a younger man that offered sizzling sex without ties that bind. And now, just in time to thwart her biological clock, Gill Macbeth had found out today she was pregnant.

Gill gave the mirror a thumbs-up, which the mirror gave back.

The twin reflected by the glass was handsome, not pretty. People told Gill she looked a lot like Candice Bergen, auburn hair, emerald eyes, seductive mouth. Her figure was strong enough to match her lover stroke for stroke and leave him exhausted, yet graceful enough that she still turned heads on the street.

"Nice bod," Gabby said, cocking his head.

She wagged a finger at him. "Cheeky boy."

"Four cheeks," the West African gray parrot mimicked.

So intelligent was the bird that he spoke with the ability of a seven-year-old child. Gabby shared his solarium-cum-aviary with a green-winged macaw named Binky. Binky was conceited because he cost twenty-five hundred dollars. Gabby was jealous of Gill's beau and wanted her all to himself.

"Music, maestro," Gabby said, in the mood to party from the way he paced his perch.

Gill moved toward her CD collection.

"Fuck Bach," the parrot opined by way of critical comment.

"Easy, Gab, or I'll wash your beak out with soap. The Killer it is," Gill said, "if that will shut you up." The piano pump of "Great Balls of Fire" filled the room. She hoped for the sake of her nerves Gabby wasn't about to sing.

Gill slid back the glass door between the dining room and outside deck where a pool and hot tub overlooked English Bay. Matching how she felt tonight, the city lay at her feet. Gill cranked a knob and the hot tub bubbled, then closing the door on Gabby's karaoke session, she padded through the chill night air to sink into the steam. Like the child in her womb, the tub was a womb to her.

Relaxing, Gill recalled the night she first shared the tub with Nick during the Ripper case.

Their toes played footsie under the water as Gill said, "How do people react when you say you were born in Medicine Hat? That's one step up from Moose Jaw."

"I'll have you know Medicine Hat is a very cultured place. Where were you born? Holetown, Barbados?"

Gill laughed. "A little south. So where's Medicine Hat?"

"Crossing from Saskatchewan into Alberta, you pass through dry short-grass country where wheat farming gives way to cattle ranching, then descend an incline into The Hat, which Rudyard Kipling described as a town 'with all Hell for a basement.'"

"It's the Bible Belt?"

"It sits on natural gas. Still, the town's not without its supernatural legends. Story is a gust of wind caught the magic hat of a Cree medicine man during a battle with the Blackfoot and sent it flying into the Saskatchewan River. The Cree saw it as a dire omen and fled."

Mouth open, Gill tilted her head back to catch some

of the rain. The wind was blowing so fast the city was stripped of its pollution. "Your turn. What do you want to know about me?"

"Why am I here? We're hardly two of a kind."

"I'm bored by predictable men and you puzzle me."

"I think I'm straightforward."

"Dream on, retro man. I see this picture in the paper of a Hell's Angel with a kiddie tucked under his arm, so I ask myself why a man like that risked death to save the girl."

"She was in the way and blocked my arm."

"Why'd you become a cop?"

"To legally beat people up."

"Crack on the head. Broken fingers. Joke's on you."

"My dad was a Mountie. So was his dad. It all began when my great-grandfather won the VC at Rorke's Drift in the Anglo–Zulu War."

"Is that why, gun blazing, you kicked in Tarot's door? I think you're addicted to danger and thrills."

"Don't see why that interests you."

"So I'm not puzzled later. The way you're going, odds are you'll end up on my slab. Glean the facts now, and I'll know why you died."

Nick laughed. "Spider woman. Madame Defarge."

Gill ran her foot up his submerged calf. "I'm not looking for ties. I'm looking for excitement. I want to whitewater raft and skin-dive for treasure. I want to downhill race and zoom on a chopper. I want someone wild to electrify me in bed."

"And I thought you lived to curl up with a good book."

Gill paddled across the tub and slithered up his chest. "Tell me your secret. What drives you?"

"My dad shot himself the day I was born, and I don't know why."

The glass door sliding back dissolved the memory. Gabby stopped singing "Milkshake Mademoiselle" to warn, "He's not for you, Gill. His nose is too big."

Nick didn't know she was pregnant yet.

Her back to the door, Gill asked, "How was the Red Serge Dinner?" She turned to add *Strip off your clothes and join us, Dad,* but what she saw in Nick's eyes made her shiver in the hot tub.

INDUNA

Rorke's Drift, Africa
Wednesday, January 22, 1879

"Hold that door!" Lance-Sergeant Craven shouted to Private Williams through the cacophony of race war battle. With his own bayonet he hacked frantically at the internal wall.

The six men were pinned like rats in a hole, their room a middle one at the back of the hospital where the Zulus had set fire to the roof. The room had no windows and no internal door, just this exit opening out on the slope to Shiyane Hill where Craven had sniped at skirmishers. The door braced shut with the lance-sergeant's bed, Williams now knocked bricks from the adjacent wall to punch a loophole for his gun. The tiny stifling room stank of sweat, urine, and open wounds. Dodging bullets to throw their weight against the wooden panels, fierce Zulus gouged the door with their assegais, splinters flying until bulging in, the barrier between whites and mutilation buckled.

"Snakes!" one patient shrieked amid the choking smoke. Delirious, he tossed on his bed in the grip of tropical fever.

"Butchered or roasted alive!" rasped another. "That's us if we don't get out!" He crawled from his cot to help Craven chunk at the wall.

"Down to my last cartridge!" Williams cried. Using his bayonet through the cracked door, he thrust a jab at the eye of a Zulu peering in.

Then clawlike black hands grabbed Williams through the breach.

This hellish, claustrophobic room was the stuff of nightmares. Damp from weeks of rain, the torched thatch smoldered, pouring sparks and smudge down into the dark confines where an oil lamp sputtered the only internal light. In through the bashed door intruded the clash of battle: the magnified roars of rifles amid war cries of *"uSuthu!"*; gibbering from those impaled on bayonets and spears; the crack of a knobkerrie crushing a skull; the rap of bullets striking biscuit boxes; the queer plump of slugs tearing into mealie bags; the *whizz* and rip of hurled throwing spears; as the fevered soldier squealed "Snakes!" repeatedly.

Grabbed by the arms and legs, Williams was dragged outside. There, Zulus speared him in a bloody "washing" frenzy, then his abdomen was slit to dissipate *umnyama*. His face gray with plaster dust and brick chips flying, Craven punched through the interior wall as Africans stormed in. Masked by gagging smoke billowing out the door, he and his helper shoved a patient into the hole as Zulus across the room pounced on two Redcoats in their beds. "Snakes!" howled one while they stabbed him sixteen times, before slitting his belly so intestines slithered to the floor like the reptiles in his fever. Hauling his helper after him, Craven wriggled through the hole into the next room, but Zulus grabbed the private by the legs for a tug-of-war. When the "rope" died from an assegai to the spine, Craven nailed the Redcoat to the floor with his bayonet, using the corpse to plug the hole.

The one-story infirmary was a disorganized maze of rooms. Chambers that didn't interconnect opened to the outside, while those that were linked had weak internal doors. Two large rooms in front opened on the veranda, backed by cubbyholes down one side and across the rear. Mattresses raised on boards within the tiny rooms was the only change that converted the house to a hospital. Chard had forewarned those confined to burrow from room to room, and failure to heed his advice meant every nook was now a cage.

Fire and churning black smoke filled the room into which Craven escaped. The Zulus who seized the veranda after Chard's withdrawal to the storehouse barrier were inside the hospital and mobbing this door. Private Hook was single-handedly defending nine patients when Craven appeared in the smoke like a ghost who can pass through walls. A spear thrust in the door struck Hook's helmet, knocking it back to slash his scalp and gush blood down his face. "Hold them, Hook!" Craven yelled

over the din of battle and cries from the wounded and
groans of fear from bedridden patients. Grabbing the
navvy's pick used earlier to punch loopholes in outer
walls, Craven swung it hard at the divider between this
room and the next. Chips and chunks flew everywhere
as the lance-sergeant hammered, *bangs!* from the pick
rivaling *bangs!* from Hook's rifle. Only one Zulu at a
time could rush the door, and as each fell to Hook's
lunger he blocked the assault of the next. Bullets they
held in contempt, but Zulus respected the bayonet, for
its reach extended beyond that of assegais. Craven
smashed a jagged tunnel through the wall, then shoved
or hauled patients into the adjoining room. Only Private
Connolly remained when Hook gave up the door, blasting the nearest Zulu point-blank to hurl him back at the
mob. Dragging Connolly behind him, Hook crawled into
the hole, the invalid yelping with pain as his leg broke
during their retreat. Frustrated cursing followed them.

Another isolated room, another blocking wall. Hook
held the last hole while Craven hammered the next,
arms pistoning the lunger back through the breach,
spurts of blood spraying in with each hit. Again Hook
as last man out had to drag Connolly.

The next two rooms had a connecting door. A window
high up in the far wall overlooked the yard between the
hospital and the storehouse. Their names reflecting the
number of Welshmen in "B" Company and not kinship,
here Private Jones, an "Old Sweat" with a black goatee,
and Private Jones, born the year before the Sweat en-
listed, were not only defending the room but trying to
evacuate patients out the window to the yard. Craven
and Hook joined the escape route, helping their men
out the exit, too. The last patient was delirious from
malaria. Dressed to go, he sat on his bed and refused to
move. The Sweat and Hook climbed out the window.
"I'll bring him!" said young Jones as he handed Craven
his rifle spiked with a lunger. As Jones ran for the patient, the lance-sergeant clambered up to the exit.

The fire had burned through the rafters and flames
licked menacingly at Craven's head. Both hands were
cut and blistered; his lungs hacked from smoke; and it
was unbearably hot up here. But along with fresh air
came a new ordeal, for thirty yards of no-man's-land

stretched from the hospital to the barricade protecting the front of the storehouse. The mealie bag walls down both sides were seized by Zulus after Chard abandoned them, so the hospital patients were hobbling and crawling a gauntlet between enemy warriors massed outside the flanking barriers. A hail of sustained gunfire from the biscuit box rampart made it difficult for Zulus to breach and cross the yard, but now and then one would risk a dash to get at the escapers.

A scream from behind wrenched Craven's head about. Zulus had broken into the room and were assegaiing the malarial patient. "Go! Go! Go!" Jones exhorted as he retreated for the window. Only the crash of burning timbers saved him from being speared. Clambering out the exit, Craven dropped into the yard.

He remembered Shaka.

This *Induna Enkulu.*

Born in about 1787, Shaka was the illegitimate son of Chief Senzangakhona of the *amaZulu* people. Banished from their village as an embarrassment, both mother and son lived in exile among the Mthethwa. The youth gained a reputation as a ruthless warrior, and on his father's death in 1816 seized the throne to rule as King Shaka kaSenzangakhona of the *amaZulu*. When he took control of the army, the Zulu were just one of a number of small Nguni tribes. It was Shaka who designed the deadly two-bladed thrusting assegai, and then the attack formation of the "beast's horns"—the *impondo zankomo*. One group of warriors—the *isifuba* or "chest"—rushed the enemy head-on, while two flanking groups—the *izimpondo* or "horns"—moved swiftly around on both sides to encircle the rear. Reserves—the *umuva* or "loins"—were massed behind the chest, and held back from battle to plug any gaps. Swiftness of foot was important, so Zulus fought barefoot. Their soles were hardened by having to parade on thorn grounds. Any man who flinched was put to death then and there. Ferocity was important, so Zulus could have no sex until they "washed their spears," and those defeated in battle were put to death. Discipline was important, so shield-bearers shading the king from the sun who allowed rays through were put to death. Respect was important, so

those who sneezed when the king was eating or failed
to grieve when his mother died were put to death. Power
was important, so when he developed an interest in em-
bryology, a hundred pregnant women were cut open for
him to see. He made "To Conquer or To Die" the Zulu
motto, and within four years, the realm of the *ama-
Zulu*—"The Children of the Heavens"—was 20,000
square miles.

He remembered Shaka.

This Battlefield Commander.

Zulus had a name for barbarians like these. Whites
were *abelungu*—"pallid sea creatures"—which the surf
spat onto African shores. Throughout the reigns of
King Shaka, King Dingane, King Mpande, and now
King Cetshwayo, they had pressed . . . pressed . . .
pressed Zululand. Zulu regiments were humiliated at
the Battle of Blood River by Boer Trekkers in 1838.
And now—the ultimate insult—British Redcoats were
invading Zululand. Earlier this afternoon across the
river at Mount Isandlwana, 1,500 of the whites and
their black slaves had been annihilated in the greatest
Zulu victory since Shaka's time. Prince Dabulamanzi
and this *Induna* were in command of the loin reserves—senior warriors of the *iNdlondlo, uThulwana,*
and *uDloko* regiments. The reserves were not released
so they had missed the battle, and consequently would
have no tales of glory to tell and no exotic loot to
flaunt. Laurels for being "the first to stab" would go
to younger men, a blow to their honor. The king had
prohibited his army from crossing into Natal, but Dabulamanzi knew he had to "wash the spears of his
boys," who were loath to return home without something to show for the day. A raid on *KwaJim*—"Jim's
place"—at Rorke's Drift would allow the 4,000 reserves to kill white Redcoats and loot their supplies.

The raid was not going well.

Outreached by bayonets, outgunned by the awe-
some firepower of breach-loading Martini-Henrys dis-
charging sustained volleys like a machine gun, and
outmaneuvered by having to rush fortified positions,
Zulus were falling by the hundred for every defender
killed. This raid could become a horrid defeat unless
something magic was done, something to inspire the

attackers into a massive onslaught to overrun the ramparts around the storehouse yard, behind which the Redcoats were building a redoubt of mealie bags to make a last stand.

He remembered Shaka.

From when he was a boy.

"To Conquer or To Die."

The cry he shouted now.

So this *Induna Enkulu,* this Battlefield Commander, reined his white horse around from where he and Prince Dabulamanzi watched the battle raging from the slope of Shiyane Hill, and rode down to the Zulu-held mealie bag wall running from the front corner of the storehouse across to the back corner of the hospital, where he dismounted from his horse across the wall in no-man's-land as patients ran the gauntlet.

Dizzy from his illness and dazed by glare from the burning hospital, a trooper turned as if not sure which way to go, then wandered like a sleepwalker toward the *Induna.*

Redcoats behind the barricade yelled at him to hit the ground so they could shoot.

The trooper shielded the *Induna* approaching beyond.

Limited to a handful of the most senior commanders in 1879, the *Induna*'s battle dress harkened back to the days of King Shaka. His magnificent "kilt" was made of twisted civet and monkey fur. Cow tail festoons circled his neck, elbows, knees, and ankles. His stuffed otter skin headband was adorned with colorful feathers. Below his grizzled beard, the snakeskin pouch around his neck with the festoon contained ten knucklebones: *izikhombi* "pointers" he used to smell out evil. For this *Induna* was a bone diviner: an *inyanga yamathambo.*

One arm carried a full-size *isihlangu* shield taken from his horse.

The other hand gripped a carved knobkerrie club.

Inspired by the magic man's immunity to shots from the ramparts, other Zulus were vaulting over the mealie bag flanks.

The *Induna* raised the knobkerrie to club the dazed trooper.

"You!"

The shout close behind caused the *Induna* to whirl.

And that's when Lance-Sergeant Rex Craven used the twenty-two-inch socket bayonet to stab the witch doctor through his heart.

THE STRATEGY WALL

Vancouver
Wednesday, December 8, 1993

For Inspector Zinc Chandler it had been a long and bumpy road back. The Ghoul, the Cutthroat, the Ripper: three psychos out for the kill. More actually, but that was a different story. And each demon had taken a piece of him.

Six-foot-two and 190 pounds, his physique was muscled from working the family farm in Saskatchewan. Rugged and sharp-featured, his face was hard and gaunt, the years of pain subtracting from handsome good looks. His natural steel-gray hair was the color of his eyes, the metallic tint responsible for his given name. The one-inch-square piece of bone cut from his brow had left an indent where the doctors had patched his brain, but recent plastic surgery had hidden that. Those scars on his forehead from the bullet wound were gone, which left the old knife scar along his jaw. There was a *new* knife scar on his back, and that stabbing had taken the past year to heal.

If reincarnation was true, he planned to come back as a cat.

The way life had treated him, nine lives were what he needed.

The aftermath of the Cutthroat shootout had forced Zinc out to pasture, five long years back on the family farm, waiting, waiting, waiting to return to Special X. Then one winter day, last December, the call to duty came, though no one, including him, realized it at the time.

Who could have known what torture and torment that Mystery Weekend would be, trapped on a secluded island with Jack the Ripper himself, that carnival of carnage that put Zinc to a do-or-die test, the result being—after recuperation—he was allowed to return to Special X.

Now, thanks to Jack having his head smashed in and his guts torn out, Zinc was the new head of Operations and back on top.

Historically, the Tudor building at 33rd and Heather was to house Langara School For Boys. Purchased by the Force in 1921, it became barracks accommodation for 200 Members. Four stables were added for 140 horses. The Heather Stables, as it was known, was now the RCMP Training Academy. New recruits were trained at Depot Division in Regina as they had always been, but here West Coast Mounties could upgrade their leadership, management, or investigative skills for promotion. Like police forces everywhere, "E" Division is chronically short of space, so Special X had usurped a chunk of the stables. Chief Superintendent DeClercq's office on the second floor was the one he had commandeered during the Headhunter case.

At three o'clock in the morning, six hours after Jack's death, Zinc rushed into that office with a fax from Germany.

"John Doe's name is Günter Schreck. German police want him for killing three cops. They must want him bad since they're flying a man here *today* with extradition papers."

"Germany after us," Robert said. "If I have a say, all they'll get is Schreck's bones. He owes Jack a life in jail first."

"Schreck's psychotic. Weird hallucinations. Thinks he's being persecuted by"—Zinc checked the fax—*"Knochenpolizei."*

"Bone Police," Robert said.

It never ceased to amaze him, the chief's eclectic knowledge, which Zinc put down to researching the books he'd published: *Men Who Wore the Tunic (Those Who Wore the Tunic* in a later edition), and *Bagpipes, Blood and Glory,* the myth of Wilfred Blake.

"He sees cops as skeletons wearing uniforms," said Zinc. "They have no flesh, so the only way to kill them is to crush their skulls."

He passed the fax and accompanying photophone picture to DeClercq, who read the print twice and compared the German mug shot with one snapped here. The glower of the same skinhead in both photos gazed upon a vision of horror and paranoia. The chief pinned the papers to his Strategy Wall.

Robert DeClercq's office was an airy, high-vaulted loft. Windows faced the Conservatory atop Little Mountain's Queen Elizabeth Park, once a quarry for rocks to pave the city's streets. Three Victorian library tables U'd like a horseshoe served as his desk. His chair was an antique from bygone days, high-backed with a barley-sugar frame crowned with the buffalo head crest of the North-West Mounted Police. Two walls were covered floor to ceiling with corkboard, for when plotting a book or solving a case, DeClercq campaigned visually. Standing before his Strategy Wall, the chief was a general about to do battle through troop markers deployed around his Headquarters map.

Tonight, the map on the wall was of Coquitlam.

Vertical lines divided the wall into thirds.

The left third, on which DeClercq now focused his attention, visualized the murders of Bert and Ernie on Colony Farm. Preliminary reports encircled Polaroids of the bodies. Each new jigsaw piece to arrive was added to the puzzle.

"Schreck killed both deputies," Robert began. "He stomped their heads, crushing them, then escaped across Colony Farm. The MO fits his psychosis. Skull-crush the Bone Police."

"He's our man," Zinc agreed. "Psycho on the run."

"Running amok? Or running toward a goal? New West Police arrested him B and Eing a sporting goods outlet. The loot he'd gathered consisted of a thermal coat, a polar tent, and other Arctic stuff. Does the Canadian Arctic somehow feed into Schreck's psychosis? Is that why he's here?"

"I'll alert all transportation links to the North. Planes, trains, automobiles, gateways, and Cassiar and Alaska Highway stops. He won't be hard to spot."

"Tag him 'extremely dangerous.' A crazy cop killer loose."

After Zinc made the call, Robert moved to the map pinned high on the central third of his Strategy Wall. Vertical Colony Farm Road T-intersected with horizontal Lougheed Highway. Along the lower edge of the Lougheed ran railway tracks. "When the sheriff's deputies called in a ten-eighteen medical problem but didn't arrive at FPI, the Forensic Institute sent doctors out. They found the bodies and raised the alarm. Our response was along the only route, down the Lougheed and south on Colony Farm Road. Unfortunately, a mile-long train blocked the way. Schreck was long gone by the time it passed. Dogs lost his scent at the Coquitlam River, and didn't pick it up on the other side. Perhaps he used the ditch network to throw them off."

From Colony Farm Road on the map, Robert's finger slid east across the Coquitlam River to Mary Hill Road. "Schreck escaped at ten after five, heading toward Dora Craven's home. Nick left her alive about that time, and later she's found bludgeoned with a crushed skull. Did Schreck pick up some kind of club as he fled, then use her house to hide from us?"

"MO fits," said Zinc.

"What bothers me," said Robert, "is the scent from the house. Dog teams tracked it from the back porch, up the path along the face of Mary Hill, toward the Indian Reserve and Port Coquitlam Town Center. If Schreck left the scent, there should be *two* trails, one climbing the hill from Colony Farm, the other as found. Instead, the dogs seem to say the killer backtracked the same route he arrived."

"Unless Schreck angled north along the ditch network," said Zinc, "then climbed the hill, reached the path, and came south to the house."

"That's fleeing in the wrong direction. Toward the cops on his tail. If only the trail from the sheriff's car didn't end at the river. And if only the dogs could tell us the scents on both sides were left by the same man."

"It's dark," Zinc said. "Schreck's in the bush. He turns the wrong way."

"None of his fingerprints were found in the murder kitchen."

"Surfaces were wiped clean."

"Hardly the act of a psychotic on the run. Schreck kills the deputies with prints all over the scene, then stops to wipe Dora's kitchen clean?"

"A crazy doesn't act rationally. Irrationality is his hall-mark. A different killer at Dora's house flouts the odds. Too great a coincidence."

"Is it?" Robert said. "Schreck kills the deputies at five-ten. Nick leaves his mom alive about that time, and soon whoever came down the path arrives at her back door. The kitchen window overlooks Colony Farm Road, so he witnesses the manhunt below, perhaps catching a news flash on the radio. An escaping madman has crushed two skulls on Colony Farm. If X clubs Dora and wipes up his prints, then flees up the path by which he came, surely the police will blame the missing psycho. Sounds like a perfect smokescreen to me."

"Okay, we keep an open mind and follow both trails till one gets blocked. The problem I have with X is his motive. Did he come to kill Dora, or decide to kill her there? If preplanned, why? If spontaneous, what set him off? Be interesting to see Kidd's report. I hear she's smart," said Zinc.

Mary Hill was down near the tip of the V where the Coquitlam and Pitt rivers joined the Fraser. Northeast across the map, Robert slid his finger up the right arm of the V to Minnekhada Lodge. "Schreck killed the deputies and killed Dora. Schreck killed the deputies and X killed Dora. Who killed Jack?"

The central third of the Strategy Wall was for the Craven murder. Moving right, they stood before the MacDougall third. Photos of Jack, disemboweled, crowded by reports.

"Whoever it was came and left by car," said Zinc. "A *third* killer would really stretch the odds. A double smokescreen?"

"Say it's X."

"Motive? Link? Why kill Dora and Jack?"

"Say it's Schreck."

"Gotta be. Then everything fits. The deputies are Bone Police, so he crushes their skulls. Dora's on his escape route, so he clubs her down. He steals a car and follows Jack from Dora's house to the lodge when Jack returns from driving Nick. Jack's with the Bone Police, so he crushes his skull. Four psychotic murders in a row."

"What doesn't fit," Robert said, "is gutting Jack. Schreck sees the Bone Police as animate skeletons. Why disembowel a psychotic hallucination without any flesh? As you said in the parking lot, 'The bludgeoning killed him. So why the disemboweling?' Good question. It's the key."

HARD ENTRY

When this city has a ghetto, it will be the East End. Late last century, the area was a timber stand for Hastings Mill, and Indians hunted elk here to sell to white settlers as a substitute for beef. The only roads back then were skidroads for logs, and skid road is the future many see now. In 1891, East Vancouver was born, thanks to the new electric interurban railway that shot east to New Westminster. The streets were laid by chain gangs from the city jail, and cows were soon limited to twenty-five per household. One of the streets, Adanac, is Canada spelled backward. The summer of 1904, Edward Odlum was standing with friends on a rise within sight of False Creek. "What a grand view," someone said, and he replied—the story goes—"Yes, Grandview would be an excellent name for the area."

So Grandview it is.

But a "grand view" it's not today.

First to settle Vancouver's first suburb were the British, of course. But after World War I, the Chinese, Italians, and East Europeans moved in. After World War II, East Indians arrived, followed by waves of refugees from the Third World, drawn by the fact Canada's immigration laws are a mess. Land and claim you're persecuted back home—it matters not whether it's California, which wants you for rape-murders, or Iran, which wants to cut off your head—and you get welfare and medical while your case is mired forever in a bureaucratic bog. The country's known as a pushover around a world on the move, so Canada's a haven for offshore crime, and those fighting foreign battles from afar.

The Bad Guys, to Special X.

Somalia was currently enmeshed in civil war. Rival warlords and their clans fought for control of Africa's multimillion-dollar khat trade, while UN peacekeepers struggled to feed starving people. Grown in the uplands of Kenya and Ethiopia, khat is a highly addictive drug trafficked throughout the Horn of Africa. To buy guns and pay men to wage their war, warlords send "refugees" to Canada, usually their families and members of their clan. The "refugees" apply for welfare under multiple names, and import khat with pot and opium grown in the "death triangle" around Biaboa to sell. The net effect is Canada finances the war, buying arms like those that killed twenty-three UN peacekeepers from Pakistan, and almost wiped out a crack American Ranger unit. Canadian paratroops sent to dodge Canadian-financed bullets torture and kill Somali youth, while the politically correct at home muzzle truth with Partyspeak.

War as soap opera.

But not this morning.

Easy for the doc to say *You must avoid alcohol and sleeplessness. And never—I repeat* never—*miss taking your drugs* ... but Chandler was a cop and cops work around the clock, so though he was subject to epilepsy from the gunshot scar in his brain, sleeplessness it was. As head of Operations, he oversaw all cases, so having worked through the night on Jack MacDougall's murder, booting the Violent Crimes Analysis Section out of bed to computer-hunt every cop hater and killer from coast to coast and beyond, now the darkness before dawn saw him drive to Grandview in Vancouver's East End, and here stop by a gun-metal gray van innocuously hidden in a church parking lot.

The fourteen-foot-long box of the van yawned and swallowed Zinc. Inside, he met the op commander of HQ's Emergency Response Team, a telecommunications pair with headsets, mikes, recorders, and a video screen, plus a negotiator should something go wrong. The radio man and woman sat at a small desk; Zinc and the negotiator on a side bench; while the OC kept pace with his shadow cast on the eight-foot ceiling by the washy black-and-white image on the screen.

"Brief me," Chandler said.

"The Somalis are in a duplex three streets away." The OC indicated the residence on the screen. "Special I installed an infrared camera up a telephone pole. Two marksmen on roofs within a hundred yards will feed us running comment from their scopes. Final check," the OC ordered telecom.

"Sierra One. Op Command. Update the front."

"Op Command. Sierra One. No sign of life. Windows dark with no movement in Alpha or Bravo."

"Sierra Two. Op Command. Update the rear."

"Op Command. Sierra Two. Alpha Half black. TV just on in Bravo Half. Upper floor, window two."

"Alpha Team?"

"Copy."

"Bravo Team?"

"Roger. Life on the top floor, second window in."

"Alpha, Bravo, hard entry in two. Phase Line Green and hold for Go from OC."

The duplex spied on by the infrared camera was a boxy, bland, boring Vancouver Special. A relic from the decade of disco, platform shoes, and $7.50 Led Zeppelin tickets, it featured a low-rise tar-and-gravel roof, a wrought-iron balcony railing with little balcony, and a flat stucco front above brick facing. Stippled ceilings and swag lamps with lime-green or burnt-orange wall-to-wall shag would showcase black velvet paintings inside. In this part of the East End, Vancouver Specials were a plague.

"The drugs are in the Alpha Half," the operations commander continued. "Khat, hemp, and poppy from Kenya by way of London, hidden in a cargo of tobacco leaves. Our tip said the Somalis rent just the Alpha Half, but watchers caught them going in and out of the Bravo Half all day."

"You're taking down both sides?"

"Two eight-man teams."

Just as Special X is the external arm of the RCMP, so Special I (for Investigation) is its electronic ears and mind's eye, while Special O (for Observation) sends out

fleshed "watchers." As the OC briefed Zinc, sixteen
shadows converged on the duplex from both edges of
the screen, darting and dodging from cover to cover
toward the side-by-side front doors. From how the point
man on the left moved, Chandler knew Ed "Mad Dog"
Rabidowski led Alpha Team.

A brawny loner with a heavy-browed scowl, the Mad
Dog was the meanest-looking Member in the Force. Son
of a Yukon trapper raised in the woods, he could take
the eye out of a squirrel with a .22 at 100 yards before
he was six. A man of repressed violence, he lived to kill:
hunting grizzly bears at Kakwa River, packs of wolves
near Tweedsmuir Park, elk on Pink Mountain, and
punks with the ERT. There was a time when people
likened him to Charles Bronson—a comment he wel-
comed before Bronson went soft—but now he aped the
screen presence of Harvey Keitel. The Mad Dog made
a point of only dating whores, for—as he put it—"Why
mess with amateurs if you can blow with a pro?" The
Mad Dog was the barbarian DeClercq sicked on savages
so he could follow with the Charter of Rights. The best
that could be said for having the Mad Dog on your side
was then you could be sure he wasn't on the other.

Though some wore baseball caps, this was Canada so
most had tuques or balaclavas. The black turtleneck was
hidden under a dark blue combat jacket with no buttons
and nylon zippers to remain antistatic around aircraft.
Matching blue combat pants with cargo pockets had
cuffs tucked into black Canadian Army boots. Over each
jacket was a dark tactical armored vest with Velcro
pockets to move around for different ERT weapons: tear
gas, pepper spray, or blasts for hard entry. POLICE
RCMP in white blared the pull-down flap in front. PO-
LICE on the fold-down flap behind. VPR, or Voice Private Radio attached to each vest scrambled orders so no
one could intercept ERT communications. An earphone
was stuck in each cop's ear.

"Oscar Charlie. Alpha Team. Phase Line Green."

"Oscar Charlie. Bravo Team. Phase Line Green."

"Go!" ordered Op Command.

The Ram-It member of each team battered one of
the two doors. A thirty-inch cylinder weighing thirty-five
pounds, with semiflex grips to swing it in a roundhouse

arc at locks, the Ram-It (or "key to the city") impacts with a kinetic force of 14,000 pounds, with extra "pop" added by the follow-through handles. *Even your smallest operative becomes a BIG ramer with Ram-It* hints the ad, and there's a two-man Ram-It II to add 10,000 pounds of he-man thrust should testosterone demand it. *Even short strokes yield high impact.*

Your Vancouver Special is cheap to build. Aluminum framed with minimal wood for a square-foot cost of $35, walls and doors are so thin you might as well *be* in the next room. Both duplex doors exploded in unison, Ram-It members stepping back to let their teams in, Alpha Team into the Alpha Half, Bravo Team into the Bravo Half, in four pairs of two a side, the Ram-It member joining the last odd man.

The Mad Dog led the *second* pair of Alpha Team, for he had to be where the danger was.

ERT Mounties don't give both hands to the gun. The two-hand stance, arms out, is for long-range targets. The *last* thing you want when you wax a door is both hands occupied, the idea being to scare the fight out of the Bad Guys NOW!, so the first-man-in-the-door on both teams tossed a stun grenade into the living room off the entrance hall, left in Alpha Half where two Somalis slept, right in Bravo Half where no one was, the bright burst and loud explosion hurling a concussion you could feel, followed by each first pair storming into the room, the Alpha two on the Somalis before they came out of shock, guns to both heads as the designated speaker yelled, "Police! Police! Search warrant! Everyone on the floor!" With each punk down, the ERT team "drops a body," so the first two into Alpha Half cuffed and guarded the dazed Somalis, while the Mad Dog rushed up the stairs toward the upper floor.

The fourth-man-in trailed him as the second pair.

The next two reinforced the ground floor assault.

The last pair started up the stairs as upper floor backup.

The Mad Dog gripped a SIG/Sauer P 226 in one hand as primary weapon, his other hand free to catch rebounding doors, or to guide him along dark halls, or to switch on lights. The 9mm pistol weighed two pounds, the fifteen-round magazine "short-loaded" by one to take pressure off the spring so it wouldn't jam. The secondary weapon slung on his back was a Heckler & Koch MP5 submachine gun, thirty rounds in the mag in front of the trigger guard. Extra mags were in the Velcro pockets on his vest.

The Mad Dog was halfway up the stairs when a door at the top jerked open.

Night vision goggles are only used if you control all light. An unexpected flash could blind the whole team. Instead, the Mad Dog beamed the Surefire torch mounted under the barrel of the SIG, activated by a pressure plate. In the room downstairs, flashlight rays crossed like swords in the dark, but here in the stairway tunnel, only the Mad Dog lit the way. Those behind followed single file, beams out so not to backlight him as a target. The tunnel was a shooting gallery for the Somali on the landing above, who gripped a Mini Uzi in both hands, commando weapon of the Israeli Army, 950 shots a minute from a 32-round clip.

The Mad Dog shone the Surefire at his unadjusted eyes.

The wincing Somali swung the machine gun to spray the cops on the stairs.

He was asking for it, so the Mad Dog let him have it. *Bam! Bam! . . . Bam! Bam! . . . Bam! Bam! . . .* Thunder boomed along the narrow tunnel as yellow muzzle flashes licked up the stairs. Shoot to kill, the Mad Dog fingered "double taps" at the man, second round following on the tail of the first, all shots at the "center of mass," both the largest target and home to the heart, lungs, and spine. *Ping! Ping! . . . Ping! Ping! . . . Ping! Ping! . . .* Casings flew from the ejection port, bouncing off the staircase wall as the SIG semiauto action used each blast to slide a live round into the spout.

In white undershirt and white underpants, his dark head and limbs lost in dark shadows at the top of the stairs, this Somali was begging *Shoot me here.* The six shots tore his undershirt, red holes sucking light from the Surefire beam, as forward motion pitched him headfirst down the stairs, the 9mm not an abattoir gun, no hurling back of mangled bodies like the guns of TV cops do, but the Bad Guy gone all the same.

"One coming down," the Mad Dog yelled to those

behind, the body tobogganing down the aisle beside their single file.

Two more gunmen appeared above.

The naked one who emerged from the same doorway as Underwear had a shortened version of the AK–47, Chinese model. From the hall that branched left from the top of the stairs to another bedroom, a thug in a leopard-skin jockstrap joined Bareballs, this Somali so big they had to form two ranks so both could command the tunnel. In one hand he carried a flashlight. The other aimed a MAC 10.

The Mad Dog snuffed his beam as Jockstrap's torch lit the hall above, reversing the shooting gallery. Trained to keep climbing until he was clear of stairs, dominating each Bad Guy in turn, the Mad Dog shouted "Police! Police!" while bounding up the steps, *Bam! Bam! . . . Bam! Bam! . . . Bam! Bam! . . .* blasting the SIG at Jockstrap in a volley of double taps, feeding him slug upon slug to cut him down. *Twelve gone,* Ed thought, keeping count of shots, so he raised the gun and . . . *Bam! . . .* put one between Jockstrap's eyes.

The arm with the flashlight smacked back to whack Bareballs. It conked him as he triggered the AK–47 down the stairs, jerking the barrel high to machine-gun the top of the tunnel. *Pffdrdrt! Pffdrdrt! Pffdrdrt!* rained plaster down, and Bareballs stumbled back into the dark bedroom. As Jockstrap cried blood from his Cyclops eye, crumpling to his knees, then crashing to the floor, the Mad Dog crested the top of the stairs. The Mini Uzi and MAC 10 were both machine pistols, unable to pierce the armor the ERT cops wore. The AK–47 was an assault rifle armed with military full metal jackets, so now was the time to make the last shot count, Bareballs collecting himself in the dark for an armor-piercing burst, as the Mad Dog gave both hands to the gun, shone the Surefire into the room, and fired the SIG.

The Mountie was trained to watch arcs of fire, to ensure he didn't hit one of the team or blast through a wall with someone on the other side. The Mad Dog's aim was true and *Bam!* the bullet drilled through Bareballs's heart, killing him instantly. What the sergeant could not control was cadaveric spasm: the Somali's finger twitching as he twisted from the shot, triggering a

Pffdrdrt! at the wall dividing Alpha from Bravo Half in this sturdy Vancouver Special.

Knives through butter.

ERT Mounties train to synchronize attacks. Third man into Bravo Half was Corporal Wayne Tarr, a wiry and fiery redhead with nerves to match. As he dashed up the stairs parallel to those next door, gunfire exploded in Alpha Half. On his last assault, Tarr was almost shot, so adrenaline hit him hard as he topped the stairs, the fact a cop killer was loose cinching him another notch, SIG itching to fire, door on the landing closed, one, two, three, turn the knob, kick it wide open, this door to the bedroom second in, from which Sierra Two reported TV glow.

The room was dark except for a *Scooby Doo* cartoon Tarr couldn't see, an armchair facing the set with its back to him blocking the screen.

As the door burst open, a figure jumped and turned toward him, a black silhouette against flickering glow, just a head, hand, and gun visible over the back of the chair.

Bareballs's bullets from next door blew through the wall, zipping from the dark to whiz past the corporal's face, chunking plaster beside him.

Tarr thought the shots came from the chair.

He fired the SIG at the silhouette until it dropped from sight.

In the Op Command van parked in the church lot, Zinc, the OC, and the others were glued to the telecom, visualizing the takedown from broadcast bursts and demands.

"He's in behind! He's got a gun! Gimme cover! I'm going in!"

"Oscar Charlie. Alpha Team. Alpha is secure. Three cold badgers. Two warm badgers. Belly down. Proned out. Cuffed up."

"Copy, Alpha. Clear the air."

"Jesus Christ!"

"Bravo Team. This is Op Command."

"EHS! EHS! We need 'em now!"

"Copy."

"EHS!"

"EHS being called."

"EHS Emerg! We got one down!"

"A Member down?"

"Negative! Members are okay!"

"EHS ambulance coming Code three."

"Oscar Charlie, we got a b-i-g problem here!"

The OC took the mike. "What kind of problem?" As he listened, jaw muscles jumped and temple veins popped out. Then he said, "This is Swann. I'm taking over this scene. Clear the air. No more transmissions. Secure the perimeter. I want Ident here now. I want Serious Crimes here now. I want Internal here now. I want VPD and HQ Media Relations here now. I want the Incident Commander here now. NOW! Is that clear?"

POWDER KEG

West Vancouver

> Ode To Teaboy
> Oh, to make a pot of tea,
> Some for you, and some for me,
> The kettle boils while teapot heats,
> Then add the bags, it's time to steep.
>
> Oh, then to pour the steaming tea,
> Into the *Equal*ed, milky sea,
> Some for you, and some for me,
> Hand-prepared by boy of tea.

Yes, there certainly had been changes around his home.

DeClercq had worked all night on Jack MacDougall's killing, and now returned home with the first light of dawn to wake Katt up for school and grab a few winks' sleep before tackling the case again. His eyes caught the poem magnetically pinned to the fridge with a Happy Face the moment he stepped in the door. Weary though he was, a smile creased his jaw, while his mind recalled the close of the Ripper ordeal. . . .

Snow billowed up as the helicopter entered ground effect. The Cowboy lowered the collective pitch lever to set them down. Indicating the overgrown tangle to the right, Craven shouted, "Someone's in the maze." The whup-whup-whup *of the airfoils died to a whistle.*

Remington pump in hand, Heckler submachine gun slung over his shoulder, the Mad Dog opened the port doors and jumped down. Guns drawn, the others followed him, facing the maze the searchlight lit as bright as high noon.

Two trees flanked the entrance to the labyrinth. About fourteen, with fear in her eyes, a girl wrapped in a rug stumbled toward them. DeClercq shuddered with déjà vu. *He was living the dream that had plagued him for years.*

In the Shakespeare Garden of Stanley Park stand two trees: "Comedy" lush as you like it, and "Tragedy" as stunted as Richard III. Between their trunks, arms outstretched, Janie runs toward him, her frightened voice crying "Daddy!" plaintively. No matter how hard she runs, she draws no closer to him.

Then before he knew it, the girl was in his arms, teeth chattering like tap dancers from the cold, hypothermia seeking his warmth.

She wasn't his daughter.

But she might be.

When sorrow is asleep, wake it not.

"You're bleeding."

"He cut me."

"Who?" DeClercq asked.

She gave him the name of the killer on Deadman's Island.

"Your name?"

"Katt Darke."

"Where's your mother?"

"Dead."

"And your father?"

"Don't have one. Now I don't have anyone in the world."

Since that day a year ago Katt had lived with him, and for the first time in over twenty years Jane's ghost was at rest. His daughter and his first wife had been killed by terrorists in the Quebec October Crisis of 1970. Genevieve—his second wife—was shot ten years ago during the Headhunter case. Since then he and Napoleon had lived in a tomb . . . this tomb opened up to air and life by Katt. Katt, the poet laureate of his royal house, scribbling screeds to commemorate major home-front events, like how he brewed a pot of tea or "Dog's" return from the vet. Katt, who saved him from becoming a morose SOB.

The "Teaboy Ode" was pinned beside "My Lomies & Me."

The first thing DeClercq did to bond with Katt was take her to Egypt. Nothing like travel in foreign lands to link inquisitive minds. Their second day at Mena House beside the Pyramids, he awoke to find Katt gone from their room. *Climbing the Stairway to Heaven,* the note on her bed read.

Around noon, Katt returned dripping with sweat. "Sorry," she said, "but I was afraid you'd nix my idea. Wait till you see the pix I took from the top of the Great Pyramid."

"You can't climb Cheops," DeClercq said.

"Not *can't,* Teaboy. *Mayn't* is the curse."

At each of the four corners of the Great Pyramid stood a guard with an automatic weapon. Katt recruited a Mata Hari for her plan: "This chick with boobs out to here," her outstretched arms explained. ("Chicks sharking muffins with dudical buns," Robert had learned was where women's lib led its latest generation. *Ah, freedom!* he thought.) Mata Hari approached Soldier Boy for a light, neckline gaping to her navel for cool air, and while Mr. Magoo's eyes bugged from their sockets, Katt darted behind him and scampered for the peak. Two hundred and one chest-high blocks later, she crowned herself Queen of the Nile.

"What say you lend me some money, Teaboy, and we celebrate, my treat?"

Celebration was a night along belly dancer strip, Katt among Arabs amused by how quickly she learned from mimicking them, shirt rolled up and jeans pushed down to bare her bowl-of-Jell-O tummy, Robert so flabbergasted he didn't know whether to laugh or cry . . . deciding next day *cry* was the answer when King Tut's Revenge hit his bowels.

"Great food, huh?" Katt yelled through the bathroom door.

"Hurry up," DeClercq said. "My round thirty-three. I may die before the chemist gets here with drugs. Remind me next time—if there's a next time—Lomotil, not Imodium."

The following day at breakfast, the poet gave a reading:

> My Lomies & Me
> Up the Nile, wearing a smile, we go
> My Lomies & me—
> From Cairo's markets dark and dank
> To Aswan's granite rocky banks
> Oh, Allah, we give thanks to you
> My Lomies & me—
>
> The chemists of this distant land
> Place this bowel-binder in my hand
> So we shan't defile these sands—
> Now shout one and all
> For three loud cheers I call
> God . . . Bless . . . Lomotil!

True, it wasn't Keats's "Ode on a Grecian Urn" or "To a Nightingale," but in this day when schools turned out kids who couldn't read, let alone with any grasp of whom Keats was, DeClercq was content with Katt's poetic missives.

Napoleon entered the kitchen as Robert reread both poems. When he crouched to nuzzle the shepherd's brindled face, he spied the honor guard of sneakers by the door. What was it with women and shoes? Were they foot fetishists, one and all? Walk down any street with either of his wives and he was yanked to every window with footwear on display. Was it genetic, or Pavlovian drooling from the torture of wearing spikes? Whatever the cause, Katt was afflicted, too. Witness her Docs, Shell Toes, Gazelles, etc. If women weren't commenting on someone else's shoes, they were adding to their own podagral collections, or complaining about the shoes currently pinching their feet. Call him sexist, but it was true.

With Katt, it was shoes *and* hats.

The Mad Hatter's room was down the hall on the left. Originally a guest room when Genny was alive, Robert had lined it floor to ceiling with bookshelves after she died, only to reconvert the library to a bedroom when Katt moved in. On her stomach with her mussed head to one side, the teenager slept soundly in her canopied bed. A dozen hats hung on hooks down the four posts, one of them the top hat she wore on Deadman's Island.

Napoleon howled like a wolf baying at the moon.

The Mad Hatter opened one sandman eye in her puffy face.

"Couldn't we get a rooster like everyone else?"

"It's Wednesday. Egg Day. Your favorite," he said. "Those not at the table in five minutes go without cholesterol for a week."

"Drag me out, dog," Katt moaned.

Robert returned to the kitchen and switched on the radio. Listening to news, he boiled eggs and toasted bread.

"*. . . yesterday in Los Angeles, Damian Williams, the black man convicted in the widely televised attack on white truck driver Reginald Denny in last year's riots, received the maximum sentence of ten years in prison. The attack, witnessed live by millions on TV, came to symbolize racial anarchy in the streets. The case began on May third, 1991, when black motorist Rodney King's beating by a gang of white police was captured on videotape. The officers' acquittal by a state court sparked the L.A. riots in which fifty-four people were killed. . . .*"

"Big end up," Katt said, padding into the kitchen, ash blond hair tufted above a blue bathrobe and sheepskin slippers. Theirs was the war in *Gulliver's Travels* over whether to crack a boiled egg at the big or little end.

"*. . . last night in a suburb just outside New York, a gunman randomly shot commuters as he walked down the aisle of a packed rush-hour train, killing five and wounding sixteen. Armed with a nine-millimeter pistol he had to reload twice, the gunman was subdued by passengers. Police identified him as Colin Ferguson, a U.S. citizen from Jamaica who brimmed with racial hatred. Those* *shot were white or Asian, races he disparaged in four pages of seized notes. . . ."*

"Teaboy," Katt said, feeling the cold pot, "you're falling down on the job."

"Sorry, Lady Katt."

Robert DeClercq was addicted to tea. It used to be coffee—seven cups a day—until he discovered tea has caffeine without the jitters. Katt coined "Teaboy" from the number of pots he brewed. Last June, they drove to Seattle—"A trip into Darkest America" in Katt-speak—to catch the Blue Jays/Mariners game. When they stopped for breakfast next morning before heading home, sure enough, the diner served cups of hot water with bags on the side.

"Must be some weird subliminal Boston Tea Party thing," said DeClercq. "Americans refuse to grasp tea results from a shower, not a dip in the pool."

"In Darkest America," Katt said, "one must be prepared." From her shoulder bag she extracted the Brown Betty from home, plunking the earthenware pot in a cozy down on the table.

"Be wanting vinegar on your fries, eh?" the waiter said.

". . . after three centuries of white monopoly rule, South Africa's black majority got its first real say in governing with Tuesday's inauguration of a multiracial council to oversee running the country until elections next April. The dismantling of apartheid, Africa's last and harshest white racist design, came quietly when blacks joined whites in the former Good Hope Theater, a building next to Parliament and not far from Table Bay where Jan van Riebeeck and ninety other Dutch settlers landed in 1652. . . ."

Katt turned off the radio when Robert served their eggs, his little end and hers big end up. As they carried their plates and cutlery down the hall to the dining room she said, "You and your CBC Radio news. How archaic and quaint. May I introduce you to the joys of picture news on TV?"

Until the kid moved in, Robert had no TV. He considered the medium a homogenizer of minds, which killed appreciation of arts refined over ten thousand years. Katt groaned she'd shrivel up and die without MTV rock videos and *Beavis and Butt-head.*

"Alakazam," she said, punching the remote for the living room tube from the breakfast table. The screen was suddenly filled with the face of an anguished, hysterical black woman screaming, "They killed my baby!"

In the background, Chandler, the Mad Dog, and Wayne Tarr stood by the duplex door.

REDCOATS

North Vancouver

Lions Gate Bridge—the gateway to the North Shore—takes its name from The Lions. From west to east, the three North Shore mountains are Hollyburn, Grouse, and Seymour. Bearing real resemblance to a pair of crouched lions, The Lions—two peaks behind—stare through the gap between Hollyburn and Grouse. Early white colonists called them Sheba's Paps, presaging Sheba's Breasts in Rider Haggard's African classic, *King Solomon's Mines.* Renamed The Sisters for more respectability, The Lions were dubbed around 1890 when Judge Gray noted the royal profiles justified calling the entrance to Vancouver's harbor The Lions Gate.

The windowless room was in a log cabin dubbed the Lions Den, an early forest fire lookout perched high on Grouse Mountain at the end of a logging road. This room was ringed by other rooms to insulate it from the cold. Leased, the pioneer hideaway was furnished with three tables and a chair. Flickering on one of the tables, since there was no power up here, an oil lamp burnished the walls bronze and cast the shadow of Evil Eye restlessly pacing the floor. Pictures spiked to the log walls were of Redcoats then and now.

Here lay Wolfe mortally wounded on the Plains of Abraham after defeating Montcalm's French to win Quebec for Britain in 1759. The Redcoat comforting him was John Craven.

A pair of prints captured the American Revolution.

Redcoats fired on Colonists in 1770's Boston Massacre, and General Cornwallis surrendered to Washington at Yorktown in 1781. Though not in either painting, John Craven was there.

Fripp's jingoistic "The Last Stand of the 24th at Isandlwana" was here. Raging around a stalwart sergeant and heroic Drummer Boy, the battle reflected Victorian fantasy of the Thin Red Line.

Dual canvases of Rorke's Drift caught Rex Craven winning his Victoria Cross. A view from the storehouse, Alphonse de Neuville's painting showed Craven helping a patient escape from the burning hospital. Lady Butler's famous "The Defense of Rorke's Drift" had Chard and Bromhead center, with Craven bayoneting a Zulu over the mealie bags. Commissioned by Victoria, the original was in the Royal Collection at St. James's Palace.

All the paintings had once been in Ted Craven's trunk. Also stolen from the trunk were two photographs of Ted in the "Four Circle" and "Wagon Wheel" formations of the RCMP Musical Ride. Like the paintings, these, too, were nailed to the hewn logs, joining a snapshot from another source: Nick Craven in a Color Guard saluting the Queen. The faces of both Mounties were defaced by X's, crisscrossed thin red lines of blood.

One of the tables was draped with Ted Craven's Red Serge, also from his trunk. On it sat the Rorke's Drift trophy box. Pacing, Evil Eye listened to African hatred whispering through the lid, urging the zombie to wreak revenge in Redcoat blood.

A sea of blood.

To that end, Evil Eye was plotting.

SUSPECT

West Vancouver

Gill Macbeth awoke to a bout of morning sickness, scrambling from her bed in which Nick was still asleep, to begin the day retching over the toilet. A week past her period and three weeks from conception, yet already the pregnancy was an ordeal.

The news was on the clock-radio when she returned to the bedroom. Nick, up and listening intently, put a finger to his lips to keep her quiet. The lead story on the news was about the duplex shootout and the death of the boy.

"Are you okay?"

"Yes," Gill said. She had yet to tell him. Fatherhood could wait until he laid his mom to rest. "Must be something I ate."

"Up to going to work?"

"Once my stomach settles. I phoned Dr. Singh. The autopsy's at nine. He put your mom on the first shift to accommodate me. Think an hour's enough to get to New Westminster?"

"Sure. After the bridge, rush hour's coming your way."

"And you?"

"There'll be hell to pay over this shootout mess. I'm off to HQ for an update on it all, then to engage a funeral home to take care of Mom. I'll see you at Royal Columbian for lunch."

Traffic approaching Vancouver was at a bumper-to-bumper crawl as bedroom communities emptied their beds for work downtown, but heading east with the sun in her eyes, Gill made good speed. Reversing the route Bert and Ernie drove yesterday at five, she took the off-ramp to the Royal City as an unmarked RCMP car crested the overpass from Coquitlam and fell in behind. When Gill parked in the Royal Columbian Hospital lot, the ghost car tailed her and parked beside.

The white got out and walked to the morgue.

The black got out and followed her.

The two met a half hour later over Dora Craven's corpse.

A morgue is a morgue is a morgue.

This morgue was fittingly in the basement of the hospital, off the delivery area where modern-day Burke-and-Hares with the Body Removal Service spirited in the stiffs. Each corpse was weighed with an overhead scales before being stored under a sheet in the walk-in cooler or, in the case of murder, in a locked crypt. The crypt keeper was kept busy last night, as first the two deputies were carried in, then Dora Craven after them, then Jack MacDougall after her. Now, pairs reversed to convenience Gill, the latter were wheeled into the theater for dissection.

The autopsy theater was institutional beige. The window in the south wall looked out at the Fraser. The dais at that end was used for storage, with steps down to the floor where the cutting was done. Here, a stainless steel table crossed the room. Off it were side-by-side dissecting stations. Each unit was equipped with a sink, garburetor, and water supply. Overhead, a microphone recorded findings. The gurney that rolled in Jack Mac-Dougall was locked feet-to-sink into the unit manned by Dr. Kahil Singh. Singh had done the autopsy on Helen Grabowski in the Headhunter case, and now was chief pathologist at Royal Columbian. The gurney with Dora Craven was locked into the other unit, where Gill Macbeth and Rachel Kidd met face to face. The rest of the room was empty working space, with stainless steel sinks holding brains in formalin.

"Gill Macbeth," Gill said, introducing herself. "A VGH pathologist, here to help out."

"Rachel Kidd," Rachel said. "Investigating officer with Coquitlam GIS. Corporal," she added.

The exhibit woman, Ident tech, tool marks examiner from the Forensic Lab, and morgue attendant confirmed their presence. Wearing surgeon's greens under a green plastic apron down to her ankles, Gill stood in the angle of the L-shaped station, Dora's body to her left with the dissecting unit on the other side. Usually cadavers are examined faceup. Here the trauma was to the back of the head so she reversed the procedure. Using her hand-held Philips recorder instead of the fixed mike, she scanned the body from head to toe with a powerful light, moving down one side, then up the other, noting bruises on the flesh and, after unbagging the hands, a Band-Aid on one finger.

Removing the bandage revealed a small cut.

"A recent incised wound one centimeter long on the

palmar aspect of the left index finger over the distal phalanx," Gill recorded.

The Ident tech snapped photos as she worked. Every find was marked with a number and two-centimeter scale. Location shot, to 2-to-1, to 1-to-1 with a macro lens, he filled each frame with as much detail as possible. Shot in close proximity to the finger, 1-to-1 captured the cut on the negative life-size.

"No defense marks on the palms," Gill noted. After she scraped the nails, the Ident tech inked and printed the fingers.

The pathologist used a scalpel blade to shave the bloody scalp. Matted hair fell away to reveal a zigzag-patterned bruise on the skin both sides of an irregular laceration. "The force of the blow that tore the scalp imprinted the mark," Gill said. "This pattern is on the striking surface of the weapon."

"A club?" Rachel asked.

"Possibly."

"With an ornamental zigzag on the head?"

"Embossed. Raised in relief. Not carved into the surface."

"Like an Indian war club?"

"Your field, not mine."

The Ident tech tried different lights with filters to enhance the mark. "Contrast photography will show it better. Can we take the skin to close the split back at the Lab?"

"Preserve the skin," the tool marks examiner said, "and we can match the bruise with the weapon when it's found."

Gill reflected the scalp from the skull to cut the skin away for the morgue attendant to treat. The skull beneath was indented with a semilunar hollow radiating linear fractures. "Single-blow blunt-force cranial cerebral trauma," she recorded.

"Instant death?" Rachel asked.

"No, but immediate loss of consciousness."

"All that blood came from the brain?"

"From the scalp," Gill answered.

At the other station, Dr. Singh examined Jack MacDougall faceup, due to the intestines spilling from his belly. Pinkish-brown last night, the coils were turning purple. When Singh rolled the body on its side to probe the back of the head, Gill and Rachel joined the group at his dissecting unit.

"Same weapon?" Rachel asked.

"No opinion. Repeated bludgeoning pulverized the back of this skull. The scalp was shredded when he was dragged faceup by the feet."

"The wounds don't link the killings?"

Gill shook her head. "The same killer or different killers, I can't tell."

Singh checked both corpses and confirmed the open question.

Back at her dissecting unit, Gill opened Dora up. Cutting from throat to pubis, she peeled skin and fat away to expose muscles covering the internal organs, cracking the rib cage with bone shears to access the lungs and heart. From the heart she siphoned forty milliliters of blood to inject into Vacutainers destined for the RCMP Forensic Lab. Red top tubes for "plain" blood. Gray top tubes for "preserved" blood. Purple top tubes for DNA blood samples.

The exhibit woman marked each tube with an exhibit number.

The tubes were signed by Gill Macbeth and the exhibit woman.

The autopsy over, Rachel Kidd checked the evidence the exhibit woman would convey to the Lab, dotting the *i*'s and crossing the *t*'s of continuity. If the case went to trial, defense counsel would try to break the "chain of continuity" to raise a doubt in the jury's mind whether exhibits may have been "tainted" before they were lab tested. Clothes, shoes, apron, samples of Dora's blood, tissue, hair, body swabs, and finger scrapings: all was in order. Satisfied, Kidd left the hospital and walked toward her car.

She stopped short.

Macbeth's BMW was parked next to the ghost car. As the pathologist unlocked the driver's door, another car pulled up and honked. Nick Craven was behind the wheel. Gill smiled, waved, and relocked the door. She crossed to Nick's car and climbed in. Through the rear window, Rachel saw Gill kiss Nick hard on the lips.

Hmmm, she thought.

Coquitlam

Staff Sergeant Bill Tipple was one of the living dead. He was eleven years into his afterlife. It was thanks to crime that he was still on Earth, instead of blown to smithereens when an overpowered, underworld bomb blew his car apart.

Zombie, they called him.

The bulls in GIS.

Tipple had made his name in the Headhunter case. A man of slight build with a pockmarked face and dusting of dandruff on the shoulders of his sports jacket, he wasn't the sort of Mountie the Force used on a recruitment poster. But what he lacked in looks he made up in energy, plus the fact he was blessed with horseshoes up his Horseman's ass. Having intruded himself into that pressure-cooker case—he was a Special I eavesdropper with Commercial Crime at the time—luck found him in the right place when the bust went down. Then the night of the Red Serge Ball to celebrate victory, he'd walked to the mall for aspirin to dull a nagging headache, and that's when a thief hot-wired his car and set off the ignition bomb.

Initial reports had Tipple killed.

When he returned from the dead, they promoted him in lieu of a funeral.

Now "Zombie" was head of the Plainclothes cops in Coquitlam GIS.

Rachel's boss.

The staff sergeant at his desk and the corporal to one side, they sat talking in the glass-walled cubbyhole off the bull pen. Two constables in the main room were munching lunch. Tipple stopped Kidd midsentence. "Close the door," he said. The route this "bounce" was taking he wanted no one to overhear. She shut the door tight.

"You know what you're alleging?"

"Yes," Rachel said.

"You know the consequences if you're wrong?"

"I'll be frozen out."

"You understand what that means?"

"Fail in going after one of our own, and I'll be shunned."

"So?"

"So any charge has got to stick."

"Okay. I'm listening. Make your case."

"Corporal Craven informed me he's an only child. I double-checked and he's the only birth registered to his mom. This letter was found in one of the drawers at the murder scene."

Kidd placed the copy on Tipple's desk so he could read:

December 2, 1993
Mother—
   It's taken my lifetime to uncover your whitewashed secret. Discussing it face to face on my birthday seems fitting. I'll call on the 7th.

"Typed and not signed," the staff sergeant noted.

"Yes, sir," Kidd said. "But he's the victim's only child and the seventh *is* his birthday. He was at the murder scene from four-thirty to five-ten P.M. yesterday. Just mother and son for a private birthday party. Dora baked a pumpkin pie whipped-creamed 'Happy Birthday.' She was doing the dishes—*two* pie plates, *two* pie forks, *two* teacups—when she was clubbed at the sink. Who would she cut the pie for but the Birthday Boy? The window above the sink reflects the room behind. Someone she knew took her by surprise."

"Craven ate the pie?"

"Says he didn't."

"Why admit being there and deny that?"

"So it looks like someone came *after* him."

"Assuming he typed the letter, what's this 'white-washed secret?' "

"Just a guess."

"Let's hear it," Tipple said.

"Craven told me his father shot himself the day he was born. His dad was a Member in Alberta, I found out. The night he died, only his wife, sister, and the baby were in the house. It was a home delivery in Medicine Hat. There was an inquest and both women were cleared. Craven told me his aunt died last month. Fell down the stairs in the house where he was born. What if he subconsciously blamed himself for his father's death, then recently turned up something implicating his mom? Might he not explode with repressed rage for depriving him of Dad and burdening him with guilt?"

"Evidence?"

She tapped the letter. "Circumstantial conjecture. The murder has all the elements of a close-relationship crime. No break-in. No robbery. And no sexual assault. Beating the face points to a killer related to the victim."

"The face was beaten?"

"The back of the skull was crushed."

"Careful," warned Tipple. "Hardly a frenzy."

"No," said Kidd. "But psychologically sound. Cold heart. Cold mind. Kills in a cold rage."

"Anything in Craven's background that shows he's capable?"

Rachel placed Nosy Parker's scrapbook on the desk. Tipple studied the Jekyll-to-Hyde photos of Nick. "Ran afoul of drugs in his teens," she said. "Demons under the surface? Hiding from Mom? He changed when she was comatose in the hospital. Dad dead from suicide and son raised by mom. Matricide profile. And his girlfriend is older than him."

"How much older?"

"Five years," Rachel said.

"Careful," warned Tipple. "I had a girlfriend much younger than me."

"Not the same. Oedipus angle. Younger man, older woman equates with Mom. And this older woman is part of the case."

"Who?"

"Dr. Gill Macbeth. She did the autopsy. I saw them smooching in his car and got suspicious. What's a VGH pathologist doing at Royal Columbian Hospital? Helping out, she said. Truth is she phoned and *asked* to do the postmortem. *Crime and Punishment?* Is Raskolnikov using her to interfere in the case?"

"Smoke," said Tipple. "Gimme fire."

"Craven arrived at his mom's at four-thirty P.M. He was wearing an overcoat over his Red Serge. When he left at five-ten, the coat was missing and he was carrying a large plastic bag. He told me he spilled tea on the coat

and left it behind. No coat was found in the house and
no murder weapon. He was the last person seen there
until we arrived. No sign of tampering and all the doors
were locked. His mom, he said, would never open the
door to a stranger."

"Theory?"

"The house was locked and Mom let him in. He had
a bone to pick with her as evidenced by the letter. The
date—his birthday—is somehow tied in. Anniversaries
always play on the emotions. Wearing the overcoat, he
clubbed her from behind. The bloody club and coat went
into the bag. When he left the house, the door locked
after him."

"Why lock the door? Why not leave it open? Schreck
on the loose, we'd think it was him."

"Schreck's a coincidence *after the fact*. He killed the
deputies and escaped at five-ten, the same time Craven
was seen leaving the house. Luckily for us, the locked
door eliminates Schreck."

"What about MacDougall? Craven's clear of that?"

"Yes, he was talking with investigators on Colony
Farm at the time."

"Schreck killed MacDougall?"

"Or someone else."

"The autopsies support your theory?"

"The sheriff's deputies were stomped, not clubbed.
MacDougall and Dora were bludgeoned, but their
wounds don't link the weapon."

"Why write his mother? Why not phone? They live
in the same city. Who writes letters these days?"

"Maybe it isn't a letter. Maybe it's a note. Dropped
by, she wasn't home, so he stuck it to the fridge."

"Fingerprints?"

"The original's being checked. Preliminary report says
just hers."

"Typewriter in the house?"

"Doesn't match. Perhaps he typed it beforehand in
case she wasn't home."

"Anything else?"

"No," Kidd said.

Tipple turned sideways to face her straight on. No
mistaking the seriousness in his voice. "Reason you're
in GIS is I asked for you. Reason you're a corporal is

my recommendation. You've got a future. Don't ruin your career with this case. I won't shut you down. Craven's in the frame. But there's far from enough to support a charge. By the book, hear me? Give yourself an out. Tug the rip cord if you smell danger. First thing you do is ask him about the letter. Cards on the table. Nothing up your sleeve. If your bluff gets called, walk away from the game."

ASSIZE

New Westminster
Tuesday, March 1, 1994

Three months after Dora Craven was bludgeoned to death, Lyndon Wilde called Rachel Kidd as a Crown witness in Morgan Hatchett's Court.

Lyndon "Broompole" Wilde QC was a blustery, short, stout, ruddy-cheeked, mustachioed lawyer. He resembled a cross between the Quaker Oats pitchman who says "It's the right thing to do," and Rich Uncle Pennybags, the chairman of the board in a *Monopoly* game. Rotund in the black silk of Queen's Counsel robes, his barrister's vest glittered with the fob chain of a pocket watch he flipped open and snapped shut when he wanted to attract the jury's attention. Perched halfway down his rubicund nose were reading glasses, another tool he utilized in court. Perusing notes through them made him look like a wise old owl. Peering over them with a withering stare conveyed the impression he just uncovered a lie. Taking them off to tap his teeth displayed rumination, while whipping them off to stab the air thrust home a telling point. On this stage, he was as skilled in the use of a prop as Alice Cooper.

The nickname "Broompole" dated from his first big prosecution. The year was 1967: the Summer of Love. Two hippies high on LSD were hitchhiking on Fourth Avenue. A van with smoked windows stopped and the nearest head got in. Before his friend could follow, tattooed hands grabbed the hippie from behind as the door slammed shut and the van peeled rubber down the street. The Headhunters Motorcycle Club had a "buttler for the meetin' meetin'" that night.

The Headhunters' Den was the anteroom to hell. The only light within was cast by lamps on a line of "hogs" down one wall. Around the room were "colors" seized from rival gangs: emblems of the Grim Reapers, Gypsy Jokers, Undertakers, L'il Devils, Outlaws, and Coffin Cheaters. The trophies they prized most adorned the bar: the skin off a killed Hell's Angel's chest inked with a naked woman forming the crossbar of a bike, and a royal blue-and-gold crest hijacked from the Special E Gang Squad of the Mounted Police.

Stripped, the hippie shivered in the glare of the lamps as demons lurked in the shadows.

Every member of this gang was a 1%er, the percentage of bikers who are a law unto themselves. For rides and meetin' meetin's like this, they wore "originals," jackets pissed on for initiation and never cleaned. The colors on back were a severed head stuck on a stake. In addition to iron crosses and swastikas on both sleeves, their leathers bore "wings" proclaiming sexual acts: Red Wings for "eating Mama on the rag," and Black Wings for "tonguing black tang."

The hippie was whipped with a bicycle chain, then kicked in the face with winkle picker shoes. The Junkman gave him a rag and bucket to wash up the blood. A plastic "buttler's hat" was placed on his head and torched so "napalm" seared his shoulders and back. To cool him off, he was submerged in a bathtub floating with ice, while the drunken spectators hooted for more. The encore was he had to dance naked with a broom and masturbate to show respect for the bikers' girls. When he stumbled, Fat Fred took the broompole and rammed it up his butt with such force he was driven across the room. The "buttler" sobbed on the end of the stick as he was hobby-horsed around the den.

The hospital called Special E.

The trial came on before Mr. Justice Colefax. The Crown was represented by Harris Foot QC and new-to-the-bar junior counsel Lyndon Wilde. Against them were nine of the best trial lawyers in B.C. The indictment listed counts of kidnapping, confining, wounding, and indecent assault. The only direct evidence was the word of two drugged hippies.

The first witness, the other hitcher, crumpled on the stand. It was '67, the jury was straight, and hallucinogens were new:

"Tell me, witness, this LSD, do you shoot it with a needle?"

"No"—a smirk at defense counsel—"you drop acid as blotter or windowpane."

"*Y-o-u* drop it, witness. Not me. Does drop it mean swallow?"

"Yeah."

"You say the two of you were high while hitchhiking on Fourth?"

"We were tripping."

"Do I have this right? Tripping means blowing your brain?"

"Your mind, man. Blowing your mind."

"And when you blow your mind, what's the effect of this LSD?"

"When you experience an event, you live one reality from cause to result. Acid expands the mind to other dimensions. When I experience an event, I live hundreds of realities, each with cosmic causes flowing to Tarot results."

"Fascinating, witness. But that presents a danger. When you take The Bible in your hand and swear to tell the truth, the whole truth, and nothing but the truth, which of your 'hundred realities' do you select to give as evidence?"

The tortured hippie was next on the stand. Harris Foot QC was in the middle of direct examination when he stopped, clutched his left arm, and dropped dead from a heart attack. Court recessed so a stretcher could carry out the corpse.

"My Lord," said the spokesman for defense counsel when court reconvened without the jury. "If you declare a mistrial and traverse this prosecution to the Spring Assize, in light of the lengthy adjournment, we request bail."

"Mr. Wilde," said the judge. "When were you called to the bar?"

"In September."

"The loss of Mr. Foot is most unfortunate. It does seem a mistrial—"

"You can't grant bail, My Lord. If the accused are released, the case will collapse. The Headhunters have a bounty on the witnesses. These nine have every reason to collect."

"Tomorrow morning, Mr. Wilde. Unless you're ready to go, it's a mistrial."

At ten A.M. the next day, the nine accused were in the dock, the jury was in the jury box, the witness was on the stand, defense counsel were at their table, and the judge was on the bench.

"Where is Mr. Wilde?" Colefax asked the clerk.

"No idea, My Lord."

With a crash, the doors to the Assize Court burst open, and Lyndon Wilde, his robes askew and collar tabs dangling, dashed to his seat with papers flying to drop his notes on the counsel table.

"You're late!" the judge snapped.

"Sorry, My Lord. I worked all night and lost track of time."

Colefax turned to the witness. "You're still under oath."

Nervously clutching disheveled notes, Wilde began, "You were telling Mr. Foot about being forced to dance with the broom. Then what happened?"

"That one"—he pointed—"grabbed the broom from me and rammed it up my rectum."

The jury jumped.

"Pardon," Wilde said meekly. "I didn't hear."

The witness raised his voice. "That one took the broom and shoved it up my rectum. Then he ran me around the clubhouse on the stick."

The jury jumped again.

Wilde dropped his notes.

Gathering them up, he mumbled distractedly, "Where was I? Oh, yes. The dance with the broom. Then what happened?"

"The gang laughed when that one jammed the—"

"Really, My Lord!" Fat Fred's counsel was on his feet. "He's belaboring the point."

"What point?" said Wilde.

"The point about my client shoving the broom into his anus."

The jury jumped.

"I am not belaboring the broompole rammed into his ass."

"Mr. Wilde," the judge said. "I'm sure we've all heard quite enough about the broompole inserted in this man's private parts."

The jury flinched.

"Get on with it."

"Yes, My Lord. Now after Fat Fred jammed the broom into your rectum and all the others laughed . . ."

By the time the jury retired for coffee, they were clenched so tight they squeaked as they walked. The act with the broom had been described not only by Wilde and the witness, but also by defense counsel and the judge. It was as if they all accepted it as fact. Young Lyndon Wilde struggled on as best he could, outgunned by nine lawyers so slick they qualified as slugs. The gang was laughing and sniggering at him, unaware the jury felt the bikers were mocking them. The judge was now leaning toward the Crown to balance the case. And the witness, pissed off, was growing stronger on the stand with each question asked.

It was a performance worth fifteen years in jail.

Earning Wilde the nickname "Broompole," for taking a losing case and ramming it up the outfinessed rear of nine defense counsel.

After convicting the biker gang, Wilde returned to his office at Foot, Peabody, and Strong. For his call, his parents had bought him a huge mahogany desk. With a Swiss Army knife, Lyndon carved a notch into the underside.

Twenty-six years had passed since then. The firm was now Strong, Wilde, and Finch. The underside of that desk had hundreds of notches, and though the old system of hiring Assize Court Crown counsel from the private bar was long gone, a vestige from those days remained. If the case was too big or too hot or too political for Crown minions to handle, the call went out for Lyndon Wilde QC.

Like this case.

Last week the Crown had feted Wilde with a roast, as good an excuse as any to tie one on. The barbs were flying thick and fast when a drunk asked "Broompole of the Bailey" for his epitaph. Slowly drawing the Havana from his grinning lips, Wilde outlined a tombstone with the burning end. "Lyndon Wilde QC," he intoned, hushing the room. "Any Crown worth silk can convict the guilty. But it takes a hell of a lawyer to convict an innocent man."

The prosecutors howled.

They thought he was joking.

He wasn't.

For Lyndon Wilde QC, winning was everything.

"Corporal Kidd," said Broompole, approaching the witness stand. "I show you a garment in a plastic bag. Do you recognize it?"

"Yes, it's the one I seized on December eighth of last year. Here's my signature on the exhibit tag."

"My Lady," said Wilde, turning to Hatchett. "Might this be marked an exhibit in the trial?"

"So ordered," said the judge. "Exhibit twenty-three."

The lawyer turned back to the Mountie, who wore Red Serge. "Please tell her ladyship and the jury how you came to make this seizure, Corporal. . . .

THE KNIFE

Vancouver
Wednesday, December 8, 1993

"You look beat."

"I am."

"Zinc—"

"I know, Alex. 'Avoid sleeplessness. And never—I repeat *never*—miss taking your drugs.' That's why I'm home. Wake me at four?''

He left her working at her desk in the writing den of the house they leased, editing *Deadman's Island: The Case of Skull & Crossbones,* and wandered to the bedroom to change for sleep. In his pajamas, he fetched a glass of water from the bathroom en suite, then returned, sat on the bed, and opened the night table drawer. Reaching for the vial of Dilantin, his antiepilepsy drug, Zinc spied the knife at the back of the drawer.

Hefting Pop's knife in his hand brought memories flooding back.

When he was a kid on the prairies, all cream soda was red . . . till Pop took him and his brother Tom to the Calgary Stampede. Back then, the Stampede was the real McCoy, not the glitz and schlock hyped today. Get off a plane and you were given a white Stetson hat, now you'd be lucky to get a smile. Bales of hay and log palisades appeared in shops, while cowpoke and dude alike dressed for the range. Flapjacks for breakfast were served free in the streets, streets blocked impromptu for square dancing by whites or tribal dances by Blackfoot, Blood, Sarcee, and Peigan. Wild cow milking or bucking broncs, Roman racing astride two steeds, bulldogging steers or roping calves, it was the Wild West going, going, gone. The bets were fast and furious for chuck wagons to win, a figure eight around barrels while outriders threw in the stove, the race on around the track as hooves and hats flew, Zinc, Tom, and Pop in the stands with Gene Autry sipping soda pops.

Calgary Cream Soda was crystal clear.

Like 7UP with vanilla taste.

That was the second-best day Zinc ever spent with Pop, Pop becoming the sort of dad he willed him to be, not a drunk and his sons, but *three* kids at the rodeo. On the final day, at a Western store, with Zinc sipping pop and a case of Calgary Cream Soda in the truck, Pop bought hunting knives for both boys.

"Man ain't a man without a knife," he said.

Zinc glanced at the knife belted on Pop's hip, the sheath for the blade a good eight inches long, the stag

horn handle finger-polished from use, then proudly held
up his knife, the happiest "man" in the world. On their
return to Saskatchewan, Pop trained the boys on a backwoods trek, showing his sons how to paddle a birch-bark
canoe, teaching them survival in the bush, *coureurs de
bois* and *voyageurs* in the Chandler past. Disney's *Davy
Crockett* was the mania of the year, so Zinc and Tom
had coonskin caps.

Late the first day, they camped by the lake. "Tom,
gather wood for a fire," Pop said. "Zinc, go cut sticks
for a wiener roast. Greener the better, then they won't
burn."

Alone in the woods like Davy, Zinc the Frontiersman
threw his knife at a tree. A grin lit his face when the
point stuck in the trunk. A frown replaced it when he
wrenched the blade out sideways and snapped off the
tip. *Pop'll kill me,* he thought, for Pop's belt enforced
respect for property.

They sat around the fire with hot dogs to roast.
"We're gonna starve if you don't strip those sticks," Pop
said. Zinc was out of excuses for not drawing his knife.
Slowly, he withdrew it from the sheath at his waist.

"Lemme see that!"

Zinc passed Pop the broken blade.

Pop held the damaged knife out against the bonfire
sparks. Zinc had been warned: "Lose it and it won't be
replaced." Eyes that could read a forest glaring at his
son, Pop growled "Shoddy work!" with contempt. Zinc
was sure the comment referred to him, then Pop un-
belted his own knife and handed it to his son. "Whatever
the job," Pop said, "this will see it done."

Stripping sticks, Zinc felt as if Jim Bowie of the
Alamo had bequeathed *his* knife.

That was the best day he ever spent with Pop.

Now, three decades and a bit later, Zinc replaced the
knife in the drawer and went to sleep.

If only he knew how important to him Pop's knife
would be.

"Zinc."

"Uh."

"Wake up. Four o'clock."

She kissed him on the forehead while he opened his

eyes. In the dreamworld of awaking, fragments of memory crossed his mind. . . .

Of those who came off Deadman's Island alive, Katt was cut by the Ripper's knife, Alex suffered a broken leg, and Zinc was stabbed in the back.

Alex Hunt. The plane to that island. Love at first sight . . .

Barely visible through the rain was Vancouver's downtown core. Huddled like a waif at its feet was the shack of Thunderbird Charters. From the shack to the plane on the water stretched a gangway and hundred-foot dock. The woman sea-legging down the gangplanks struggled against the storm, suitcase in one hand, umbrella opposite bucking the wind to block sheets of rain. She wore a black tight-waisted top over black jeans tucked into black cowboy boots, and a black trenchcoat flapped about her like Dracula's cape. Blond hair pulled back in a ponytail held by silver heart-shaped clips, wayward strands snake-danced about her face, masking it. Nearing the plane, she looked up, and Zinc's heart was gone.

Eyes the hue of Caribbean lagoons.

Narrow, delicate chin around a kissable mouth.

Fine-boned nose just the right length.

But how she moved, this ballerina, was what captured him.

Grace under fire.

The quest of his dreams.

Zinc touched the indent in his forehead, subconsciously hiding it.

He wished—God how he wished—he was the man he once had been.

So he might stand a chance with her . . .

Alex Hunt. On Deadman's Island. The night the murders began. . . .

So here he stood in front of the mirror dressed in his regalia: the standard Red Serge of the Force except for the black-bordered cuffs, harnessed into a stripped Sam Browne without the usual sidearm, his blue breeches yellow-striped and his riding boots fitted with spurs. At least the Stetson covered the indent in his forehead.

Half filling a glass with water from the decanter on the washstand, Zinc popped his third Dilantin of the day. He

*set the pill bottle down on the table beside his bed as a
reminder to take the fourth cap before he went to sleep.
Opening the door, he stepped into Castle Crag's deserted
upper hall . . . deserted that is till Alex opened her door.*

She stopped on the threshold.

"My, my," he thought she said.

Then Alex put two fingers to her lips and wolf-whistled him.

"Likewise," he replied, nonplussed.

*Alexis wore a plain cream dress with simple gold jewelry, but she might as well have been wearing Queen Elizabeth's crown. "How much to hire you as a boyfriend
for the weekend?" she asked, slipping her arm through
Zinc's to guide him down the hall.*

"You want a buffer between you and Bolt?"

*"I definitely want him to leave me alone. That man
radiates danger."*

*"Being your boyfriend's a job I'll gladly take on for
free."*

*"Good," said Alex, and before he knew it she had his
hat in her hand, plunking the Stetson down on her head
at a jaunty angle.*

*His hand rose automatically to his indented brow. "It
doesn't bother me," Alex said, gently intercepting him.
"Don't let it bother you."*

So that was that.

He had a new girlfriend.

At least till Sunday, beggars would ride . . .

Alex Hunt. In the year and a month since Deadman's Island . . .

*When Zinc came out of the hospital—hospitals had
ruled his life since the shootout in Hong Kong—Alexis
lured him south to her Oregon house to recuperate. For
weeks she hobbled around on crutches with her leg in a
cast, while Zinc walked up and down Cannon Beach,
mending body and mind. One morning, he returned to
find her scribbling at her desk, drafting the outline for a
new true crime book. Without being told, he knew the
tale she planned to tell. . . .*

Now, gazing up at her bent over the bed, Zinc felt as
happy as he had ever been.

If only he knew the tragedy fate was plotting for them.

THE POISONED TREE

To love this city, you gotta love rain. Drizzling rain. Drenching rain. Dismal rain. Driving rain. Dreary rain, rain, rain, rain. . . . The clouds from the west have crossed the Pacific, and must drop what they've sucked up to scale the North Shore peaks. West Coast sunshine comes in two forms. Dry sunshine like what beamed down this morning. And liquid sunshine like what flowed down Lonsdale now.

Rachel parked at the foot of the hill in the Seven Seas Seafood Restaurant lot, then turned up her collar, opened the door, popped her black umbrella, and stepped out into a puddle. The restaurant was an old boat permanently moored near shore, its beacon *Seven Se* underlined with blue neon waves, the *as* flickering as if the rain short-circuited those two letters. The gray water beyond was dulled by gray mist, as smothering dark gray clouds mottled the sky, the downtown core of the city across the harbor inlet so vague it might be a mirage, this gray on gray on gray washed by depressing gray rain.

Her back to the inlet, Rachel sloshed and splashed uphill.

To her left was Lonsdale Quay, a big red Q looming high, one of those trendy markets on pilings every seaport spawns these days. To her right were the abandoned sheds of Burrard Dry Dock, once the finest shipyards in B.C. and builders of the *St. Roch* RCMP boat that plowed Sergeant Larsen with eight crew along the icy Northwest Passage in the 1940s for history's first two-way voyage through the Arctic. Rusty gray with broken windows, the sheds were now sets for Vancouver-filmed TV series like *The X Files*.

To Bean or Not To Bean was up the street.

The billboard outside inquired: *To Bean or Not To Bean, Is That The Question?* Aromas from aged Sumatra, spicy Sulawesi, Arabian Mocha Java, and dark French enticed customers in from the rain. Around the corner, a stairway off the side street climbed to an apartment.

Up Kidd went and knocked.

Having bounced her suspicions off Staff Sergeant Tipple, Rachel had driven to Special X to question Nick about the "Mother letter."

"You missed him by ten minutes," the Mad Dog said. His eyes were squinted from stress, anger, and lack of sleep.

"Say where he was going?"

"Home. Personal time. Got to make arrangements for his mom."

"Know where he lives?"

"Lower Lonsdale. Above a coffee store called To Bean or Not To Bean."

The woman who answered Rachel's knock was Filipina and young. She was dressed in a sweatsuit with her hair pulled back in a scrunchie. A vacuum on the carpet down the hall, a bucket and mop outside the bathroom door, laundry for the cleaners hanging on a knob, the essence of exotic cooking wafting from the kitchen: Rachel figured she was Nick's girl Friday. Was he also screwing her?

"Mr. Nick not home." Friday checked Rachel out. As if trying to figure how she fit into Nick's life. As if wondering if he was screwing Kidd.

The black Mountie took in the white Mountie's home in a glance. Where you live, she believed, says who you are. Just as Craven lived in retro town, so his living room was that of a retro man. The CD box sets were all fifties rock. The bookshelves were lined with classics in uniform editions, as if he'd joined a club to make up for illiterate time. Nooks and crannies were crammed with Mountie kitsch, probably from the flea market down the street: Mickey Mouse, Garfield, Barbie, and Cabbage Patch dolls in Red Serge. Hung on the walls were Mountie movie posters. *Susannah of the Mounties,* with Shirley Temple, cute as could be. *Northwest Mounted Police,* "*I thought you Canadian girls were cold . . . like your northern climate!"* printed beside Gary Cooper. *Saskatchewan,* with Alan Ladd, *"Actually filmed in the Canadian Rockies!"* blared the poster, out a few hundred miles from the gopher-hilled plains.

Her eyes fell on the tunic.

Grimed when he scaled the rickety bridge on Colony Farm, Nick's Red Serge hung on a doorknob in the hall, waiting for Friday to go to the dry cleaners. Was that blood on the cuff of the right sleeve? Rachel flashed a smile and her regimental badge.

"You work with Mr. Nick?" the Filipina asked.

Nodding, Rachel reached for the tunic. *Don't say a word. Let her think what she thinks.*

"You take to clean?"

Another nod.

"He say nothing to me. Where you take?"

"Special cleaning at Headquarters." Stretching the truth.

"Receipt," Friday said, holding out her hand.

As Kidd wrote on the French side of her RCMP card, she recalled the promise Craven extracted from her last night:

"Remember this is Canada, not the States. Fruit of the Poisoned Tree is much weaker here."

"Spit it out, Nick. What's bothering you?"

"I hope you're not tainted by the American Bill of Rights? Promise me, whatever it takes, you'll nail who killed my mom. Whatever it takes. *Understand? Use your brain. No candy-assed Charter of Rights and Freedoms bullshit."*

"I promise," she replied.

Vancouver

The RCMP Forensic Laboratory was a mushroom-shaped building at 5201 Heather, a few doors along the street from Special X. In 1937, Surgeon Maurice Powers was one of the first graduates in forensic medicine in North America. Assembling equipment in a vacant bedroom off the Officers' Mess, he established the first laboratory at Depot Division in Regina that September. Sections specialized in documents, toolmarks, firearms, toxicology, and spectrograph analysis. Powers died in a plane crash in 1943, but his legacy continues to grow.

In 1987, the Pitchfork case revolutionized police work. Two teenaged girls were sexually assaulted and murdered in the same small English village. The crimes were separated by more than two years. From the bodies, police collected evidence in the form of vaginal smears and semen stains. After the second murder, a youth confessed to both crimes. To buttress his statements, DNA analysis was performed. DNA showed the victims had been raped by the same man, but not by the youth confessing to the murders. Using a "blooding" dragnet of unprecedented scope, police asked all mature males in the village to submit blood samples for DNA analysis. Several thousand samples were collected, but none matched the semen from the two bodies. The case was solved when police learned Colin Pitchfork convinced a coworker to submit a blood sample in his place.

Pitchfork was the first case in which "DNA fingerprinting" was used. The RCMP was quick to jump on the genetic bandwagon. Molecular Genetics became a service centralized at the Ottawa Lab. But now the demand for genetic comparison of body fluid or tissue samples from crime scenes with suspects was exploding. The logistical problems in sending all exhibits from across Canada to one lab prompted Ottawa to decentralize. A top geneticist—Colin Wood—had been sent west to set up DNA testing here.

Rachel parked in the Lab lot and ran through the driving rain, umbrella protecting the tunic she carried double-sheathed in clear dry-cleaner's bags. As she was buzzed in the Laboratory door, the Craven case exhibit woman came out.

"What's with the tunic?"

"I'll explain later. Who took the Biology exhibits from you?"

"Dermott Toop."

"Did he go back upstairs?"

"No, I think he's still in the Exhibit Receiving Room."

Rachel signed in at the front counter just inside the automatic door, then crossed to the receiving room. The room was small with a clock on the wall, cupboards, fridge, and a desk. On the desk was the box of exhibits she'd checked for "continuity" after the autopsy this morning, including the Vacutainer samples of Dora's blood. The black man who sat on the edge of the desk reading a Request for Analysis form looked up as Rachel knocked on the jamb. The sight of her spread a smile across his face.

The corporal entered and closed the door.

The forensic specialist approached and gave her a lingering kiss. "Bed was cold without you last night," he whispered.

"Big case. You'll have to wait. We can't do it here."

"Why not? Exhibit Receiving Room? Have I got an exhibit for you."

"Flash that offensive weapon and I'll turn you in."

"All I'm asking. That we turn in."

"Maybe tonight, if I'm not lynched on the northern forty by then." Kidd backed off and held the Red Serge tunic out to Toop. "Blood on the cuff. I think he's the killer. And I better be right."

"Girl," he said. "What *have* you done?"

"My job," she replied.

There was nothing like past British Colonies—the present Commonwealth—to teach an outsider the meaning of "ethnocentric." Native Canadians lived here at least ten thousand years before British "discovery," but they were labeled Canadians nonetheless. Cartier, Champlain, and La Salle explored New France, but after the Plains of Abraham were French Canadians. Chinese Canadians and Indo-Canadians and other ethics were labeled, but British Canadians don't exist. They're simply Canadians of historically pure stock, in the same way Brits are unlabeled Australians, New Zealanders, South Africans, Rhodesians, and the rest.

African-American Canadian, that's what Rachel was.

The label felt like Kidd was dragging a train.

African was the *last* word she felt applied to her. Except for the brand of skin color, there was no proof of the link. Sometime before the Civil War her genes arrived as slaves—perhaps on the boat of the man who penned "Amazing Grace"—but from where, when, how, and why were long lost.

Central Africa, surely, as her skin was the blackest black.

Dermott Toop was the color of a coconut shell.

She envied him his history and anchor in the past.

Toop was not adrift.

African-Canadian firmly applied to him. His great-granddad had "washed his spear" in the Anglo-Zulu War, distinguishing himself at Rorke's Drift and Ulundi. His dad was born in 1923, when Colonial whites consolidated their economic stranglehold on the country. Blacks were merely a source of cheap South African labor. Pay was a pittance to toil in the mines, where his dad saw blacks killed in accidents by the hundreds. In the forties, he joined the ANC, and organized strikes challenging white domination. Defying the "kaffir regulations" in 1952, he was jailed for being on the street after eight without special permission. He sat on benches for *Europeans Only,* and then in 1956, was almost whipped to death for having sex with a white woman.

Up to 1960, the African National Congress espoused passive resistance. That changed in March after sixty-nine blacks were killed in Sharpeville during a protest against the pass laws. Toop's dad died in that massacre by South African police, which turned the civil rights movement into civil war.

"My mom came to Canada as a refugee," he said, the last time he and Rachel lay in bed. "After she married here, she had me sent out."

"Ever been back?"

"No, but I want to. I may take a job in forensics there after the election."

"I'll miss you."

"You could come. Together we could help rebuild South Africa's police."

"Not my frontier," Rachel said.

African firmly applied to him, but not to her. In Kidd's case, the label was a control device. Invisible apartheid papers of Multicult. Be proud of your outside heritage, just as we unlabeled Canadians inside are proud of ours.

Good fences make good neighbors.

Amen, Rachel thought.

Subsections in the Forensic Lab changed as science advanced. So encompassing was the DNA revolution that it recently shrank their number to eight. Hair and Fiber, Serology, and Molecular Genetics combined as

Biology. A cop with exhibits for the Lab filled out a Request for Analysis form. The form Toop was reading covered Biology testing of the exhibits in the box. Rachel wrote out a new form for Nick Craven's tunic.

"I think Corporal Craven bludgeoned his mom," she said. "Dressed for the Regimental Dinner last night, he wore a topcoat over his Red Serge. Blood spattered the coat, which he then removed, and the cuff of his tunic bared when he clubbed her."

"Craven's right-handed?"

"Yeah, I checked. Samples of Dora's blood from the autopsy are in that box. Are you set up to do forensic DNA analysis yet?"

"Just," Toop said.

"Derm, I'm out on a limb. This case could bring me down. Screw it up and the old white guard will have my black ass. If the blood on the cuff isn't Dora's, I'm royally fucked."

"The DNA jockey setting us up is a genetic whiz. Wood's back tomorrow and I'll give him the tunic first thing. He'll test it himself and you'll have results by the end of the month."

"Three weeks." Rachel sighed. "Tenterhook time."

"Don't worry." Dermott winked. "The only one royally fucking you is gonna be me."

WHITEWASH

Though it went unmentioned, the incident yawned between them, dividing the two men along the fissure of race. *When you look long into an abyss, the abyss also looks into you,* Nietzsche wrote. So neither man looked down.

Chan's great-great-grandfather had worked the Cariboo mines, emigrating to Canada in 1859. Not once in five generations had the family left B.C., until joining the Mounted took Eric to Hong Kong.

When China reopened to tourists in 1979, Chan convinced his daughter Peggy, then eighteen, to undertake a pilgrimage back to her roots. He thought the family too Western, and not Chinese enough. Peggy embarked on the journey to please her dad.

From Canton, she took the train west to Kunming, then through Hunan and Guangxi toward Guizhou, hunting a part of China tourists had yet to see. Find somewhere untainted by the West, Chan had said, then imagine what it was like before the gunboats arrived. She sat in the swaying railcar, Walkman clamped to her ears, listening to Bruce Springsteen as the rural farms slipped by. After Guiyang she ate some fruit, which gave her diarrhea.

Most of that afternoon was spent in the railcar's toilet, a shit-spattered hole open to the tracks. One attack came on so fast she almost didn't make it, a desperate dash during which the stereo fell to the floor. With no time to stop, she left the Walkman behind, and when she returned it was gone.

Sign language and faltering Cantonese apprised the ticket-taker of her plight. He joined Peggy in a search of the train. Two cars forward they found the amazed thief, a senile old man in peasant's rags stroking his dangling mustache. Wide-eyed, he sat bolt upright for all to see, marveling at The Boss's *Born to Run*. The ticket-taker ripped the Walkman from his ears.

The train pulled into the next station as Peggy returned to her seat. No doubt the old man had heard the Walkman playing on the floor, and unable to find its owner had toyed with curiosity. Smiling, Peggy decided to find him and let him listen for a while. Her thoughts were interrupted by a tapping on the window.

The old man stood shaking on the platform outside, flanked by members of the *Gong An Ju*. The Public Security cops wore green with peaked army caps, yellow headbands distinguishing them from the Red Army. One cop stepped back as the other drew his gun. Peggy screamed "No!" as the old man was shot through the head. Blood spattered the window, then one cop waved, pleased to be of service to China's new friends. The train pulled out of the station as Peggy began to shake.

Chan met his daughter at the airport and drove her home. Not a word was spoken along the way. Then came the nightmares, insomnia, and depression, followed by attempted suicide. First Peggy was in therapy, then in Riverview. Each weekend, Eric and his wife visited her there. Finally, six months ago, they brought her home, and DeClercq was invited to dinner that Friday to celebrate. The Chans lived close to Special X so the Mounties walked.

"You're a new man," Eric said, "since Katt moved in."

"Redemption," Robert agreed. "She rescued me from myself."

"And the dog?"

"Good as new. You'd never know he was stabbed. He loves Katt and she loves him. Been a long time since I felt this good."

"Me, too," Eric said.

"It's working out? Peggy being home?"

"She has her ups and downs, but Sally is ecstatic. Having our only child home has—"

Hammering.

Frantic hammering from the house as they turned in the gate, hammering, hammering, hammering as if a life-and-death race to get someone out, or keep someone in. The men ran to the door, which Eric unlocked. Hammering banged above. The men ran up the stairs. Sally kneeled in the hall with hammer and chisel in hand. The men ran to the door, which she was trying to chip open. "Peggy's locked in," Sally cried on the verge of hysteria. Water seeped out from under the door to creep slowly down the hall.

A decade had passed since DeClercq had last waxed a door, but like riding a bike, once learned, the technique stays, so bracing himself, back and hands against the opposite wall, he pushed off hard and pistoned his foot toward the lock, slamming the wood beside it which shrieked in protest as it gave, bursting into the bathroom behind a spray of splinters.

Naked, Peggy sprawled submerged in the overflowing tub. Sightless eyes stared up from below through black hair on the surface. Beside the tub were empty vials of pills, and an open bottle of Javex bleach. The smell of the chemical wafted strong in the mist as the whitewash leeched color from her blistering skin. Scrawled across the mirror in lipstick was I LOATHE MY RACE.

Sally choked and buried her face in Eric's chest.

Shock leeched color from her husband's face.

"Take her downstairs," Robert said, "and I'll take care of this."

Though it went unmentioned, the incident yawned between them, dividing the two men along the fissure of race. It was there, but there were more pressing matters to discuss.

Every organization has terms for those at the top. At "E" Division Headquarters it was The Third Floor or The Brass. The deputy commissioner's office was on the third floor of the Operations Building. "You're wanted on The Third Floor" was the summons, so Robert splashed up Heather from 33rd to 37th, and climbed the stairs to Eric's new domain. The change in rank had switched who went to whom.

"Go right in," said the DC's assistant, feeding a computer on the desk guarding the door.

Spacious but not ostentatious, the third floor office was 24 by 12. The wide executive desk to the left was backed by windows overlooking the entrance court, a view denied—the joke said—to those groveling on the carpet. The beige carpet stretched across to a pair of love seats, wing-back chair, coffee table, and plants in the far corner, where those not "on the carpet" could relax. There, from a love seat, Chan motioned DeClercq to the wing-back chair.

"There's hell to pay," Chan said, "over the Somali ERT assault. An all-white team guns down a ten-year-old black boy with a TV remote in his hand. Watching early-morning cartoons, for God's sake."

"Special O got it wrong," said DeClercq. "The tip was the traffickers rented Alpha Half. The watchers saw them in and out of Bravo Half all day, so we took down both sides to nab them all. Turns out a mom and her son lived in Bravo Half. The Alpha plumbing plugged, so she let them use her toilet."

"A *black* mom. And *black* son," emphasized Chan.

"A tragedy no matter what color," said DeClercq.

"No, a bigger tragedy *because* of color. After Jack was killed last night, a radio station opened a special line so

callers could extend condolences. Instead, what came is
ethnics screaming "Racism!" and "Nazis!", white exclu-
sionists decrying the upsurge in violence fostered by colored immigration and lax refugee laws, while editorialists
warn us against any perceived whitewash over today's
events. Imagine what would happen if Vancouver were
L.A."

"It's not," said DeClercq.

"We also have the Vancouver Police breathing down
our necks. The shooting's in their jurisdiction, so the
finger's pointed."

"They gave permission for the assault. Their team was
tied up in a hostage standoff."

"Well, now they're looking for damage control from
us. Tarr's suspended. What sort of hothead blasts an
unarmed kid?"

"Desk job?"

"*Suspended.* Out the door. The works. Let *him* watch
cartoons instead."

DeClercq shook his head. "Easy, Eric. Don't pander
to the mob of political correctness. The room was dark.
There were guns going off and bullets through the wall.
The tape shows Tarr thought the pop-up had a gun.
There was a hand piece in the boy's fist. A split-second
call had to be made. I'm not saying it's the right one,
just let Serious Crimes and the Public Complaints Commission handle it. Ground Tarr, but don't hang him out
to dry. We all deserve a hearing before we're lynched."

"Tell that to the black kid's mom."

"Let me pose you a problem as a cop. Two black men
rob a pizza parlor. Alerted by radio, you home in on a
car nearby with a black driver and passenger. Does the
fact this city has a small black population justify you
taking them down?"

Chan ignored the bait. "The reason you were called
is Craven's suspended, too."

"On what grounds?"

"Coquitlam Detachment's pegged him as a suspect in
his mother's death." Chan dropped a copy of the
"Mother letter" on the coffee table. "He's the last person seen leaving her house. The house was locked and
she didn't let strangers in. His overcoat is missing and

blood was found on the cuff of his Red Serge. The cuff of the arm he'd use to wield a club."

"Whose theory is that?"

"Corporal Kidd's."

"*Black* Corporal Kidd's?" emphasized DeClercq.

"So what?"

"So black, white, red, yellow, or polka dots, she stepped over the line with this. Did she ask Craven if he typed the letter? The *unsigned* letter? No, he tells me. Did she have a warrant or reasonable cause to toss his residence? Not that I can see. Before she took his tunic to the Lab, did she ask him about the blood? No, he tells me. He didn't type the letter and he left his mom alive. The blood got on his Red Serge when his hand caught on a nail while crossing a bridge on Colony Farm last night. The search was bad. The seizure's illegal. So Nick gets back his tunic."

"You hate the Charter of Rights as much as I do."

"Yes, but it's there, so I endure it. *Maintiens le Droit.* Isn't that our motto?"

"You're protecting one of your men. Like you once did me. But now I have broader considerations. A white ERT cop shoots an innocent black boy. While blacks cry racist, the media scrutinize us for bias, searching for hints we're closing ranks around our own. The Member investigating Craven is black. She thinks the trail of blood leads to him. What would you have me do? Shut Kidd down? And give the media proof to say we white-wash our own?"

"Eric, Nick's case is not about race."

"It is when our only *black* corporal is involved."

"That's bullshit. You see this morning's news? You want us to end up like that? White police beat a black man senseless on tape—the perfect smoking gun, every cop's dream case—and what does the jury see watching that film? A black youth hits a white man with a brick and does a victory dance on tape—the perfect smoking gun, every cop's dream case—and what does the jury see watching that film? Not what's happening, but which race is mine? And that determines the verdict in spite of the evidence. The California jury system is rotting. It doesn't weigh evidence, it touts race, when what's required is citizens pulling together out of a sense of duty and shared moral values for the best interests of society. How long till a trial comes along that exposes that racial maelstrom for the sinkhole it is? Nick's case has nothing to do with race, so don't feed it in. Stick to the facts."

"Don't lecture me."

"Then don't be color-blind."

"Craven had Macbeth do the autopsy. Why'd he feed his girlfriend into the murder?"

"Because she's thorough, so he knew nothing would be missed."

"We'll see. Craven is suspended till his Red Serge is tested. If the blood's his, he'll be cleared. In the meantime, Special X is suspended from that case. I want no interference with Kidd."

"That's a lot of suspensions for one day, Eric."

"You keep race at bay your way, I'll keep it back in mine."

"Nick's case isn't about race," repeated DeClercq.

"These days everything's about race," said Chan. "And when it comes to that issue, I think I'm much more sensitive than you."

BLACK CAT

New Westminster
Tuesday, March 1, 1994

The trial, three months later . . .

The designation QC in B.C. is a joke. Past days of political patronage made it a brown-noser's badge, and ass-kissing the powers-that-be remains the route to go. A Queen's Counsel ought to be the best there is, and QC solely a mark of professional distinction, but truth is the most courageous lawyers practicing criminal law are shut out because they do the job too well. Lyndon Wilde was QC because the Crown passed out the initials, while Vic Knight—the paladin of the defense bar—had no QC after his name. Vic Knight considered that his badge of distinction.

Hatchett loathed Knight.

Her seething animosity went back to a trial before she became Chief Justice of the Supreme Court, back before she served on Cal Cutter's Court of Appeal, back to her first assize as a trial judge.

Knight was defending.

The charge was first-degree murder, and the Crown's circumstantial case turned on taped statements by the accused. The victim was a child whose stripped skeleton was found buried near the Fraser River nine months after she vanished. Death caused during a sexual assault is first degree, so the Crown used lack of clothes to infer that motive.

The accused was an oddball in the Valley farm town where the victim lived. Misdiagnosed as retarded at an early age, he'd spent all but the past year in mental institutions, and since his release had been a vagrant on the streets. Pressured to crack the case, GIS hauled him in.

Statements made to a person in authority must be proved by the Crown to be voluntary: not the result of hope of advantage or fear of prejudice induced by the police. Before the British Parliament shipped Canada's Constitution home with a Charter of Rights and Freedoms in 1982, finally freeing the country from quasi-Colonial status, statements made by an accused to an undercover cop escaped the "voluntary rule" if he was blind to the hidden "authority."

Questioning a suspect is never conducted according to the Marquis of Queensberry rules. The Mounties use the full extent of the law lawmakers give them. It took Serious Crimes and GIS several hours to break the oddball down, and when they were through he was a psychological mess, curled up in a fetal ball on the grilling-room floor. Again and again, visible cops hauled him up from the cells, using the good guy/bad guy Mutt and Jeff technique, probing his emotions with photos of the corpse, threatening hypnosis or polygraph tests, asking him to imagine how such a crime occurred, then once his imagination was going, shipping him back to the cells where his cellmate—the invisible cop—asked him what he told them.

His statements led to the charge.

Hatchett took one look at the oddball in the dock and thought, *My friend, you're going down.* In the legal profession a judge like her is called a "streamliner": one who decides beforehand how a case should end, then streamlines the evidence admitted toward that result. A voir dire, or "trial within a trial" without the jury present, was held to determine the admissibility of the statements.

"Sergeant," Knight asked the visible cop about the grilling upstairs, "short of physical violence, injecting truth serum, or electroshocks, what third-degree method *didn't* you use?"

"None," said the cop forthrightly.

"Do you think what he said to you was voluntary?"

"No," he answered.

Hatchett ruled out the upstairs statements as she preplanned to do.

Which left the invisible cop.

"Mr. Knight," Hatchett said at the end of the day, "will you be calling evidence on the *voir dire*?"

"Yes, My Lady."

"Who?"

"A psychiatrist."

"*Which* psychiatrist?"

"Dr. Jasper Goodman."

Hatchett bounced her palm off her forehead, telling him what she thought of that without leaving biased comment on the record.

The headshrinkers' parade is the phoniest charade in any trial. There are Crown psychiatrists; there are defense psychiatrists; and on the stand you wonder if they're testifying about the same accused. Cynics might say it all depends on who's paying the bill. Dr. Jasper Goodman, in thirteen years as a shrink, had never given evidence for the Crown. Crown counsel and Crown-minded judges alike thought him a charlatan.

"Dr. Goodman," Knight said the following day, "did you examine the accused in light of his psychiatric history?"

"I did."

"What, if any, conclusions did you draw?"

Goodman placed his hand on two stacks of documents each a foot high. "As a child, Dan was misdiagnosed as retarded, when in fact he has dyslexia, a learning disability. Through oversight—Dan's an orphan—he spent twenty years institutionalized with people half his IQ, leaving him mentally ill. He suffers from what we call a 'borderline state,' and finds it difficult to separate fact from fantasy, or fantasy from delusion. He'd be totally unreliable as a witness, and any statements made by him should not be believed without independent corroboration."

Knight argued what Dan told his cellmate were not the words of an "operating mind," and since they might be fantasy induced by the officers upstairs, should be excluded as unsafe and unreliable. Hatchett accepted Goodman's opinion for most of the statements, but ruled there were "islands of rationality re: the crime," and since these were "internally consistent, each with the others," provided "buttressing corroboration that made them safe to be weighed by the jury."

Legalese is a deadly language. If a judge says the moon is made of green cheese, it's made of green cheese . . . until the appeal. The truncated statements went in and the jury heard them.

Then came the wild card.

"Mr. Knight," Hatchett said, "your client has disappeared."

The lawyer turned to find the prisoner's dock empty. On checking, he found Dan curled up in a fetal ball on the floor, fingers stuck in his ears. Astute enough to realize the trial was a railroad, Dan had withdrawn his presence.

"My Lady," said Knight, his mind sparking fast, "I don't think he's fit to continue."

To stand trial, an accused must be mentally sound enough to instruct counsel. Hatchett had no alternative but to adjourn so Dan could be assessed at FPI. A week later, court reconvened for a fitness hearing. The same jury would determine whether Dan was fit, so the Crown had to call two shrinks who, given Dan's history in the document piles, supported Goodman. "He's fit enough to be tried," they stated, "but don't trust any confession without objective backup."

On the chessboard of the courtroom, Knight had the queen in check.

The only thing more important to Hatchett than imprisoning scum was her winning record with the judicial elite. Thanks to the "Crown" shrinks backing Goodman, a conviction based on the statements she had let in—for it was too late to close the barn door—was doomed in the Court of Appeal. Only an acquittal would save her winning streak.

From that point on, there were two defense counsel in court. When it came time to sum up, Hatchett ordered the court reporter to type without tape recording, then played two-faced for the jury. The Crown theory was put in a monotone. The defense theory rang out in the blast of Clarence Darrow. It looked balanced in print, but if you were there, Wow!

The jury acquitted.

Dan was released.

And soon killed again.

All that court attention was the highlight of his life.

To this day, Hatchett believed Knight had coached him to fall down in the dock.

And finally, with this trial, she would settle the score.

When judged for art direction, color, and pizzazz, British courts opened on Broadway, Canadian courts off Broadway, American courts in Poughkeepsie. With no wig or haughty use of "ithue" for "issue," Hatchett's Court was stuck in the twentieth century, unable to pretend Mozart or Johnson was on trial. It may have slipped a notch, but not as far as Down South, where judges dressed like refugees from a Baptist choir, dowdy black robe tossed over street clothes, while the accused sat hidden among his "defense team," hard to differentiate the attorneys from the crooks, were they planning to try a case or play a game of football, how many lawyers do you need for a group hug? Yes, American courts could use a shot of Andrew Lloyd Webber, just as Hatchett's Court could use a shot of justice.

Hanging Judge Begbie's Heritage Courtroom provided the perfect stage: carved oak, with velvet bunting, and polished brass. Hatchett sat high on her throne in this Court of the Crimson Queen, face to face with the scum in the dock, isolated as he should be. No fat overblown "defense team" here, just two barristers a side, senior and junior, and let's get on with it. Corporal Kidd was on the stand, dressed in Red Serge, standing tall like Mounties do when they give evidence, civilian witnesses sit, but not the Force. Lyndon Wilde QC in black silk, starched white, and striped gray morning pants could be a Victorian undertaker at a royal funeral. The perfect stage for a prima donna to preen, he tugged his pocket watch from his vest, flipped it open, confirmed the time, snapped it shut, and said, "Thank you, Corporal. I'm through with direct." Then turned to Knight. "Your witness."

The Vulture rose to his feet.

Six-foot-four, lean, lanky, and stooped in black on black, Knight had short black hair, dark hooded eyes from late nights in the law library, a Nixon beard that needed reshaving before he could clean his razor, and a deep resonant voice. Sporting black trousers to augment his robe, he had the Paladin, Johnny Cash, Oliver Stone look in court. Crown lawyers called his waterfront home "The House That Drugs Built." Crown lawyers called him "The Vulture" because he made carrion from flesh on the bones of their cases.

"Corporal Kidd," Knight began, "why are you in Red Serge?"

"I was told to wear it."

"By whom?"

"Mr. Wilde."

"Why?"

"You'll have to ask him."

"You're on the stand, you're wearing it, so I'm asking you. Tell the jury when you usually wear Red Serge."

"For regimental functions and formal occasions."

"Do you wear it on Canada Day?"

"Not for several years."

"Why?"

"It's wool with a tight collar and July first is too hot."

"Have you worn it for any other trial this year?"

"No."

"Last year?"

"No."

"The year before?"

"Mr. Knight," Hatchett snapped. "The Red Serge is my order."

"And why is that, My Lady? Because there's a—"

"Don't question me. This is my Court and I determine the rules. Now get on with it, and leave the dress code to me."

"Are my collar tabs straight enough?"

"I'm warning you, Mr. Knight."

"Corporal Kidd, explain again, what made you think this murder was an 'inside job'?"

"Winifred Parker, the first witness, the neighbor across the road—"

"Nosy Parker."

"Yes, Nosy Parker, saw no one but Nick Craven—"

"Corporal Craven."

"Yes, Corporal Craven, approach the murder house from Mary Hill Road. When I arrived, the front and back doors were locked with no sign of burglary or tampering. Corporal Craven told me he'd locked his mother in, and that she would never open the door to a stranger at night."

"So, from that you deduced she knew her killer and let him in?"

"Yes."

"Okay, if we assume only Corporal Craven used the front, and Dora Craven was locked but not bolted . . . not bolted, right?"

"Yes, locked but not bolted."

"And Dora Craven was locked but not bolted in, and she didn't open the door to anyone she didn't know, and no one got in by burglary or tampering, is that enough to prove your theory?"

"Enough for me," said Kidd.

"The back of Dora Craven's house overlooks Colony Farm?"

"Yes."

"Can Nosy Parker view back there from her house on Mary Hill Road?"

"No."

"Is there a public footpath across the face of the hill?"

"Yes."

"A dark, unlit path Nosy Parker can't view?"

"Yes."

"One end turning down to Colony Farm and the other going toward Port Coquitlam Town Center?"

"Yes."

"And does that path skirt the back porch and rear door of the murder house?"

"Yes."

"Shortly before Dora Craven was killed, were there two murders on Colony Farm Road?"

"Yes."

"A psychotic madman named Günter Schreck murdered two sheriff's deputies taking him to Colony Farm's Forensic Psychiatric Institute for a court-ordered mental remand?"

"Yes."

"How did he kill both deputies?"

"He crushed their skulls."

"And then he escaped across Colony Farm?"

"Yes."

"In the direction of Dora Craven's home?"

"Yes."

"Where you soon found her dead in the kitchen?"

"Yes."

"Dead from a crushed skull?"

"Yes, but she was clubbed. The deputies were both stomped."

"Clubbed like a Mounted Policeman was also clubbed in Coquitlam that night?"

"Yes."

"And he was clubbed at a time when Corporal Craven was miles away on Colony Farm talking to officers investigating the deputies' deaths?"

"Yes."

"Clubbed at a time for which Corporal Craven has a rock-solid alibi?"

"For the Member's clubbing, yes."

"So if Dora Craven's house was found unlocked or burglarized, with a skull-crushing madman loose nearby, given those facts and nothing else, surely logic would point a finger at Schreck?"

"If," said Kidd.

"Take a look at Photo thirteen in Exhibit two entered

by the Crown. Is that the locked kitchen in which Dora's body was found?"

The clerk passed Kidd the exhibit. "Yes," said the Mountie.

"What's that on the floor in the far corner?"

"Two bowls and a box."

"A cat food bowl? A water bowl? And a cat's litter box?"

"Yes," said Kidd.

"So Dora Craven wasn't the *only* person living in the house?"

"A cat's not a person."

"Obviously you've never lived with one."

The jury laughed.

"Have you, Corporal?"

Kidd shook her head. "I'm allergic to cats."

"The night of the murder, did you see the cat in question? Did you meet Jinx?"

"Yes."

"Where?"

"Scratching the back door."

"Inside or outside?"

"Outside," said Kidd.

"Scratching the scratches we see on the door in Photo nine?"

"Yes."

"Was the cat in the house when the door was opened with a skeleton key?"

"No."

"You saw Jinx later?"

"Yes, when I returned from questioning Parker."

"So if Jinx lived *in* the house with Dora, and you met Jinx *outside* wanting in, is it logical someone let Jinx out earlier?"

"Yes."

"Have you any reason to assume Dora Craven herself didn't let the cat out?"

"No."

"And if she opened the back door to let Jinx out, what if Günter Schreck was lurking outside? Would that not explain how he got in uninvited without leaving a mark?"

"His feet would be muddy."

"Perhaps he removed his boots to sneak up to the door. I repeat: if she opened the back door to let Jinx out, what if Günter—"

"It might," said Kidd.

"If he killed Dora Craven and fled, would closing the door behind him leave it locked but not bolted like when you arrived?"

Kidd nodded.

"Yes or no, Corporal?"

"Yes," she said.

"I think it's time we took a closer look at madman Günter Schreck. . . .

MADMAN

Vancouver
Wednesday, December 8, 1993

Any blonder and the German would be an albino. His Nordic face bore angles like iceberg facets, with eyes the pale blue of Arctic floes, under hair and brows the platinum of polar caps. Having dropped skis in a travel bag beside his suitcase near the door, shedding his alpine jacket revealed a turtleneck sweater over skintight ski pants. The Cariboo—where the Hanging Judge lashed and strung up American rowdies—was fast becoming a region for German cowboys, and Whistler, he told Zinc, was now known in Europe as North America's best ski resort. The agents at the Federal Intelligence Service in Cologne competed for the perk of flying the extradition papers here. When DeClercq returned to Special X after arguing racial politics with Chan, he found Zinc and the German discussing Schreck by the Bert and Ernie section of the Strategy Wall.

"Jürgen Müller, Robert DeClercq," Chandler introduced them. "Jürgen corrals right-wing militants and neo-Nazi groups."

The two shook hands.

"Wolfgang Schreck," the German said. "This name is known to you?"

"The Werewolf," DeClercq replied, again surprising Zinc with his research breadth. Müller frowned as if he wished the name *were* unknown.

"Schreck's father?" Chandler guessed.

"Grandfather," said Müller. "Hanged in 1948, after the 'Doctors' Trial.' He worked with Josef Mengele at Auschwitz-Birkenau, developing 'plague bombs' for Göring's Luftwaffe. Both men were fascinated by twins and used them as TP's."

DeClercq caught the question mark in Chandler's eyes. "Test persons," he said.

"The Angel of Death—the camps' name for Mengele, because on a whim he could condemn or spare—yearned to solve the genetic blueprint of twins, in the hope he could duplicate it in German women to produce multiple births of blond-haired, blue-eyed Aryans. The Werewolf used twins to study plagues, injecting one with typhus, cholera, anthrax, and other pathogens, while the double provided the perfect 'control' to assess each germ's effect. One camp had a tower off the medical labs, and up there the Werewolf did vivisection when the moon was full. Here is a quote"—he flipped open his notebook—"from the Nüremberg Trials. 'The Jew knew it was over,' testified Schreck's assistant, 'so he didn't struggle when they led him naked into the lab and tied him down. Then Schreck picked up the scalpel, and that's when he screamed. Without anesthetic, the doctor cut him open from chest to groin—' "

Both DeClercq's and Chandler's eyes flicked to the photos of Jack MacDougall's disemboweled corpse further along the wall.

" '—and he screamed and screamed with his face all twisted in agony. He made this unimaginable sound, he screamed so horribly, and those screams could be heard around the camp. The doctor dissected him alive to see what the disease did to his insides. He made the double watch the procedure, then vivisected him, too, to compare TP's.' "

Müller closed his notebook.

"When Germany split West and East after the war, the Werewolf's family was trapped in the Russian Zone.

They lived about two kilometers east of the Branden-burg Gate, where Günter Schreck grew up in the heart of our new darkness. Schliemannstrasse in the Prenz-lauer district has barely changed since the Soviets fought their way from door to door in 1945. The Schreck tene-ment was in near ruins, its facade half shot away, with heaps of war rubble still piled in the courtyard. There's a saying in German: 'We don't fry up extra sausages,' which means: 'We don't encourage not identifying with a group of some kind.' Schreck identifies with Hitlerites, and as you know, in East Germany before the Wall came down, antifascism was a central article of Soviet faith. The department that dealt with neo-Nazis was the Communist Ministry of State Security. In 1989, People's Police searched Schreck's home."

Müller faced DeClercq. "The Werewolf's collection. You know about it?"

"Wolfgang Schreck harvested tattoos."

Müller turned to Chandler. "It all began with Ilse Koch, the Bitch of Buchenwald. Her husband was com-mandant of that camp. She discovered human skin made an excellent lamp shade, so inmates were killed to deco-rate their home. Prisoners with tattooing were culled for Schreck, who flayed their skin, treated it, and had the image framed. His favorite was a masterpiece of Hänsel and Gretel. When the People's Police searched Günter's home, they found his grandfather's horde of tattoos in an alcove shrine to the führer. Hitler's portrait was pinned to the wall, along with a swastika and anti-Se-mitic slogans: 'The chosen people of Satan killed Jesus Christ, Martin Luther, and Adolf Hitler. America is the long arm of world Jewry. Germany is becoming the crown colony of Judas.' The upshot of the search was Schreck was sent to Ravenscrag."

"Brainwashed?" said DeClercq.

"Electroshock. The works. The jolts they gave were thirty times normal therapy. Because the two electrodes zapped the *sides* of his head, Schreck thinks the shocks wrenched his brain sideways in his skull, so his front-to-back brain waves could align with the current. Skull width shorter than skull length, his brain is now vised to cause him constant mental pain. Just before the Wall came down in November eighty-nine, Schreck was back on Schliemannnstrasse in the Prenzlauer."

"A time bomb," said Chandler.

"Who's gone off several times."

"You paint a vivid picture. Your English is better than mine!"

"Müller grinned. "I have two girls in their teens. In Europe, MTV is broadcast in English. I told you we competed for the perk of flying here. He who best spoke English won."

"The Bone Police," DeClercq said. "How'd that come about?"

"You grasp the nightmare we inherited with German reunification? War-related angst is the most important question in our political culture. It creeps into every debate on major policy issues, much the same way racial questions lurk within U.S. discussions. Ours is the sum of all guilts. There are *verboten* words like *Endlösung* and *Sonderbehandlung* missing from our language— 'final solution' and 'special treatment' respectively—and we often replace 'Jewish' with *Mosaisch,* as in 'the people of Moses.' I took my girls to a rock concert. The band from Britain tried to rouse the fans by telling them to punch the air with right hands to yells of 'Boom, boom, boom!' The crowd wouldn't do it. Why? Because a mass of raised right hands would look too much like newsreel footage of a Nazi rally.

"In 1990—the year we reunified—workers found a buried section of the führer bunker intact in central Berlin, complete with murals of black-booted SS troops and happy Aryan families. That was an omen for Schreck and his ilk. Since then, 26 have been killed and 1,738 injured in 4,800 neo-Nazi attacks on 'un-Germans.' With 41,900 members in far-right groups, not counting 25,000 in the Republican Party, our department has tripled in size to keep them under watch. For some it's simply nihilism, they destroy because they like it, while others are caught in the void between the frigid austerity of the Communist past and binges of new capitalist excess. But Schreck's the real thing.

"He thinks *Untermenschen*—or subhumans—betrayed him to the People's Police, which electroshock revealed as skeletal zombies intent on torturing him. The arson

attack that killed five Turkish women in Solingen, the
gasoline bombs in Duisburg, the baseball bats in Olden-
dorf, the human swastika on Alexanderplatz, the assault
on the U.S. luge team in Oberhof—those monkey noises
and shouts of 'Nigger out'—they all have the earmarks
of Schreck's handiwork. But we want him extradicted
for murder. His paranoid delusion Bone Police are after
him—*Knochenpolizei* born from electroshock—has
grown to encompass *all* police in conspiracy. Before his
trek to Canada, he crushed the skulls of three cops who
got in his way."

"Why's Schreck here?" Chandler asked. "What brings
him to Canada?"

"The magnetic North Pole," replied Müller.

"Of course," said DeClercq. "Depolarization. Stand
on the North Pole, and hopefully that will counter the
polarization that twisted his brain. Which explains the break-
in at the sporting goods outlet." He directed the German to
the New West Police report on the wall. "His loot contained a thermal coat, a polar tent, and other Arctic
gear. We wondered if the Canadian Arctic somehow fed
into Schreck's psychosis. The magnetic North Pole's off
Cape Columbia, Canada's northernmost tip. Get there
and he could cross the ice to it."

"We know Schreck killed these two deputies," said
Zinc, indicating the photos of Bert and Ernie dead. "He
stomped their heads to crush their skulls. But since he
sees only cops as skeletons, why crush the skull of a
civilian nearby?"

The three men moved to the Dora Craven section of
the wall.

"That's how he kills," suggested Müller. "The Bone
Police *must* be killed that way, and with others it's an
easy method."

DeClercq moved to the photos of Jack MacDougall's
body. "If Schreck crushed this skull as one of the Bone
Police, why then disembowel a fleshless skeleton? Or is
the gutting somehow tied to the Werewolf's vivisection?
And if so, why gut a *dead* man?"

"Perhaps you seek too much logic from a madman. If
Schreck slips in and out of lunacy, as my sources among
the neo-Nazis say, his delusion may adopt both past and
present insanities."

Chandler turned to face the windows where darkness blackened the city. "He's out there somewhere. I wonder what Schreck's up to now?"

MORTUARY

In Harvey Dingwall's line of work, yuks were very important, so that's why *Tales from the Crypt* played on TV, the old black-and-white set on a new VCR, the ideal medium to match this atmosphere, as one half-hour show followed another. The scene on-screen at the moment was of a screaming man beating frantically on the lid of a buried coffin, having realized his nine lives inherited from a cat were actually eight since the cat had used a life up when it died. As Harvey rammed the trochar into Mr. Saddlebags' groin, using the sharp foot-long half-inch-diameter metal tube to puncture organs, collapsing them so they didn't bloat while he was on display, *Open Casket* read the tag tied to Mr. Love Handles' toe, the Crypt Keeper puppet appeared on-screen to wrap up the episode.

Harvey yukked along with the Crypt Keeper's ghoulish cackle.

Gallows humor.

Mortuary puns.

Davis, Craig, and Ingels was B.C.'s oldest funeral home, a gray stone Gothic mansion on Kingsway out past Main, its mullioned windows drilled by rain as branches scratched the roof. Tomorrow, Mr. Rodney Craig—fourth generation—would lay on a dignified open casket walk-by for Mr. Saddlebags' bereaved, so Mr. Dingwall had to do the yeoman's work tonight. Wearing an autopsy apron similar to Macbeth's, an owllike man with roving hands when beauties graced his slab, no need for *Playboy* with a sexy job like his, this the night reality behind the day fantasy of dark suits and wet hankies in the chapel out front, Harvey worked in the cramped, humid mortuary masked by the somber facade,

two "patients"—neither a beauty—on the slanted slabs
in the poorly lit charnel room, hemmed in by cruel machines, ugly instruments in dirty cupboards, and foul-
smelling embalming fluids and powders. On a stool was
the makeup kit.

Having perforated the pecs and abs of his patient, like
a baked potato skin or crust for apple pie, Harvey
switched the trochar for a suction pump. The same
sound as a vacuum cleaner, it slurped Mr. Saddlebags
clean of stagnant blood, so his vascular system could be
infused with mummy juice. The head was the focus in
open casket sales, so the mortician jabbed catheters into
a carotid artery and jugular vein. The face flushed pale,
makeup came next.

Nothing thrilled Harvey more than tickling a beauty's
fancy while he painted her face, the paint box on the
stool worthy of Van Gogh, enough makeup for *Phantom
of the Opera* here, but this guy was butt, so Harvey put
him off.

He turned to the other slab.

A lovable, cute, rotting zombie out of the grave, the
Crypt Keeper cackled as he wound up another tale. In it,
a mortuary fed a subterranean banquet hall for gourmet
ghouls. " 'Rah, ree, reen! Sis, boom, bean! Stick 'im in
the ash can! His bones are picked clean!' Hee, hee!
That's the organization's cheer, creeps! No choking!"

Harvey yukked along with the Crypt Keeper's grisly
mirth.

Ms. Smash Head was the other patient tonight. She
lay naked on the twin slab, released earlier today from
Royal Columbian Hospital morgue. The toe tag called
for embalming *and* cremation. Why the extra treatment
Harvey could never understand, jacking up the price for
redundancy, no need to mummify what would soon be
ash. "But do *both* this time," Mr. Craig had warned.
"No shortcuts when the sale's a cop."

Harvey checked his watch.

Almost time.

Cremations were done under cover of night. Didn't
want smoke belching out during chapel mourning service, human smoke spreading human ash by day far and
wide, do it at night when all community-responsible industries do their polluting.

Out of sight, out of mind.

The mortician's creed.

The arms of the Y-stitch down Ms. Autopsy's torso V'd from her shoulders to halfway down her sternum, the handle of the incision then dropping to her pubic bone. No need to use the trochar on organs the postmortem had emptied from her, just open the stitches to reveal the plastic bag of guts repacked inside, to fill the cavity with a perfumed mix of sawdust, alcohol, and formaldehyde. While open, he'd suction-pump the blood to infuse mummy juice, then sew her up with the same overlapping stitch to prevent leakage. No need to do the head, which looked like Frankenstein's Bride, a brain incision over the crown from behind both ears; who was going to see her?

Had she been younger, he might have done her face anyway.

Then pizza time.

The crematorium was along the hall because it rose to temperatures of almost 1800 degrees Fahrenheit. Heat was the *last* comfort you wanted in a mortuary. The huge brick gas-fired oven was walk-in size, for bodies cooking gave off combustible gases. Harvey would encasket Ms. Smash Head—another waste—then roll her in, fire the jets, and burn, baby, burn. Later, he'd collect the ashes and pieces of charred bone, removing coffin nails to dump the cremains in a tumbler, so rocks could grind the fragments to dust. Ashes to ashes and dust to dust would then be packed in a funeral urn for sale to the cop tomorrow.

Harvey was about to cut the autopsy stitches.

What was that?

Breaking glass?

In the buffer room between the chapel and the mortuary?

Had one of the branches scratching the roof broken a window?

Harvey left to investigate.

From the door he could see the smashed-in pane, as his hand fumbled for the light switch in the dark. Wind moaned mournfully in through the breach, but no branch intruded that he could see. Stepping into the darkness, he recoiled to one side when he glimpsed a black figure at the corner of his eye, which remained black even as white light lit up the room, then *whap!* Harvey's lights went out instead, the force of the blow bludgeoning his skull blackening everything in sight.

When Harvey eventually came to, the first thing he did was dial 911.

Guy who breaks into a mortuary must be a pervert, right?

God knows what he might do to the patients.

The last thing Harvey wanted was face-to-face battle with a sick fuck.

Then he remembered the Crypt Keeper on TV.

The *very* last thing he wanted was cops thinking *he* was a sick fuck.

So Harvey shambled back to switch off *Tales from the Crypt*.

Except for two details, the mortuary was unchanged from how the mortician had left it. But now the ghostly glow came solely from the TV, casting a black-and-white flicker about this halfway house for the dead, an ether from the other side where mystery lurks, RIP to sinners who squandered the entrance fee, the zombies who return because there's nowhere else to go. And by this hellish pallor from beyond, the black one had slashed Ms. Smash Head's belly with a blade, leaving the autopsy stitches still sewn, but slitting the plastic bag containing her guts, so the coils of her repacked intestines were disemboweled down the slab.

On-screen, the Crypt Keeper cackled to wrap up his final tale.

Hee, hee, hee.

But this time Harvey didn't yuk along.

RETURN FROM THE GRAVE

West Vancouver

Robert DeClercq took a deep breath and let it out slowly. Would the troubles of this depressing day never end? "Katt," he called to the kitchen after hanging up the phone. "Got to go out. I may be late. So don't wait up."

The cooking smells of steak *frites* hung heavy in the hall. The teenager poked her head through the door, dish towel in hand. Theirs was the war of meat eaters everywhere: do you eat the tenderloin first or last? "First," she'd said at dinner, "so you get the best part hot." "Last," he'd responded, "to savor the *better* part after."

"You'll miss the new CD by Nine Inch Nails," Katt said now.

"Keep it down," Robert warned. "Windowpanes are expensive."

"No louder than 'The Who Live at Leeds,' " Katt said, the retort once used on her mom, the now-dead Luna Darke.

Snugged in his parka and beaver-skin hat (the head-gear of Arctic Mounties with flaps tied on top), Robert locked the front door and braved the foggy frost. Here where he'd survived attacks by Cutthroat's Alley Demons and later Garret Corke, Napoleon (spleen gone but knife wound healed) stood guard. "Take care of her, boy," the Horseman said, nuzzling his dog.

The path climbing to Marine Drive was slippery and treacherous, black ice moonshadowed by hoary firs along both sides. Behind him, from the miasmic bay beyond his waterfront home, foghorns on phantom freighters groaned and mourned.

Recently, DeClercq had purchased a new "preowned" car, the term for those who find "used" a dirty word.

For years he'd driven French imports—a Citroën before the Peugeot—till Katt advised him, "Bob, it's time to shed the dorky wheels. You don't shark chicks in Flintstone-mobiles."

The chariot in the carport off Marine Drive was a BMW M5 four-door with a racing engine and wide-oval low profile tires. Discovery of Blake's headless corpse on Windigo Mountain had propelled *Bagpipes, Blood, and Glory* onto bestseller lists here and in Britain. Even the Americans—cautious with books set outside their realm—had put aside the umpteenth retread of Lewis & Clark to buy enough copies to fatten his bank account. Combined with royalties from a rewrite of *Men Who Wore the Tunic*, retitled *Those Who Wore the Tunic* to bring it up to date, his sideline scribblings had financed the cool car.

"Oh, Bob," Katt moaned, face buried in her hands. "The vehicle of old fogeys and yuppie swine. And white, no less."

"Study hard, my culture guru, and you'll have your pink Ferrari."

"A Honda Civic DX Hatchback, aztec green, with a CD player will do," she said, producing a glossy brochure from her room.

Tonight, the old foge-mobile (Beethoven's *Pastoral Symphony* playing inside, no less) snaked its way northwest from Lighthouse Park, slipping here, sliding there on black ice rinking the road, Eagle Harbor, Fisherman's Cove, and Whytecliff Point invisible on the foggy ocean side, the hump of Hollyburn Mountain looming blackly to the right, until he reached the ferry dock at Horseshoe Bay.

Parking the BMW, he boarded *The Queen of Capilano* as a foot passenger for the twenty-minute crossing. The Mounted's Marine Services would bring him back.

Three to four miles wide and seven to eight miles long, Bowen Island clogs the entrance to Howe Sound. In 1860, British surveyor Captain George Richards named it for Rear Admiral James Bowen, hero of a sea battle with the new French Republic in 1794. Squamish natives had already given it names like *Kwumch-Nam* ("Noise as When Stamping Heels") but that didn't count. The first white settlement was a lumber camp back when logs were hauled down skid roads to the sea. The skids were greased with dogfish oil, so the man who greased them had a cabin to himself. No one could stand to live with him because of the smell. Twenty square miles of rain forest walled in by rocky bluffs were soon dotted with stump ranches among the firs and salal. Robert's destination was one of the pioneer sites.

Though west of West Vancouver, Bowen is policed by North Vancouver RCMP. *The Queen of Capilano* docked at Snug Cove, where one of the island's two constables met the chief superintendent. She filled him in while they drove down island to the grave above Queen Charlotte Channel.

"The Asian who bought the property is building his dream home. Yesterday, workmen tore down the ramshackle pioneer house. Afraid the ground would freeze with this chill in the weather, today they began to backhoe the foundation. A few feet down, they uncovered a skeleton wrapped in plastic. We checked the previous owner, Luna Darke, and found you sold the property as trustee for her daughter. So the call."

"How old's the corpse?" DeClercq asked.

"Pathologist says a year. That jibes with a notebook found on the body."

"Name?"

"Pete Trytko. Boston private eye."

The crime scene was cordoned off with yellow tape repeating CAUTION POLICE DO NOT CROSS in black. The pit beyond resembled an archaeological dig. Crisscross arcs lit the grave as bright as high noon, sheening one side of the earth and timber heaps around the rim. A backhoe and other mechanical beasts lurked in the dark, spooked by the skeleton wrapped in torn plastic with tatters of flesh and cloth clinging to its moldy bones. A skeletal arm reached from the shroud like a zombie summoned to walk with the undead. The crushed skull peeking through the tear reminded Robert of Lindow Man in the British Museum. Dressed in white coveralls with boots and hood attached, Ident cops staked the pit with a crosshatched rope grid to guide their forensic hunt. Those who made murder their business—coroner, pathologist, exhibit man, file coordinator, field investigator, body removal grunts—stood on the rim cracking

jokes about fleshing out the case while plumes of con-
densed life curled from their lips. Athletic and lean, with
short brown hair, a clipped brown mustache, and muddy
brown eyes, Corporal Rick Scarlett was the NCO in
charge. Like Tipple, he was a veteran of the Headhunter
Squad, partnered back then with Katherine Spann as
one of the Flying Patrols. Spann outshone him, so she
made Special X, and Scarlett returned to duty with GIS.
When Craven became an X-Man during the Ripper case,
the corporal replaced him at North Van Detachment.

"Rick."

"Chief."

"Thanks for the call. What have we got here?"

"Skull crushed. A dozen blows. Hammer most likely.
Backhoe ripped the plastic when it dug up the corpse,
baring a trench coat pocket at one end of the tear. In
it, we found these."

Sheathing his piano-player hands in latex gloves, De-
Clercq opened the plastic pouch Scarlett offered him.
Stuck together when the corpse decomposed, a wallet
and small black notebook fell into his palm. A laminated
PI license issued to Pete Trytko by the State of Massa-
chusetts was tucked in the wallet. The book contained
jotted notes. Reading between the lines, DeClercq
grasped the *who* and *why* of Trytko's death. The last
entry was December 4, a year ago. . . .

Bowen Island, British Columbia
Friday, December 4, 1992

Damn airlines, Luna thought, hammering one of the
small wheels on the bottom of her suitcase back into
line. *If they don't lose your bags, they wreck them.* Hers
had been damaged on a recent cross-country junket, a
quaint Canadian custom where taxpayers fund CanLit
authors Ottawa thinks they should embrace but no one
buys. Surviving in the marketplace is strictly for the
States.

Someone knocked at the door.

Mainland residents had learned to triple-lock their
homes, adopting the bunker mentality that comes with
"world-class status," but here on rural Bowen that
wasn't the practice yet. Luna walked from her bedroom

to the porch door, and swung it open to face a stranger on the dripping deck. He raised a Polaroid camera and flashed it in her eyes.

"Hey!" Luna grumbled, raising the hand without the hammer to shield her face, the hammer hidden by the half-open door. "What gives, man?"

"Luna Darke? Lenore Dodd? Nona Stone? Name's Pete Trytko. Boston private eye."

Luna froze.

The man on the porch backed by rain smelled of last night's booze, his eyes as bloodshot as the label of Johnnie Walker Red, quaffed no doubt as a bracer to ward off this harsh Canadian cold. In that regard he fit the Hammett/Chandler archetype, but everything else about him said the guy was a wuss. The dandruff on his trench coat. The face like Elmer Fudd. He even wore one of those dorky hats with flaps hanging over the ears. "Chiclets" replaced several teeth knocked out by a philandering husband caught in the wrong bed. Compared to him, Columbo was a dude.

"I'm Luna Darke," Luna said, "but not the other two. You've mixed me up with someone else."

Trytko withdrew a composite drawing from inside his trench coat. The likeness was Luna, take away fourteen years. "Snatching a mother's baby burns your features into her mind. Game's up, lady. I wanna see your kid. If she doesn't mirror my client, I'll eat my hat."

Tough guy, Luna thought, *with a tiny cock.* "Katt's not home."

"Fourteen years to find her, I got time to wait. Police gave up eventually, but not Mrs. Baxter. First you cost her kid, then her accusing husband: 'How could you be so trusting, you naive bitch?' Eighty thousand bucks she's paid, working herself to the bone. That kinda fee and commitment, I wait till Hell freezes over."

"Get off my property, or I'll call the cops."

"Call 'em, lady. Makes no difference to me. No way you're disappearing until the kid's informed. I want the question in her mind if you try a bunk. No matter where you go, she'll want the answer. Jig's up, Nona. Get it off your chest."

"What'll it take to prove you're wrong?"

"Nothing short of a DNA test on the kid. You or Mrs. Baxter? Who will her genes match?"

Cat and mouse, a Mexican standoff, they stood eye to eye. Then a single tear rolled down the woman's cheek. A man's gotta do what a man's gotta do, said Trytko's smirk. "How'd you find me?" Luna asked.

"Snatching a baby, no ransom, is a nutcase crime. Gotta be a woman who desperately wants a child. Gotta be a woman who can't have one of her own. Flashed the composite in every ward on the East Coast. Finally got a lock on you in Maryland. Traced the car you rented to Washington state, then your marriage of convenience up here. Citizenship, huh? Before you dumped the guy? Only thing not recorded was your daughter's birth. Storks don't bring babies in my world."

Another tear.

"So where's the kid?"

"In the front room. Watching TV."

The PI stepped into the kitchen, easing Luna aside, her right hand visible, her left behind the door. "Let's get this over with," he said.

"Yes. Let's," Luna agreed, whirling like a Cossack with the hammer in her hand, striking the man's forehead as hard as she could, the nose of the weapon punching through his skull in a crunch of bone, ripping splinters with it as she yanked the hammer out, Trytko dropping to his knees like a penitent before God, as "Yes. Let's," repeated, another blow cracked his skull, Luna bringing the weapon down in both hands like an ax, the metal snout caving in his crown like a volcano, spewing red lava in an eruption of blood and brains, hitting the walls, spraying her, raining down on the floor, Trytko shaking like all that booze had brought on the d.t.'s, one leg banging in counterpoint like a hoedown foot, the third blow driving his head *splat*! against the tiles, a pool of blood spreading crimson red across the white, as "Yes. Let's. Let's. Let's," Luna mashed his skull, flattening his brain like a pancake until his death shudders stopped.

Luna dropped the hammer.

Her breath came in gasps.

Then she looked at the kitchen clock.

Katt would soon be home.

What time was she off school today for that damn rotating strike?

Fucking teachers.

So afraid of work.

Pull yourself together.

Got to clean up this mess.

First she fetched a plastic sheet from the broom closet, always on hand in case a "Squamish" sprung a leak in the roof, then she wrapped the corpse in it and tied the shroud with twine. Humping the bundle to a cleaner area of the floor, she wiped the plastic of blood and humped the body again, repeating the process until it left no telltale trail. Stripping, she washed her skin of blood with a dishrag from the sink, then opened the cellar door and dragged the corpse downstairs, bumping it like Christopher Robin lugging Winnie-the-Pooh. The body stretched out on the earthen floor, she returned to the kitchen.

Working frantically with a mop, brush, and pails of water, Luna scrubbed, wrung, and rinsed until the blood was gone, then scoured the floor with ammonia, vinegar, and Comet. Some of the tiles were cracked from the hammer blows.

She washed herself again.

Wrapped in a rubber raincoat like a lobster fisherman, with rubber boots on her feet and gloves on her hands, Luna descended the cellar stairs to dig a makeshift grave. Thank the Earth Goddess pioneer homes were built on dirt foundations.

Pick . . .

Shovel . . .

Pick . . .

Shovel . . .

Four feet down . . .

Then Luna rolled the plastic bundle into the underground hole, filling it in to stomp on the mound until it looked like . . . a grave.

Think, girl, think!

Up the stairs and out the door, she sloshed to the side of her home, and there unlocked the slanted chute that once fed wood to the cellar. The ramshackle house clung to the slope south of Snug Cove, this side gazing across the incline toward Point Grey and the States, both now swallowed up by the hungry storm. Down was to the left, up to the right, with runoff collecting in a trough parallel to the wall, before it tumbled below to Queen Charlotte Channel. Across the strait, Lighthouse Park winked through the rain.

On hands and knees, Luna built a dam across the trough.

Soon the rain rivulet was diverted down the chute, gurgling into the cellar where it inundated the floor, smoothening the mound of the grave into an even layer of silt.

Luna dismantled the dam.

Then relocked the chute.

Then went in, shucked off her clothes, and took a long, hot shower.

Everything bloody was in the washer when Katt returned home, Luna drying her hair by the stove. The kitchen was spick-and-span with no trace of murder about. A day or two and the cellar would be dry, its floor the same flat layer of earth it was before the killing. Until then Luna didn't want Katt poking around, alone in the house while she was gone for the Mystery Weekend.

"Mom, you look spooked. Like you've seen the Devil himself."

"Pack a bag, Katt. We've got a ferry to catch. You're going to help me win fifty thousand dollars."

Wednesday, December 8, 1993

For a year DeClercq had wondered why Luna Darke took Katt to Deadman's Island. The teenager wasn't on the guest list found at Ravenscourt. Reading Trytko's notebook, he now knew why.

Corrine Baxter.

The name of the PI's client glared from the page.

He glanced from it to the zombie clawing from the grave.

The skeletal fingers reached for Katt.

SUICIDE CLUB

Cloverdale, British Columbia

The Moaning Steer was yer vintage Canuck country and western bar. Log shack at the crossroads, sawdust and spittoons on the hardwood floor, pool table over which honky-tonk women in tight jeans bent, brass boot rail, horns mounted over the doors. Johnny, Willie, and Merle wrung few tears from the jukebox here, elbowed out by k.d., Anne, and Stompin' Tom. "Three Cigarettes in an Ashtray" played, lang's howl cuttin' through smoke as thick as dust. Dust gathered on bourbon bottles behind the bar, while VO, Canadian Club, and Crown Royal sold by the case. Yer Bud Man, yer Marlboro Man were booted out the door, kicked by Moosehead and Kokanee. Shots of the Calgary Stampede back when and the Cloverdale Rodeo now hung askew from the logs, joined by Western legends like Sam Steele, "Bub" Walsh, the Mad Trapper of Rat River, "The Shooting of Dan McGrew." The only Yank welcome here was Big Clint, for having the sense to shoot *Unforgiven* in Alberta. Patrons of The Moaning Steer knew you couldn't find the West in America no more. Yanks were too enamored with pretty boys in big hats.

The man shooting Scotch by himself was yer typical cowboy Canuck. Big hands, wary eyes, weathered leathery face. Plain shirt, cuffs up, worn jeans, and boots. The way he hunched over a shot glass said he was in a funk, oozing the warning he'd kick yer teeth down yer throat if you bothered him.

All heads but his turned when the Slicker entered the bar.

Stranger on the farm.

The Slicker paused at the till to pay the barkeep off, flashing a BYOB brown bag while slipping her a fifty, covering drinks the Slicker wouldn't buy. Then the stranger crossed to Cowboy Canuck.

"Mind if I join you?"

"What do *you* want?"

"Company."

"Fuck off. I'm in a foul mood."

The Slicker placed the brown bag on the branded table and peeled down the wrapper in a slow striptease. Johnnie Walker Red? No. Johnnie Walker Black? No. Johnnie Walker *Blue*!

After the sixth shot, Wayne Tarr opened up. The Slicker heard about his days with the rodeo, breakin' broncs and rasslin' steers and nuttin' ornery bulls. He told the Slicker how his wife left him for a lawyer, saying she couldn't stand the stress of ERT assaults, he rammed the doors in, he corralled the punks, he shot it out if necessary, and *she* broke under the stress? No "Stand by Your Man" in that bitch, and no "Little Bitty Tear" let him down.

After the ninth shot, Tarr began to rail. "Yanks crossed the border to build Fort Whoop-Up and sell whiskey to the Reds, so we raised the Force, marched West, and they ran for the States. Almighty Voice tried a last war cry, so we cornered him on a bluff, fired one cannon east, another cannon south, and blew him to pieces. The Mad Trapper shot some cops and holed up in the North, so we tracked him by plane with tear bombs and blew his ass away. That's how men with spurs handle punks.

"Now look at us.

"The country's overrun with foreign filth. People of color squawk and people of pallor run for the hills. Some Negro . . . some black . . . some Afro-fucking-not-even . . . some African-fucking-not-even-Canadian waves a gun at me—Shit, they're like greased pigs in the rodeo. They change the name so often you can't get a handle on *what* they are—some jig kid points a gun at me in a dark room, and *I'm* suspended while the Public Complaints Commission considers charges. I put my life on the line for them and *that's* the thanks I get. The Force backs squealing jigs over me! I oughta . . . I oughta . . . I oughta shoot myself at the Red Serge Ball, that's what I oughta do."

Unknown to Tarr, this was the first meeting of the Suicide Club.

MIDNIGHT RAIN

Coquitlam

Racism, sexism, jingoism: only now did Rachel Kidd fully grasp how her future hung in the balance, for if Nick's mom's blood wasn't on his Red Serge, any or all of those *isms* would have a politically correct front to freeze her out. By seizing Nick's tunic, she'd cast the die of her fate.

Still in her clothes, Rachel lay lights-out on the bed in her top-floor flat, staring up at the rain that snaked across the skylight, lost in thought while waiting for Dermott Toop.

"Make your case," Tipple had said, so now that she was committed to her kamikaze run, tonight the case had taken a bizarre twist.

Watching the rain, Rachel puzzled it out.

Schreck escaped from Colony Farm near Dora's home. Around the same time, Nick beat his mom to death before the RCMP dinner. Schreck—a known cop hater—followed MacDougall from Dora's house to Minnekhada Lodge, there clubbing and disemboweling him in the parking lot. Nick had an alibi for MacDougall's death—he was talking to Members down on Colony Farm—but finding the letter to his mom cast suspicion on him, so tonight he linked the Schreck MO to his mother's murder. Nick broke into the mortuary and disemboweled her body, so the combination of clubbing and gutting would match MacDougall's death, for which Nick was alibied. With a madman on the loose, that's a madman's act, so the implication is—for some psychotic reason—the same lunatic committed *both* mad crimes.

Very clever, thought Kidd.

The apartment door opened, closed, and was locked.

Footsteps creaked the floor of the hall approaching the bedroom. Dermott Toop entered, switched on the lights, and tossed *The Vancouver Sun* onto the quilt.

"See that?" he fumed.

Squinting, Rachel waited for her vision to adjust, then scanned the offending article on the paper's front page:

> *ARREST OF 2 BLACKS*
> *DEFENDED ON BASIS*
> *FEW OF RACE IN CITY*
>
> *A Vancouver Police Board report saying it is okay to arrest blacks as suspects based on their race alone means "open season" on the city's black community, says the Congress of Color.*
>
> *"I think the situation with blacks is unique since you don't see that many blacks in the city," states one board member, defending the ruling police did nothing wrong in arresting two blacks at gunpoint for a robbery they didn't do.*
>
> *"It is not merely disturbing," warns the Congress. "It's absolutely frightening. Why is it acceptable that black men in the area when a crime is committed are, by being black, automatically suspect, while whites nearby aren't targeted when whites commit a crime? Is that not clearly a double standard?"*

Rachel put down the paper.

"You didn't finish reading."

"Derm, I've a lot more on my mind than racial politics that don't hamstring me. If the blood of Craven's mom doesn't test out on his tunic in three weeks, the story in the paper will be:

> *CANNING OF BLACK*
> *DEFENDED ON BASIS*
> *ALLEGATION FAILED*

Let's make the world outside go away for now."

"Talk about stereotyping us!" Toop raged. "Whoever backs that report has no idea what discrimination is! How visible must a minority be before such bullshit is ruled out? Since when does human dignity have anything to do with the presence of your race in numbers? As a black South African, I thought I was in a country where apartheid doesn't exist. Race! Race! Race! No matter where we go, a black man's gotta hide. Just *once* I'd like whitey to see what it's like at the shitty end of the stick!"

"Derm." Rachel sighed. "Let it be for tonight. Did I not hear boastful talk at the Lab about someone being royally fucked? I'm here. The bed's here. Are you going to love me or not?"

Toop loosened his tie. He swept the paper aside. "You know it, girl. I guarantee someone's going to get *royally* fucked."

West Vancouver

"It's like I'm living Kafka's *Trial,*" gasped Nick, still breathing heavily from sex with Gill. Above them, Pacific rain drummed the roof. "*Someone must have been spreading lies about Nick C.,*" he recited, "*for without having done anything wrong he was arrested one morning . . .*"

"You're not arrested," Gill said, snuggling in the dark.

"I would be if some had their way. It *is* like *The Trial,* you know. The bank clerk in that novel. Having to 'justify' myself against phantom charges, and influence those who may effect acquittal, while not knowing what I've done, what I'm guilty of, or why I've been singled out for judgment."

"Nick, the books you're reading are too rich for your mind. The *crème de la crème* should be mixed with a little pulp."

"Your fault," he said.

The first night Nick was in Gill's home during the Ripper case, he'd approached her bookcase with trepidation. The shelves were home to Shakespeare, Austen, the Brontës, Wordsworth, Dickens, Conrad, Proust, Faulkner, Maugham, and Greene, while he was reading Grisham's *The Firm.* Hoping they were a false front hiding her dope supply, he'd tested some of the volumes, but no such luck. Moving knock-kneed toward her CD collection, he'd found Tchaikovsky, Bach, Mozart, Beethoven, and Brahms. Even her taste in rock was high-end: King Crimson, Pink Floyd, Bonzo Dog, the fifties roots. At least they had the Killer, King, and Fat Man in common. Afraid she'd quickly tire of a bimbo mind, Nick had joined the Classics Club that sent the uniform Great Works that Kidd spied in his home.

"I sense a ghost stalking me, Gill. Someone holds me to blame for something I know nothing about. Someone who for some hidden reason set out to frame me from the start. How else do I explain the letter found in Mom's kitchen? That's my birthday and I'm an only child. Whoever it is is using the Force to try me. I'm under suspension and Special X is off the case. That leaves Kidd—my nemesis—with a free hand. She'll be even more suspicious after tonight. Mutilating Mom will look like a cover-up. As if I'm trying to link her murder to that of Jack."

"No," said Gill. "The ghoulish gutting's obviously Schreck. Not having an alibi for tonight's atrocity is bad luck. You don't think 'ghost' knew you were walking alone in the rain?"

"Who knows?" said Nick.

"There's nothing better you can do than listen to De-Clercq. He's right in suggesting you leave town soon. I booked you on a flight to Maui in the morning. Take the ashes if they're ready."

"What about her cat? I must go to Mom's home. Kidd wouldn't let me near it last night."

"That's exactly what you shouldn't do. Again it'll look like you're trying to manipulate the facts. You've suffered a trauma. You're on leave. And Hawaiian sun is waiting for you. Go, and leave the cat to me, her house till you return, and the Lab to clear your Red Serge of any taint."

Vancouver

Finished.

Alex plucked the final page from her laser printer and slapped it facedown on top of the manuscript pile. *Break out the champagne,* she thought, leaning back from her desk, hands behind her head. *Crack a box of cigars,* she thought, as rain spattered the windows and pounded on the roof.

When Alexis was young, she and her parents vacationed each summer on Oregon's coast, abandoning inland Portland where her father was a high court judge. While seagulls dipped and glided around sea-slapped Haystack Rock, foaming wave after whitecapped wave broke on the crescent shore of Cannon Beach. Mist exploded from the rock like artillery shells lobbed by the mythical cannon which named that part of the state. An early fear was toddling the beach hand in hand with Dad, the surf pounding to one side as they neared a house all shiplap and shutters weathered gray by the sea. "The Old Witch lives there," wailed her father, playing off *Snow White and the Seven Dwarfs,* which they'd recently seen. Wide-eyed, Alex stared at the gnarled tree guarding the door like a hunchbacked monster with six crooked arms and too many claws. Releasing her father's hand, she moved to the oceanside, so he was between her and the gables' evil eyes. Then donkeylike she tugged him away from the hag's abode.

Four years ago a car crash had claimed Alex's mom, followed three months later by her dad's first fit. The tumor seized him epileptically while sitting in court, and the consequent neurosurgery had carved out part of his brain. Unfortunately, the doctors could not get it all.

That's when Alex bought the Witch's House.

There, after radiation treatment, she'd nursed Dad as best she could. She fed him well, read to him, and walked him along the beach, still sharing a laugh when she used him to protect her from *their* house. The tumor returned with a vengeance, and treatment was out of the question, so Alex bravely watched the cancer eat him up alive, while the house became a house of horrors that soon had a room of death.

The dark side of her father's work—abnormal psychology—lured Alex like forbidden fruit. Her writings scratched the itch to know where demons spawn, so *House of Horrors: The Case of H.H. Holmes* began at the beginning. What Jack the Ripper was to Britain last century, H.H. Holmes was to the States. He was America's premier serial killer.

The modest success of that book in 1991 led her to plan a series called *Trapdoor Spiders.* Her second book was to be *Room of Death: The Case of Dr. Marcel Petiot,* until her publisher sent a letter received the day she

decided to go to the Mystery Weekend that trapped her
on Deadman's Island:

> *Wiseman & Long, Publishers*
> *500 Fifth Avenue*
> *New York, N.Y. 10110*
>
> *November 27, 1992*
> *Alexis Hunt*
> *423 Madrona Way*
> *Cannon Beach, Oregon*
> *97110*
> *Dear Alex:*
>   *Americans like to read about Americans. A French-*
> *man fifty years ago won't do. Besides, we've got plenty*
> *of "trapdoor spiders" here. Write a book on Ed Gein,*
> *the Plainfield Ghoul. He inspired* Psycho, The Texas
> Chainsaw Massacre, *and* The Silence of the Lambs.
> *Or one on Jeffrey Dahmer, the Milwaukee Cannibal.*
> *Either subject, and you've got a contract. Same terms*
> *as the last.*
>
>   Best,
>   Chris

Deadman's Island changed her life. That ordeal not only
brought her Zinc, whom she took home to the Witch's
House to recuperate, but it also inspired her in a most
horrific way. The book she'd been writing over the year
since then was *Deadman's Island: The Case of Skull &
Crossbones.* They say write about what you know, and
she *knew* about that. Plus, enough Americans had died
to get around the jinx, for publishers in New York think
books set in Canada get a kiss of death.

Surprise, surprise, the advance was $200,000.

Which was now earned, for Alex had finished.

"Zinc, you awake?" she whispered from the door to
the bedroom.

"Umm," he said.

"The book's done, so I have a favor to ask. Do you
think DeClercq would read it and give me his opinion?
I read his nonfiction. It's good."

And with that request, she set them on a course to
tragedy.

West Vancouver

Somewhere in this city, a mom grieved for her son, gunned down by a Special X mistake. Somewhere beyond, a mom pined for her daughter, kidnapped from her fifteen years ago. Walking this beach with Napoleon, DeClercq felt sick over Katt . . . sick at heart. His mind and emotions were in turmoil from this vortex of a day. It was like all the tears cried in the world rained down on him.

Midnight rain.

The police launch from Bowen Island had stopped at his dock. Tomorrow morning he would taxi to his car. Past the oceanside knoll with its driftwood chair and antique sundial, *The time is later than you think* etched around the face, he'd trudged up from the log-strewn beach to his home. Katt was curled up in the living room, cramming for an exam. The German shepherd was stir-crazy and wanted out. So fetching rain slicker and gumboots, Robert had ventured out again to comb the shoreline toward Lighthouse Park.

White, black, white, black . . . the revolving beacon whitened and blackened his face.

For a moment he wondered what he'd do if he alone knew the secret—say he'd dug up the cellar *before* he sold Luna's house, so Trytko's death and the PI's notes were his to control—would he have destroyed the bones to keep Katt for himself? Just thinking such a thought shocked his conscience, for how could he live with himself if he foisted the gut-wrenching anguish he endured over Jane on another parent?

He knew what he had to do, and he'd do it.

Issue closed.

To loosen the knot in his gut, he focused his mind on Nick. Chan was right in saying, "You're protecting one of your men," but that's because he believed Craven innocent, not because come-hell-or-high-water he backed those in his command. Suspicion fell on Nick from the "Mother letter":

December 2, 1993
Mother—
   It's taken my lifetime to uncover your whitewashed

*secret. Discussing it face to face on my birthday seems
fitting. I'll call on the 7th.*

As a tactician who depended on his squad, DeClercq
vetted each Member personally. Nick and his mom had
lived in Vancouver since 1957, and that he loved her
and kept in touch was plain to see. Assuming he did
uncover her "whitewashed secret," why type such a letter or note if he could phone or visit?

It didn't make sense.

Unless it was a frame.

The blood on the tunic was easy to explain. He'd seen
the cut on Nick's hand from crossing the rickety bridge,
and if not for this rain having washed away all trace,
he'd have sent a tech to the river to check each nail.

But convinced though he was of Nick's innocence,
Robert was nagged by logic. If the "Mother letter" was
a frame, did that not acquit Schreck of Dora's murder?
And if her killer wasn't Nick or Schreck, who might it
be? Most vexing of all was the disemboweling tonight
at the mortuary, described to him over police radio on
the launch.

Suppose Schreck killed the deputies, Dora, and Jack.
All had their skulls crushed, and Jack was eviscerated.
The German cop had stated, "Perhaps you seek too
much logic from a madman." Suppose, instead of gutting
a skeleton, Schreck was slashing Jack's uniform. If so,
why did he break in to gut Dora's corpse, when one:
she was a civilian, not Bone *Polizei,* and two: he could
have disemboweled her in her home?

The answer was to capture and question Schreck.

The path from the beach up to his house served the
Greenhouse door, then skirted left around the residence
to the front entrance. Pausing outside to gaze at Katt
framed by the inner door to the room beyond, Robert
faced his double on the Greenhouse glass. Fiftysome-
thing, with dark and wavy hair graying at the temples,
an aquiline nose hinting arrogance he didn't have, a
shadow of beard showing through the skin of his narrow
jaw, the light behind his brooding image haloed the teenager in the chair, until reaching out, finished her studies
for the night, Katt—unaware she was being observed—
flicked off the lamp and darkened the inner man.

Coquitlam

Like flashbulbs popping in his brain, white skulls probed his mind, appearing suddenly in his dark matter to snatch one of his thoughts, accessing consciousness to drag his plans to the fortress of the *Knochenpolizei* to dissect, revealing his innermost secrets to the Bone Police. They must be using an electromagnetic device to penetrate his electromagnetic field, transmitting their skulls as hot bursts of light through the screen of his mind, inducing electroshock dread and terrifying shifts in mood to frighten him into exposing himself to their torture patrols.

Poooff! Another skull flashed and faded within his head.

Since shortly after yesterday's escape from Colony Farm, Schreck had been in this hideaway near the Indian Reserve, upstream from Mary Hill by the one-lane bridge across the Coquitlam River. He'd kicked the nuts of the man who answered the door up to his chin, then caved in his head and hauled him down to the root cellar to rot, where, as luck would have it, he'd chanced upon a cache of cocaine and a gun.

A .357 Colt Python.

Now tucked in Schreck's waistband.

When late last night the first torture patrol came sniffing around—the Redcoats trying to trick him by wearing brown uniforms—he'd aimed the gun through the crack of the root cellar door at each skull that peered in the windows by the rattled locks, checking for signs of forced entry into the empty home.

Going door to door, eventually the skeletons moved on.

The keys to the car in the cluttered yard hung on a hook in the kitchen, a mess of dirty dishes from five take-out meals. The sleek black car was an old Corvette waiting for Schreck to drive it to his rendezvous with death, after a blitzkrieg Götterdämmerung with the Bone Police.

Hours ago, he'd feared the thump at the door was a torture patrol, but it was just a paperboy flinging the Coquitlam free edition.

Schreck could read English.

He understood the print.

And the map on the front page showing the route of tomorrow's Red Serge funeral parade.

WHITE GHOST

West Vancouver
Thursday, December 9, 1993

Nick awoke to an insistent rapping on the door. At first he didn't recognize where he was, for this wasn't Gill's bedroom where he thought he fell asleep, then he heard whispers along the hall from the living room, Mom and his aunt discussing something he could not discern, and Nick knew he was in Medicine Hat in the house where he was born.

Rap! Rap! Rap! . . .

Psss. Psss. Psss . . .

Someone answer the door.

Nick threw back the covers, swung out of bed, and pulled on his robe. On tiptoes, he crept to the bedroom door and turned down the hall, the flames of the hearth in the parlor casting shadows on the wall, one his aunt on a stool leaning toward his mother, the other his mom on a straight-back chair breast-feeding two babies, both infants sucking hard as if in competition, Nick sensing intuitively one of the newborns was him.

Rap! Rap! Rap! . . .

Psss. Psss. *"Twins . . ."*

Someone answer the door.

The shadows vanished from the wall as Nick glanced into the parlor, where the stool and nursing chair sat empty by the fire, while Rap! Rap! Rap! *the knocking on the door grew more insistent, as someone outside cried, "See what you've done!"*

Nick marched over, pulled the bolt, and yanked the door open.

The cold, cruel world without was white with snow, swirling, whirling, clouding, and shrouding the man on the porch, caking him like a snowman while Nick's eyes teared, the wind so icy he stepped back toward the warm womb of the hearth, while the white ghost framed in the doorway raised an arm, the motion shedding the crust of snow to bare a gun, a Smith & Wesson .38 issued to the Force, hammer cocked as the muzzle locked against the ghost's temple, the blast blowing blood out the other side of his head, staining the snow tumbling there the color of Red Serge.

A voice behind whispered, "He shot himself because of me, brother."

But when Nick turned, there was no one there.

He awoke to an insistent rapping on the window, as a tapping twig was battered by rain. Nick turned like in the dream and saw Gill asleep on the pillow beside him.

UMNYAMA

Rorke's Drift, Africa
Wednesday, January 22, 1879

The fighting was at its fiercest.

Fourteen patients who'd escaped from the hospital were now behind the biscuit-box barricade. The shrunken position in front of the storehouse offered far greater security than the extended perimeter. The storehouse at back effectively protected those manning the mealie bag ramparts around the front yard from Zulu snipers firing down from Shiyane Hill. The reduced defense works meant Chard could deploy his men in tighter concentration. In front of the store, Commissary Dunne labored to convert two large piles of mealie bags dragged out earlier into a round castlelike redoubt. Tall he was, but Dunne had to stand on top of the bags to raise the fort to eight feet while bullets and assegais whistled past. If Zulus overran the perimeter, the last stand of the 24th would be at the redoubt. Wounded huddled by their feet, a firing line of riflemen would climb onto a step inside and aim overtop. Those defending the ramparts would retreat and form two lines outside, one kneeling, one standing with backs to the fort. First Chard, then Bromhead should he fall, would call out, "Fire one . . . Fire two . . . Fire three . . . Fire one . . . Fire two . . . Fire three . . ." to blast an unceasing hail of coordinated lead at the Zulus until the last Redcoat died.

But that was if . . .

Darkness had closed in around Rorke's Drift, which should have marked the Redcoats' end, but in a twist of fate the hospital's flaming roof lit the battlefield as bright as day. Every Zulu in no-man's-land between here and the blaze was a backlit silhouette gunned down long before he could reach the barricade. Several times the enemy tried to torch the storehouse, but firing through loopholes along the rear wall, a lieutenant and corporal with the Army Service Corps blasted them back. From the makeshift surgery on the storehouse veranda came the screams of conscious wounded operated on by the doctor. This was an ordnance depot, so ammunition was in plentiful supply. As chaplain, Reverend Smith made his rounds of the barricades in a long black coat, faded green, to pass out cartridges with the Word of God. One soldier was cursing and swearing with every shot.

"My good man, stop that cussing," implored Smith. "We may shortly have to answer for our sins."

"All right, Mister," came the cowed reply. "You do the praying, and I'll send the black Bs to Hell as fast as I can."

With the death of the *Induna* Craven impaled on his lunger, Prince Dabulamanzi himself had ridden down from Shiyane Hill, and now exhorted his warriors from behind the garden wall. By flouting King Cetshwayo's decree not to enter Natal or attack fortified places, he could only justify his actions with victory. The more anxious he became, the more recklessly he ordered suicide runs. Zulus stamped the ground with one foot while clashing their spears on their shields, then yelling the war cry "*uSuthu!*," courageous lion hunters rushed the walls again.

The recoil of the Martini-Henry was notorious. The thump, thump, thump with each shot became more and more pronounced as chamber and barrel fouled. Shoulders were now so bruised from four hours of battle that Redcoats alternated sides to fire, or held their rifles at arm's length. Barrels grew so hot that fingers and palms were scorched, so soldiers held them with rags or picked up the weapons of their dead comrades. Heat softened brass casings to jam them in chambers, requiring frantic work with ramrods in the press of attack. Bayonets broke or bent from overuse. Hands were splintered while fumbling for shells in ammunition boxes. Uniforms were tattered and begrimed. Faces were dirty and splashed with blood. The sick and wounded cried out for water, with fighting men seized by that burning thirst the psychic stress of combat afflicts. Some tried to get at the rum cask, but their sergeant would have none of that during duty, and threatened to shoot anyone who swigged. Soon Hook found the cries unbearable, so leaping over the biscuit boxes and sprinting across the yard, he made a sortie to drag back the water cart abandoned near the hospital. Lucky sod, he survived.

Away from the glare of the burning roof, the stone kraal that formed the barricade along the far edge of the storehouse yard was dark with shadows. Soon a fight erupted along the outside wall of the cattle pen, which gradually forced whites back to the interior partition, and then back to the wall separating the kraal from the yard. During the struggle, a private felt someone clutching at his leg, and glanced down to find a black hand reaching out of the straw. A snake would not have shocked him more, so frantically he jabbed at the straw with his bayonet, each thrust wrenching a pitiful howl from beneath.

The Zulu breakthrough was thwarted by the redoubt. Manned by Commissary Dunne and two others, it offered a second line of fire all round. Kraal walls were high and hard to scale, so a Zulu no sooner showed his head above the interior partition than it was blown off. Shooting down this close from atop the redoubt, it was near impossible to miss.

The most vulnerable point was the northwest corner where the biscuit-box barricade met the mealie-bag wall across the front of the yard. Shots from the wall could not reach under the rocky ledge on which it was raised, and with the abandoning of the rampart to the left when Redcoats retreated from no-man's-land, Zulus now crept under the ledge past that corner to enfilade the front breastworks. To meet this threat, Bromhead, Craven, and five others reinforced the northwest corner, exposed to cross fire from snipers who had come down from Shiyane Hill to shoot from the barricade at back and the front garden.

A bullet hit another defender in the chest and he dropped.

As stretcher-bearers evacuated him to the redoubt, yet another took a slug to the chest. He fell against the biscuit boxes, but kept hold of his rifle to remain at his post.

The next was shot through the skull, scattering his brains about the yard.

Scrambling over the front rampart, the Zulus were upon them, black on white and white on black hand to hand, totally different cultures brought together to kill, the warriors in each Zulu regiment out to prove a name: *uThulwana* "Dust-raisers," or *iNdlondlo* "Poisonous snakes," or *uDloko* "Savage," or *iNdluyengwe* "Leopard's lair"; the Redcoats of the Union Jack out to show their Colors, in praise of God, Queen, Country, and the White Man's Burden, having traveled a long way to impose *Pax Britannica* on ungrateful Africa, as *clang!* clashed both warrior cultures here in the northwest corner. A seven-foot *iNdlondlo,* his headband a ball of black widow-bird feathers with ostrich plumes flaring, crested the wall and hammered a knobkerrie down on a helmetless skull, just before Craven snapped off his lunger impaling the giant's chest. Despite the bayonet, the Zulu raised the club again, so the lance-sergeant shot him in the face. Before Craven could reload, an *iNdluyengwe* in leopardskins vaulted up onto the breastwork and pounced into the yard. He was about to assegai Bromhead when Craven presented the empty rifle pointblank at him. Thinking it was loaded, the Zulu jumped back over the wall without delivering his blow. Private Scanlon screamed as a spear rammed through his stomach, turning Craven's head toward this attacker, as a *uThulwana* with a Brown Bess musket fired over the wall. Craven's shoulder blade was blown to pieces. He tried to keep his feet but couldn't and crumpled to his knees. The Zulu wrenched the spear from Scanlon and came for him. The assegai raised high to pin Craven to the dirt, suddenly the Zulu's face was gone as Bromhead whirled and blazed his revolver. Blood sprayed Craven from head to toe. Scanlon was gibbering, "Don't let them rip me!" Reverend Smith was cautioning, "Don't swear, boys, and shoot them!" A spear zipped past to impale someone. Bromhead said to Craven, "Sorry to see you down, mate," then helped him tuck his immovable arm into his waist belt and get to his feet. Loading his revolver, Bromhead gave it to Craven and took Scanlon's rifle for himself. Scanlon went on caterwauling, "Don't let them rip me!" Bromhead and Craven were now shooting side by side. Then Corporal Schiess, a Swiss NCO of the Natal Native Contingent, who had been wounded earlier by a slug that tore open his foot, left the safety of the biscuit boxes to hobble a few paces along the abandoned barricade to the left, hoping to get a gun on those under the breastwork ledge. As he craned over the barrier, his hat was blown off by a Zulu rifle from the other side. Schiess jumped up, spiked the gunman, shot the warrior next to him, bayoneted a third who came to their aid, then clambered back into the corner.

"Don't let them rip me!" Scanlon wailed.

"No one will torture you while I'm alive," assured Craven.

"It isn't torture. It's *umnyama*," said Schiess. He knew Zulu ways from the NNC.

"What's that?" Craven asked, firing Bromhead's gun at the regrouping enemy.

" 'Blackness,' " said Schiess, reloading his rifle. To illustrate, he touched one hand to his forehead and dropped it to touch his chest, then raised it to touch one shoulder and pulled it across to touch the other: a Sign of the Cross.

HELLO, GOOD-BYE

Vancouver
Thursday, December 9, 1993

"Hello."

"Corrine Baxter?"

"Yes, that's me."

Butterflies tickled his stomach as he spoke into the phone. "My name is Robert DeClercq. Chief superintendent with the Royal Canadian Mounted Police. Do you know Pete Trytko, a Boston private eye?"

Hesitation. "Yes. He disappeared."

"When was that?"

"A year ago. Somewhere out West. The Boston Police can tell you more than me."

"We found Trytko's body buried on a rural island off Vancouver. Your name's in his investigation notes. Were you a client?"

"Yes, for many years. I hired him to find my kidnapped daughter."

"That took him West?"

"If so, he didn't say. The police think he was too involved in a messy divorce. Pete snapped pictures of a husband in the wrong bed. The man responded by punching out his front teeth. Pete was a terrier, tenacious as they come. He dogged his quarry like a bloodhound after he got punched, unaware the man had links to the Mob. The police here think that's why Pete disappeared."

"How long were you a client?"

"Fourteen years."

"Long time."

"You have children?"

"She died," said DeClercq.

"I'm sorry. So you understand? Kathleen's my baby. I'll *never* give up."

"I know it hurts, but tell me how she was kidnapped."

"What happened to your daughter?"

"My job got her killed."

"No other kids?"

"A teenage ward. I'm her guardian."

"You're lucky. I can't have more. And single women don't top adoption lists."

"Your husband?"

"He left me. Said I was to blame. Remarried. Four kids. I haven't seen him in years."

"The kidnapping?" Robert said gently. "How did it occur?"

"I was in the hospital after Kathleen's birth, nursing her when someone knocked on the door to my room . . ."

Listening to Corrine Baxter while he scanned Trytko's notes, Robert watched the crime play in his mind's eye.

Luna Darke, the "Erotic Witch" of CanLit circles, was a compulsive mother and an oversexed vamp. She was a woman men fucked on the sly but would never marry, afraid she'd boff their best friend as soon as their back was turned. As with most hypersexuals, the cause was child abuse: raped by her father before she was five. Her mother knew but cast a blind eye.

Darke—not her real name—was pregnant by thirteen. Over the next four years she had three kids. Her boyfriend was a vindictive man who caught her screwing around, the punishment being he disappeared with their family. Luna—not her real name either—hadn't seen them since. Later that year, an ectopic pregnancy left her barren. She suffered a nervous breakdown and had to be confined.

Nona Stone—Darke's real name—left the Maryland psych clinic in 1978. Hitching to Boston, she spent the next day stalking maternity wards, shopping during visiting hours for the perfect child, a cute-as-a-button baby girl. Beads around the newborn's neck gave her the mother's name. Phoning the ward as a "relative" gleaned more information. Corrine was nursing the infant when Nona appeared at the door.

"Mrs. Baxter?"

"Yes?"

"My name's Lenore Dodd."

"Are you a nurse?"

Nona smiled. "I'm studying nutrition. One of our assignments is to interview new mothers. Would you give me an hour once the baby's home?" She waved a research outline, complete with graphs and charts. "You might benefit from what I've learned."

Corrine nodded. "Give me a call."

Two weeks later, Nona phoned the Baxter home. Corrine, weary from walking her baby all night with a bout of colic, listened to suggestions for remedies. Within the hour, Nona was at her door.

Sipping tea in the kitchen, they talked about Pablum and Dr. Spock. When the baby cried in her crib, Corrine went to comfort her. Entering the nursery, she was struck on the back of the head, the blow stunning her long enough for Nona to tie her securely and stuff a gag in her mouth. Panic-stricken, she came around to find the imposter packing a bag with baby clothes, followed by the infant who was zippered in on top.

Baby and baby snatcher vanished out the door.

Hands still tied, Corrine ran crying to the next-door neighbor's for help. "She's taken my baby! She's taken my baby!" she mumbled through the gag. The street was deserted, the kidnapper gone.

The upshot was another mother lost her family.

Corrine's precious baby.

Whom Luna raised as Katt.

"Might Trytko have tracked the kidnapper without telling you?"

"He might," Corrine said. "I paid him eighty thousand dollars over the years. If a lead beckoned when I was short of cash, he followed it, knowing I'd pay him later."

"Fair man."

"And dogged. That's why I stuck with him. If anyone could find Kathleen, it would be Pete. You have his notes. What do they—"

An audible intake of breath at the Boston end of the line.

"Oh, my God! You found her?"

"Probably. I think Trytko found her and that's why he died. His notebook states *Nona Stone = Lenore Dodd = Luna Darke.* He tracked Darke to the West Coast, where she'd married a Canadian for citizenship. Trytko's body was buried under her home. Darke raised a daughter, now fifteen. There seems to be no record of the girl's birth."

"Is she okay?"

"Katt's safe and sound. Her supposed mother died a year ago."

"Katt? That's her name?"

"Short for Katarina. Or Kathleen," he added.

"Thank you," Corrine choked, emotion drowning her voice. "I pray it's true. So many nights I've awakened from this dream."

"Our main concern," Robert said, "must be Katt. If she's your daughter, a month will tell. If not, I'm loath to shock her needlessly. This past year she's been through the mill. Can you wait a month, for Katt's sake?"

"A blood test?"

"By the DNA expert in our lab. I'll need a blood sample to match with hers."

"It'll be hell, but I can wait. If the kidnapper's dead, where's Katt living?"

"With me," said DeClercq. "I'm her guardian."

PITCHFORK

Loners and groupies. The way Robert saw the world, those were the two subspecies of *homo sapiens.* Loners and groupies. The difference between the leopard and the cheetah.

The month was November, just before Thanksgiving. Corporal DeClercq was in New York for an extradition hearing. The play was *Rosmersholme.* Kate had the lead. He'd never forget the thrill that shivered through him that night, how Kate held the stage to rivet his attention, sitting anonymously in the crowd as she enslaved his heart.

A heavyset security guard blocked the door to backstage.

"Got a pass?"

"No."

"Then for you this isn't the way."

"Pass enough?" DeClercq bluffed, flashing a badge that meant nothing in the States.

What was a little fraud compared to love at first sight?

So there he was, heart in his throat and sweating under his arms, wandering backstage corridors searching for the dressing rooms, expecting arrest at any moment for his amorous deceit, asking the way until before he knew it he was at her door, and knocking without a damn thing to say. . . .

The month was March, just before Easter. Sergeant DeClercq was in London following a tip. If teddy bears it was to be, his kid would have the best teddy bear in Britain. Hamleys of Regent Street boasts six floors of toys, so rainy Monday morning found him alone with hundreds of bears, lining up thirty to inspect the troops, culling them one by one for the cutest, before adding thirty more to repeat the process. Content he had the bear of bears an hour later, he looked around for someone to pay.

"Over here, luv." A disembodied voice hidden by the till. "Five minutes more and I'd have called the police."

On his way out, a display case caught his eye. The Iron Duke faced Napoleon astride his horse as a hundred lead soldiers fought Waterloo. The price card in front read *£23*. *Fifty bucks*, he thought, converting money. He recalled the joy of lead soldiers in his youth. Boy or girl, his kid would know that joy. Flourishing his arm summoned the clerk. "Twenty-three pounds. Steep price," he said. "They're hand-cast and hand-painted," said the clerk. "Then wrap 'em up." "Yes, sir. Which one do you want?"

The birth was a twenty-four-hour ordeal of induced labor, spinal anesthetic, and steel forceps. At four in the morning, Kate asleep and himself utterly exhausted, Robert leaned against the wall of the hospital, waiting for the elevator. NURSERY, the sign beside him advised. Next to a dark hall with a single window lit at the far end. *Jane?* he thought. *Got to be.* So he detoured toward the light.

Because the incubator was draped with plastic, all he saw at first was an amorphous form. Then he found a clear hole for the nurse's glove, and kneeling, peered into the substitute womb. He glimpsed a hand with nails so small a microscope was needed, and then her angelic, cherubic face. . . .

He was gone.

A loner no more.

Kate's Aunt Paula sent a god-awful bear, synthetic *pink* fur with beady little eyes. Jane was home, in her crib, lying awake on her back. "The Battle of the Bears in a blind test," Kate announced. In beside the infant went London teddy, Jane's face scrunching as stiff fur touched her cheek. "Daddy's Scratch Bear," dubbed Kate. In beside the infant went the pretender to the throne. Jane's face registered soft-caress contentment. "Pinky wins," Kate declared, and Scratch Bear was banished to the corner.

The October Crisis of 1970. British diplomat James Cross kidnapped by the Front de Libération du Québec, prior to the murder of Labour Minister Pierre Laporte. DeClercq the cop who located the Chenier and Libération Cells, motivating a vendetta against his home. Machine pistols tore Kate apart at the door, then five-year-old Jane was abducted for revenge. The killers clashed over what to do with the child, so Robert found her with her neck broken in a backwoods shack.

He still had Pinky. Loved to death.

And Daddy's Scratch Bear. New as the day it was bought.

But he was alone again.

And now Katt.

DeClercq had come in early to phone Corrine Baxter from work so Katt didn't overhear the call at home. The funeral parade for Jack MacDougall was in Richmond at eleven, so time to spare, he strolled up Heather Street to the Lab. The day was gray and overcast, matching his mood.

Buzzed in for vetting by Security just inside the door, he skirted the exhibit room where Nick's tunic had passed from Kidd to Toop, and climbed to the second floor, where Biology had its examination room.

The room was split in half by a glass fence. On the far side was the analytical lab, where men and women in white coats extracted DNA and prepared the gels. On this side of the glass stood two large benches and a bio hood. Protection from infection, the hood was used to open vials of blood like those taken from Dora at the autopsy. On the near bench lay Nick's Red Serge. Since yesterday when he received the exhibit from Kidd, until he carried it here this morning, the tunic was in a locker to which Toop had the only key. Now he treated a bit of fabric from one of the stains on the cuff with hemochromogen, a reagent that crystallizes if hemoglobin is present. Viewed under a microscope, the test proved positive for blood.

Next Toop cut a circle of cloth the size of a dime from the stained cuff and stuffed it in a plastic tube called an Eppendorf. From here on, all testing would be done in this tube by the Ottawa geneticist, Colin Wood. Toop summoned Wood from the analytical half of the room to pass the Eppendorf. DeClercq came in as they signed the Exhibit Transfer Receipt:

RCMP GRC	EXHIBIT TRANSFER RECEIPT — REÇU DE PIÈCES À CONVICTION		
	TO BE HELD ON LAB CASE FILE — CONSERVER AU DOSSIER DU LABORATOIRE		
SECTION BIOLOGY	LAB FILE No — DOSSIER DU LAB 93 - 73642	DATE 93/DEC 8	
RE OBJET	NICHOLAS JOHN CRAVEN MURDER : DORA CRAVEN PORT COQ		
EXHIBIT NOS. PIÈCE Nº	122		
FROM - Name DE Nom D. Toop	TO - Name A Nom C. WOOD	Section/Dept. Sect/Serv BIOLOGY	

Just as the history of a city defines the city today, so DeClercq thought he grasped how these two came to join the ranks of *loner sapiens.* For he sensed both men were loners like himself.

Dermott Toop. Thirtysomething. Lowest on the totem pole of bigotry. Vancouver: a city of whites and Asians with few blacks. Shunned by *two* races if he was raised here. Tourists wondered why they never saw Asians and blacks together? Vancouver: racists rife throughout its history. Banning the Indian potlatch. Inciting riots in Chinatown. Turning away Sikhs on the *Komogata Maru.* The British Properties covenants forbidding nonwhites from buying in. The darker the color, the greater the bias. Had blood attracted Toop because all blood looks the same?

Colin Wood. History unknown. Transferred by Ottawa to organize DNA typing in this lab. Lean and pale, with dark hair and hooded eyes. Half his chin defaced by an ugly purple birthmark. Was he driven to genetics by the need to know what went genetically wrong? The biologist angled his head to offer his good profile when DeClercq approached.

Loners, for sure.

"Good morning, Dermott."

"Morning, Chief. Have you met Colin Wood?" asked Toop.

"By reputation," DeClercq replied. "Welcome to 'E' Division."

Eppendorf in one hand, Wood shook with the other. Toop saw DeClercq eyeing the exhibit and looked as if he feared the cop might grab both tube and tunic and dash from the Lab.

Words have wings, thought DeClercq. "Settling in?" he asked.

"Yes," Wood replied. "We're already doing tests. I should have everything humming within six weeks. I like it here."

"Must be satisfying to be involved in the greatest advance in crime detection since regular fingerprinting began in 1901."

"Not at forensic conventions. The absence of a DNA warrant law in Canada astonishes Brits and Yanks. There is something wrong with a country that allows mandatory breath tests for drunk drivers but not involuntary gene tests for murder suspects. They howl when I relate what we have to do."

DeClercq nodded. "Tiptoeing after suspects to pick up dirty condoms and snotty tissues. Scooping up urine after they take a piss. Depositing *Playboy* in a cell in hope the suspect'll masturbate so we can get his semen. Embarrassing, isn't it?"

"Especially when the British are so advanced. Not only did they pioneer genetic fingerprinting; not only can they toss the gene net of a 'blooding' like in the Pitchfork case; and not only can they forcibly take DNA from suspects; but now they're developing the world's first *nationwide* DNA database. Around them, I feel like a hick."

"Mark my words," said DeClercq. "I'll change that. I've almost completed a survey of unsolved murders and unsolved rapes in which DNA was recovered at the scene, yet where suspects remain free to murder and rape again because we can't test them."

"Politicians will shelve your survey."

"It's not for them. The way to move our government is snitch to the media, then watch those at the trough run squealing for cover. Politicians are con artists at heart. So I police them."

"Meanwhile," Wood said, "we sit on our thumbs." He swept his arm around the near-empty room. "All gussied up with nowhere to go."

"Not exactly," said DeClercq. He passed the geneticist a brown paper bag. "I retrieved this tampon from a bathroom basket. Soon I'll have a DNA sample from her maybe-mother to match. I need you to prove or disprove kidnapping."

KNOCHENPOLIZEI

Richmond, British Columbia

The coffin was draped with the Union Jack, for Jack was going home, home to the heather and a grave next to his mom. Because he held an officer's rank in the RCMP, his cloth cap was pinned to the flag at the head of the coffin, peak facing the foot. Below the cap, space was reserved for the ceremonial cushion, black velvet fringed with gold, bearing Jack's insignia: the orders, decorations, and medals he was entitled to wear on his uniform. The cushion now sat on the floor of the hearse next to the head of the coffin. Hilt at waist level so the blade ran down the center of the casket, Jack's sword sheathed in a metal scabbard with a gold knot was fas-

tened to the flag. The wreath was sewn to the foot of
the coffin when it was dressed by the Commander of the
Bearer Party.

The commander was DeClercq.

Under a mourning sky of drizzling rain, the hearse
turned right off Gilbert Road into Minoru Park. Cars
parked on both sides ended at a great green playing field
that stretched to high-rise apartment blocks beyond. The
hearse turned left along a lane lined with maple trees,
blazing in autumn but bare branches now. White letters—MINORU CHAPEL—carved in brown announced a
cozy gardened church nestled in woods to the right. At
the end of the maples, the lane angled right to four white
posts that marked the front walk to the chapel door.
Peaked, with stained-glass windows and its steeple on
the left, Minoru Chapel dated from 1891. Minoru being
a racehorse in Queen Victoria's stables, what better
place for a Mountie's funeral? Beneath the somber steeple bell tolling *bong . . . bong . . . bong . . .* eight Pallbearers, four a side, lined the walk. Of equal rank to the
deceased but never higher, they would escort but not
help carry the coffin. All wore Red Serge Review Order
of Dress, with Stetson, stripped Sam Browne, and medals displayed. Midway from elbow to shoulder on the
left sleeve, each Pallbearer wore a black mourning band.

The chaplain was at the curb to meet the hearse.

. . . bong . . . bong . . . bong . . . the bell tolled on.

The Bearer Party lined the laneway in front of the
chapel, two ranks facing inward at right angles to the
Pallbearer lines. As the hearse with Jack inside pulled
up, it passed two Headdress Bearers, then the riderless
charger, the Insignia Bearer, and the Commander of the
Bearer Party, before it drove between the two ranks of
Coffin Bearers, four each side. The Coffin Bearers, in
Red Serge, wore sidearms supported by Sam Browne
straps over the left shoulder, with lanyards from gun
butts up to circle their necks. DeClercq, as officer in
command, wore a sword slung from a frog and supported by a strap over the right shoulder. As it went by,
he saluted the coffin. The hearse came to a halt just
beyond this formation.

. . . bong . . . bong . . . bong . . . the bell ceased tolling.

In the sudden silence, the horse neighed.

After the chapel service, there would be a funeral procession to the airport, where Jack's coffin would be loaded onto an Air Canada flight to London, escorted by a Member in Red Serge. Presenting the flag to the next of kin is not Force tradition, for that's a custom born of the American Revolution, where folding the flag in a triangle symbolizes the tricorn hat of Revolutionaries. The protocol of a Regimental Funeral comes from British cavalry regiments. In the procession, the charger would be led by a constable immediately behind the Insignia Bearer, Zinc. As this was Jack's "last ride," his jackboots were reversed in the stirrups, heels to the front and left boot in the right stirrup, right boot in the left.

The constable calmed the horse.

Not only was the church filled with mourners, but Members and officers from other forces—municipal cops from areas not policed by the Mounties, with Washington cops and Special Agents from the FBI—overflowed into the gardens quadrangle left of the chapel, and into the small parking lot in front, so the only vehicle allowed here was the hearse. Other cars were parked back in the entrance lot or on Gilbert Road.

The funeral director opened the rear door of the hearse. When DeClercq barked the order "Bearer Party . . . Change Formation . . . March," each Coffin Bearer took two steps forward, halted, then turned to form two files facing the casket. DeClercq moved into position along a center axis behind the files, followed by Chandler, then both Headdress Bearers side by side.

"Remove Headdress."

The Coffin Bearers removed their hats and tucked them under their outside arms. The Headdress Bearers advanced along both flanks, then walked back collecting and stacking hats. One took Chandler's. DeClercq would carry his own.

"Collect Insignia."

Zinc advanced to the rear of the hearse, marching between the Coffin Bearer files. Removing the ceremonial cushion from near the head of the coffin, he marched back to his position behind DeClercq.

"Dress to Receive."

The Coffin Bearers closed in to the bumper of the hearse.

"Unload."

The front two Coffin Bearers grasped the handles of the casket and carefully pulled it out headfirst. The coffin was drawn along the files until all eight had a secure grip on the casket's handles.

"Dress . . . to Advance."

Coffin at the shoulder, the eight stepped several paces to the rear to swing the foot of the coffin about so they were now aligned facing the church. Off to the right on Gilbert Road beyond the Gateway Theater, the growl of a souped-up car gearing down could be heard. Tires squealed with torment.

"Slow . . . March," ordered DeClercq.

Leading with the inside foot to the coffin, left file Bearers stepped off on the right foot, right file on the left. The chaplain led the procession toward the chapel, the Bearers with the coffin passing between the two Pallbearer lines, both lines at attention. DeClercq followed Jack's coffin through the white posts and onto the walk, with Chandler and the two Headdress Bearers close behind. The charger and its constable would stay outside.

The growling engine and squealing tires took another corner.

Through the open door ahead, DeClercq glimpsed the chancel of the chapel. True to Force tradition, the pew front left was vacant for the Queen, should she wish to attend as honorary commissioner. Commissioner François Chartrand sat in the pew behind, Eric Chan to his left as deputy commissioner and commanding officer of "E" Division.

The only warning was a black streak along the lane skirting the right side of the chapel from the entrance parking lot to the small lot in front where the hearse was parked. DeClercq caught the dark blur at the corner of his eye a moment before the Corvette skidded to veer sharply left through the dripping maples just short of where the lane turned in front of the chapel. The motor revved to a snarl as tires churned turf chunks from the soggy lawn, then like a panther in a leap, the Corvette gunned toward the procession.

"Eyes right!" DeClercq shouted to those in harm's way, a second before the charging car rammed the Coffin Bearers.

The Pallbearers hit from behind were thrown across the fenders like kills brought home from the woods by a victorious hunter. Two right file Bearers run over by the car were spit out behind with tire marks and broken bones. The coffin went flying before it crashed to the ground, splitting open so Jack's arm flopped out in the mud of a barren flower bed. The Corvette plowed through the stunned mourners beyond, hurtling down one side of the gardens quadrangle left of the church, fishtailing to wheel in a doughnut across the far end, skinny trees shorn off and grass gouged up, before swerving this way up the opposite side, careening right beside the church to complete the square.

Carnage lay everywhere.

Bordered by a rockery with rosebushes at the four corners, the quadrangle was a sunken garden into which mourners scrambled to escape from the Vette. A sundial at its center commemorated the twinning of Richmond and Pierrefonds, Quebec, on the 3rd of July, 1968. A wheelchair ramp breached the rockery, and down this came the bloodstreaked vehicle. Around and around it roared like a Cuisinart, cutting down people or grinding them along the rocks, before vrooming up the ramp like a Batmobile out of hell.

DeClercq was waiting.

The Order of Dress for an RCMP funeral is stripped Sam Browne, so Officers and Members alike were unarmed. American cops in Canada cannot pack guns, so they were unarmed, too. The only Mounties with sidearms were the Coffin Bearers, who for a funeral must wear the holster on the right side no matter how they're handed. It was from the Sam Browne of an unconscious Bearer that Chief Superintendent DeClercq drew the Smith & Wesson six-shot .38.

He stood over Jack's broken coffin as the Corvette attacked, rumbling out of the sunken garden for another ramming run back across the body-strewn walkway to the chapel. Hunched over the wheel behind the snout of the muscle car, a skinhead with eyes brimming paranoia and hate spat the curse "*Knochenpolizei!*" at DeClercq, as closer and closer the face of death zoomed in. *Schreck,* he thought.

Feet shoulder width apart for solid balance, body

squarely facing the target, both arms stretched out and
elbows locked, the Mountie gave both hands to the gun.
Risky it was if the shots ricocheted, but a far greater
risk was the killer car, so aiming at Schreck, DeClercq
squeezed the trigger, one, two, three . . .

Pingg . . . pingg . . . pingg . . . three slugs deflected
off the windshield, for this was a drug pusher's car with
bullet-proof glass.

The car hit the coffin, which swung like a compass
and knocked DeClercq off his feet. The Corvette's hood
scooped under him and bounced him over the roof,
where he landed in a mud bed. Back through the maples
the way it came, the car turned left toward the entrance
lot to escape. The hearse was mobbed by mourners using
it for cover, bogging the only vehicle anywhere near to
give chase.

The Mounties may have moved away from their
mounted tradition, but Chandler was raised as a farmboy
in Rosetown, Saskatchewan, so riding was second nature
to him. Grabbing the reins from the constable still trying
to calm the horse, he kicked Jack's boot from the left
stirrup and swung into the saddle.

He gave the charger both spurs.

At a full gallop along the lane lined with maples, Zinc
saw the car screech right in the entrance lot just ahead.
He cut the corner of Richmond Family Place, jumping
the horse over obstacles in the way. Jogging left, then
right, the car burst out onto Gilbert Road, the mounted
Mountie thundering close behind. Across two lanes
cleared of traffic for the Red Serge procession, the Corvette careened left in a skid and almost flipped, then
Schreck put pedal to metal and accelerated south.

When the demonic hot rodder looked in the rearview
mirror, he saw a Redcoat skeleton mounted on a skeletal
horse charging after him.

"Ten-thirty-three! Members are down! Ten-thirty-three!"

The call came into the Operations Communications Center of Richmond Detachment from the first Member at the scene to reach a radio. "Subject vehicle's a black Corvette, license YNZ 101! Heading north or south on Gilbert Road!"

"Ten-four," said the dispatcher, breaking to broadcast an all-points alert.

"It rammed the funeral at Minoru Chapel, Dispatch! We need all the Emerg we can get!"

"Ten-four," she said, and asked the complaint taker at the next desk to call Richmond General. "Is the subject armed?"

"Yeah, with a car! Whether he's got a weapon within, I don't know."

"Code five," the dispatcher broadcasted, raising the takedown response to *Use caution, operation may be dangerous.*

The radio room constable then summoned the watch commander.

The last thing Cody's father said as he and Cody's mom were leaving to catch a flight to Cancún was "Drive the Zed and you're toast." The Nissan 300ZX was the old man's pride and joy, one of just 300 cars produced in a numbered edition in 1984 to celebrate Nissan's fiftieth anniversary. The Zed was silver with a black bottom and black leather seats, two stereo speakers stuffed *inside* the cushions so your ass could vibrate to music as you cruised along, turbocharged in front with a spoiler in the rear. The Zed was in the carport and there it would have stayed had Sweet Sue Prior not walked by the house in the rain. To Cody's loins, Sweet Sue was a bodacious babe, and word was she and Jess Brown were on the outs. So doubting his dad would notice a kilometer or two, he drove the Zed up the street parallel to Sue, the window down on the passenger's side.

"Hi, Sue."

"Hi, Cody."

"You look wet."

"Nice wheels."

"Where ya goin?"

"Richmond Center."

So here he was driving south on Gilbert Road, Sue in the seat beside him sweet as could be, wondering how impressed she'd be by lunch at Burger King, Home of the Whopper, Cody's favorite meal, before whisking her back to his house, Home of the Real Whopper, ha, ha, ha, and there seducing her to the mellow strains of Megadeth, when suddenly a black Corvette screeched out of Minoru Park and almost creamed the Zed.

"Wow!" said Sue.

The sound of pounding hoofbeats turned Cody's head left. He knew the Mounties had suffered budget cutbacks recently, but only now did he realize how deep the cuts had been, for here was a Redcoat *on horseback* thumbing him over.

"Wow!" said Sue.

Cody's dad once told him if you're ever stopped by a cop, meet him outside like a gentleman and he may not write the ticket. So Cody stopped, got out, and reached for his wallet with his driver's license, only to have the cop hand him the reins and state, "I'm commandeering this car," before he climbed in and drove off with Sue.

I'm toast, Cody thought.

"What's your name?"

"Sue."

"And I'm Inspector Chandler. Sue, you're deputized into the Mounted Police. Now get on the cellular, call 911, and ask for Richmond Detachment."

"Wow!" said Sue.

Busy air.

The call came into the OCC of Richmond Detachment as Mounties dashing from the chapel scrambled into cars and radioed in as they fanned out north and south along Gilbert Road.

As Zinc had one hand on the wheel and one shifting gears, Sue held the phone to his head so he could speak and hear.

"Black Corvette. Plate YNZ 101. Inspector Chandler in pursuit south on Gilbert Road. I'm driving a commandeered car, a silver Nissan 300ZX. As soon as a Member is in position, I'll break off. With me is a civilian named Sue. She'll call out our position for vectoring in."

"Ten-four," said dispatch. "All Members clear the air. We have a car in position as Primary. Update where you are, Sue. You have the air."

The Zed sped south toward the South Arm of the Fraser River.

"Blundell Road . . . Francis Road, Hasty Market on the corner . . . Williams Road, light's turning . . . Oh shit, that was close! . . .

Lane to lane, then back again, the Corvette snaked this way and that down Gilbert Road, the ZX on its tail several streets back, houses and three-story apartment blocks zipping by, with cars wrenched left and right to keep from being hit as they were cut off. The Steveston Highway marked the break between urban and rural Richmond. There, Schreck veered left in a suicidal skid and gunned east.

The engine of the Vette gnarred while the muffler rapped. Slick sprayed out behind the wheels. The madman inside laughed his head off, spittle spotting the windshield and .357 Colt Python stuck down the front of his pants prodding his cock. City to the left, farms to the right, some with rundown farmhouse relics from pioneer days, plastic on the roof joining moss-covered shingles to keep out rain and birds.

In the rearview mirror, the traffic light at Shell Road turned amber. . . .

Then red.

"Hang on, Sue!"

When Zinc braked for the red light at Shell Road, the ZX hydroplaned on the slick and didn't respond, the cross-traffic beginning to cross in front of them, then a tire caught, the Zed spun, and he and Sue were hurled pinwheeling through plywood boarding around a building site. Mud spewed up like a twister as they tore across the lot, and finally came to a halt on the car's belly with both front wheels in the air overhanging a water-bottomed drop.

The Zed seesawed on the edge of the excavated pit.

"Don't *breathe,* Sue."

"What kind of food do you like?" he asked. "Japanese," she replied. "Then Japanese it is," he said. "And I know a good place," she added. He was a rookie Member from Peace River, Alberta, recently posted to the Deas Island Freeway Patrol. His eyes were on the tempura and teriyaki side of the menu when she lightly touched his hand and said, "It's nice to date a man not a wuss when it comes to sushi."

Today, his bowels were feeling a little insecure, what with all that raw fish worming its way through his virgin digestive tract, so after lurking near the john over a cup of coffee, he tossed the car keys to Sam and asked the gas jockey to fill 'er up while he was in the toilet for a purge.

When he finally came out and walked to the pumps, drizzle graying the intersection of Number 5 Road and the Steveston Highway, dripping off the Chevron sign on the southwest corner, Sam told him, "Ben, your radio's gone wild." In his initial rush for security, the sushi king had left his portable radio behind on the seat of the patrol car.

As Constable Ben Roszmann neared the driver's side door to check it out, he heard Zinc Chandler say, "Lost the Corvette in an accident at Shell and the Steveston Highway."

"Jeez, look at that guy go," Sam, standing at the pumps, said to Ben, who turned in time to see the black Vette streak by.

"Code five. Members down," dispatch repeated.

Adrenaline pumping, Roszmann jumped into his car, cranked the ignition, then roared off in hot pursuit so fast the nozzle still pumping gas was yanked from the fuel tank.

*　　*　　*

Beyond Number 5 Road, the Steveston Highway forked in two. Route 99 South to Seattle branched right. Route 99 North to Vancouver lay ahead, the Corvette crossing 99 on the Steveston overpass, before squealing around a cloverleaf underneath the overpass to enter the freeway extending Interstate 5 north of the U.S./Canada border toward Vancouver.

Vancouver City Center 19 kilometers read the passing sign. A concrete barrier divided traffic going south from these three lanes. Engine revved to 70, 80, 90 miles an hour, Schreck weaved left and right through the slower cars.

In the rearview mirror, keeping pace and beginning to gain, a cop car with siren wailing and red-blue wigwags flashing was hot on his tail.

The driver was a skeleton.

The car was made of bones.

It wasn't a club, but a .357 slug would smash the Bone cop's skull.

The Mounted Police have substituted horsepower for horse power. Roszmann at the wheel, the car chasing the Corvette was a Camaro Z–28 specially souped up for the Force with a 5.8-liter, 300-horsepower Corvette engine, and tires a foot-wide rated at 240K an hour. Scorching by civilian cars on the road, it slopped gas as they pulled over to clear the way.

"Charlie four. I got him. North on Ninety-nine. Under Blundell overpass, heading for Westminster Highway."

"Ten-four, Charlie four," the dispatcher said. "The watch commander is plugged in. Report, all those in position to intercept."

"Bravo nine, Dispatch. North on Ninety-nine, just beyond Westminster overpass."

"Do you have a spike belt?"

"Affirmative."

"Then lay it down *fast* with flares and cones."

"Delta three, Dispatch." A French Canadian voice. "I'm east on Westminster Highway, passing Number Four Road. ETA Ninety-nine at intercept."

"Ten-four, Delta three. The watch commander is in control. Charlie four. Chevron called. You're leaking gas. The next fill wait till the cap's back on. Delta three,

proceed over Ninety-nine on Westminster overpass and
turn right down Exit Thirty-six against traffic. U-turn
north on Ninety-nine to relieve Charlie four as Primary
Pursuit. Charlie four, break off and plug the hole. We
don't want Ninety-nine a blazing inferno. Bravo nine,
yank the spike belt as soon as the subject is crippled,
then follow Delta three as Secondary Backup."

Eyes squinting hard to peer through the windshield
streaked with drizzle, Roszmann could just see Westminster Highway.

Beyond the tunnel formed by the overpass, Bravo 9
lit the first red flare.

The constable in Bravo 9 skidded to a halt on the shoulder of Highway 99 and scrambled out. Removing the
Hollow Spike Strip from the trunk, he darted across the
freeway and laid it down as best he could, the belt too
short to cover three lanes. The large hollow spikes set in
an aluminum backing angled south toward the oncoming
Corvette. As the car ran over it, the tires would blow.
The constable would then yank the belt to free pursuing
Members, who'd have no trouble taking down the Corvette clanking on its rims.

As the Corvette sped toward the spikes, he ignited the
first flare.

Die Strassensperre, thought Schreck.

To avoid what he thought was a roadblock, the madman left the freeway by Exit 36, down which against the
traffic Delta 3 was ordered to go. The Corvette ignored
the red light at the top of the ramp, and wrenched left
across the Westminster overpass, then left again on the
far side of Highway 99 to zoom down the access ramp
to 99 South.

Having U-turned from north to south, Schreck fled
back the way he came.

"He's going south on Ninety-nine," Roszmann reported,
as he shot up Exit 36 toward the four-car collision under
the light, caused when the Corvette ran the signal. "Got
to break off. I'm corralled."

"Ten-four," said the dispatcher. "Plug that tank."

"Bravo nine, Dispatch. He missed the spike belt. And I can't get across the barrier."

"I got him," Delta 3 said, the accent French. "He cut across in front of me just before Westminster overpass. I'm on the ramp heading south and going to chomp his ass."

"Ten-four, Delta three. Take Primary Pursuit. Call out the coordinates for intercept."

Flatlands whipped by on both sides at 100 miles an hour. The Corvette shot under the Steveston Highway overpass and into the George Massey Tunnel under the South Arm of the Fraser River. The sign said *Use Lights, Remove Sunglasses Thru Tunnel.* Schreck did neither as the Corvette weaved wildly down into the narrow passage lit by yellow lights. *Thum-thum . . . thum-thum . . . thum-thum . . .* was the thrum as it traversed rubber pegs dividing both lanes, striking the walls on either side to throw back sparks, causing another collision as it ascended the up-curve toward the river's south bank, which blocked the tunnel to cut off Delta 3. The engine howled deafeningly in the close confines, drowning the hum of tires burning rubber up the incline, a square of light appearing ahead, then suddenly shafts of daylight rained down through the concrete rafters above, seconds before Schreck emerged to cross Deas Slough, with boats rocking on the gray waters to his right, under an eagle winging in the sky, while he hooted in triumph over *die Knochenpolizei.*

The Corvette streaked toward Canada's border with the United States.

Hot pursuit across the border by the police of one country into the territory of the other to apprehend a fugitive is not authorized by law. So now a sergeant in Richmond OCC was on the phone to the U.S. Border Patrol and Washington State Police. "Time is tight so I'll cut to the chase. Coming toward you at a hundred miles an hour is a black Corvette, plate YNZ 101, driven by a cop killer named Günter Schreck. Possibly armed and dangerous as can be, he'll see you as skeletons who must be rammed and crushed. He's killed police in Germany and just attacked us in an attempted mass slaughter. His estimated time of arrival at Douglas Crossing is only minutes from now."

TAKEDOWN

Ghost Keeper to natives, Staff Sergeant Bob George was a full-blooded Plains Cree from Duck Lake, Saskatchewan. Though not descended from one of the West Coast totem tribes, he was a medicine man strengthened by his spirit quest as a boy, when he was sent alone into the wilds to learn who he was. As such, he was veteran of many a sweat, and so this morning found himself in a sweat lodge off a foggy inlet up the coast, surrounded by peaks soaring on three sides, a place sacred to natives and as close to "Heaven" as you'll find on Earth. With him were troubled Indian kids sent here by tribal elders to rediscover the magic known before white colonization.

But Ghost Keeper was Staff Sergeant Bob George of the Mounted, too, veteran of the Ghoul, Cutthroat, and Ripper cases, and Jack MacDougall had been a friend who helped him up the ranks. So after the sweat at sunrise, this hefty man with black hair, bronze skin, and wide cheekbones had donned Red Serge to sail on the *Lindsay* for the funeral.

The RCMP names its boats for past commissioners—Lindsay was CO from 1967 to '69—and this was a fifty-eight-foot Class I catamaran capable of thirty-six knots . . . but not in fog. Fog hazed Georgia Strait south from the inlet to Tsawwassen Ferry Terminal where George had parked his Jeep, and caused him to miss the funeral. As he was driving east along the causeway from the docks offshore to the Mainland, George turned on his police radio and heard: "Charlie four. I got him. North on Ninety-nine. Under Blundell overpass, heading for Westminster Highway." That meant

the chase going on across the Fraser to his left was
retreating north away from him toward Vancouver and
the North Shore Mountains beyond. The sea to either
side was choppy and gray, the bluff ahead to the right
misty gray with rain, the snow cone of Mount Baker in
Washington state behind shrouded out today. A sign
arching over the causeway read USE OF SEAT BELTS IS
COMPULSORY IN BRITISH COLUMBIA. Over that flew a
blue heron.

The flatlands of the Delta were losing ground to monstrous housing, but here horses in a paddock snorted
plumes in the cold air while munching bales of hay, and
Lombardy poplars planted long ago as windbreaks still
stood tall. Over the Southern railway tracks flanked by
power lines, the road ran straight as an arrow ahead to
Ladner, originally Ladner's Landing after two American
brothers who struck it rich in the gold rush, bypassing
the Hanging Judge's noose to marry twin sisters instead
and pioneer the Delta. As he passed a Jiffy John beside
a slough, stuck in the middle of nowhere as near as he
could tell, George heard: "He's going south on Ninety-
nine. Got to break off. I'm corralled."

The Cree's pulse quickened.

He's coming this way.

The pace was slower through Ladner, farmers poking
along in pickup trucks while the municipal hall, courthouse, and hospital went by, the light at Ladner Trunk
Road almost catching him, but then George broke out
and stepped on it.

"Delta three. Accident. The tunnel's blocked and so
am I. Cancel pursuit from this side," the French Canadian said.

George grabbed the mike and radioed in. "Dispatch,
Staff Sergeant George. I'm off duty in my car—a white
Jeep with plate ZYZ 223—on Highway Seventeen East.
Intercept with subject dead ahead."

"Ten-four, Staff," the dispatcher said. "Hang on while
Tach One checks for backup."

For policing, every city and district in B.C. has the
option of contracting with the Mounties or setting up its
own force. Delta elected the latter, so clearing the tunnel

meant the chase passed to the Delta Police. But this was Schreck, Members were down, and George was the spearhead channeled into Richmond OCC.

"This is the watch commander. Hear me, Staff?"

"Ten-four," replied George. The watch commander on the air was rare indeed.

"Tach One"—radio channel 43-Vancouver out of HQ to blanket the Lower Mainland—"reports Member backup too far away. Delta Police will Secondary. See them in your mirror?"

"Ten-four. Wigwags back by Crescent Slough."

Highway 99 came into sight ahead, traffic emerging from the tunnel moving left to right. Signs were coming thick and fast to fork Highway 17 . . . *600 Meters to Hope, Seattle . . . River Road, Richmond, Vancouver* with an arrow pointing straight across the overpass . . . *99 South Hope, Seattle* on-ramp curving right. . . .

The watch commander: "The intercept is cop killer Günter Shreck. Are you armed?"

"Affirmative. I'm in uniform."

The watch commander: "Sidearm unsnapped and prepared?"

George cinched the seat belt tight as could be, and pulled the leather flap loose from the holster with his right hand, exposing the butt of the Smith, its lanyard snaking up to circle his neck.

"Ten-four," he said.

The watch commander: "The Corvette's registered to a known drug dealer and probably stolen. The subject is possibly armed from the same source. The windows of the Corvette are bullet-proof glass. If the window lowers, assume he's going to fire. You have the eyeball. You're number one. Use extreme caution. If you see a gun, take him out."

Suddenly there it was, streaking from the left, a black Corvette zooming out of the tunnel and aiming for the States, going at least 100 miles an hour toward the Highway 17 overpass as George entered the on-ramp to 99 South, centrifugal force pulling the Jeep as he wheeled around the curve. "I got him," George said, glancing to the left as his boot slammed the gas pedal to the floor to pick up speed. "I got him," George repeated, locking his trajectory on a collision course with the Corvette now barreling under the 17 overpass. "Takedown!" George said, pumping himself as the on-ramp became Highway 99, the white dividing markers gone as his speed hit ninety miles an hour, Corvette and Jeep grinding together at an acute angle as George whispered something else lost in the crunch of metal on metal but picked up by the mike. . . .

The tension in Richmond OCC was palpable. All they had was the open channel feeding George's voice. "I got him . . ." Intercept. This was it! "I got him . . ." Repeated as the speaker pulled them like a magnet. "Takedown . . ." No turning back. The die was cast. Then just before the ramming, "All my relations . . ."

"What the hell does that mean?" asked the dispatcher.

The watch commander shrugged. "Must be some sort of native thing."

. . . boats rocking on the gray waters to his right, under an eagle winging in the sky, while he hooted in triumph over *die Knochenpolizei.*

The Corvette zipped past River Road Exit 29, closing on the turnoff to Highway 17 and the Tsawwassen Ferry Terminal, Schreck glancing west at the wigwags of approaching Delta cops.

The Corvette shot under the overpass as his finger pushed a button to lower the bullet-proof window on the passenger's side. Wind whooshed by the car and tickled the stubble on his shaved skinhead. If the Bone Police tried to box him in, he'd be ready to blast apart their skulls.

BAAANGGGGG!

A white Jeep rammed the front of the Corvette, its fender slamming his fender at an angle, metal crumpling and crushing like two accordions joining together, Jeep jumping the right side of the Corvette off the road so both vehicles fused window to window, this flying wedge hurtling into a demolition alley three lanes wide, with concrete barriers along both shoulders. Tortured tires peeled rubber as smoke streamed behind. Sparks flew when the force of the Jeep scraped the Corvette along the barrier dividing traffic north and south. V-joined like Siamese twins, both cars bounced right to veer across the three lanes toward the opposite barrier.

Schreck yanked the .357 Python from his pants, and swept the muzzle of the Mag around toward the skeleton in the other car. This Bone cop in Red Serge with a *red* skull had feathers sticking from the zigzags where his head plates fused.

"*Untermensch!*" Schreck shrieked.

And opened fire.

But this "subhuman" had talents sorely lacking in "the master race." He didn't need a spyglass to see the world in front of him, and he didn't need a compass to tell him where he was, and he didn't need an Elmer Fudd hat with earflaps tied up to know he was a hunter. All he needed was him.

Before he saw the muzzle, George saw the open window—*If the window lowers, assume he's going to fire*— so the Mountie released the seat belt and threw himself sideways a moment before his window exploded to shower him with glass.

The uniform may be snazzy, but it wasn't fashioned for show, every piece of it serving a practical purpose as well. The lanyard was security like a child's mitten string, so in the heat of battle, the gun was always at hand.

As he ducked sideways, George wrenched the lanyard to jerk his sidearm free, grabbing the Smith in midair with his left hand. He didn't need his eyes to pinpoint Schreck's position. The Cree's internal compass had a fix on him. All that periscoped up to brave the line of fire was his fist with the .38.

Bam! George fired.

The muzzle swung a degree left.

Bam! George fired.

The muzzle swung two degrees right.

Bam! George fired.

The muzzle swung four degrees left.

Bam! George fired.

The muzzle swung six degrees right.

Bam! George fired.

Then, because this was the you-or-me shot and only one man was coming out alive, the Mountie popped up and *Bam!* fired again.

The flying wedge slammed the barrier to the right, dumping George onto the floor as the cars veered to the left again, slamming the central barrier to bounce back to the right where this barrier ended and grass along a hedge began. The interlocked wrecks plowed turf past an old farmhouse beyond, snapping a DON'T LITTER sign like a toothpick, before churning to a halt under WHITE ROCK 27, SEATTLE 202.

Delta Police cars screeched up behind.

Delta cops jumped out, sidearms drawn.

Schreck was slumped over the steering wheel of the Corvette, three red holes in the right side of his head and the left side blown away to splatter his brains all over the bullet-proof glass behind.

The watch commander, short of breath but trying to play it straight: "Confirm all weapons are secure and all Members safe."

Silence.

The watch commander: "Confirm all weapons—"

"Fuck," said George. "I thought I was dead."

The watch commander: "I will take that as a confirmation."

HUMAN ASH

Maui, Hawaii

Nick arrived at his apartment hotel on Napili Bay to find a message waiting from DeClercq:

Schreck was killed this morning in a shootout with us. A search for evidence to link him to the murder of your mom is underway. The DNA test on your tunic should be done by the end of the month. Until then, "Get away from it all."

Friday, December 10, 1993

Twilight saw Nick 10,000 feet up in the "House of the Sun," watching dawn break over the rim of Haleakala Crater, to creep down into the volcano's deep throat of silverswords and cinder cones. Daylight saw him back at Napili Bay, jogging his five miles before the scorch began, running by golf course after golf course footing Pineapple Hill, to justify a breakfast of macadamia nut pancakes at the Gazebo.

Cooled by the shade of monkeypods, coco palms, and wili wili trees, Nick's garden apartment overlooked the foaming surf.

He unpacked the urn from his suitcase.

Then he walked up the beach.

Kapalua takes its name from the ancient Hawaiians. *Kapalua* means "arms embracing the sea." Rugged crags of lava rock reached out into the blue to form Kapalua and adjacent Napili bays, Kapalua the best snorkeling cove on Maui, colorful clumps of coral alive with even more colorful fish. Halfway across the eight-mile strait to Molokai, a humpback whale breached as Nick stood out at the tip of the arm dividing the bays. The distant shoe-shaped island forged by two volcanoes gathered mist from the horizon to hide its jumbled peaks. There at Kalawao Cove in 1866, lepers were dumped without shelter, food, or hope, until the "Martyr of Molokai" landed in 1873, and sacrificed his life to their disease to redeem them to God.

Mom told him that story when he'd asked about the picture.

The picture in the attic above her desk.

The desk where she sat at the end of each month to juggle their dwindling funds.

"That's where I'd like to be redeemed when I die," she'd said.

Near as he could tell, the photo was taken here.

Around the tip of the point and a glassy tide pool at his feet, incoming waves tumbled left to Napili and right to Kapalua. The sun behind cast his shadowy image across the ocean mirror. Leaning over the tide pool, he cracked the lid of the urn as the sea sprayed him. Arms

out, he sprinkled Mom's ashes onto the pool, and tapped
what remained in the jar into his right hand, as if to
hold her one last time, before he spread his fingers to
give her up to the tide.

Before him lay the primal womb from which we all
evolved.

Mom's ashes grayed the surface of his shadowed
reflection.

The hands of the silhouette reached for him like a
black twin.

BLOOD TIES

Vancouver
Friday, December 31, 1993

Deputy Commissioner Chan, sitting in his office at 37th
and Heather, phoned Chief Superintendent DeClercq,
sitting in his office at 33rd and Heather, and asked him
to be at the Lab in-between at 4:30 sharp.

The last time DeClercq walked to Biology Section's
Examination Room on the second floor of the Lab,
Colin Wood had told him, "I should have everything
humming within six weeks." Only three weeks had
passed, but tests were humming now.

Deoxyribonucleic acid—DNA—determines how he-
reditary traits are passed on. The DNA in each cell of
an individual carries the genetic code for building that
human. Each cell's nucleus has 46 chromosomes com-
posed of coiled DNA. A DNA sequence on a chromosome that encodes a particular inherited trait is a gene.
One hundred thousand genes make up a complete genetic code. Uncoiled, the DNA in each human cell is six
feet long. Since only identical twins have the same genetic code, only one person in the world has that DNA.

The DNA typing procedure used by the RCMP has
four steps. Three weeks back, after he'd tested the stain

on Nick's tunic for blood, Toop had cut a dime-size piece from the cuff to stuff in the Eppendorf handed to Wood. Wood had carried the plastic tube along with samples of Dora's blood around the glass bisecting the room to the analytical half.

There he'd begun testing.

Step One saw the sample in each tube digested with proteolytic enzymes, centrifuged and washed to extract pure DNA. From the fume hood where this occurred, Wood carried the tubes to the left side of the lab where the DNA in each was digested with *Hae*III. This "restriction enzyme" scans DNA for sequences it recognizes and cuts the strands at those sites. Different people's DNA cuts at different places, producing different combinations of fragment lengths.

Step Two saw the lengths sorted by a method called electrophoresis. Agarose is a jelly with pores through which DNA lengths can pass. The tubes of cut-up samples to be matched are loaded into slots at the "origin end" of a slab of gel. Like a racetrack, the slots feed parallel lanes. When electrical current is applied across the gel, the samples migrate through the slab away from the origin end. The smaller the fragment, the faster it migrates, so when the electrical current stops, the DNA pieces in each lane halt in separate bands.

Step Three saw the fragment bands transferred from this gel slab to a nylon membrane by Southern blotting. From the Examination Room, Wood carried the membrane to the radioactive Hot Room. There, placed in a bottlelike tube and bathed with "probe," the membrane stewed in a Robbins incubator. A DNA probe is a short piece of DNA tagged with a radioactive label. The genetic sequence of the probe seeks out and *only* binds to complementary sequences on the membrane fragments. Once this binding was done, Wood washed excess probe off the membrane and overlaid it with a sheet of X-ray film. He then stored both layers in a freezer at -70 degrees C. There, radiation from the probe-marked bands registered bar codes on the X-ray film. Since the bands to which a probe binds vary from person to person, each bar code is a "genetic fingerprint."

Running the film through a processor produced this autoradiogram, which—at 4:30 on New Year's Eve—

Wood and Toop laid before Chan, DeClercq, Tipple, and Kidd, gathered in the Lab:

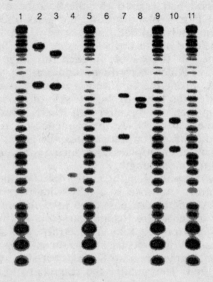

"The DNA 'fingerprinted' on this autorad is a polymorphic area on Chromosome five. By polymorphic I mean it varies from person to person," said Wood. "Lanes one, five, nine, and eleven contain Molecular Weight Markers. Markers are DNA fragments of known size. Marker lanes are rulers we use to measure the size of unknown DNA fragments. Lanes two, three, and four contain internal controls to make sure the gel has run properly. Two is the Male Cell Line, three is the Female Cell Line, four is the Blood Internal Standard. The lanes with known DNA samples are six, seven, and eight. The bands differ because the samples came from different people. Lane six contains the sample of Dora Craven's blood from the autopsy."

Wood paused while all eyes focused on Lane six.

"Lane ten contains questioned blood taken from the cuff of Corporal Craven's Red Serge tunic. The match is obvious."

Wood placed four more autoradiograms on the table.

After the first autorad, he'd stripped the membrane in
hot water to remove the probe before repeating the test
with a different one. All five probes had matched Lanes
six and ten.

Step Four saw the autorads go to Toop for computer
work. A computer scanned the bar codes to determine
the size of each band. The probability of two samples
both binding for that probe at that point was statistically
known, so multiplying the chance of each autorad having
a match by the chances of the other four—1/50 x 1/9 x
1/8 and so on—produced the probability of Lanes six
and ten matching on all five autorads.

"One in one hundred billion," said Toop. "The odds
the DNA in the blood on the cuff didn't come from
Dora are one in one hundred billion."

"Could your tests be wrong?" asked Chan.

"Nothing in science is ever black and white," said
Wood. "Every new test developed goes through an initial stage of exaggerated infallibility, followed closely by
doubt. The scientific basis for DNA typing is sound. It
will withstand those skeptics who question its forensic
use. The areas ripe for attack are laboratory error and
faulty statistics. Were samples mixed up so they tested
in the wrong lanes? Did sloppy continuity contaminate
a sample? Are the population databases random enough
so the statistical odds aren't biased? However, I know
the importance of this test to the Force, and guarantee
the blood on the cuff given to me matches blood taken
from Dora at the autopsy."

"What about twins?" asked DeClercq.

"Twins," said Wood. "The one exception. Since they
split from the same fertilized egg, identical twins do have
the same DNA."

"Which means they produce the same autorads?"

"Yes," agreed Wood.

DeClercq was about to leave the Lab when Wood took
him aside.

"I also have results from the kidnapping case," he
said.

HAPPY NEW YEAR

West Vancouver

Six o'clock. News time. The close of another year.

Click!

"*. . . from Los Angeles. This was the year of gangsta rap, the violence-soaked subgenre of hip-hop that's now its prevalent form. Snoop Doggy Dogg, the current hot artist, is touted as the first to have his debut album* Doggy Style *enter the* Billboard *charts at number one, following such gangsta successes as Dr. Dre, Eazy-E, Spice 1, and Ice Cube. Dogg could make history as the only artist charged with murder while number one . . .*"

Click!

"*. . . a black community leader in Montreal has urged subway riders to be on guard against possible racist attacks after two men tried to push a black woman onto subway tracks. Police say those involved may be skinheads. Earlier, black groups received anonymous calls and letters warning of revenge after an immigrant from Chad fatally pushed a white Quebecer into the path of an oncoming train . . .*"

Click!

"*. . . in emotional rallies reflecting South Africa's deep ethnic and racial divides, three factions in the bitter battle for political power celebrated conflicting holidays December sixteenth to honor anniversaries soaked in the nation's blood. Threats were loudest from twelve thousand white Afrikaners circling a sandstone monolith outside Pretoria to mark the 1838 Battle of Blood River where several hundred Boer guns mowed down thousands of spear-chucking Zulus. In the seething black township of Soweto close to Johannesburg, ten thousand supporters of the African National Congress party cheered and danced as Nelson Mandela reviewed the guerrilla army he formed thirty-two years ago to fight white apartheid laws. Mean-*

*while, in the rival black KwaZulu tribal homeland of
Natal, Zulu Inkatha militants mobilized for election violence to come . . ."*

The front door opened.

"I'm home," Katt called from the hall.

Click! The TV screen went black as Robert punched
the remote.

"Prepare to be scared . . ." Katt's voice coming down
the hall, bleeding into the spooky fanfare of a cheesy B
horror film.

A black Ride snowboard, held in front, served as a
masking cape.

Between it and the woolen toque glared squinty evil
eyes.

Flourishing the booted board bared crooked vampire
fangs.

Lipstick down her chin was dribbled blood.

"Not bad, huh?"

"You're sniffing rubber cement?"

"Au contraire, Bob. We wimmin just liberated drama
class. The play committee met up Grouse today. Combined a little boarding with our Christmas hols assign-
ment. Wally—Mr. Walmsley to you—told us to decide—
or he would—who plays whom in *Dracula* this March.
Après-ski in the Grouse Nest, I queried why some guy
should have the preordained right—"

"Your vocabulary's growing."

"I sleep in a library."

"Skillful interweaving of French. I'll have you bilingual soon."

"Bob, this is a saga of dramatic import. Pfeiffer. Fos-
ter. Streep. Madonna. All the great thespians may have
to clear the way for me."

"Lay on, Macduff."

"I questioned why some guy should have the preordained right to suck my neck while I cowered or fainted
in a see-through nightie. I demanded we vote on reversing gender roles. Unfortunately, Kirk Mitchell"—
Katt cracked a wicked grin—"had to leave for his hot
date with Pam Brodie. He's gonna be pissed to learn
his lust cost the male vote. Now *I'm* Countess. Jenny's
Renfield. And the costume committee is sewing scant
p.j.'s for hickey fodder guys."

"Kirk Mitchell? Isn't he the muffin you're sharking?"

"The very same."

"And Pam Brodie? Is she—"

"Trash, Bob. Loose trash."

"How'd that come about?"

"You mean why am I spending New Year's with you instead of in Kirk's arms?"

"Sort of."

"Social machinations, Bob. The etiquette of men. I was about to ask Kirk out, when Wade—he's this sexist dork with an Elle Macpherson calendar in his locker—asked me to the Led Zeppelin party at Whistler."

"Led Zeppelin's playing a ski bash at Whistler!"

"Drugs, Bob. Come on. You're a cop. I'm sure Kirk heard Wade asked me out, and since both play basketball on the school team, and I told Wade I already had plans to wash my hair, Kirk could hardly go out with me and still—"

"To the Zeppelin party?"

"Of course not. I planned to lure him down Lover's Lane. So he asked Pam, who incidentally—"

"Loose trash, I hear?"

Katt hissed and flicked her tongue like Anthony Hopkins. "One bite." She wiggled her fingers beside her eyes. "One look . . . we vampires are hypnotists . . . and p.j. Kirk is MINE!"

"Sharked by jaws," said DeClercq. "I don't think I want you sucking blood from a guy who fools around with loose trash."

"Hey, I'll swallow a condom. . . ."

Katt sniffed the air. "Something's amiss. I don't smell moussaka cooking. I don't see *The Big Sleep* and *The Maltese Falcon* by the VCR."

"Held up at work. Change of plans. We're going to La Cucina."

"New Year's Eve? We'll never get in."

"We're regulars. They'll water the soup. We'll sit in the parking lot. But first we have to talk."

DeClercq sat on the sofa and patted the cushion beside him. Laying down the snowboard, Katt shed her wet parka to curl up next to him. Sweat and flying snow had plastered curls to her brow. Her cheeks were rosy from mountain exercise. "Is this a *Father Knows Best* chat?" she inquired. "If so, you need a Perry Como sweater."

"Katt," he said gently. "I'm not your father."

"Teaboy, you're *better* than any father to me."

"There's no easy way to say this, so I'll just get it out. Luna Darke wasn't your mother."

A furrow creased the space between Katt's cobalt eyes, deepening as the words sank in. "You're saying I'm adopted?"

He eased his arm around her. "You were kidnapped, Katt." The jolt that galvanized her muscles matched the electric chair. He tightened his hold. "In 1978, a newborn baby girl was snatched in Boston. The real mother has searched for her child ever since. For reasons we'll discuss later, I suspected that baby was you. I had the Lab compare your blood with DNA from Boston. Your real mom's name is Corrine Baxter. I'll be calling her."

"Is it the money?"

"Huh?"

"I cost too much?"

"Katt—"

"You can have it. Everything in the trust. Every goddamn cent from selling the Bowen house. I don't need to go to college. I don't need—"

He pulled away and gripped her shoulders with both hands. Her eyes were unfocused, staring through him, as her mind flailed like a punch-drunk boxer.

"After all I've done to make you love me? I *won't* leave here to live with some stranger. I *won't* go back East and down to the States. I'm Canadian. You can't *force* me!"

"Katt, you're American, and the decision's not up to me. I have to do what's morally right." Rising from the sofa, he fetched the framed photo of Jane from the mantel. The four-year-old sat laughing in a pile of red-gold-brown-orange-amber maple leaves, head thrown back so her hair caught a glint of sun. "I feel what your mom's gone through because I went through it with Jane. Fifteen years of torture searching for you. You're not an object. You have a say. So you and your mom will have to work it—"

Katt stood up.

"Come on, dog. Let's go for a walk."

He watched them from the Greenhouse with a punctured heart, Napoleon bounding down the beach toward Lighthouse Park, two black silhouettes against the onyx bay, Katt kicking stones like asteroids across the pinpricks of far Point Grey.

Happy New Year, he thought.

Vancouver

Avoid alcohol, the doc had warned, so Zinc filled a champagne flute with mineral water for himself, then uncorked a half bottle of Veuve Clicquot for her. *Bang!* the cork popped like a mortar shell, while fizz bubbled from the neck over his hand.

"What shall we toast?" Alex asked, serving steamy bowls of cioppino by candlelight.

"To the success of your book in the New Year," he said, crossing the hall carpet to the hardwood floor of the dining room.

"Any comment from DeClercq?"

"He's a busy man. Losing both Eric and Jack weeks ago left him shorthanded. He promised he'd read it, so we'll hear soon.

"Happy New Year," Alex said, hand reaching out for the flute. A spark of static electricity passed between them, causing her to flinch. The glass slipped from her fingers, crashed to the floor, and broke.

"I hope this isn't an omen of what's to come." She sighed.

It was.

Cloverdale

Which is the saddest song? "Old Shep" by Elvis? Or "Raggedy Ann" by Little Jimmy Dickens?

This was the calm before the storm at The Moaning Steer, unhappy hour for drowning the cares of the last twelve months, before the country-rock band Road Apples began at nine to see in the New Year. The newspaper on the table rehashed newsworthy events of 1993, including the shooting of the innocent Somali boy by "that racist cop," according to black comment. The photo beside the print caught Wayne Tarr.

Tarr sat slumped at his usual table downing shooters of Scotch, as Little Jimmy cried his heart out from the jukebox. While the Mountie suspended by Chan stared at brands in the wood under the empty glasses, a bottle of Glenlivet descended miraculously to one side, before a pile of CDs followed. From the CD covers, angry black men posing in-your-face scowls glared hatefully up from the raps at Tarr.

The Slicker sat down, cracked open the bottle, and filled the empty glasses.

"Happy Fuckin' New Year," said Tarr, snapping back a shot.

"Unhappy Fuckin' New Year," he added, snapping back a shot.

"Did you mean what you suggested the first time we drank?"

"Wha' was that?" Tarr slurred, third dram down his gullet.

"About having the guts to kill yourself at the Red Serge Ball," said Evil Eye.

The second meeting of the Suicide Club was now underway.

Vancouver International Airport

Gill waved to Nick as suitcase in hand he cleared Canada Customs with other tanned passengers from Maui. "Welcome home. Car's outside. We'll stop at the nearest motel," she whispered, leaning over the rail to hug him in Arrivals, "so I can demonstrate sexually how much I missed you. Dinner at The Teahouse to see the New Year in, then you can demonstrate sexually how much you missed me."

"Still no word on the DNA test?"

He asked the question as arm in arm they neared the exit doors, where Kidd, Tipple, and two burly Mounties entered to intercept them.

"The stains on your Red Serge match your mother's blood." The burly pair seized Nick as Rachel Kidd said, "Corporal, I'm arresting you for the murder of Dora Craven."

MEMENTO MORI

Rorke's Drift, Africa
Thursday, January 23, 1879

When the bloodball of the African sun came up the following morning, the only Zulus around were heaped in piles of dead and dying about the barricaded storehouse yard. The first cold gray light of dawn gave way to red shafts of glory that dazzled off 20,000 spent cartridge casings scattered about the entrenchment. A heavy pall of smoke filled with the acrid stench of roasted flesh hung over the British post like a wreath. The defenders were ringed by a Hell on Earth of utter devastation. At their boots were slit shields, snapped spears, battered helmets, broken rifles, and empty ammunition boxes on a carpet of tramped grain spilling from torn mealie bags. Hordes of flies were mired in the sticky blood splashed on the fortifications. Six hundred dead Zulus hemmed in the whites, piled up in places where the attack was the fiercest almost to the top of the barricade. Limbs were tightly entwined with each other in grotesque thrashing from violent death. One warrior seven feet tall in life lay sprawled back with his heels on top of the parapet and his head nearly touching the ground, the middle of his body supported by dead comrades packing the base of the wall. Of the four hundred-plus Zulus wounded, those not evacuated by their cohorts were flopping and groaning in agony.

"Color-Sergeant Bourne."

"Sir," said the young man, responding to Chard.

"Call the roll. Report losses. And see the men get a tot of rum."

"Sir," said Bourne, and off he went.

The battle had been a grueling ordeal for the Zulu attackers. Most were middle-aged men who without proper food for days had run twenty miles across country from Isandlwana to ford the Mzinyathi River and charge right into six hours of sustained hand-to-hand combat in the teeth of devastating fire with little to show for their efforts. A military rule of thumb is ten percent losses will destroy an army's morale, and they'd lost twenty-five. They had no water, no medical attention, and soon every assault was over the bodies of their friends. The final charge had been at ten P.M. last night, and after midnight the shooting had waned. Two hours before dawn, they'd drifted away.

The question was would they return 20,000 strong?

Chard took precautions.

Details were ordered to rebuild and strengthen the rampart walls, and to remove thatch from the storehouse roof, and to pull down the still smoldering hospital by means of ropes through the loopholed walls, and to chop down bushes and trees in front of the yard, and to post lookouts with warning flags up on the stripped rafters. While thatch was being dumped in the stone kraal, the Redcoats were surprised by a lone Zulu feigning death who jumped up and fired his rifle at them, then ran for the river. He missed, and so did those who shot at him, causing Chard to remark he was glad "the plucky fellow got off."

Others were not so lucky.

The Redcoats were down to a case and a half of ammunition. Patrols were sent out to collect weapons from the Zulu dead. Private Hook—who'd kept the attackers at bay while Craven hammered through the hospital walls—marveled at the horrific carnage around the yard. One soldier kneeled up against the wall, but didn't respond when Hook said, "Hello, what are you still doing here?" Tilting back his helmet revealed the blue mark where he was shot in the head. Where the Zulus had killed whites and been able to reach them, the bodies were mutilated in the usual fashion, stomachs ripped and disemboweled. Most of the African dead wore the married man's *isicoco* headring, "ring-kop" black wax woven into their hair. A macabre *impi* still besieged the post. Strangely, many slain blacks had dropped to their elbows and knees, and now remained hunched up like that with knees drawn into their chins. While heading for the river, gathering spears along the way, Hook passed a "dead" Zulu still bleeding from his leg. The Zulu made a grab for the butt of Hook's rifle. Hook dropped all the spears but one, then assegaied the man. Another patrol discovered a number of wounded blacks abandoned during the retreat huddled in the orchard and garden in front of the hospital. Having put the bayonet through most of them, they saved the last two to lynch from a transport scaffold.

Some found later would be buried alive.

Back at the post, there was a narrow miss. During the struggle for the hospital, wounded Private Waters hid in Reverend Witt's wardrobe closet. Tension got the better of him, so he wrapped himself with a black cloak and dashed out back, where he crawled through the grass toward the cookhouse to work his way over to the safety of the storehouse yard. Finding the cookhouse manned by Zulus firing at the defenders, Waters took a handful of soot and smeared it over the white skin of his face and hands. Through the night he lay "dead" out back as Zulu rushers tramped on him, and now, forgetting he'd put on blackface, ran toward the post. Redcoat marksmen almost cut him down.

Waters accounted for, Bourne altered his casualty report. The final list would be fifteen defenders dead, two mortally wounded, and sixteen others suffering less severe injuries.

Left outside the stone kraal during the fight, the Royal Engineers wagon had been wrecked. The looters had spared one bottle of beer, which Chard now shared with Bromhead in a hearty toast to having come safely out of so much danger.

Lance-Sergeant Craven was hunting for trophies.

Memento mori.

Blackened by powder and splattered with blood, his red tunic tattered and his helmet gone, Craven gripped the lunger he'd used in the final stages of the defense in his good hand. The stench of charred flesh from the hospital was nauseating. Vultures were feeding outside no-man's-land as he walked across. Trooper Hunter, the dazed patient, lay crumpled on the ground with six stab wounds in his chest. The Zulu who speared him was piled on top. Beyond them was the *Induna* Craven spiked during the escape.

The battlefield commander.

Memento mori.

The Zulu's "kilt" of twisted civet and monkey fur was soaked with blood. Bloodstains mottled his cow tail festoons. Near him lay the full-size *isihlangu* shield and carved hardwood club. Stabbing his lunger into the dirt, Craven picked up the knobkerrie, hefting it in his hand. Satisfied, he stuck the weapon into his belt near his useless arm. The sun at his back, he stood over the Zulu covered by his shadow until he spied the snakeskin pouch around the man's neck. Crouching, Craven tore the pouch from the witch doctor's throat and used his teeth to tug open the drawstring. Ten eyes inside stared back at him.

The Redcoat pocketed the pouch, pulled the lunger from the ground, and walked away.

His shadow came off the Zulu like a black ghost.

Following him.

PART II

WHITE MAN'S BURDEN

Take up the White Man's burden—
    Send forth the best ye breed—
Go, bind your sons to exile
    To serve your captives' need;
To wait in heavy harness
    On fluttered folk and wild—
Your new-caught, sullen peoples,
    Half-devil and half-child.

—KIPLING

GLADIATORS

The Chief Justice of British Columbia was not a man to be taken lightly. For thirty-three years Calvin Cutter had clung to his Seat of the Scornful, going to the bench an already conservative maritime lawyer, then veering right as criminal cases hardened what little elasticity there was in his brain. A brain the defense bar dubbed the "Black Hole of Cal Cutter"—so dense the good arguments that went in never came out in his judgments.

The CJ had so many pet names it was hard to keep track of them all. A roly-poly man with sphincterlike lips, some called him "Moon Face" because his features resembled a human behind. Others called him "Rum, Sodomy, and the Lash" because his chambers painted blue had galleon prints on the walls, boats in bottles, a ship's steering wheel, and a brass telescope aimed down at the yachts on False Creek. "The Smiling Viper," "Mr. Catch–22," "The Iron Fist in the Iron Glove," the list was never-ending. The CJ's latest dub was "Three Monkeys." See All Evil. Hear All Evil. And Speak All Evil . . . his judgments.

Before Hatchett stepped down (actually a step up) to become Chief Justice of the Supreme Court as head of the trial division, she sat beside Cutter on the Appeal bench in what defense lawyers now called The Dark Ages. Appeals are heard by three judges, and Cutter as CJ set the coram for each appeal, so he and Hatchett ended up on all the big cases, forget the third wheel for he or she was but a dissenter from the deadly Cutter-Hatchett One-Two Punch.

Hatchett saw Craven's case as the perfect means to strike a blow at "American rowdies," so from the moment he was charged, she assigned the trial to herself.

When bail was requested, she ordered Nick detained, leaving his lawyer no option but to apply to Cutter for permission to appeal under Section 680 of the *Criminal Code.* In effect, the application was the Cutter-Hatchett One-Two Punch reunited.

Section 680 was a gate. With Cutter on guard, the room to squeak through was narrow indeed. Usually, such a request was made by written submission, but as the CJ had recently turned down the Somalis who'd survived the ERT assault, he thought it wise for an oral hearing to show how balanced he was.

Gill Macbeth arrived late.

Back when the North Shore was little more than bush, the Guinness Family—fine Irish beer and *Book of Records*—bought the mountainside for "The British Properties." They built Lions Gate Bridge across the First Narrows to Stanley Park so buyers could reach the downtown core. The three-lane span is now Vancouver's worst bottleneck, which can't be widened because that would usurp more of the park, so a serious accident can hold traffic up forever and—like this morning—make every commuter late.

The Law Courts in Vancouver resembled a piece of cheese. Thirty-five courts on five tiers were stacked up the right angle of the glass wedge. Greenery spilled from each level like the Hanging Gardens of Babylon. On sunny days the Great Hall under the sloped roof sizzled lawyers alive. On winter days like today the Great Hall was a freezer, and lawyers milled about sniffling from colds. Gill rushed in the Smithe Street door by the statue of Themis, blindfolded Goddess of Justice with scales in her hand, and zigzagged up the stairs to the fifth level, turning left along the balcony to the Heritage Court. Through stained-glass doors marked COURT OF APPEAL, she slipped in as Nick's lawyer finished his submission.

"... may it please your lordship, this applicant is a Mounted Policeman with a sterling record. There is, I submit—with the greatest of respect for Chief Justice Hatchett—no 'substantial likelihood the accused will, if released from custody, interfere with the administration of justice,' as her ladyship ruled. I therefore ask that you refer her decision to the Court of Appeal for review."

Nick's lawyer, John Peabody QC, sat down.

Lyndon Wilde QC rose to his feet.

The Old Courthouse along the street was a columned edifice with two stone lions guarding the front steps. When the new Law Courts opened in 1978, the government saved money by finishing the courtrooms in concrete and felt. So outraged was Cutter at this legal travesty that he *demanded* a Heritage Court like those in New Westminster and the one he'd left. Eight Greek pillars carved from red oak soared behind the CJ, canopy above broad bench and five chairs flanked by crimson curtains forming his royal box, with carpet the color of blood on the floor, befitting an arena where Cutter was Nero lording over lawyers in The Pit, itching to give his gladiators the thumbs-up or thumbs-down.

"My Lord Chief Justice," Wilde said, "the evidence will show the applicant typed a letter threatening his mother. He was the last person seen at her house before her body was found. The house was locked, no tampering, and her blood was found on the sleeve of his Red Serge. Found on the sleeve of his striking arm, and his mother was clubbed."

Cutter glared around his court as if searching for Nick, but those with counsel don't appear in the Court of Appeal.

"The applicant was involved in a younger man/older woman sexual tryst," said Wilde.

The CJ, a bachelor, squinched his nose as if able to smell rutting in the air.

"Here the charge is matricide, so May-December sex takes on Freudian tones. The applicant's mother-substitute is a pathologist in Vancouver. What compelled her ladyship to order detention is he surreptitiously sent this woman to New Westminster to perform the autopsy on his mother. A clear case of interfering in the administration of justice, I submit. Your lordship may also be influenced by the fact the Crown will proceed by direct indictment," said Wilde. "The applicant can stand trial within two months."

Imperial profile to the gallery where Macbeth sat, Cutter studied the wooden clock on the wall as Peabody replied.

"My Lord, the age difference is a mere five years. Dr. Macbeth leads her field. The applicant asked her to perform the postmortem so no forensic clues were overlooked."

As Peabody sat down, Cutter read his ruling from a page of prejudged reasons.

"In exercising my discretion under Section 680 of the *Code,* the test I put to myself is might this Court reverse Chief Justice Hatchett's order to detain? The applicant has shown a penchant to undermine the rule of law. If released, he may try again. My answer's 'No' to the test, so the applicant will remain in custody until his trial."

Cutter got up and wheezed out.

A railing separated The Pit from the gallery. Gill blocked the swing gate as Lyndon Wilde, smirking with triumph, left the arena.

"How dare you!" Gill snarled. "What was that May/December crap about?"

"It's called Knowing Your Judge, Lady Macbeth. Any hint of 'perversion,' and the CJ closes what passes for his mind."

"This may be a game to you, but it's Nick Craven's freedom and my reputation. My professional integrity is paramount to—"

"What's paramount to you is some stud between your legs. I've seen your type before," Wilde said with hard contempt. "The *professional* whore. The woman who can't keep her cunt out of the job. The female lawyer smitten by a rogue of a client, who smuggles in a gun and busts him out to get boned. How'd you bed Craven? On the job? Shove your 'professional integrity.' I see through you like glass."

"Is this how you relate to all women?" Gill asked.

"Just *professional* bimbos who put on the act. Grow up, *Doctor.* If Sir Walter Raleigh is dead, expect wet feet."

"You slandered me in your submission, and now you slander me here. You better hope I'm not recording what you say."

"Take a look around. You're standing in a court. A tape recorder here will run your ass out of town. Which is what I'll do if you mess with my case. A game it is, *Doctor,* and I'm the best. Play with me, and I'll chew you up and spit you out."

* * *

Main and Cordova is the guts of skid road, home to the drunk, junkie, loser, and the lost. Three-twelve Main is the Public Safety Building, headquarters of the Vancouver Police. Two twenty-two Main is the Provincial Court, where anyone charged with crime in this city enters the judicial system. Behind the courts at 275 East Cordova, across from the old Coroner's Court, now the Police Museum, is the Vancouver Pretrial Center, Nick's new abode. Breath pluming from the cold and blood still aboil from Lyndon Wilde QC, Gill walked in the door.

Technically she was here for personal reasons, but when the visits reception officer logged her in as professional, Gill didn't balk. She signed the book, then stored her possessions in one of the metal lockers. Buzzed through the door to the Holding Area, she passed electric frisk by an Outokumpu Metor 114 metal detector to move on to the Mantrap. The Mantrap steel door fired like a shotgun, opening into a cramped cubicle like an elevator, one-way glass to Gill's left, the door ahead securing the Secure Area. Red on white, the sign on the door read EXCESSIVE PHYSICAL CONTACT WILL RESULT IN IMMEDIATE TERMINATION OF VISIT. One door of the Mantrap was always locked.

Bang! fired the door.

The space beyond the Mantrap confined open visits. Inmates and outsiders sat face to face on futon chairs across low tables, six pairs at a time. To the left was a door marked GV-18, for "door 18, ground visits." Only professionals entered here, and "popped" through with a pneumatic *bang!*, Gill faced a muscled woman from Visits Control, who ushered her past nooks for "glass visits" by telephone to door GV-19.

With a key, she locked Gill in.

What would henceforth be known as Nick's "office" was a 10- x 6-foot room entirely viewable from the 18- x 18-inch judas window in the door. A hard bench ran the length of the far wall. Centered against the left wall was a cream-colored table with two brown chairs. A pair of bare fluorescent tubes provided light. The floor was rust tile. Beside the table, the only window looked out on the exercise yard.

Bang! . . . *Slam!* . . . *Bang!* . . . *Slam!* . . . heavy doors fired pneumatically slammed shut, then GV-19 was unlocked and in came Nick, sporting a white T-shirt stamped VPSC, a green work shirt and matching pants without a belt, and white runners secured by Velcro straps.

"I heard," he said. "Peabody phoned. Cutter on the bench, jail was preordained."

Mindful of the physical contact warning, Gill gave Nick a professional kiss on the cheek. "You okay?" she asked.

"I'm Section 38.1 of the *Rules and Regs*. Separate Custody. PCPC. Protective Custody gets kiddie diddlers, skinners, rats, and finks. I'm a cop so I need guarding more than them. At the moment, there are just two of us in the Digger. Me and Arnold, who I'm told is 'a bit of a cannibal.' "

"Hannibal Lecter?"

"Hardly. He looks like Caspar Milquetoast."

"Dare I laugh?"

"Feel free," he said.

Fleetingly, their hands touched as they sat at the table, a caress from palms to fingertips. Then Gill said, "Nick, fire your lawyer."

"Too harsh," he soothed. "With Cutter, who could get me bail? All cops hire Peabody. He prosecuted, you know?"

"That's the risk. The man is Crown-minded. 'May it please your lordship' this, and 'With the greatest of respect' that. Form is important to Peabody, and don't rock the boat. That's how he made QC and will go to the bench. Do you think a hit man or pusher would hire that Pinstripe?"

"I don't want their kind of shyster."

"Why?" said Gill angrily. "You'd rather spend life in jail? Cops are so dumb when it comes to counsel. You don't hire the suit who fights with one hand behind his back, you retain the pit bull who goes for the jugular. The best defense advocate is always in shit with the judge, not kissing his ass."

"Who do you think I should hire?"

"You're on the witness stand in a big case. If you crumple in cross-exam, a killer walks free. One-on-one, who do you fear and hate most?"

"The Vulture," said Nick.

"He's the lawyer you want."

What began as a scoff turned into a snort. "Knight is owned by the Mob. All the Big Guys run to him. He's in the pocket of every hitter in—"

"Don't be silly. Drop the cop-speak. I know Knight better than you. The man's a free agent, not mouthpiece to the Mob. The reason hitters run to Knight is he gets them off. Is that not a good enough reason to hire him for you?"

"You know what he costs? An arm and both legs. I squandered my savings, and can't get Mom's estate while charged with her murder. The bottom line is Knight's too rich for me."

"Not for me," said Gill.

"I pay my own way," Nick snapped. "I'm not a kept man."

"I'm hiring Knight for you."

"No, you're not."

"Oh, yes, I am. Now shut up and listen. That first night at my place, I told you I wanted excitement, not ties. You know I'm an independent woman of independent means. But for sex, I don't need a man to complete me. I've taken something from you, Nick, you should know. I was going to tell you the night your mom died. Then I was going to tell you the night you were arrested. Too much turmoil got in the way, and now I can't wait for a happy moment. I'm seven weeks' pregnant with your son or daughter."

It took a second to hit him. "You're—"

"I'm not finished. If you want to rot in prison, that's your choice. And the fastest way to get there is let John Peabody take on Lyndon Wilde. But don't expect me to bring your child out on weekends, or explain that Daddy's there because he refused to fight, he wouldn't be 'kept' by me, so now he's kept by the queen, because out of foolish male pride he let Broompole convict him of killing his mom!"

Nick stared out the window at the cold gray prison yard.

"It's your money," he mumbled.

"It's our lives," she replied.

KNIGHT'S GAMBIT

The Digger, or Separate Custody, was on the sixth floor of the Pretrial Center, high atop the Tower where inmates slept. Because Nick was a cop his cell had "the good view," a narrow panorama of the Pan Pacific Hotel, where Charles and Di stayed during Expo '86, and Yeltsin checked in for his summit with Clinton. On the opposite side, Arnold the Cannibal enjoyed "the bad view" of the skids.

Nick's cell—*04*—was shaped like a cleaver. The single bed and slatted window by its foot edged the top of the blade. Across from the window, a stainless-steel toilet and sink were tucked into the stubby handle. The door ran along the bottom of the blade, and etched into its paint was the philosophy KILL. The floor was gray, the walls and ceiling taupe. The space between the door and the bed was for pacing. There was a smoke detector, a fluorescent light, and an emergency button to "guard up" the door. Hands behind his head, Nick lay faceup on the bed contemplating his unborn kid being fatherless from birth.

Like me, he thought.

Hemmed in physically, emotionally, and legally, he was so claustrophobic he felt driven to pound his fists against the walls.

The judas window in the door was a grilled square of glass with a steel cover. The steel port lifted as a face stared in. "Your lawyer's here, nigger," said the guard.

To themselves, they were Correctional Officers. To outsiders, they were guards. To the inmates, they were screws. Until lately, screws wore brown, for the first uniforms were World War I surplus. Up to twenty inmates surround each screw, so their dress evolved to blue for "more authority" and to distinguish them from sheriff's "Brownies" in charge of remand. Screws branch into two subgroups: right-wing rednecks—"Chilliwack militia"—

Chilliwack's a Valley "hick town" to hip Vancouverites, those screws who call inmates "maggots" or "shit rats," and left-wing bleeding hearts—"fixing the broken machine"—who espouse reform instead of merely clamping down the garbage can lid.

This guard was militia.

A Mickey Spillane tough, all crew cut and cut the crap, he released Nick and led him across the TV common room to the elevator access door. "Pew, secure movement to Visiting. Count of one," the screw growled into the intercom.

Bang! fired the door.

The segregation unit had eleven seg cells. As Nick left Secure Custody for Visiting, another screw lifted the port to Arnold's cell, then jumped back when he saw the cannibal's face pressed against the glass, grinning at him.

Slam! shut the door.

"Don't call me nigger," Nick warned the guard.

"I'll call you anything I like. Where's your sense of humor, Craven? You and Pancakes are in segregation, so that makes you two the niggers of the joint. Nothing personal."

"Pancakes is Arnold?"

"That's what I call him. You can call me Gallows. For gallows humor. We had the Paper Bag Rapist in seg a while ago. I'm the joker who hung the Gumby doll in his cell with a little paper bag over its head."

"Why Pancakes?" asked Nick.

They rode the elevator down as Gallows explained. "Pancakes was a hermit up Revelstoke way. He butchered a rural family that had a little girl. Cut her stomach open and ate the contents. Twenty guesses what she had for breakfast?"

"He should be jailed up-country. What's he doing here?"

"Same as you. Court remand to accommodate counsel. You'd be in Surrey Pretrial if not for your lawyer, and he'd be up north if not for his. Pancakes was PC'd with the other scum, but he kept sneaking up behind them and whispering, 'What'd you have for breakfast? What'd you have for lunch?' A diddler snapped and went berserk, so we had to open the armory and SWAT the PC unit, cuffing them all facedown spread-eagled on their beds. That's when the SCO transferred Pancakes to PCPC. Nice company you keep."

Gallows grinned and nudged Nick in the ribs. "To welcome him to seg, I taped a few autopsy photos to his wall. Took 'em down when the moppers bitched the floor was white with cum."

The elevator opened on the ground floor where they crossed to an orange door marked VISITING. The intercom was RFA'd by the screw, the request for access inducing another "pop."

Bang! fired the door.

As he was passed to the muscled woman from Visits Control, Nick thanked the guard for escorting him down. "After all the militiamen, nice to get a bleeding heart for a change."

"See you, nigger."

The woman led Nick to GV-19 and locked him in. The Vulture—dark, lean, and lanky—was waiting in Nick's office. He still wore legal robes under his trench coat, for he was here over the dinner break while waiting for a jury. His chin hadn't felt a razor since five A.M. so his jaw resembled a kid's smeared with chocolate ice cream.

"I know you, Craven."

"And I you, Knight."

"You don't like me. Hate me, perhaps?"

"I don't like you. Hate's a strong word."

"To what trial do I owe your animosity? Or is it a matter of general principle?"

"Inderjit Parmar," said Nick.

"Right. The carvings from India hiding all those drugs. You made a mistake in removing the junk from inside at Canada Customs."

"It was imported. The smack was in our hands."

"Imported in fact, but not in law. For that it had to clear Canada Customs, and all that came through was the carvings and a bit of junk you missed. How could my client possess something that didn't exist in law?"

"The judge tongue-lashed me over sloppy work. You screwed us when you said you were pleading to *all* the drugs."

"Did I? Or did you just *think* that's what I said?"

"Either way, you set me up."

"When I was young, I lost a lot of trials I should have won. Older now, I win a lot of trials I ought to lose. It balances out, so justice gets done. My client got off. That makes me a good lawyer. Law is the only profession that sells luck. The more luck you have, the more you have to sell. That's why Gill Macbeth retained me for one hundred thousand dollars. Now the time has come to redirect your hate. Before driving here, I went to see Wilde, so he'd know it was me, not Peabody opposing him. You know he carves a notch under his desk for each big win? He invited me to get down on my knees to see the spot chosen for you."

"Christ," said Nick, "you two play games with human lives."

"Don't you? The question is, Are you playing to win or lose? You need me because I play to beat Wilde. This may seem like you are the stakes, but I play for my reputation." The lawyer offered his hand. "From now on call me Vic."

"Vic and Nick." The two men shook. "Sounds like a vaudeville team."

"Wilde has a chessboard beside his desk. He plays against a computer to keep his mind sharp. In chess, a gambit is an opening in which a piece is sacrificed to gain some advantage. Direct indictment sends you straight to trial with no preliminary hearing to test the Crown's case. That's Wilde's gambit, but it is also mine. Where the evidence is direct—someone is seen committing the crime—a prelim allows the shaking of eyewitnesses before trial. The evidence against you is wholly circumstantial, so a prelim would merely hint our defense to Wilde. Our gambit is go for the jugular by surprise attack."

"You haven't asked if I did it."

"I don't care. My only ethical restraint is not to knowingly offer false evidence or lying witnesses. What you don't tell me, I don't 'know,' so keep the truth to yourself unless I specifically ask. What will this jury believe, not truth, concerns me."

"I'm disillusioned," Nick said dryly.

"Illusions are a luxury you can't afford. Motive, opportunity, and means are our focus. Here's the case we must meet:

"The motive is matricide, evidenced by the letter. As

you're Dora's only child, it was typed by you. What would be most helpful is an evil twin—"

Nick blinked.

"—or barring that, a way to show the letter is a frame. Did you search your mother's house after her death?"

"No," said Nick. "Corporal Kidd pushed me away the night of the murder, then I was warned to stay clear of the place, and when I returned from Maui I was arrested at the airport."

"The first thing we do," Knight said, "is toss the house for answers. I'll get a court order allowing us a search."

"Me, too?"

The lawyer nodded. "The opportunity alleged is the birthday visit, as evidenced by a neighbor who saw you come and go. Since you're the last known person in the locked house, and everyone says your mom wouldn't open the door to strangers, only you had opportunity to kill her. Wilde showed me the Ident photos. Your mom kept a cat?"

"Jinx," Nick replied.

"Good, I'll use that to crack the door. Breach the house and there goes sole opportunity. With Schreck on the loose, he's prime suspect."

"If it's him, how do we explain the letter?"

"Open question until we see what the search turns up. The means," the lawyer continued, "is a club, which was taken from the murder site. The only evidence tying the means to you is blood, so our first line of defense is get your tunic excluded."

Nick groaned. "I'm a cop. I loathe the Charter of Rights."

"Hopefully I'll change your mind before this trial is over."

"Our second line of defense?"

"A Band-Aid," said Knight.

BAND-AID

Gillian Macbeth was on the witness stand at Nick's trial.
Nearing the close of direct examination, Lyndon Wilde
QC closed in.

"Does that conclude your evidence concerning the
postmortem you did on Dora Craven?"

"It does."

"Doctor, tell the jury about your relationship with
the accused."

"We've dated."

"Have you slept together?"

Gill turned to Hatchett. "Is my sex life relevant? I
resent the inference."

"Your resentment is irrelevant. Answer the question,
Doctor."

"Yes," Gill said.

"And did the accused come to your house the night
of his mother's murder?"

"Yes."

"With a request?"

Knight was on his feet. Judging from broadcasts on
TV, Americans expect attorneys to play jack-in-the-box,
objecting to this or objecting to that as "Incompetent,
irrelevant, and immaterial." Canadians are a suspicious
breed. Object and the jury wants to know what damning
truth you're trying to hide. "Will Mr. Wilde be cross-
examining his own witness? If so, I'd prefer to do it
myself."

"You'll get your turn," Hatchett said. "Answer the
question, Doctor."

"He asked me to perform the autopsy on his mom so
he would know nothing was overlooked."

"So he would know nothing was overlooked," echoed

Wilde. "Is that why he waited outside the morgue while you did the job?"

"We had a luncheon date."

"Doctor, are you bankrolling his defense?"

"Objection," Knight interjected. "Solicitor-client privilege."

"This isn't America, Counsel," Hatchett said. "If you have an objection, get on your feet. I won't have sloppiness."

Knight rose and bowed with a chivalrous arm swept under his vest. "I object, your ladyship."

"I'm warning you, Mr. Knight."

"So you keep saying. May I trouble you for a ruling on my objection?"

"Sustained," Hatchett snarled through tight teeth. The damage, however, was done by the question itself. The seed Wilde planted in the jury room was: *If you're paying for his defense, would you also cover up for the man? For your lover who's meddling with evidence sought by the Crown?*

"Doctor, what's the meaning of 'Oedipus complex?' "

Gill's eyes narrowed. "It's a Freudian term linked to psychoanalysis. Oedipus was a king in a Greek legend who murdered his father and married his mother. An Oedipus complex is the unresolved desire of a child for sexual gratification through the parent of the opposite sex. At first there's identification with, then later hatred for the parent of the same sex, who is thought by the child to be a rival."

"Desire by a son for his *mother,* is it not? Father by daughter is 'Electra complex?' "

"Yes," said Gill.

"An illustration of hate is the flip side of love, agree?"

"Perhaps."

"How old is Corporal Craven?"

"Thirty-seven."

"How old are you?"

"Forty-two."

"Interesting," Wilde pondered aloud, "in a case of matricide." He flipped his pocket watch open to consult the time, then sharply snapped it shut like a leghold trap. "Particularly where a son asks his older lover to cut up his mom."

The prosecutor turned to Knight and smugly said, "Your witness," but before he could sit down, Gill took a Parthian shot. "If *you* were dating a woman five years younger, would that be 'interesting in a case of patricide?' "

"If she wrote a letter like the one in this case," Wilde shot back.

"Mr. Knight?" said Hatchett, a wicked smile on her pursed lips.

"In performing this autopsy, Doctor, were you the only pathologist in the morgue?"

"No, Dr. Singh was at the station beside me."

"Also doing postmortem?"

"Yes, another clubbing."

"The clubbing of a police officer, I believe? Who was also disemboweled?"

"Yes," said Macbeth.

"Was Dora Craven disemboweled?"

"Not that night. But I was later told—"

"Hearsay," Hatchett snapped. "Don't say anything more."

"Did you and Dr. Singh consult?"

"Yes, back and forth."

"So there's no way you could sabotage evidence for the Crown?"

"One, I'd never do that. Professional ethics. Two, the postmortem was witnessed by experienced police. And three, Dr. Singh and I reviewed each other's work since we wondered if the clubbings were related."

"And were they?"

"We couldn't tell. The bludgeon used in this case imprinted the zigzag shown in the photographs onto Dora Craven's scalp. The other scalp was shredded when that body was dragged faceup."

"Apart from the head, there was another important injury here?"

Hatchett looked up from her bench book.

Wilde cocked his head and frowned.

Macbeth seemed perplexed. "To what do you refer?"

"Exhibit six, Photo ten," Knight advised Hatchett. The jury rummaged through their albums and thumbed to the picture. "The Band-Aid we see on the victim's index finger? Did that cover the cut we see exposed in Photo fifteen?"

A flipping of photographs. "Yes," the pathologist said.

"And was that cut recent?"

"Yes," Macbeth replied.

"As recent as the day she died?"

"Definitely."

"And would such a cut bleed?"

"Yes, for a while."

"In your professional opinion, can you attribute a cause?"

"It looks to me like an incised wound made by a sharp blade."

"By a kitchen knife?"

"Possibly."

"A wound suffered by a cook?"

"Yes, the sort of slice you get when a knife slips while cutting food."

"The sort of slice you get when a knife slips while cutting food," Knight echoed, aiming a meaningful glance at Wilde. "Thank you, Doctor."

The Vulture sat down.

SKY-HIGH

West Vancouver
Wednesday, January 12, 1994

On the passenger's seat of the stolen four-wheel drive sat the Rorke's Drift trophy box. Parked waiting, Evil Eye listened to African hatred whispering through the lid, urging the zombie to wreak revenge in Redcoat blood.

A sea of blood.

To which end, the psycho was advancing.

Evil Eye's plot was taken from 1988's Commonwealth Conference in Vancouver, where Sikh terrorists paid an attendee with terminal cancer a fortune for his soon-to-be-fatherless family in exchange for blowing India's prime minister to bits. Tipped to the plan, and despite Maggie Thatcher rebuffing their suggestion of a general rectal search, the Force had thwarted the assassination just in time, though Gandhi didn't escape a subsequent attempt back home. This time, the Force itself was the target.

Today was a dry run.

To test the equipment.

Nothing revolted Evil Eye more than a happy family.

Like this family.

The car was parked by the side of the road at this end of a cross-country trail on Hollyburn Mountain sky-high above English Bay. The four-wheel drive was parked further on, where Evil Eye sat in the driver's seat and watched with binoculars.

Though snow was new to the city sprawled below, up here in Cypress Bowl it had flurried on and off since Christmas, whitening ski runs and cross-country trails. Now a slushy tumble fell from clouds so low it seemed you could reach up and touch them, which the young girl tried to do while her parents and older brother knocked packed snow from their ski equipment before lashing it to the roof rack.

Adults in front, kids in back, the family got into the test vehicle.

When the car began the long zigzag switchback down the mountain face to West Vancouver along the shore of English Bay, Evil Eye followed with a remote control in hand.

The mountain road was deserted.

Today was a workday.

The Christmas vacation was over and students were back in school.

Just preschool kids and their yuppie parents could fart away the morning.

Like this doomed family.

As the test vehicle approached the curve where the trap was set, the young girl turned in the back seat to wave at Evil Eye through the window.

The psycho waved back with the remote control, one finger pushing the button to blow the detonators. *Boom!*

went a small wad of cyclotrimethylenetrinitramine putty behind one tire, the blast spinning the family car like a whirling pinwheel across this hairpin curve, as *Boom!* blew another wad of putty beneath the barrier along the edge of the road, blasting the railing sky-high to open a yawning gap in the fence above the precipitous plunge down the mountainside, through which the out-of-control vehicle spun off the slippery road for launching like a shot put.

Boom! echoed the explosion below as Evil Eye drove on.

TROPHY BOX

Port Coquitlam

Pursuant to court order, two sheriff's deputies in brown uniforms drove Nick caged in back of a brown car from the Pretrial Center to the crime scene. Snowflakes drifting lazily from a somber gray sky slushed the windows, slicked the road, and curtained off the street. Half human, half snowman, Vic Knight stood at the curb in front of Dora's home. The Brownies parked where Nick parked the day his mother died.

A Coquitlam Mountie broke the evidence seal on the back door. Paint scratched from the wood near his boots revealed where Jinx had wanted in. The house had been sealed in early December after forensic techs finished combing for clues, and hadn't been entered since. Stomping snow from his shoes, Nick stepped into the kitchen where his mom had died.

Claws of emotion picked at the scars patching his heart. Where Mom had stood at the sink every day of his youth, preparing meals or washing dishes while he tussled with homework at the Formica table, there were ugly brown stains from her blood. The fading photo of her as a girl feeding a sty of pigs (he'd nicknamed her Piglies, a term of endearment she endured with grace);

the canisters of Murchie's tea (Queen Victoria blend her favorite) lining one shelf; woven garlic braids from the Tree of Life Garden; wherever he looked there were signs of her. Signs of her, but never again Mom herself.

"I want this over," Nick said flatly. "Let's get it done."

Kitchen to parlor to hall to bathroom to his and her bedrooms, Knight and Craven searched the cramped pioneer house.

"Anything missing?"

"Not that I can tell."

"Basement?"

Nick shook his head. "The house is built on stones with a sump."

"And up there?" Knight asked, pointing to a set of stairs off Dora's walk-in closet.

Nick took a deep breath. "Mom's private space. Off bounds to me as a kid."

We all have a decade that defines who we are—the ten-year stretch we'd live in if we had a time machine. Nick's mom was shaped by the fifties, an era she never left. Preteens, he stood at the bottom of these creaky stairs, listening to her play 45s up there while she sewed. "Teddy Bear" by Elvis, "Ain't That A Shame" by Fats, "Breathless" by the Killer, Jerrah Lee. Though he was only three when 1960 dawned, in many ways Nick was a creature of the fifties, too. "Here Comes Summer" by Jerry Keller, "A Lover's Question" by Clyde McPhatter, "The Great Pretender" by The Platters, "Since I Met You Baby" by Ivory Joe Hunter: the songs from the attic still haunted him.

"Climb," said his lawyer. So for the first time in years, Craven climbed.

From his mother's bedroom facing Colony Farm, the closet steps ascended to the front of the house where a door opened right into the peaked attic. A bare bulb on the landing cast the only light, until Nick flicked the switch in her time machine.

The fifties was an era of Cold War tension, H-bomb angst, redbaiting, racism, and stifling conformity. But not to Dora. For here was her collection of golden age dolls, rescued from garage sales for a buck and change: Toni, Miss Curity, Little Miss Revlon, and bountiful Barbie with what it takes to make a grown man cry . . . Here was her collection of cartoon watches: Mickey Mouse, Porky Pig, Howdy Doody, Popeye, and Woody Woodpecker . . . And here were her collections of brass buttons, board games, carnival glass, music boxes, playing cards, puppets, and other refugees from rummage sales. Amazing the floor didn't buckle under the weight. The peaked roof was plastered with a photo collage, yellow edges curling as time passed by. Brando as *The Wild One* and Jerry Lee Lewis on full-stride piano and Elvis in his gold lamé suit. Crowding around these icons like groupies were overlapped photos of fashion models, all clutch coats and wasp waists and hoop skirts and saddle shoes and pink pedal pushers with cat's-eye glasses. . . .

"Mom was a pack rat," Nick said, "who sewed consignment clothes here to make ends meet." He pointed to a dressmaker's dummy masked by shadows.

"A farm girl?" Knight asked. "The photo of pigs downstairs?"

Nick nodded. "Lethbridge, Alberta."

"You were born when she was how old?"

"Eighteen."

"Married?"

"Spur of the moment. She eloped at sixteen without her parents' consent. Dad was a Member, ten years older than her. Drove to Reno. Came back hitched. And never talked about him after he died."

"When was that?"

"Fifty-six. Suicide. Got drunk and shot himself the night I was born."

"Strange," Knight said, eyeing Dora's collage. "The prairies. The fifties. Demand to conform if married to a cop. Yet all the men on her fantasy wall are outcasts and rebels."

Nick shrugged. "New life. Birth of rock 'n' roll. We moved here the month after Dad died."

"From Lethbridge?"

"Medicine Hat. That's where I was born. Mom stayed with Aunt Eleanor—she was a midwife—till after my birth."

"Complications?"

"The doc predicted twins. A prairie quack. He was wrong."

"Wait a minute . . ." Knight said.

"I already checked. I'm the only birth registered to Mom. I searched B.C., Saskatchewan, and Manitoba vital statistics, too."

"Was Eleanor your aunt? Or your mom's?"

"She was my dad's sister. Eight years younger than him, two years older than Mom. Died in November from a fall in the house where I was born."

"Your mom have any siblings?"

"An only child. Her parents were strict Mennonites and she married outside the faith. 'So never darken our door again.' "

"She didn't remarry?"

"No," said Nick.

"What sort of men did she date here?"

"None but me. Night and day she worked herself to the bone."

"Attractive?"

"Worry and stress ruined her face."

"Was it she couldn't replace your dad? Or had she had enough of men? Men in the flesh"—Knight swept the collage—"if not in fantasy."

"She was a good mom," Nick said simply.

"So I see."

The lawyer crossed to a battered desk besieged by teddy bears. Bears on the floor to the left were black, bears to the right were beige. The bear on the desk was half-made: sewn but not stuffed. On the wall facing the chair was a picture of Hawaii.

"Black bears go to Africa. To Somalia," said Nick. "Beige bears go to Children's Hospital. A pastime after she quit work at Riverview last June."

"Doing what?"

"Laundry and food. For thirty-five years."

Squatting, Knight pulled a mutant from the pile of beige bears. But for tufts, the fur was gone from its threadbare head, while bits of strawlike stuffing stuck through holes not patched with yarn. Both glass eyes retained an intelligent stare, and minus a black strand or two a nose tipped the worn snout, but when Knight unwrapped the baby blanket cinched under its chin, the bear's body had less substance than a plucked anorexic chicken.

"This poor beat-up thing will never find a home."

"That," said Nick, "is *my* teddy bear."

"Name?"

"Teddy Bear."

"Now that's original."

"Damn right," Nick said. "*The* original name. Teddy's bear, actually."

Knight had his client talking, loosening up. Cops were tough nuts to crack and loath to show faults. Us and them, and lawyers were definitely them. The bear in the lawyer's hand, like those on the floor, was tailor-made to form and retrieve boyhood memories. "Roosevelt, wasn't it? Theodore, not Franklin?"

"Turn of the century, a Washington cartoonist drew a caricature of him, gun down, refusing to shoot a bear cub. In Brooklyn, a Russian immigrant sold toys made by his wife in their small candy store. He had her sew a plush brown bear and placed it in the window beside a copy of the cartoon with a label *Teddy's Bear.* Worried he needed White House permission to use the President's name, he screwed up courage to write Roosevelt. Teddy replied he couldn't imagine what good his name would be in the stuffed-animal business, but the merchant was welcome to use it. For the psychological good of the world, what President ever made a better decision?"

"Your mom tell you the story?"

"Yeah," Nick said.

"Your bear was her model?"

"Sewed when I was born. She gave me two. Beige and black. The black one's lost."

"How'd he get so battered?"

"Insecure childhood and lots of love. Nothing will see you through times of turmoil like a faithful teddy bear."

Knight passed him the tattered relic. "Meet your new cellmate."

"Didn't you have a teddy bear?"

"No," Vic said.

"That explains why you're now a lawyer. All that festering boyhood emotion crying to get out. Repressed, frustrated, you beat up those caught in the playpen for bully boys.''

A rare thing happened. Vic Knight laughed. "A teddy bear will make me a kinder and gentler lawyer? Just what you need."

Kneeling, Nick rummaged through the pile of beige bears like a kid sorting toys in a toy box. "Mom would be pleased if I salvaged your soul with a bear sewn by her—"

He stopped.

Turned.

And scowled at Knight.

"Her files are gone. The cabinet was here." Clearing bears from the floor revealed parallel scars gouged beside the desk. "Mom kept a file for the current month downstairs in the kitchen drawer. In it went bills and letters, whatever came by mail. Each month, she juggled money to get us through. A new file meant the old file was stored here."

"How far back did the files go?"

"I have no idea. But the cabinet dated back as far as my memory."

"The letter found in the kitchen drawer was in her current file. If something stored up here compelled the killer to club her to death—"

"Club . . ." Nick said, with a quick blink the lawyer caught. Trained to detect the telling lie, the pregnant pause, the lost memory that suddenly flashes through a witness's mind, Knight knew his probing had just struck gold.

"The trophy box," said Nick.

VICTORIA CROSS

Of all Imperial decorations, the Victoria Cross—the VC—carries the highest prestige. In 1856 the only medals awarded to British fighting men were for good conduct and long service. The queen wanted recognition of "Officers or Men who have served Us in the presence of the Enemy and shall then have performed some single act of valor or devotion to their Country." She decreed "neither rank nor long service nor wounds nor any other circumstance or condition whatsoever save the merit of conspicuous bravery or devotion shall be held to establish a sufficient claim to honor."

From the beginning, since it was first struck at the end of the Crimean War (best known for that fateful Charge of the Light Brigade), the bronze medal has been cast from Russian guns seized at Sebastopol. The medal, suspended by a 1½" red ribbon, is worn on the left breast and takes precedence over all other awards. The VC is a cross pattée with the Royal Crest (Lion over Crown) in the center, above a semicircular scroll with the words "For Valor." Engraved on back is the name of the bearer and date of his brave deed.

Queen Victoria insisted the medal be forfeited on conviction for "any infamous Crime." Gunner Collis of the Royal Horse lost his for bigamy. Forfeiture stopped in the reign of King George V: "Even were a VC to be sentenced to be hanged for murder, he should be allowed to wear the VC on the scaffold."

The most VCs awarded for a single action were eleven to the defenders of Rorke's Drift. The most VCs won by any regiment in battle were seven by the 24th Regiment of Foot at Rorke's Drift. . . .

"Fittingly, I found the box on Victoria Day," Nick told Knight in the attic. "I was nine, inquisitive, and alone in the house. The rule was I could play anywhere but up

*here. I yearned to know if the attic hid secrets about my
dad. . . .*

Nick stood in his mother's closet and gazed up the
stairs. Flicking the wall switch at the bottom spilled light
from a bare bulb down the steps. *Creak . . . creak . . .
creak . . .* his feet began to climb.

Topping the stairs, he paused to squint into the dark
attic, and froze when someone stared back from the
shadows. Locked in a Mexican standoff, neither
moved . . . until Nick tugged a cord within to flood the
peak with light. A dressmaker's dummy in a scant bikini
silently laughed at him.

Mom's attic was crammed with relics from rummage,
jumble, and garage sales. Beside the padded female form
on a wooden stand stood a new Singer sewing machine
and an old treadle model. Supplied from crates of castoff
clothing yet to be cut up, fabric scraps were laid out on
a cutting board. Used patterns from yesteryear poked
from boxes lined with bobbins and odd spools of thread,
behind which, stored in the darkest corner, Nick found
a dusty, cobwebbed trunk labeled TEDMOND "TED" CRA-
VEN, RCMP.

The key in the lock unlocked it.

The boy raised the lid.

On top was the brown, wide-brimmed Stetson of the
Mounted Police, a Smith & Wesson .38 pillowed on the
Red Serge tunic beneath. Caressing the service revolver
his dad used to shoot himself, Nick stuck the handgun,
fugitive style, in the waistband of his jeans. Then he
carried the Stetson and tunic over to the dressmaker's
dummy.

A stack of 45s hovered on the record changer. Nick
played them as he dressed the dummy in his dad's Red
Serge. Whirling the overhead fan brought the tunic to
life. Tilting the Stetson forward hid the featureless face.
"Hi, Dad," he whispered.

*In eighteen and fourteen we took a little trip,
Along with Colonel Jackson down the mighty
Mississip'.
We took a little bacon and we took a little beans.
And we met the bloody British near the town of New
Orleans . . .*

        *   *   *

Returning to the trunk, he removed the rest of the clothes. Beneath lay pictures of Redcoats—Mounties?—unlike those Nick had seen. Redcoats comforted a dying man. Redcoats fired on civilians without guns. Redcoats fought black Africans. Redcoats galloped the Musical Ride. At the bottom of the trunk, Nick found an oblong box.

> *We fired our guns and the British kept acomin'.*
> *There wuzn't nigh as many as they wuz a while ago.*
> *We fired once more and they began to runnin'*
> *On down the Mississippi to the Gulf of Mexico . . .*

REX LANCELOT CRAVEN was carved into the ebony lid. Engraved on the brass plaque below was RORKE'S DRIFT. Inside were two compartments lined with velvet. On red plush in the upper half lay a tarnished lunger, the twenty-two-inch socket bayonet of the British Colonial Army. Pinned across the blade was a bronze medal. In feeling the tip of the lunger, Nick drew blood.

> *They ran through the briars and they ran through the*
> *brambles*
> *And they ran through the bushes where a rabbit*
> *couldn't go.*
> *They ran so fast that the hounds couldn't catch 'em*
> *On down the Mississippi to the Gulf of Mexico . . .*

On black plush in the lower half lay a Zulu knobkerrie two feet long. Atop the stout handle was a round polished knob, its striking surface nestled facedown in the plush. Looped around the handle was a snakeskin pouch, which Nick opened and turned upside down in his palm. Ten knucklebones tumbled into his hand. Carved on each bone was an Evil Eye.

"Nicholas!"

Oh, oh.

"What are you doing up here!"

The scratch of a needle on vinyl cut Johnny Horton off midwail, ruining the record like those trashed by outraged Brits in 1957. Mom crossed to the trunk and loomed over him. Thanks to Johnny, he hadn't caught the sound of her car returning or footsteps creaking the stairs.

"Well?" Mom said. "You know the rule."

The best defense, Nick figured, was self-attack. "Did Dad shoot himself because of me?"

"Oh, baby." Mom sighed, shaking her head. "No way, honey. What gave you that idea?"

"He died the night I was born."

"Who told you that?"

"I overheard you talking with Aunt Eleanor."

"What'd you hear?" Eyes narrow, frightening him.

"She asked if I knew Ted died the night I was born? You said no, and you'd never tell me. She said best to let sleeping dogs lie. Why'd she call Dad a dog, Mom?"

"Just an expression. Where were you?"

"Playing James Bond behind the couch. You and Aunt Eleanor were Russian spies."

"Anything else?" Mom eased the gun from his jeans.

"She told you the doc who predicted twins had died from a heart attack. He was a quack proved wrong by my birth, you said. He died from drink, Aunt Eleanor said, so that was that."

"I'm listening."

Nick shrugged. "You left to make tea. Aunt Eleanor went to the bathroom. And I reported to M."

"M?"

"Gee, Mom. Don't you know James Bond?"

"Who's M?"

"Monty. Our cat." Nick laughed.

She took the bones from his hand and refilled the snakeskin pouch. "Is that Dad's medal?" he asked as she closed the box.

"No, your great-granddad's," said Mom, reopening the lid. Unpinning the medal, she pointed to the name, rank, and regiment engraved on back of the laureled clasp. Etched in a circle on the medal's reverse was the date 22.1.79.

"What is it?" Nick asked.

"The Victoria Cross. Your great-granddad won it for bravery in the Zulu War. Because today is Victoria Day, you're off school."

"I know," said Nick, reciting the chant of British Empire school kids:

"Hip, hip hoorah,
The 24th of May
Is the queen's birthday.
If you don't give us a holiday
We'll all run away.

"Why is the queen's birthday called Victoria Day, Mom, when Elizabeth is our queen?"

"Good question," Mom said, sitting her son down on the floor and cuddling him like she did when it was Story Time, like when she read him *The Jungle Book,* and *Pugnax the Gladiator,* and *Biggles Defies the Swastika,* and *Prince Valiant Fights Attila the Hun,* and *Freddy and the Clockwork Twin. . . .*

"The odd thing, Nick, is Britain doesn't celebrate Victoria Day. Which proves the adage Colonials are more British than the British."

"Are we Colonials?" Nick asked.

"Yes, and proud of the fact. For last century when Victoria was queen, it was true the sun never set on the British Empire. . . .

"You said the club was facedown?" Knight queried Nick. "Did you take it out?"

"No," he said.

"Too bad. I wish we knew the club had a zigzag on the knob."

BUM RAP

Cloverdale

Electric drums from the concrete jungle boomed in this room, 2Pac's "Crooked Ass Nigga" loud as could be, a wall of sound with gunshots and siren noise included, a drug dealer on a rampage with a 9-mm gun, a cop yelling "Freeze!" popped in the knees 'cause he didn't shout "Punk, please!", and Ice-T's "Cop Killer" blaring after that, the speed metal band Body Count driving the words home, then "Crooked Ass Nigga," then "Cop Killer," then "Crooked Ass Nigga" again, the CDs a gift from Evil Eye to pump up the cop, Tarr clenching his teeth tighter as each "coon rap" drilled into his brain, a brain reeling from five, six, seven Scotches too many, *How dare those fuckers blackball me for one jig kid. . . .*

It takes a special kind of cop to volunteer for an ERT team, some because it's an action test of balls and machismo, others because they yearn to play with all those kick-ass toys and feed off adrenaline, and one or two like Tarr because they could get killed.

Latent suicides.

For them, the problem with suicide is it's seen as a coward's exit, instead of the ultimate brave act that Tarr thought it to be. The past year he'd suffered from the mental illness of chronic depression, which led him to the ERT team as a death wish, the pump of adrenaline quelling the blues for a while if he survived, as death crouched waiting for him behind the next door, or maybe the next, wax enough doors and odds were one would have your number, Valhalla ahead for the Viking who died in battle, not a coward's spat-on grave.

How dare those fuckers blackball me for one jig kid. . . .

A kid who probably jigabooed to coon rap like this shit. . . .

Crooked ass nigga, my ass . . .

Cop killer raps. . . .

How dare those fuckers suspend me for such a bum rap. . . .

Stealing my chance at glory. . . .

The drapes in the living room were drawn against the day. The Sports Network flickered silently on the TV. *Fuck, don't white guys play basketball anymore?* His hand reached for the bottle of Scotch on the table that propped up his feet, the surface marked with rings from too many glasses of slopped booze, papers tumbling from it to pile up on the floor, one a divorce petition from The Bitch filed by the law firm of her shyster hump, surrounded by newspaper pictures of Tarr and jig group spokesmen calling for his badge. *Shit, I might as well be a cop in fuckin' L.A.*

"Did you mean what you suggested the first time we

drank?" the Slicker had asked Tarr in The Moaning Steer on New Year's Eve. "About having the guts to kill yourself at the Red Serge Ball."

"Why?" he answered.

"Seems like a weak way to make a point if the only death is yours."

"What point's that?"

"The point that you don't blackball a gutsy cop to suck the joints of p.c. fools who pander to cop-killing crooked ass niggas."

"You got a better idea?"

"As a matter of fact I do."

So Tarr had listened to the idea, agreeing to join the Suicide Club, unaware of how deep the depths of his depression sank, or how suicidal blue he'd get the longer he was weaned from the adrenaline rush that pumped the ERT team.

Tarr grabbed the .38 off the table propping up his feet.

He flipped open the cylinder and emptied it of six shots.

He fed the cylinder one bullet, gave it a spin and snapped it shut.

He cocked the hammer and placed the muzzle to his temple.

"Did you mean what you suggested the first time we drank? About having the guts to kill yourself at the Red Serge Ball."

"You bet," Tarr said now. "If I last that long."

He pulled the trigger.

THE IRREGULAR

Vancouver
Thursday, January 13, 1994

"They must be treating you well in here, from the grin on your face."

"Actually, it's hell. But the company is cool. The other

inmate in seg is a cannibal. Well, maybe not. Eat stomach contents but not the stomach itself, does that qualify as maneater? Pancakes won't look me in the eye. He stares at my belly."

"Then why the grin?"

"As Gallows the Guard brought me down to Visiting, I remembered Mom taking me to the PNE when I was eight. Every detail is as vivid as if it were today. Clanking through the turnstile of the Exhibition. Pausing at the stockyards to see horses, pigs, and cows. Mom hustling me away when a stallion got a hard-on two feet long. Best of all was the midway, of course. The Hall of Mirrors that stretched me thin as a toothpick. A glance at the Girlie Show when Mom turned away. Riding the Octopus and Tilt-a-Whirl. The reason for the grin is what happened next. We were in the gauntlet lined with games of chance, barkers importuning us to step right up and win a prize at ball toss, balloon darts, or topple the milk bottles, me pestering Mom to play, Mom warning me every game was a scam suckers lose, me telling her that was wrong 'cause look at the guy ahead of us with a stuffed bear, Mom replying he was a shill paid to stroll around and lure dumbos in, me wheedling, 'Come on, Mom, can't we play, huh, can't we?' until she stopped and demanded, 'Nicholas, give me a quarter from your allowance.' "

"Lesson time?" augured DeClercq.

"The game was called Toss Until You Win. The goal was to lob a rubber ball onto a plywood sheet drilled with holes the size of the ball without a smidgen to spare. You had to hit them directly or the ball bounced off. The barker running the game called the prizeman 'Doctor.'

" 'Nicholas,' Mom told me, while slapping down the quarter, 'the world is full of cheats out to steal your money. Half your weekly allowance bought a toss of this ball, and like that'—she threw it at the sheet—'you are a poorer boy.'

"Next thing we know there are lights and bells going off all over the place. 'Bring out a ham, Doctor!' the barker yells. The prizeman opens a fridge and pulls out a leg of pork half the size of me. 'See what you've done,' Mom says. 'Now we have to go home. Carry ham all

day in this sun and it'll go bad.' So home we went to
eat pork every meal for a week."

DeClercq laughed, and suddenly knew—if there was
doubt before—Craven was innocent.

Silence filled Nick's "office."

Finally broken when Robert said, "You asked to see
me?"

"I didn't kill her, Chief. I loved—still love—my mom.
It's like I'm trapped in a Hitchcock movie. *The Wrong
Man* is me."

"And her blood?" said DeClercq.

"How that got on my cuff I don't know. I picked my
Red Serge up from the dry cleaners and changed before
I went to Mom's and the Regimental Dinner. Following
the murder, Kidd refused to let me near the scene. Assuming she didn't plant it to frame me after seizing my
tunic—she did have access to Mom's blood from the
autopsy—all I can theorize is the killer crossed the old
bridge after the crime, then I followed and unwittingly
picked up some of her blood."

"Why would Kidd frame you?"

"Her ass is on the line. Nail me and she's heading for
sergeant. Fail and there's backlash. Maybe she's a black
who secretly hates whites."

"That's what you think happened?"

"No," said Nick. "It answers the blood but not the
letter." From the pocket of his green prison shirt, he
withdrew a crumpled photocopy and smoothed it on the
table. For the umpteenth time, both Mounties reread the
Mother letter:

December 2, 1993
Mother—
    It's taken my lifetime to uncover your whitewashed
    secret. Discussing it face to face on my birthday seems
    fitting. I'll call on the 7th.

"Why type this letter if I was planning murder? If the
killing was spur of the moment, why send it to Mom
when she's near as the phone and I see her weekly?
Why would Mom—if it was from me—store it in her
monthly mail file? She'd kept a file in that drawer since
1957. Knowing that, if I killed her, why leave such evi-

dence of motive behind? I might as well put a noose around my neck."

"Who do you think sent the letter? Is it a frame, too?"

"You won't laugh, Chief?"

"This isn't a laughing matter."

"When I was born, I fear Mom delivered twins. That explains the letter—sent as an introduction—and the birthday mentioned being the same as mine. If something was wrong with the birth—what I have no idea—might that not explain my dad shooting himself the night I—*we*—were born, and why my brother or sister was put up for adoption?"

"Any evidence?"

"Not concrete. There's no record of a second birth in any registry from here to Manitoba. My new lawyer is checking the rest of Canada. I do know a doctor who saw my mom predicted twins, from a conversation I overheard her have with my aunt. My aunt—now dead— was midwife for delivery. Mom said the quack was proved wrong by my birth. Aunt Eleanor said he died from drink, so that was that."

"Anything else?"

"I've been having dreams. Mom and my aunt conspire while Dad shoots himself. A voice behind me gloats, 'He shot himself because of me, brother.' When I turn, no one's there."

"Dreams may be mirages."

"Or buried memories." So Nick told the chief about the relics taken from Dad's trunk and the file cabinet gone from Mom's attic. "Who but a twin would steal that combination of loot?"

"Perhaps your mom emptied the trunk years ago?"

"No, dust at its bottom outlines a recently taken box."

"Have you told Coquitlam?"

"No," said Nick. "A twin sounds like a lame excuse to explain the Mother letter. The only proof of what is missing is my word, and obviously what I swear means sweet fuck-all to Kidd. Convicting me will balance out racial politics. I'm a scapegoat for the politically correct. Chief, I'm living a nightmare and I'm begging for your help. How can I defend myself locked away in here, when my only hope is answers to questions out there?

All I'm asking is a fighting chance. I need a cop investigating to *clear me*."

"Nick, I'm under orders to keep out of your case. So is Special X."

Silence reigned again until Robert knocked for the guard. "You know what they call you in the ranks?" Nick said to the sound of the key.

"I shudder to think," the chief said as the guard released him.

"The Last Honest Man," Nick said as the door slammed shut.

"I know the paranoia in being framed," said Zinc, sipping coffee in DeClercq's office at Special X while he recounted his meeting with Nick. "I still shudder at what Cutthroat did in Hawaii."

Though newer investigations dominated the Strategy Wall, the Schreck-Craven case remained pinned up to one side. The official line was Schreck killed the deputies and Jack MacDougall during his psychotic war with Bone Police. Ramming the funeral certainly linked him to the latter crime. Smoke-screened by Schreck's attacks, Nick clubbed his mom, then later disemboweled her to tie his matricide to Schreck's MacDougall murder for which Nick had an alibi. DeClercq remained unconvinced the jigsaw pieces meshed, so the Schreck-Craven puzzle remained up on the wall.

"Schreck killed the deputies. No doubt about that, agreed?"

"Case closed," Zinc confirmed.

"The question before us is who killed Dora Craven? Nick says he's innocent and my gut believes him. Accept that as true in considering the question. We also know Nick didn't kill Jack. His alibi for that crime is airtight, agreed?"

"Agreed," said Zinc.

"If Nick killed neither Dora nor Jack, the obvious suspect for both murders is Schreck. But how, given the facts we know, did he do that? The Corvette that rammed Jack's funeral was registered to a Port Coquitlam punk named Bud Beck. A search of Beck's home near the Indian Reserve revealed his skull-crushed body in the cellar. His watch was broken and crystal shards were found just inside the front door. Schreck fled from Colony Farm at ten after five. By timing how long it takes to go north up the Coquitlam River to Beck's home, GIS says Schreck arrived at the time on the broken watch. If so, he had *no time* to detour and club Dora."

"Unless the time on the watch was wrong," Chandler said.

"Drugs were found in the cellar and a pusher meets clients on time."

"If Schreck fled north and hid in Beck's house, no way did he *later* go south to Dora's through the manhunt searching Colony Farm."

"That's why the dogs didn't track him up to Dora's door. He didn't club her."

"Schreck killed the deputies, but not Nick's mom. Nick killed neither his mom nor Jack. That," said Zinc, "begs the question, Did Schreck kill Jack?"

"Beck's neighbor swears the Corvette wasn't driven the night Jack died. He's bedridden from a work injury. The only time the Corvette rumbled out was the morning of the funeral. So if Schreck followed Jack from Dora's house to Minnekhada Lodge, what car did he drive that night?"

"If Schreck didn't kill Jack, why'd he ram Jack's funeral parade?"

"He wasn't after Jack. He was after us. The parade offered him a chance to crush the Bone Police in mass. The funeral route was mapped on the front page of the newspaper found in the Corvette. The paper was a local rag delivered to and missing from Beck's Port Coquitlam home."

"So Schreck hid in Beck's house from the time he left Colony Farm until he drove to Richmond to ram the funeral?"

"The dragnet was intensive. That's how he slipped through."

"Schreck killed the deputies, but neither Dora nor Jack. Assuming Nick didn't kill Dora, and knowing Nick didn't kill Jack, we're looking for someone still loose out there."

"Nick's twin," said DeClercq.

"You believe that?"

"Hypothetically. Assume Dora delivered twins: Nick and X. For some reason, the births caused Nick's dad to shoot himself. For some reason, Nick was kept and X was sent away. A child who fears becomes an adult who hates, and X lived in fear growing up. Now an adult, he or she comes looking for Mom. X finds Dora, and sends her the Mother letter. After Nick leaves the birthday party for Minnekhada Lodge, X approaches Dora's house along the back path. Remember the dogs tracked a scent coming and going there? When X raps on the back door, Dora admits her hateful abandoned child. X is searching for his/her roots, so Dora shows the twin his/her dad's trunk. Hate explodes so X hits her with the club in the trophy box, then empties the trunk of relics and leaves by the same path."

"With the file cabinet slung over his/her back?" doubted Chandler.

"X didn't steal the cabinet. Much easier to empty it of files."

"In your hypothesis, who killed Jack?"

"X," said DeClercq. "Using the club and bayonet in the trophy box. Unfortunately, the zigzag mark the club imprinted on Jack's scalp was shredded when X dragged him into the shadows."

"But why kill Jack?"

"That we must find out. What nags me is the theft of Redcoat relics from the trunk. The Redcoat pictures, trophy box, and Ted Craven's Red Serge. X hates Dad as much as Mom. In different ways, both abandoned him/her. Dad's a dead Mountie beyond revenge. Did X slash Jack's Red Serge as a fetish?"

"If Jack wasn't ripped to disembowel, why gut Dora in the mortuary?"

"That we must find out."

"To embark on that means flouting Chan's hands-off order."

"I can't do that. Not 'the Last Honest Man.'"

"What we need is something concrete to draw us in. Same as the old search warrant conundrum. You can't get a warrant without reasonable and probable grounds, and to get the grounds you've got to do the search. Catch–twenty-two."

"Do you know what an irregular is?"

"Someone who doesn't eat enough bran?"

Robert winced. "Try again."

"Someone who fights outside regular regiments of a military force. A partisan."

"After the Sepoy Mutiny of 1857, the British Colonial Army was in an Old Testament mood. The Duke of Cambridge, the army's commander-in-chief, pledged support for 'all who have the manliness to inflict the punishment.' Indians called the Imperial response 'the Devil's Wind.' Soldiers shed their uniforms for irregular garb: tweed coats, and turbans, and even a cloak made from the green baize of a billiards table in the Officers' Mess. Stripped of army livery, they also shed army constraints, and rode out into the country for revenge. Sepoys were lashed to cannon muzzles and blown to bits. Those who turned their backs on avengers were shot for insolence. Indians near the Bibighar, site of a massacre of British women and children, were forced to lick caked blood from the floor, then hanged. Once the Queen's Peace was restored, these 'irregulars' disbanded to reassume their former regiments as regular troops."

"The moral being," Chandler said, "when the job is beyond a regular force, an irregular is needed?"

"Precisely," said DeClercq.

"Who do you have in mind?"

"You asked me to edit Alex Hunt's manuscript. I'm impressed by how she ferrets out facts. Is she planning to research another true crime book?"

JUJU

Zinc sat in the TV room of their leased Vancouver home, waiting for Alex to return from house-hunting in Deep Cove, a video cued on the VCR.

"Africa."

He loved the word.

He rolled it around on his tongue.

Conjuring hundreds of memories of action, danger, and adventure from his youth.

"Afffriiicaaa."

When Zinc was eight his mom's Mum flew from London to Saskatchewan for Christmas. She stayed a month. Once Tom, his younger brother, was shuffled off to bed, Zinc would settle in with Granny for Juju Storytime. A full-fledged, card-carrying Daughter of the Empire, she read him terrifying tales from a battered book about "fuzzy-wuzzies and wogs."

Rudyard Kipling. "The Mark of the Beast." *Before we could stop him, Fleete dashed up the steps, patted two priests on the back, and was gravely grinding the ashes of his cigar-butt into the forehead of the red stone image of Hanuman . . .*

H. G. Wells. "Pollock and the Porroh Man." *It was in a swampy village on the lagoon river behind the Turner Peninsula that Pollock's first encounter with the Porroh man occurred . . .*

W.W. Jacobs. "The Monkey's Paw." *"To look at,"* said the sergeant-major, fumbling in his pocket, *"it's just an ordinary little paw, dried to a mummy . . ."*

Edward Lucas White. "Lukundoo." *The swelling on his right breast had broken. Van Rieten aimed the center line of the light at it and we saw it plainly. From his flesh, grown out of it, there protruded a head, such a head as the dried specimens Etcham had shown us, as if it were a miniature of the head of a Balunda fetish-man. It was black, shining black as the blackest African skin; it rolled the whites of its wicked, wee eyes and showed its microscopic teeth between lips repulsively negroid in their red fullness . . .*

"Mum!" Zinc's mom barked. "Are you scaring the boy again?"

White sons stained red with the Glories of Empire learned young you didn't fuck with the juju relics of conquered lands.

Which made him wonder about the snakeskin pouch of knucklebones Nick had described.

The chill of the front door opening shut down such thoughts in Zinc's mind.

"Chinese food okay?" Alex called down the hall. "I hope you haven't slaved for hours over a hot stove. The house I saw's a possible if we both mortgage our souls to the devil."

"I'm in the TV room," Zinc called back.

Alex appeared at the arch with a bag of Cantonese food in hand. "Good. A video by the fire. I hope it's a mushy romance."

He tossed her the video case, which Alex caught in her free hand. Above the scene of Redcoats and Africans locked in epic battle—did she not recognize the young officer shouting in their midst? Yes, he was listed in the credits above Richard Burton—four looming letters carved with African symbols made up the title *ZULU*. The back of the case bore a review from Martin and Porter's *Video Movie Guide:*

> *Several films have been made about the British Army and its exploits in Africa during the nineteenth century. Zulu ranks with the finest. A stellar cast headed by Stanley Baker and Michael Caine who charge through this story of an outmanned British garrison laid to siege by several thousand Zulu warriors. Based on fact, this one delivers the goods for action and tension.*

Alex frowned at Zinc and said, "Popcorn, bwana?"

Zinc replied, "Do you know what an irregular is?"

ZULU

Friday, January 14, 1994

Though Alex Hunt knew as much Colonial history as any royalist, her education was worthless in helping to solve this case. The exploits of Washington, Jefferson, Franklin, John Paul Jones, and Paul Revere were drilled into her, but she'd never pass a test on Lord Roberts of Kandahar or the Hero of Tel-el-Kebir. The Iron Duke of Wellington she knew, of course, and Gordon of Khartoum (thank you, Charlton Heston), but the gap was her

Colonial history was taught from the point of view of the muzzle end of Redcoat guns.

So it was back to school.

The Department of Asian Studies boomed at UBC, but given the population of blacks, there was no Department of African Studies. Professor Ken Mbhele of the Department of History, however, came from Africa, so under a gloomy canopy threatening to dump snow on academe, Alex entered the Buchanan Tower between the Main Library and George F. Curtis Law School, and rode an elevator up to the twelfth floor. The elevator opened into a hall hung with grad class photos and a case boasting publications by faculty members. *Mau Mau: A Lesson for Apartheid* by Kenneth Mbhele caught Hunt's eye.

A typist in the History office directed her to a line of doors behind the elevator bank. As Alex passed door 1218, then 1219, she spied the African mask at the end and hurried toward it. On the jamb was a nameplate: DR. K. MBHELE. The scowl on the carved wooden mask was as hateful as gangsta rap lyrics.

"Enter," said a thick South African voice when she knocked.

The office was barely wide enough to stretch out her arms. Shelves lined the flanking walls from ceiling to floor, crammed with books, boxes, reviews, and loose papers. Windows beyond the desk looked down on Buchanan quad, then over the Museum of Anthropology to the peaks across English Bay. The man who turned from the desk to face the opening door was dressed in khaki, and in his midthirties, with a tight Afro and mustache and goatee framing his face. His dark skin was blotched with white, prompting Alex to wonder if Mbhele had the disease pop star Michael Jackson claimed lightened his color.

"Yes?" said the professor.

"Doctor, my name is Alex Hunt." She passed him her published book. "The office said you'd be in today, and that your specialty is African history. In working on a third book—the second will be published soon—I hit a snag. Writer-to-writer, I hope you'll give me insight on the subject."

"Mau Mau?" asked Mbhele, one hand offering a chair

while the other indicated several copies of his book on the shelf.

"Rorke's Drift."

"I'm Zulu, Ms. Hunt. I'd dance if your interest was Isandlwana instead. Perhaps a British historian is more to your need?"

"History is history, is it not?"

"If you believe that, you also reject the need for Women's Studies. History is herstory, is it not? So can men not be trusted to canvass your female perspective adequately?"

"I'm American, Doctor. We also faced British guns. The battle was fought in your country, so Zulu outlook interests me." She recognized Isandlwana from Burton's introduction to the *Zulu* video. "Isandlwana and Rorke's Drift. I want the whole picture."

So, as Alex made notes, the African told her.

"Isandlwana," Mbhele said, "was the most crushing defeat the British Army ever suffered battling 'native' troops. In January of 1879, Lord Chelmsford led 3,500 men across the Mzinyathi River at Rorke's Drift, moving into Zululand to camp on the grassy slopes below Mount Isandlwana. There Chelmsford made the mistake of splitting his column, and while he was away campaigning with half his men, on January 22nd 20,000 Zulus overran the British camp. Chelmsford returned to find his base a smoking defeat of burnt wagons, torn tents, rubbish, and ripped corpses, 1,357 of his troops dead on the battlefield.

"You grasp the magnitude of our victory?" the Zulu said. "Armed with modern rifles and well-supplied, with support from artillery and a rocket battery, versed in African warfare and camped on ground of their own choosing, the British were annihilated by a tribal army armed with spears, clubs, and shields. But do they trumpet Isandlwana in light of the 'glorious' Defense of Rorke's Drift?"

Scribbling fast, Alex began a new page.

"Chelmsford had left one company of the 24th Regiment behind to guard supplies at Rorke's Drift. King Cetshwayo had warned his army not to charge entrenched positions, but those held back in reserve from Isandlwana disobeyed. Over six hours of constant hand-to-hand battle with barricaded whites, Zulus died by the bloody hundreds storming the post. Despite overwhelming odds, the British held Rorke's Drift, so it—not Isandlwana—entered the English language as a synonym for Imperial heroics."

"So Rorke's Drift was the *minor* battle that day?" Alex said.

"Not to hear them tell it." By heart, the African recited a poem for Hunt:

> "Her sons in gallant story,
> Shall sound old England's fame,
> And by fresh deeds of glory
> Shall keep alive her name;
> And when, above her triumphs,
> The golden curtains lift—
> Be treasured long, in page and song,
> The memory of Rorke's Drift.

"The British were literate. We Zulus weren't. They didn't want to lionize a major defeat, so Rorke's Drift portrays them as holding the Thin Red Line, while we're the butchers of Isandlwana who disemboweled the Redcoat dead."

"What!" Alex said, almost dropping her pen.

"When a Catholic encounters evil, he crosses himself. In the same way, Zulus believe killing someone in battle releases evil forces of 'blackness,' or *umnyama*. These can only be countered by cleansing rituals known as *zila*. To dissipate *umnyama* lingering about a corpse, the belly must be ripped open from sternum to groin. If the ritual's ignored and decomposition gasses swell the abdomen, a supernatural taint will attach to the slayer and swell him, too. Redcoats at Isandlwana and Rorke's Drift were disemboweled, which the British published as barbaric savagery. The truth is *they* chose the hour of battle, and while *umnyama* is always a danger, the night of January twenty-second to twenty-third was the new moon, a time when evil is so pervasive that if not cleansed it might curse the whole Zulu Nation."

"What brought the Zulu War to an end?"

"The Battle for Ulundi on the plain outside King Cetshwayo's royal kraal. Launching another invasion of

Zululand, Chelmsford included 900 cavalrymen among his 5,000 troops. Nearing our capital, the British formed a hollow square, riflemen four deep with fixed bayonets spiking all four sides, field guns and Gatlings at the corners, and the 17th Lancers, colors flying, at center with a band. When 20,000 of us attacked the square, the four firing lines blasted sustained volleys, dropping us by the hundreds so not a single Zulu got within thirty yards of them. Then when our *impi* faltered, the lancers burst from the square, trot, to canter, to gallop, to a pounding cavalry charge, impaling us on their lances and cutting us down with their sabers to trample underfoot, until not a Zulu was left alive on the killing plain."

"I see," Alex said.

"Do you?" Mbhele replied. He pointed to an African map on back of his office door. "North of the Kalahari Desert is Lake Ngami. When David Livingstone arrived in 1849, he found Eden. News of this miracle of creation drew hunters from Britain. From 1865 on, average annual kill was 5,000 elephants, 3,000 lions, 3,000 leopards, 3,000 ostriches, and 250,000 other fur-bearing mammals. The carnage was even more frenzied than the massacre of North American bison. It didn't stop until four million kills left nothing worth the hunters' powder and shot. British Colonials converted Eden into tusks, skins, and plumes.

"A century later, to destroy Mau Mau rebels hiding in Kenya, British forces strafed the Aberdare Mountains with rockets, bullets, and bombs. No Mau Mau died, but the assault was devastating. Blind elephants with shattered tusks and severed trunks trampled everything they encountered. Enraged buffalos with jaws and udders shot off charged trees and rocks. Lurching, snorting rhinos dragging mangled limbs turned on the birds that cleaned them. The tiny velvet monkeys that fell from the trees in shock savaged their companions as the planes roared overhead.

"It's fair to say," Mbhele said with irony in his voice, "the British respected Africa's wildlife as much as they did us. They're civilized on the surface"—pinky out, he held a phantom teacup to his lips—"but underneath, they're a vicious lot. The end result of their Zulu War was apartheid, torture, prison, and death. For his part in the Soweto Uprising of 1967, the first of the great convulsions to shake South Africa, my father was jailed on Robben Island with Mandela, to die on a contraption called the Airplane, suspended from iron bars with arms and legs tied behind his back."

Alex closed her book. "Thank you for your insight, perspective, and time."

"You haven't told me the snag you hit that brought you here?"

"I'm hunting for a trophy box from Rorke's Drift. The name Rex Lancelot Craven is carved into the lid. If my source is correct, inside are two compartments lined with velvet. On red plush, the upper half has a bayonet and Victoria Cross. On black plush, the lower half has a Zulu club and snakeskin pouch. The pouch contains ten bones, each carved with an eye."

Mbhele rapped his head as if to jog his memory. "I saw that box somewhere," he said. "Not the actual case, but a photograph."

"Where?"

"Patience, Ms. Hunt. My memory is human. I recall I saw the photo while researching Mau Mau history for my book. Yes. Now I remember. I saw the trophy box in back issues of *The Times*."

From Mbhele's office in the Buchanan Tower, Alex walked to the adjacent Main Library, passing the Ladner Clock Tower, the most phallic prong of architecture she had ever seen. The Main Library dated from 1925, a neo-Gothic heap of cold gray stone, up the front steps of which Alex climbed, reaching double doors and a sign of the times: NO ROLLERBLADING, NO SKATEBOARDING IN THE LIBRARY, to enter a medieval vault and climb again to the Main Concourse, a soaring banquet hall of a chamber with timber rafters way up there and card catalog and computers down here, the librarian at the central Information Desk directing her through a door beyond marked BOOK STACKS, STACK LEVEL FIVE, where she pushed through a turnstile and trudged up even more steps among sixty-seven miles of musty bookstacks creaking under the weight of 3 million books and 5.5 million nonbook items such as maps, recordings, and microforms. Turning right, then right again, Alex followed the path of GOVERNMENT PUBLICATIONS AND MICROFORMS signs to the Microforms Desk.

Under call number AW1 R103, the Main Library had a complete collection of *The Times* of London from 1785 to November 30, 1993.

The Microforms librarian led her to an alley lined with thousands of small brown boxes. "What year do you want?" he asked.

Mbhele had told Alex the Mau Mau Rebellion lasted from 1952 to 1960. It was an antiwhite insurrection by the Kikuyu tribe of British-ruled Kenya, fought to drive Imperialists from the land so ancient customs could be restored. To prevent infiltration by British spies, Mau Mau was bound together by horrific ritual oaths used to ensure complete devotion to the cause. By the close of 1956, 100 whites, 2,000 African loyalists, and 11,000 rebels had been killed. Another 20,000 Kikuyu starved in detention camps, where "intensive efforts" were made to resubject them to the Queen.

The year Nick was born seemed to Alex the best year to start.

"Nineteen fifty-six," she replied.

The librarian removed box *The Times Reel 103 July 1955 to July 1956* from the shelf, then withdrew a spool of film. Hunt followed him into the stacks to a carrel where he threaded the spool through a microfilm reader. Seated facing the three-foot-square screen, she slowly turned the handle to advance through history, published day by day in *The Times*.

"Magnify here," the man said, tapping a top center lever. "High to the left. Low to the right. Call if you want to print."

He left Hunt to her work.

So here she sat, right hand going round and round, tracking yet another black-versus-white war, eyes scanning every page for Mau Mau coverage linked to the trophy box.

As column after column passed before her eyes, the American drew parallels to trends in her country: White Supremacists and armed militias and men hidden by sheets; the pounding hate of ghetto rap and rioting in Harlem, Watts, and Central L.A.; the breakdown of justice where whites and blacks on juries protect their own against conviction for attacking the other race, as tribal hatred kills the common good and white or black vigilantes fill the void, borders crumbling as the global exodus demands in, the spider's web of Internet a hatemonger's dream, population exploding as resources shrink, and bigots who don't feel *All right, Jack,* hunt for someone to blame.

But suddenly that angst was gone as she rolled another page, for there in the January 27, 1956 issue of *The Times,* on a page of reports out of Africa, the main column devoted to the Mau Mau Rebellion, with sidebars on Rhodesia, Tanganyika, and South Africa, Alex saw the photograph of Lance-Sergeant Rex Craven's Rorke's Drift trophy box. It was—*The Times* told her—now possessed by a Canadian heir, RCMP Constable Ted Craven of Lethbridge, Alberta. Of interest to all appalled by Mau Mau oaths would be the snakeskin pouch with its witchcraft bones.

Alex sought out the librarian, who inserted a copy card into a microfilm printer, and, for twenty cents a page, ran off magnified copies.

CHESSBOARD

Monday, January 17, 1994

The crux of the Crown's case against Nick involved proving his mom's blood stained the right sleeve of his Red Serge tunic, so this morning Wilde and Kidd were in the lawyer's harbor-view office tightening the evidence. The snowfall threatened on Friday had bypassed the city for the Interior, and now weak winter sunshine streamed from a cloudless sky. Wilde's office doubled as a black museum full of relics from his greatest wins, displayed in glass cabinets arranged around the marble chessboard floor like chess pieces. In the cabinet to Kidd's right the sawed-off end of a broomstick lay diagonally across colors won from the Headhunters Motorcycle Club. In the cabinet to her left arsenic graphs followed a patient's decline. Kidd sat facing Wilde, who sat behind his desk facing "The Trial of Oscar Wilde" mounted behind the Mountie. At the far end of the desk, a chessboard was in play.

"I see you play white?" commented Kidd.

"White gets the advantage, since white always goes first."

"So I've learned," the black said dryly.

"The setup on the board is a fork. Black is about to lose a rook no matter what it does. Saving this rook means that rook's taken. Save that rook and this rook goes. Black's forked in more ways than one," the lawyer punned.

"Court's a chess game to you?"

"And checkmate's my play. Strategy takes the board every time. Craven says he left his mom alive at five-ten. We've got the man who dry-cleaned his tunic. Since one of the brass buttons came off the uniform's sleeve, requiring the cleaner to sew it back on, he swears the cuff wasn't stained when Craven picked his Red Serge up shortly before the murder. You know he didn't enter the house while you were there or get near his mom's corpse before it went to the morgue. That leaves Knight three moves on the board:

"One, Craven innocently stained his tunic with her blood *before* he left the house;

"Two, Craven's tunic was tainted by other exhibits between the time you seized it from his home and Wood performed the test;

"Three, the DNA test was faulty."

A knock on the door interrupted them. Wilde's secretary entered with a FedEx letter. "From Knight," the lawyer said as he ripped it open. Reading it once, then reading it twice, he passed the puzzling correspondence to Kidd.

The original of this courtesy copy to Lyndon Wilde QC had been sent to Staff Sergeant Tipple at Coquitlam GIS. Under Knight's letterhead, the top sheet read: *The trophy box in this picture copied from the London* Times *is missing from the attic of Dora Craven's home, and so is the cabinet with her monthly records. Since both are essential to Corporal Craven's defense, I ask that you*

*undertake a thorough search for them. I may inform the
trial judge you were asked to pursue this lead seven weeks
before plea.*

Clipped to the covering letter was a blowup of the
trophy box.

"Africa?" said Rachel. "How does that fit into the
case?"

"The club," said Wilde. "It must be the club." He
poked the knobkerrie in the trophy box. "If Knight's
not careful, this could explode in his face. Who but Craven would know about the box? Is that where he got
the club to bludgeon his mom? I wish the knob were
faceup so we could see if the striking side is carved with
a zigzag pattern."

"Africa?" Rachel repeated. "I know where to start.
Dial this number, and put us on speaker phone." She
fed Wilde seven digits, which he punched in. One, two,
three rings . . .

"Biology."

"Dermott Toop, please."

"Derm, it's for you."

Far-off voice: "Take a number and I'll call back."

"He's in the middle of a test and can't—"

"Tell him Kidd's on the line and it's important."

"Kidd's on the line and says it's urgent."

The far-off voice: "Put her on speaker phone."

"Derm?"

"I hear you, Rach. Something wrong?"

"Defense threw us a curve ball in the Craven case.
You're South African. Know anything about a trophy
box from Rorke's Drift? Contains a Zulu club and a
pouch of bones, with a bayonet and Victoria Cross. *Rex
Lancelot Craven* carved on the lid."

"You need my cousin, Rachel. Got Three-Way Call
on that phone?"

Yes, Wilde nodded.

"I'm in Lyndon's office. Give me the number, then
hold on while I dial." Depressing the receiver till she
heard three short tones followed by a dial tone, Rachel
called UBC. Just one ring . . .

"Hello. Ken Mbhele."

"Ken, my name is Rachel Kidd. I'm a friend of your
cousin. Hold a moment while I connect Dermott to this

line." She pressed the receiver again. "Derm, we're all set."

"Ken?"

"Hello, Dermott."

"Rachel needs your help. Ever come across a trophy box from Rorke's Drift?"

Mbhele groaned. "Powerful magic, that box. A woman was here Friday asking about it, too."

"Who?" Rachel said, jumping in.

"A writer named Alex Hunt. She's working on a book about—"

"That fucking DeClercq," sneered Wilde.

DeClercq looked up from the stack of paperwork on his desk to find Chan at the door. "It must be serious, for you to come to me."

"I've had a complaint about you."

"From whom?"

"Lyndon Wilde. He alleges Special X is nosing into the Craven case. Seems he's keeping track of who visits Nick, and you did last Thursday. Then Friday has Zinc's girlfriend at UBC, and what she uncovers is sent to him through Vic Knight. He claims you're using Alex Hunt as a puppet to flout my order."

"A weak circumstantial case, if you ask me."

"You think Nick's innocent?"

"I'm certain of it, Eric. But I'm trying to adhere to your—"

Chan's palm became a stop sign. "The night you sat with Sally and me at our first Red Serge Ball, how high a backlash price did you pay? And when you stood up for Jack when they tried to kick him out for being gay, I heard some call you names behind your back. And had you not backed Zinc in that Cutthroat mess, where would he be now? And then there's Peggy, and you were there again. I respect your loyalty. When Nick became a suspect and we disagreed, I said, 'When it comes to racism, I think I'm much more sensitive than you.' That was out of line and I want to take it back. As far as Wilde's concerned, I told him I was shocked. In this day and age, who'd dare think Alex was under Zinc's thumb? The Craven case meshes with her other work, so the last thing I'd do was tell him to keep the little woman in line. I fear I may also have said, 'When it comes to sexism, I think I'm much more sensitive than you.' "

ASYLUM

Coquitlam

Boarded up and pillared like a Deep South mansion, moonlight silvering its eerie facade, West Lawn loomed above the Riverview road, as Alex drove the switchback up to the asylum.

Unknown to her, Evil Eye followed.

The earliest recorded case of insanity in B.C. was in 1850. Back then, male lunatics were deported to Napa Asylum in California or jailed. When B.C. joined Canada in 1871, the province was told "the Dominion Government has declined to take charge of the lunatics in B.C. as it might be too large an undertaking." Such has been the attitude of the East always been to Lotusland. To appease the people of New Westminster, who hoped their city and not Victoria would be the new capital, Victoria decided to build the B.C. lunatic asylum here as a consolation. To the outrage of New West, it was built on the cricket pitch, with chain gangs from the local jail raising the two-story "nuthouse." When the first inmates arrived in 1878, Dr. John Ash, the member for Comox, suggested to the legislature that it not be made too comfortable or those with no right to be inside would flock in. Robert Smith of Yale voiced he always felt New Westminster the proper place for lunatics. The first brick laundry was built in 1894, all washing done by hand by the Chinese patients.

By 1901, the asylum was packed. No wonder when the main causes of patient madness were listed as heredity, intemperance, syphilis, and masturbation. So in July 1905, eighteen inmates trudged upriver to clear Colony Farm and the benchland above. By 1911, the patient farm was producing 700 tons of crops and 20,000 gallons of milk per year, and uphill on Mount Coquitlam, Essondale Mental Hospital was taking shape. On April 1, 1913, the doors of West Lawn confined 340 chronic males, followed later by Center Lawn (the psychopathic unit), then East Lawn for chronic females. In 1942, electroshock therapy began, and by 1957 when Dora Craven started work in the new Essondale laundry, psychosurgery—lobotomies—was in vogue.

Tonight was the second trip Alex made to Essondale—now Riverview—Hospital.

The first was this morning.

Having found photographic proof of the Rorke's Drift trophy box, she had turned her attention to the missing files. "If the killer stole them after murdering Dora, why take the heavy cabinet?" Zinc had asked on the weekend. "I doubt he, if it's a he, could lower it from the attic by himself. In any event, why not just remove the files?"

"You don't think the killer took them?"

"No," he replied.

So after dropping Zinc at the airport this morning—he was off to an Interpol conference in Ottawa—Alex drove inland to Riverview. From 1957 until she retired last June, Dora worked first in the laundry, then after it closed a decade ago and cleaning was shipped out, on the food line in East Lawn. Dora's life centered around work and her son, so odds were if she had a confidante, that person also worked at Riverview. Coquitlam GIS had pegged Nick early as prime suspect, so Alex wondered if Kidd had questioned all Dora's work-mates in East Lawn. That's what she'd done this morning, and that's how she heard about Flora.

Flora launched the Home Cooking Restaurant in Port Coquitlam. Dora came in every Saturday for lunch. Flora was a movie buff so classic films played on video above the counter. A joke with the regulars was to act along, Flora doing Bergman while Moe the Plumber was Bogart in *Casablanca,* Flora doing Davis while Dora was Baxter in *All About Eve.* When Vancouver joined L.A. and New York as the top three filming centers, Flora changed serving food into set catering. Depending on the job, sometimes Dora helped out.

Flora and Dora.

The Home Cooking pair.

Lunar shadows lurked in the grounds of the lunatic asylum, stalking her car as Alex snaked up the hillside to West Lawn. At Colony Farm Road, where Bert and Ernie had turned right toward the Forensic Institute huddling by the river, she had turned left, then right, to angle up the slope, skirting the sign RIVERVIEW HOSPITAL SITE MAP 300 METERS, the headlights on HOSPITAL TRAFFIC ONLY stenciled on the road, the winter trees bared of leaves to their skeletons, through which Colony Farm stretched flat below, moonlight sheening its ditches, rivers, and pools, the sole sound—but for her car—the squeal of steel wheels on train tracks edging the highway. Where Holly Drive forked into Pine Terrace she branched left, switching back up Fern Terrace toward Pennington Hall, as West Lawn, Center Lawn, East Lawn lined the hillside to her right, three antebellum plantations out of *Gone With The Wind*. Forming a reverse Z up the rise, Boxwood Drive zigged back in front of West Lawn, but Alex drove up Clover Street to park behind. The dousing headlights caught a sign: CAUTION! OVERHEAD HAZARDS. WATCH FOR FALLING OBJECTS.

Like Poe's House of Usher, West Lawn was crumbling down.

Alex parked beside the only other car. The elderly woman behind the wheel climbed out. "Spooky, huh?" she whispered, when Hunt joined her in the creepy shadow of West Lawn. "Easy to see why it's used as a horror movie set."

"What was filmed here?"

"*Jennifer 8,* with Andy Garcia and Uma Thurman. *The X Files,* of course. *Tales From The Crypt* comes in after *Psychotic,* which I feed."

"Dora worked on *Psychotic*?"

"Only for a day. Then the star broke his wrist, so production shut down. I went to California for a month and just got back. Didn't hear poor Dora was dead until after Christmas."

"Thanks," said Alex, "for meeting me tonight."

"You're much younger than you seemed on the phone. It's obvious your nerves are stronger than mine. No way would I work alone in here at night. Her files are that important?"

"Maybe," Alex said.

"As I mentioned on the phone, West Lawn is gutted. It's the oldest building at Riverview. Both Center Lawn and East Lawn are still hospitals. West Lawn is no more than a shell. There's no heat, and no power, until both generators return. I hope you brought a good flashlight and batteries."

From the sack in her hand, Hunt withdrew a six-volt Duracell. The lantern shot a beam at the building when she switched it on, spotlighting five stories of brick with dormers high above, upper windows broken and those at this level boarded up, the circle sweeping here and there like a prison break. Nineteen steps climbed to an iron door.

"Were you and Dora close?" Alex asked.

"Close enough," Flora said as they ascended.

"Did she talk about her son?"

"All the time. Hard to believe he killed her, from how proud she was."

"Did Dora mention having twins?"

"News to me! You must be mistaken. Not a word was said." From her parka Flora produced a key worthy of Fort Knox. This went into a lock capable of securing the Crown jewels.

The door swung open as West Lawn breathed a sigh. Halitosis of decay fouled Hunt's nose. The lantern beam stabbed in over a tiled floor, while hesitant footsteps picked a path through the rubble. Each step echoed into black vaults beyond.

"How'd her files get here?" Alex asked.

"Filming involves waiting, waiting, waiting," said Flora, "for prima donnas to demand something *now*! When I suggested Dora find a task to kill time, she told me she'd been meaning to cull some old files for years, so I had the boys swing by and pick them up. Then we shut down. So here they are."

"The files moved when?"

"End of November."

Slamming the door, Flora locked it from inside, as Evil Eye—car hidden—skulked shadow to shadow around back of West Lawn.

Moonlight on steel.

*   *   *

One summer at Cannon Beach when Alex was a teen in braces, she'd read the "Had-I-But-Known" novels of Mary Roberts Rinehart. The plot was standard: foolish female finds herself involved in a situation she's been warned to avoid, then to prove how pigheaded she is, forges on risking life and limb until she's plucked from the jaws of death, hopefully by her lover. See-through nighties are a big help. "Had I but known then what I know now, these awful murders would not have occurred," she opens in retrospect, while the reader shouts, "No, you fool, stay clear of the asylum!" But our plucky heroine will not be deterred.

Recalling such "HIBK"'s with a grin as she shut the door behind Flora, the old woman having shown her where the files were, Alex turned the key to lock herself in. This being the age of hero(ine)s with balls, forget plucky airheads and plucking lovers, and besides, hers was off in Ottawa, back down the circular staircase she went to the ground floor, unaware Flora was having her throat cut outside.

Had she but known . . .

The ground-floor kitchen was as makeshift as could be: a portable stove, fridge, and sink in what was once a Quiet Room, where if she listened hard she could hear hallucinations lingering from bedlam frights. Moonlight seeped through gaps around boarded-up windows. Plaster crumbled from the ceiling to crack underfoot. Pipes and wires were exposed in patches torn from the walls. The last vestige of a hospital was the iron bed to one side with restraint straps. And next to it stood the cabinet full of Dora's files.

Her realm shrinking to the pool from the lantern's beam, in parka, scarf, gloves, and mukluks against the cold, Alex got down to work.

The records began the year Nick was born: 455 thin files, one for each month, advancing from January 1956 to November 1993. The first eleven months of 1956 were filed by Nick's father, until December 7th when he shot himself. Only with that final month did Dora take over, completing her husband's work for the year to compute a tax return.

In file *February 1956,* Alex found reference to the trophy box. A letter from London dated January 28:

Dear Sir:

I note your Rorke's Drift trophy box reproduced in
The Times. *My name is Nigel Hammond, and I'm the*
London agent for South African buyers who repatriate
artifacts removed from that Colony in Imperial times.
To this end I shall be in Canada the first week of
March, and shall stop in Lethbridge to discuss the Zulu
izikhombi *bones in the box.*
Yours truly,
Nigel Hammond

The first week of March, according to Force memos on
file, saw Nick's dad involved in a manhunt north of the
Arctic Circle, so if Hammond did make it to Lethbridge,
only Dora was home. As there was no follow-up letter
concerning the bones, which Nick found in the box in
the attic ten years later, obviously the Zulu relics
weren't returned.

Alex removed the Hammond letter, then refiled the
file. In the darkness about the lantern pool, something
scurried by.

Half an hour later, in file *January 1957,* the word
placement caught her eye. It was in a letter mailed to
Lethbridge from Medicine Hat, written to Dora by Ted's
younger sister, Nick's Aunt Eleanor:

Sister Superior of Sacred Heart vows the placement
has the sanctity of confession. She is someone I loved
as a child. A thankful donation to Sacred Heart would
be in order.

Alex removed the Eleanor letter, then refiled the file.
From the darkness about the lantern pool, rodents
watched her.

As time advanced toward the hours of the next day,
Alex combed diligently through the files, tracking Dora
struggling to make ends meet, imagining Nick growing
up as his mom grew old, but for thirty-odd years there
was nothing more concerning the Rorke's Drift trophy
box or Sacred Heart "placement." Finally, she reached
the last file, *November 1993.*

A rare letter from Eleanor to Dora:

*Sister Superior just phoned to say the placed twin
has returned. She revealed nothing about us, which led
to a threat. I don't have your unlisted number, so this
letter. Do you release Sister Superior from her vow
of silence?*

Removing the *placed twin* letter, Alex refiled the file and
closed the cabinet. It was almost midnight by her watch.
Lantern knifing the darkness, she picked her way
through the rubble toward the stairs, her footsteps echoing down the hollow hall, then up the spiral staircase to
the second floor. Here peeled paint and grilled moonlight led to the exit. Unlocking the steel door and pulling
it open, Alex stepped into midnight and turned to lock
up, then jumped when fleet sneakers ran up the steps
behind her.

Before she could react, a bayonet pinned her hand
holding the letters to the door.

The lantern tumbled down the steps and smashed to
extinguish the beam. A glove clamped over Hunt's
mouth to muffle her yelp of pain. When the lunger
yanked free from her pinned palm, the letters found in
Dora's files fluttered to the ground. At the corner of
her eye, Alex caught a black mask within a black hood,
madness in the pupils glaring from moonlit whites.
Adrenaline powering her with do-or-die strength, Hunt
lurched back as hard as she could and kicked her attacker's leg, sending him or her or it stumbling down the
steps. She wrenched the key from the lock and shoul-
dered in the door, intent on seeking asylum from the
insane by locking herself alone in the insane asylum, but
fumbling fingers dropped the key, which clanged down
the steps, bouncing between the feet of the psycho lunging up.

The stench of fear met the stench of madness halfway.

Shoving the door behind her, Alex dashed into West
Lawn. Ahead across the tiled floor she fled for marble
stairs. The door crashed open a moment later, the black
silhouette stark against moonlight behind, and Evil Eye
followed close on her heels. One two three . . . she
veered left to scramble up fifteen steps, a barred window
on the landing overlooking a court outside, then one two

three . . . she reversed and ran up seven more steps.
Now on the third floor, the psycho a breath behind, a
slash of the bayonet slitting across the back of her parka,
her heart in her throat as she sprinted down the corridor
jogging right, her mental compass flummoxed by twists
and turns in the maze, room after room after room
flashing by on both sides, moonlight paling as darker
then darker then darker grew the hall, glass splintering
underfoot along SHIT scrawled large on the wall, until a
swipe from the lunger slashed hair from her head as its
tip drew blood from her neck.

A recurring nightmare in her past was fleeing down a
hall, with something monstrous—she dared not look—
gnashing fangs behind. A door ahead beckoned, reach
it and she was safe, her hand extending in slow motion
to touch the knob, then like a poorly spliced film missing
frames, she was back down the hall with the door ahead,
having lost precious ground that the demon behind
had gained.

That was bad.

This was worse.

The set director of *Psychotic* had vandalized West
Lawn, painting the peeling plaster with tormented self-
portraits, reminding Alex of the wretches she'd encountered this morning, shuffling around the asylum grounds
with nowhere to go, many with cigarettes in hand but
no matches, begging one by one for a light when she
parked by East Lawn to question the food line. The
faces along the hall grew grimmer as the moonlight
waned, misshapen heads and wonky eyes and throwback
devolution, the last figure squatting with knees drawn up
and head laying on its side, eyes aligned vertically with
the sword rammed down into his ear, the hilt a Christian
crucifix with Jesus on the cross.

Save me, Alex prayed.

Bursting upon the spiral staircase winding up and
down, not a hint of light below to guide her way, crash
into something and the blade would spear her back,
Alex corkscrewed clockwise up the most filmed stairs in
B.C. So many patients had hurled themselves down the
well in the early days that blacksmiths sealed this drop
inside a wrought-iron cage, so walls to the left, bars to
the right, up, up, up she went. Eleven steps, turn . . .

eleven steps, turn . . . the bayonet slashing behind, shredding her parka and slitting her jeans, a few cuts drawing blood. Eleven steps, turn . . . eleven steps, turn . . . until she hit the top.

Sprinting back the way she came two stories below, Alex passed toilet stalls without toilets in rooms with bashed-in doors, linoleum turning to wooden slats that creaked and heaved as she trampled, moonbeams spilling through dormers left and right, luring her to dead ends should she alter course. *There must be stairs, must be stairs descending soon,* she thought. *Stairs to the exit open to the night . . .*

Alex tripped.

The shadow of the psycho pounced onto Hunt. Splinters drove through her gloves to pierce both palms when she hit the floor and skidded. The bayonet's shadow warned it was coming down, so Alex rolled a jiffy before the blade stabbed the slat under her head. On hands and knees she crabbed around a pillar supporting the roof, a scramble of ring-around-a-rosy with Evil Eye behind, ignoring the pain that seared from her wound to grasp a grating half wrenched from a dormer to yard herself back on her feet. Releasing the grill, the bars intercepted the lunger in a stab, steel upon steel clanging like dueling swords.

Yanking open a fire door led to another hall, Alex moving so fast she missed the stairs to her left, so on she ran through squares of moonlight down the corridor, the dreamscape of the asylum grounds flitting below to her right, conical shrubs pruned to perfection awash in lunar glow, vast lawns with skeletal trees sloping to Colony Farm. The dormers cast a shadow chase across the rubbled floor, nooks and crannies echoing the footfalls behind, the psycho gaining as Alex ran through an open frame, wires dangling from the door like snakes trapped in a box. *God!*, the stairs within were blocked by crisscrossed timbers, the lunger slashing as she entered the dark unknown, dodging right to escape the blade raking her shoulder, left hand hooking to swing her around the corner ahead, then suddenly there was no floor beneath her feet.

Alex found asylum by plunging down a wedged-open elevator shaft.

CHARTER OF RIGHTS

Like Hanging Judge Begbie in Colonial days, Morgan Hatchett was on a crusade to thwart "American rowdies." Few of those she loathed were American in fact, but all were infected with the "American disease." For what she saw south of the border was a country of cities, towns, streets, school yards, parks, and even backyards stalked by Bill of Rights predators, perverts, and punks. *Bleak House* court cases ground on for years as Bill of Rights nitpickers pretended pinhead legal points were of life-or-death importance. And now—God Save the Queen—the disease was rampant here. What happened to the good old days of British law when crime charged in March, tried in April, appealed in May, ended on the gallows or with hard time in June? What the people wanted was a Charter of Responsibilities, not the Charter of Rights based on the U.S. Bill of Rights that pinko Trudeau yoked on the courts in 1982. For with that abortion came "American disease," the deadly symptom of which was scum whining, "Gimme my Rights!"

True, the deadly Cutter-Hatchett One-Two Punch could bloody the Charter in the Court of Appeal, but it was a liberal—Elizabeth Toussaint—determining who tried what below. When Toussaint was appointed to the Supreme Court of Canada, Hatchett lobbied Ottawa for the vacant administrative job. No sooner was The Hatchet ensconced as the Chief Justice of the trial court than every important Charter case was channeled to the right wing or usurped by herself. With her in control at this level, Charter Rights were doomed. With Cutter to stack his Court and back her on appeal, Charter Rights were doomed there, too. That left the Supreme Court of Canada to take the heat . . . freeing a man who dragged a sixty-five-year-old woman from a wheelchair and raped her because he was too drunk to form criminal intent . . . freeing a man because police took a DNA sample from one rape and used it in another . . . Yes, in these scarlet robes she'd hold a thin red line . . . until public outrage forced the SCC to buckle.

The battle was hand-to-hand.

"Section 8 of the Charter of Rights and Freedoms," Knight said, reading from the blue *Revised Statutes of Canada* in both hands, *"Everyone has the right to be secure against unreasonable search or seizure."* The book dropped with a thud. *"Semayne's Case*, 1604," he argued, grabbing the dustiest legal volume Nick had ever seen, "77 English Reports, page 194: *That the house of every one is to him as his castle and fortress, as well for his defense against injury and violence, as for his repose . . ."*

"We're not in law school, Mr. Knight."

"Perhaps you should be, Judge."

"I'm warning you! For the *last* time!"

The book dropped with a thump onto the Charter as Knight snatched a dustier volume. *"Entick v. Carrington* in 1765 . . ."

"Not so fast, Counsel. Back to *Semayne's Case*." In front of her to be read through glasses perched on the tip of her nose was the judgment she'd already written prior to legal argument. *"In all cases when the King is party, the Sheriff (if the doors be not open) may break the party's house, either to arrest him, or to do other execution of the K.'s process, if otherwise he cannot enter."* Whipping off her glasses, Hatchett wagged them at Knight. "Limitation, Counsel, that's what concerns us here."

"Concerns *you*, not me," Knight snapped back. "That case firmly enunciated the principle that 'a man's home is his castle,' and not even the King himself had right to invade its sanctity without authority of a judicial warrant. That's what *K.'s process* means. Corporal Kidd had no warrant to enter my client's home, so even without the Charter, I should win this point. And I want it on record you're reading from reasons you've already prepared."

"One more comment like that and you show cause for contempt. I'm reading from questions to clarify a major point in this case. The issue raised by Corporal Kidd's seizure of the accused's tunic from his home without a warrant concerns police authority to enter a private dwelling in exigent circumstances to prevent evidence being destroyed."

"Exigent circumstances are not a limitation on the law in *Semayne's Case. Colet v. The Queen,* 1981 Supreme Court Re—"

"Shut up. I'm speaking. Under the common law, situations of urgency will always permit police entry, as in the case of hot pursuit, or of a person in danger of death, or to prevent evidence being destroyed. Nothing in the Charter extinguishes that. Had Corporal Kidd not seized the tunic it would have gone to the cleaners and we would not be here. All the accused lost was a chance to cripple this case."

"He wasn't even home! What the accused lost—what we *all* lose by this intrusion—is the security guaranteed by the common law *and* the Charter that police will not invade our homes. That's the fundamental precept of a free society."

"No, Mr. Knight. Order and crime prevention is the precept. If we can't walk every street in this city, we aren't free."

"The Fourth Amendment to the Constitution of the United States reads: *The right of the people to be secure in their—*"

"The land of circus trials? Don't waste my time. I find I'm none the wiser after reading American Law."

"None the wiser perhaps, Judge, but so much better informed."

"That's it!" Hatchett stormed, throwing down her pen. "Apologize for your behavior, or show cause why I shouldn't hold you in contempt."

"Apologize?" said Knight. "Here's my apology. Your ladyship is right, and I am wrong as your ladyship usually is."

"You're saying I'm usually wrong! Court Reporter, read that back!"

The reporter cleared his throat. "Your ladyship is right, and I am wrong as your ladyship usually is," he quoted.

"It's on record, Counsel. I cite your apology as the contempt."

"Mr. Reporter," Knight replied with a gotcha grin. "Be sure you put a comma between the words 'wrong' and 'as.' "

That was earlier in the trial, but this was now.

Nick's Red Serge tunic with blood on the cuff was ruled admissible as evidence, a foregone conclusion before the trial began, with lengthy reasons damaging the Charter to follow.

The tunic before the jury, Lyndon Wilde QC called the last witness for the prosecution.

"The Crown calls Colin Wood," he said, and checked his pocket watch against the clock high on the wall behind the dock.

MALARIA PILLS

Thursday, January 20, 1994

Hissing . . .
    Bubbling . . .
    Breathing . . .
    . . . *blip* . . . *blip* . . . *blip* . . .
Zinc was back up The Peak in that hospital room in Hong Kong, recuperating from surgery to mend his brain. Intensive Care Unit sounds were old friends of his, the hissing and breathing from an oxygen mask, the bubbling of a suction tube hooked in a mouth, the . . . *blip* . . . *blip* . . . *blip* . . . of a cardiac monitor tracking heartbeats. The bed was similar to his: wraparound curtain, emergency button, and overhead poles with nutrient bags dangling snakelike tubes. The only difference was the patient in the bed.

Alex lay in a coma in the ICU of Royal Columbian Hospital, her leg fractured in two places and her palm punctured. Other cuts and bruises traumatized her body.

Tuesday morning, a yardman had found a throat-cut woman stabbed twice in the abdomen hidden near the old bakery behind West Lawn. Following a trail of blood into the asylum, Coquitlam Members were led to an elevator shaft wedged open for filming. Shining a flashlight down two stories revealed Alex crumpled on top of the elevator stopped at the third floor. Zinc was on the next flight back from Ottawa.

A CAT scan revealed no injury to her brain. It was dangerous to anesthetize her in a coma, so operating on the broken leg was postponed. Doctors set the fractures and put her in traction. For two nights, Zinc sat vigil by her bed, and here DeClercq found him nodding off in a chair.

"Zinc?"

"Uh?"

"Morning. Time to go home. I'll see you're called if Alex comes to."

The inspector rubbed his eyes and washed his hand down his face.

"I'm sorry," said the chief superintendent. "I was daft to suggest an 'irregular' do our job."

"We both thought it a good idea, and so did Alex. The fault lies with the asshole who stabbed her at West Lawn."

"Docs still noncommittal?"

"Last I heard. She may be out for weeks or she may come around today."

"The wound through her palm approximates the width of the bayonet in *The Times*. Tool Marks gauged the blade from the standard diameter of the Victoria Cross in the photo."

"How'd Chan react?"

"The gloves are off. Alex being American involves Special X. We're free to investigate any connections to Nick's case."

"Speak to Wilde?"

"His reply was 'So what? West Lawn housed hundreds of madmen over the years. Someone drawn to the building by psychosis took umbrage at burglars inside his former home.' "

"The man's deadly."

"That's why we like him appointed to prosecute."

"Anything in Dora's files?"

"Nothing about the trophy box or possible twin. I culled them myself."

On the bed, Alex stirred and one eye blinked open. Galvanized, the Mounties leaned toward her. Through the oxygen mask and around the suction tube, Alex muttered, ". . . twin . . ."

They sat on either side of the bed and listened to her story, about finding Flora, then finding the files, then finding the letters. . . .

Nigel Hammond, writing from London, on January 28, 1956: "Saw box in *The Times*," mumbled Alex. "Traveling to Lethbridge, first week in March, to buy Zulu bones. *Iza*–something. Can't remember. Ted in Arctic. Only Dora home."

Eleanor Craven, Ted's sister, writing to Dora from Medicine Hat, January 1957: "Sister Superior of Sacred Heart vows placement has sanctity of confession. A nun she knew as a child."

Eleanor, from Medicine Hat, November 1993: "Sister Superior phoned to say 'placed twin' back. Vow resulted in threat."

That off her chest, Hunt breathed a sigh of relief and fatigue. Zinc clutched her hand when she closed her eyes. "One question," said DeClercq, "and we're through for today. What do you recall about the person chasing you?"

"Black mask. Black hood. Rest a blur. Afraid if I looked back I'd trip over rubble. Maybe Flora saw something. Ask her."

Now was not the time for guilt over Flora's death, so both cops said nothing and got up to leave. DeClercq withdrew a colored cardboard cutout from his pocket. He held it up for Alex to see and said, "Katt forged this for you."

The cardboard medal he placed on her pillow bore a cross pattée with the Royal Crest over a scrolled "For Valor."

The Mounties stood bathed in sun beside Chandler's Ford, halfway between where Dora died and where her son would stand trial. The glare off the river was blinding so they faced away.

"The killer took the letters. They weren't found," said DeClercq. "He jumped Flora coming out and she told him about the files. By culling the files, Alex cleaned them and brought him the evidence."

"Him or her," Chandler clarified. "What will Wilde say?"

" 'That's what trials are for,' " answered DeClercq. "Nick saved Alex from the cliff on Deadman's Island. My bet is Wilde'll think she's paying him back. We use the man because he's tough and loves to win. Unfortunately, this time he's on their side."

"Their side is our side."

"Welcome to Wonderland, Alice."

"Sacred Heart and Nigel Hammond. Two new leads. We need something concrete Wilde can't explain. Which lead is mine?"

"Hammond," said DeClercq. "Failed Catholic though I am, I know the byways of the Church. Nick is the only birth registered to Dora. Every province, territory, or northern state's been checked. Adoptions in the fifties were unregulated and loose. Baby on the doorstep. Homes for unwed mothers. Daughters sent out of town. Scandals hushed up. Anonymous placement of the twin would not be hard. Every city with a cathedral has a Sacred Heart. My gut says the one we want lost its Sister Superior in November."

"The dates?" said Chandler. "Is Hammond the twins' father? Ted's in the Arctic when he arrives. Dora falls for Hammond, then he's off. Nine months later, his kids are born. Which might explain why Ted shot himself that night."

"I'll check if Medicine Hat still has a record of the inquest."

"Hammond wrote from London as an agent for African interests. I worked the Ghoul case with Scotland Yard. DCS Hilary Rand is a commander now. If Hammond's alive, she'll find him."

"He may not be in Britain."

"I'll have her search wide."

"The fifties saw African independence delegates in London. From 1955 on, decolonization boomed. Ghana

went independent in 1957. Guinea 1958. Nigeria 1960.
Tanzania 1961. Uganda 1962. Kenya 1963. And so on.
The white flash points were South Africa and Rhodesia.
If Hammond was capitalizing on native son demands sto-
len relics be returned, he may be an *African* entrepre-
neur. How's your yellow fever?"

"Two years to go."

"My gut tells me you better start popping malaria
pills."

SHADES

University of British Columbia

The History office told DeClercq Professor Mbhele was
at the Museum of Anthropology, so from the Buchanan
Tower he crossed Northwest Marine Drive to venture
out onto the cliffs above Tower Beach, where he entered
the huge 'Ksan doors of the MOA. Inside, instead of
flashing his badge, he paid the $6.00 admission, then
walked down the sloped Ramp through the Cross-Roads
to the Great Hall, the Kwagiutl carving to his right a
human house-post holding a human head from Xumtaspi
Village on Hope Island.

The Great Hall filled with totem poles was a spectacular gallery inspired by the post and beam dwellings of
B.C's First Nations. Fifty-foot-high walls of glass admitted ever-changing natural light. Backlit in front of the
glass doors to the Haida House complex outside stood
the Oweekeno Pole from Katit Village at Rivers Inlet,
the nine-foot beak of Hokhokw, the Cannibal Bird, jutting above the doors like an arch. On a platform to the
right sat two large potlatch feast dishes: one carved to
represent Sisiutl, the double-headed serpent; the other
Tsonoqua, the Wild Woman of the Woods. Beyond the
dugout canoe with high projecting bow and stern to the
left was a mammoth totem cut into four sections, carved
before 1860 and removed in 1957 from Tanoo Village in

the Queen Charlotte Islands. The Cormorant on piece two was being sketched by a man wearing khaki, with a tight Afro and mustache goatee framing his face. Nearing him, DeClercq noticed his dark skin was blotched with white.

"Dr. Mbhele?"

"Yes?" A thick South African voice.

"I'm Chief Superintendent DeClercq of the Mounted Police." He produced his regimental badge. "Last Friday Alex Hunt came to see you. I need to know what the two of you discussed."

"How is she? I heard on the news."

"Battered and broken. But she'll pull through."

"Anything to help," said the African. "The subject we explored was the Anglo-Zulu War last century. I was told she hoped to find a trophy box from Rorke's Drift, and when she described it, I told her I'd seen a photo of the box in *The Times*."

"This photo?" said DeClercq, holding up the microform copy from UBC Library.

"Yes," Mbhele replied.

"Like yourself, Doctor, I'm a historian. Military strategy at Isandlwana and Rorke's Drift I know. What I lack is knowledge about Zulu death rituals practiced in the war. Like *umnyama*."

"Does this concern the policeman disemboweled last month?"

"Yes, and the body slashed in the mortuary."

"How do those crimes relate to us?"

"Us?" said DeClercq.

"I'm Zulu, Chief Superintendent."

The Mountie passed him the photocopy of the trophy box. "The print's too small to read, but several sheets of handwriting are visible tucked inside. The newspaper article with the picture says the notes pertain to the 'witchcraft bones' displayed, how they were seized from a 'Zulu witch doctor' killed at Rorke's Drift by Lance-Sergeant Rex Craven VC, and how the 'bone diviner used the fetishes to conjure evil spirits.' "

Mbhele snorted. "Bigots," he said. "I'm sorry if I hurt your sensibilities."

"I'm French Canadian, Doctor. The British thrashed

us, too. Nothing you say about them will hurt my sensibilities."

"Are you Catholic?"

"Once upon a time."

"Then you know all about Communion? Practiced also by the Anglican Church? Of which the Queen is Defender of the Faith?"

DeClercq nodded.

"The museum in which we're talking is built on the ancestral lands of the Musqueam Nation. The Indians who lived here were pagans to British invaders because they communed with the spirit world. The totem I'm sketching is a fine example. It once stood outside the front of a dwelling called 'Plenty of Tliman Hides in This House,' and stories behind the crests were owned by a family of the Haida Raven Clan. From bottom to top, now from left to right, the carvings are: Bear, Cormorant, Eagle, and three Watchmen. The Watchmen sat atop the totem to warn of approaching danger."

"I bet they screamed bloody murder when the first British ship arrived."

The African indicated the second of the four totem pieces. DeClercq studied the cracked and unpainted gray pole. "Note how the Cormorant appears partly human. The bird's beak with human eyes, the bird's feathered wings with human hands. This totem suggests communion through transformation. Is the bird becoming human or the human becoming bird? Or is it that by communing they make up One World?"

"The point?" said DeClercq.

"The point is what the British couldn't understand they banned. So totem-raising potlatches were outlawed in 1885. Six years *after* Rorke's Drift and the nonsense in Craven's notes. Communing with shades has nothing to do with conjuring evil spirits."

"I'm listening," said DeClercq.

"Whites failed to see that in Africa a human being is a whole entity, not divided into body and soul, but made up of body *and* soul—*umzimba* and *idlozi*—with no clear division between the two. We do not say, 'Here is the body and there is the shade,' because the shade *is* the man, not a part of him. For us, what separates life from death is almost nonexistent, like what separates the fetus from the newborn child, so our dead remain as real as elder living relatives. They are 'living dead' to us, so the importance of the shades in everyday Zulu life cannot be overestimated. The shades appear to survivors in dreams, visions, omens, or through the medium of a diviner."

Mbhele fingered the bones in the trophy box photo. "*Inyanga yamathambo*. Bone diviner," he said.

"The shades choose those they wish to divine their will. One chosen to be a diviner enters into the state of *ukufukamela*, during which time the shades *brood* over him, bringing forth something else like a hen does when brooding over eggs. Excess brooding by the shades is to be avoided, for that brings about *ukuhlanya*: psychotic insanity. To be a diviner is to be the servant of the shades.

"The most common word for a diviner is *inyanga*. An *inyanga yezinthi* divines with sticks. An *inyanga yamathambo* divines with bones. The term *isanusi* refers to a male diviner who has the ability to smell out evil and witchcraft. Though this kind of diviner is rare today, last century they were the diviners of the king. To be accused by *isanusi* of witchcraft or sorcery meant death by impalement, since they were *izinyanga zokufa*: death specialists. To smell out evildoers, they divined with ten knucklebones, five from a female left hand and five from a male right. Such bones are called *izikhombi*—or pointers—because like fingers they point at what the shades see."

"So the bones in the photo were taken from a death diviner?"

"Yes, they are powerful relics indeed. Ten is the complete life: *imphilo ephelele*."

"How are the bones used?"

"The realm of the shades is opposite to the realm of the living. Light reverses with dark, left reverses with right. Because we're black, shades are white. When King Shaka first saw whites, he thought he saw shades. The left hand is the evil one, yet it divines, so bones are thrown out like dice with the left hand, then each position is noted by pointing with the left forefinger. If the bones point in every direction, *imphilo*—health—is everywhere. But when they point in a certain way, evil is fingered."

"So how does *umnyama* fit in?"

"We distinguish three sources of power. Power from the Lord-of-the-Sky. Power from the shades: the lineage of the clan. And power from medicines. Christians think God is the source of good and Satan the source of evil, but we think both good and evil originate with the Lord above. Evil is everywhere, and sometimes it's channeled through witchcraft. One way to guard against evil is by divining insight from the shades. Another way is *zila:* cleansing rituals.

"Days before Isandlwana, King Cetshwayo's army was summoned to Ulundi. A ceremony was held to cleanse the nation in preparation for battle. On the second day of the ritual, war doctors treated a wild black bull with medicines, then had it killed and cut into strips that were tossed among our warriors. The doctors led them in groups of three down to the banks of a stream to vomit into a deep, narrow hole. *Ukuphalaza*—vomiting—casts out evil, so a sample was taken to the king and added to the *inkhata,* a grass coil bound in python skin that embodied the unity of the nation. The pit was buried to keep evil out of the hands of the British.

"Both Isandlwana and Rorke's Drift were fought at the worst time. The night of January 22nd/23rd was the new moon, an inauspicious time for war as the malicious and all-pervading evil influence of blackness—*umnyama*—is unleashed. If uncleansed, not only might a killing pollute the killer with blackness, but so much combined evil might bring misfortune to the outcome. Ripping the abdomen of the dead is a cleansing *zila,* for if a body bloats from undissipated *umnyama,* the killer who didn't cleanse will bloat, too."

"Is divining communing?"

Mbhele shook his head. "We use ritual slaughter to commune with the shades. If there's been a killing, the shades have been approached. Shades manifest themselves sometime between the invocation—*ukubonga*—during the slaughter, and later when choice organs—*isiko*—from the body are burned. We commune by *ukuhlabela amadlozi:* 'slaughter for the shades.' "

"Powerful stuff," said DeClercq.

Mbhele shrugged. "The kosher meat Jews eat comes from *shehitah* ritual slaughter. In Holy Communion, you Catholics and the Anglicans drink wine with 'This is my blood,' and eat bread with 'This is my body.' Does that not sound like *imizimu* to you? In my eyes, the British commune as ritual cannibals."

The Zulu puffed himself up in a fair imitation of Queen Victoria, then wagged his finger at the communing Cormorant. "What arrogant hypocrites."

"Thank you, Doctor. You've been most helpful. I'll leave you to your work."

"May I ask a question?"

"Certainly."

"Do you think the killer you hunt is a Zulu?"

"No," said DeClercq. "Do you know the Greek myth about Pandora's box? Ignoring taboo and blind to consequence, she opened it and released all the evils of the human race. Only Hope remained at the bottom of the box."

"Shades aren't evil."

"Not to the right mind. But neither was a Beatles' song about a playground slide till 'Helter Skelter' was played to Charles Manson. The signs of the zodiac spoke to the Zodiac Killer. And so did his neighbor's dog to the Son of Sam. Whatever shades this killer released, I suspect they brooded him insane."

EVIL EYE

North Vancouver

The pull of the trophy box was too strong for Evil Eye to resist. An African voice inside urged the psycho to lift the lid. Overcome by irresistible impulse, Evil Eye opened the Rorke's Drift box.

Outside, moonlight shone around the Lions Den, the log cabin perched high on Grouse Mountain at the end of a logging road. The windowless room at the heart of the cabin was bronzed by the flickering oil lamp that cast Evil Eye's shadow like a black ghost onto the Redcoat pictures spiked to the logs. All three tables in the pioneer hideaway were used tonight. Spread across the left table was a ship's blueprint on a poster announcing "E" Division Headquarters 'Red Serge Ball would be held aboard the *Good Luck City* this March. Tubes of plastic explosives stolen from RCMP Bomb Squad seizures weighed down both sheets. Piled on the right table were research books: *Zulu: Isandlwana and Rorke's Drift: 22nd–23rd January 1879; The Story of the Victoria Cross; Zulu Thought-Patterns and Symbolism* ... Before this table sat the only chair.

The table between was draped with Ted Craven's Red Serge. On his tunic sat Rex Craven's trophy box. Inside were the notes the lance-sergeant wrote after defending Rorke's Drift, detailing the battle, how he stabbed the *Induna,* how the witch doctor used the "pointers" in the snakeskin pouch to divine from shades, and why Africans feared *umnyama.* That night in Dora's kitchen before she died, rooting through the box she brought down from the attic, the twin had found the notes tucked beneath the red-and-black velvet halves displaying trophies in this box.

The night Evil Eye first heard the voice.

This voice urging the psycho to throw the knucklebones.

This voice backed by African drums pounding within the psycho's mind while silence filled the juju room in the Lions Den.

Zombielike, Evil Eye emptied the knucklebones from the snakeskin. Carved on each bone was a hypnotic evil eye that glared at Evil Eye. The black ghost lamplight cast across the log wall moved rhythmically to the call of the drums as screams brought the Redcoat pictures to life.

The psycho stared at Lady Butler's "The Defense of Rorke's Drift." The viewpoint was from the front of the hospital looking toward the storehouse. The air as dark as gunsmoke was filled with sparks and smudge from the burning thatch. Lieutenant Chard, at center, drew Bromhead's attention to a gap in the defenses. Behind them, Corporal Schiess leapt onto the rampart, hand cupped to his mouth to shout. Private Hitch, arm hurt, carried ammo packets to the thin red line holding the barricade along the left. There, Lance-Sergeant Rex Craven lunged with his bayonet into the sea of brandished shields and contorted black faces dashing wave after wave upon the whites, dimly glimpsed as they were squeezed out of the frame by the steadfast stand against the savage mass of Darkest Africa.

"One more picture like this," Lady Butler's spouse warned her after she was commissioned to paint by Queen Victoria, "and you will drive me mad."

A warning unheeded by Evil Eye.

Transfixed, the psycho watched the battle ebb and flow until a carpet of dead and dying Africans sprawled right up to the Redcoats' boots.

Evil Eye tossed the knucklebones across the table like dice.

Inyanga Yamathambo.

Bone Diviner.

In the picture, Chard and Bromhead shared a bottle of beer. The other Redcoats drank a tot of rum. Slowly, a ghost came into view among the whites, unseen by all except Evil Eye. The screams that came from the picture were deafening, a symphony of agony emitted by spectral images too vague to discern, but through the hazy forms of which wandered Black Ghost. The shade was an old man with a grizzled beard. His "kilt" was of twisted civet and monkey fur. Cow tail festoons circled his neck and limbs. His stuffed otter-skin headband was adorned with feathers. Through his chest was a lunger wound, and stolen from about his neck was the snake-skin in Evil Eye's hand.

Again the psycho threw the *izikhombi* "pointers" to divine the shade's will.

"*Isiko,*" commanded Black Ghost.

The *isiko* was to be a Redcoat's heart.

NEW RECRUIT

West Vancouver
Friday, January 21, 1994

Robert DeClercq was in the kitchen cooking up a feast, wearing the apron and chef's hat Katt had sewed him for Christmas, listening to CBC Radio analyze the upcoming South African election, unaware killers behind the news would soon stalk one of his men to the ends of the earth.

"*. . . when results are compiled after the April twenty-sixth vote, the last white-minority stronghold in Africa will be gone. Barring an unforeseen tragedy, the next South African president will be Nelson Mandela, undisputed patriarch of black liberation. Dominated by Mandela's African National Congress (ANC) and the National Party of F.W. de Klerk, the election campaign that began this month has been marred by violence. South Africa in its present form will die with the vote. Parliament—which now has separate houses for whites, Indians and mixed bloods, but not for blacks—will transform to a single national all-race legislature. Gone will be the racist laws of colonialism. Gone will be the tribal homelands of apartheid. Including KwaZulu. . . .*"

The specialty of the house at Chez DeClercq was cannelloni. His secret was the delicate balance between his savory meat filling with fresh oregano only and his—*shhhhhh!*—divine heart-clogging double-cream sauce. Dinner under control in the oven, he uncorked a bottle of wine, a cheeky little Chardonnay with just a hint of wood. Heretic that he was, Robert felt California vineyards had surpassed the overpriced French, and now, thank Bacchus, South African wines would be politically correct.

"*. . . promising to correct the 'racially distorted' economy, Mandela's African National Congress plans to give a third of the nation's farmland to blacks. Blacks were*

*dispossessed in 1913 when 87 percent of all land was re-
served for whites. The ANC may also nationalize some
industries. Though expropriation isn't mentioned, the
manifesto clearly plans to give blacks a share of what is
now owned by whites. Mandela accuses de Klerk—with
whom he shared last year's Nobel Peace Prize—of white-
washing death squads in the police and a secret 'third
force' in Government Security dedicated to sabotaging the
transition to democracy and black majority rule. . . ."*

The front door opened.

"We're here," Katt called. A twitching nose poked
around the jamb of the kitchen door. "Cardiac arrest.
My favorite meal."

The teenager squatted to hug Napoleon. The German
shepherd butted her back toward the front door.

"Take him for a walk, Katt. Or take over in here."

"Coming, Mom?" she asked as Corrine Baxter came
into view.

"You go. My feet are killing me. New shoes," her
mom explained.

DeClercq nodded knowingly.

*". . . the Afrikaner Resistance Movement, embracing
Nazilike symbols and policies, has decreed, 'We are the
rightful owners of this country. We are the ones who
brought civilization to South Africa.' Afrikaners are boy-
cotting the election because the government and ANC refuse to guarantee them a* volkstaat—*or white homeland—
in the Orange Free State and Transvaal . . ."*

The front door closed behind Katt and Napoleon as
Corrine said, "You look like a chef at the Ritz in that
hat."

"Puts me in the mood to sling hash," Robert joked.
"Katt sewed the apron and embroidered the bib. The
get-up's for her. I'm not *that* vain."

Stitched on front was an ornate cup swirling steam
with a spoon on its saucer and tablets of Equal beside.
Garçon de Thé ringed the needlework.

"Translation?" asked Corrine.

"Teaboy," said DeClercq. He showed her the "Ode
to Teaboy" on the fridge.

Baxter read it and laughed.

With ash blond hair and deep cobalt eyes like Katt—
mother and daughter, but for age, displayed the same

genes—Corrine Baxter was an artist in thought, dress, and fact. In Boston she bought old houses to redecorate as mansions, earning her living by reselling them at a profit. Instead of disrupting Katt by yanking her out of school (denying her the *Dracula* joy of vampirizing Kirk Mitchell), she'd bought a house in North Vancouver to transform. The powwow tonight was to discuss Katt's future.

"Wine?" Robert said, bottle in one hand, glass in the other.

"I nefer drink . . . vine," Corrine replied, mimicking Katt doing Bela Lugosi. "But for you"—she took the glass—"I'll make an exception."

"*. . . South Africa is often seen in simplistic black and white: Black versus White, Good versus Bad, Oppressed versus Oppressors. But racial conflict isn't the only tension, for tribal, language, and class divisions also fan discord. A turf war between the ANC and Inkatha Freedom Party of Mangosuthu Buthelezi has killed 10,000 blacks over the past decade in Natal and the tribal homeland of KwaZulu it surrounds. Buthelezi's nephew is King Goodwill Zwelithini, Lion of the Zulu Nation and head of its Royal House. A bearded man who lives in a palace with five wives, Zwelithini was crowned eighth monarch of the Zulus in 1971 to guard the interests of his 8.5 million subjects. In practice he's the puppet of Buthelezi's Inkatha Party in its power struggle against the ANC. . . .*"

"So?" Robert said. "How goes the battle?"

"Bonding with Katt's like wrestling a wildcat hand to paw. She's . . . she's . . ."

"A live wire?" supplied DeClercq.

"That she is. What's your secret? She thinks the world of you."

"My friend Chartrand is commissioner of the Force. What I know about command I learned from him. He gives orders by advising you of his opinion and asking if you can help. No one likes to be told what to do, and he'd no more think of doing that than asking you to help where your help wasn't needed. The CO commands voluntary respect.

"Luna Darke was a practicing witch. We're lucky Katt's as stable as she is. The trick is to make her want to prove she has everything under control. Which often she does.

"When Katt came here from Deadman's Island, we had a talk. I told her I was a loner who feared she'd cramp my life. Only if she was responsible, worked hard at school, and read every book in *our* library could she stay. Sneak that she is, the shelves are now stocked with what she wants to read. Katt thinks she pulled a fast one, but it got her reading."

"Why such a good 'dad' to her?" asked Corrine.

"You don't know what you've got till you lose it, and I lost my first chance. As you said on the phone: Lonely, isn't it? I hunt mutants spawned by criminally negligent fathers. Guys too busy with themselves to center on their kids. Later they sit in back of a court wondering where things went wrong. As Plato said: Keep your dick in your pants if you're not up to the job. Katt's my salvation."

Corrine drained her wine. "You make this decision hard."

The front door opened.

"We're back," Katt announced.

"Why so soon?"

"It's raining Katts and dogs."

The teenager entered the kitchen and spied the bottle of wine. "This bilingual house adheres to French drinking laws?" She found a glass, held it out, then asked, "What shall we toast?"

"Half pints get half measures," Robert said.

The glass Katt held up had plenty of room left for the bouquet. She measured the distance between the rim and surface of the wine. "As Plato said: Here's the gap between adults and teens. To you this glass is half full. To me it's half empty."

Baxter eyed DeClercq.

"Plato said a lot of silly things," he replied.

Cozy in this kitchen with its savory aroma, Corrine said, "Boston's home, so that's where I want Katt to live."

Here it comes, Robert thought. *The long good-bye.*

"Katt tells me if she moves there her future can't be. Since she was born in Boston, she's American. Which means she has to live here to apply for citizenship. If not, she's barred from recruiting because she's Ameri-

can, and can't follow her dream of being a Mountie just
like you."

Robert looked at Katt, who looked everywhere but at
his eyes. *You little schemer.*

"I've got a great idea," said Katt enthusiastically.
"The best way for Mom to see what we Mounties are
all about is for you to take her to the Red Serge Ball."

"Let's eat," said DeClercq.

Unaware the warning tolled the bell for one of his
men, he switched off the radio as the CBC continued:
"*. . . on Monday, Zulus armed with traditional spears,
shields, and clubs stormed from a Soweto hostel to hear
King Zwelithini demand an independent Zulu Nation in
Natal. 'A Zulu king is not just another black leader who
should be approachable by just anybody.' The speech
meshed perfectly with Buthelezi's warning the Zulus are
under siege and will fight to the finish against the ANC.
As South Africa moves toward the postapartheid era, civil
war may be only a shot away. . . .*"

HAIR OF THE DOG

Cloverdale

Last night was the fourth meeting of the Suicide Club,
so Wayne Tarr woke up to a raging throbbing full-blown
hangover. To quell the pain of nails being driven into
his brain, he poured himself a tumbler of Scotch with a
shaky hand. Nothing like a little hair o' the dog the
morning after.

The drapes in the living room were drawn against the
day. The Sports Network still flickered silently on the
TV. JR Country played Conway Twitty wringing every
tear out of "Lonely Blue Boy." When Tarr set the bottle
of Scotch down it tipped and spilled, pouring the amber
spirits across the divorce petition from The Bitch, and
next to that a light blue card:

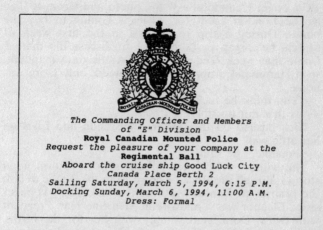

The Commanding Officer and Members
of "E" Division
Royal Canadian Mounted Police
Request the pleasure of your company at the
Regimental Ball
Aboard the cruise ship Good Luck City
Canada Place Berth 2
Sailing Saturday, March 5, 1994, 6:15 P.M.
Docking Sunday, March 6, 1994, 11:00 A.M.
Dress: Formal

As he drank, Tarr aimed his thumb and index finger like a gun at the blue card.

"Kaboom!" he said.

SACRED HEART

Vancouver

"Criminal lawyers are storytellers," DeClercq told Craven three weeks after Nick asked for his help. Snow fell outside the window of the Pretrial Center, and on the table between them lay witness reports. "The lawyer who tells the best story wins the trial, so here's the story you offer Knight. . . ."

Ted and Dora Craven lived in Lethbridge, Alberta, where Ted was a Member with the Mounted detachment. Ted was the grandson of Lance-Sergeant Rex Craven, and heir to a trophy box from Rorke's Drift. Among the relics in the box was a pouch of bones, a photo of which appeared in *The Times* on January 27,

1956. Nigel Hammond saw the photo and wrote to Ted as the London agent for Africans hoping to buy the bones. During a trip to Canada in the first week of March, he'd stop in Lethbridge to discuss the matter. Come that week, Ted was in the Arctic on a manhunt, so if Hammond dropped by as planned, only Dora was home.

"You think he fucked Mom?"

"Is that not possible?"

Nick flashed on the posters of Brando and Elvis on her attic wall.

"Possible," he said.

The winter of 1956 was Alberta's worst. Storm upon storm followed the Rockies down from the Arctic to lash the prairies to Kansas south of the line. Ted's younger sister Eleanor was a midwife in Medicine Hat. Pregnant with twins, Dora went to stay with her for the births. Ted joined them on his days off. The night all the snow in the Arctic was dumped on Medicine Hat, besieging the city to block streets and choke doors to the house, the twins were born. Both births were witnessed by Ted and Eleanor, then later that night, whiskey drunk, Ted shot himself.

"Dad committed suicide because we weren't *his*?"

"If Hammond went to bed with your mom, is that not possible?"

Nick matched the dates. "Possible," he said.

"What went on in the house that night we may never know. The inquest into Ted's death wasn't transcribed. There is, however, a note in the file that Dora's face was bruised. Eleanor swore that was caused by thrashing during the births. Or did Ted beat her from rage caused by paternity?"

Something else about the two births was wrong. The cuckolding might explain her husband's suicide, but not why Dora kept one twin and rejected the other. Why was the birth not recorded to her, and what would motivate Eleanor, *despite her brother's death,* to place the twin through Sacred Heart, with a vow of secrecy from Sister Superior? Was the twin defective in a way that affected *both* women?

Whatever the reasons, a lifetime passed. Then last November, the "defective" twin came searching for Dora, having somehow learned it was "placed" by Sacred Heart. Refusing to breach her vow of silence, Sister Superior was threatened. The nun told Eleanor, who then wrote to Dora, shortly before she fell down stairs in the house where the twins were born.

"No Sacred Heart in Canada has a record of placing your twin. But the one that taught your aunt as a child suffered a break-in last November in which files were stolen. Its Sister Superior died that same night in an unsolved hit and run. The next day, your aunt fell down the stairs."

"You think my twin found Eleanor through his file, then went to Medicine Hat and forced her to expose his mom?"

"His *or* her mom," clarified DeClercq.

In early December, Dora received the letter found in the drawer:

Mother—
    It's taken my lifetime to uncover your whitewashed secret. Discussing it face to face on my birthday seems fitting. I'll call on the 7th.

On the 7th, as Nick was driving to the Regimental Dinner from his birthday party at Dora's, the twin came along the path from Port Coquitlam to knock on the back door. Face to face with her unknown child for the first time since 1956, Dora cut the birthday pie to eat with him or her, then tried to explain why she did what she did in Alberta. When she related the trophy box was how she met Hammond, the twin asked to see the African link to its dad. So Dora went up to the attic and brought it down.

"We're dealing with a psychotic. Of that I'm quite sure," said DeClercq. "Wherever Sacred Heart placed the twin, it was abused. Stripped of mumbo jumbo, psychosis works like this. A child escapes mentally from abuse by repressing thoughts, which it locks away in the dungeon of its subconscious. To return to consciousness, jailed thoughts trick the jailor by disguising their origin in breaks with reality. Hallucinations, delusions, and obsessions are classic breaks. A psycho sees visions that don't exist, or hears phantom voices. A psycho becomes the zombielike puppet of supernatural forces. A psycho fixates on a fetish or symbol with links to the abuse. The perfect example is the Son of Sam. David Berkowitz shot people in New York because the dog of his neighbor housed the spirit of a six thousand-year-old demon that ordered him to kill. 'It wasn't me,' the psycho confessed after his arrest. 'It was Sam working through me . . . Sam used me as a tool.' "

"So what's my twin's psychosis?"

"Your sibling's the zombie of the African bones in the box. . . ."

Her back to the twin, Dora stood washing dishes at the sink. The twin sat at the kitchen table, mesmerized by the bones. The evil eye carved on each bone's a link to the realm of the shades. Rex Craven described their juju power in notes the twin found in the box. It was a moment ripe for psychosis to emerge and crush the cause of the placement abuse. The shades linked to the bones compelled the twin to smash Dora's skull in with the club.

Through the window above the sink, the twin looked down as police cars converged on Colony Farm. Within a minute, dogs fanned out to search for Schreck. The twin climbed to the attic where Dora got the box, and at the urging of the shades emptied Ted's trunk. Returning to the kitchen to wipe away prints, the twin donned Nick's tea-stained coat to hide Dora's blood, then closing the door which locked behind, ran up the path away from the Schreck manhunt.

"You see the logic in the madness?" said DeClercq. "The psychotic use of symbols for revenge? The Rorke's Drift trophy box symbolizes the tragedy of the rejected twin. The Redcoat relics represent Rex, Ted, Dora, and you. The Zulu relics represent Hammond and his rejected child. Both father and offspring want revenge for their rejection. The shades want revenge for Redcoat conquest in the Zulu War. To advance the latter means advancing the former, so the twin becomes the zombie of African hallucinations. What other explanation fits events that followed?"

"Jack?" said Nick.

"The psychotic link to Rorke's Drift turns florid. Hallucination, delusion, and obsession control, so Jack is clubbed with the knobkerrie and disemboweled with the bayonet. He's a Redcoat stand-in for Rex, Ted, Dora, and you. Unfortunately, the zigzag imprint shredded when he was dragged."

"But Mom wasn't gutted?"

"Training on the job. The twin didn't finish Rex's notes until *after* it left Dora's house. That's when the psycho learned about the *umnyama* curse, leading to the mortuary break-in to finish the job."

"You think it'll kill again?"

"When the pressure of psychosis builds."

"Another Member?"

"Yes," answered DeClercq. "The twin's obsession is fixated on Red Serge. Our uniform stands for everything your double hates."

"Including me."

"Including you. Who reaped the mother love denied to it? You standing trial for Mom's death is the ultimate revenge."

"How do we find my double?"

"First we find Nigel Hammond. Why were the relics not returned that March? Did he contact your mom after Ted died? Was there mention of him in the Sacred Heart file, prompting your twin to contact him recently as a result? The address Alex recalls on Hammond's letter in fifty-six was a block of London flats leveled in the sixties. Nigel Hammond is a common name in Britain. Unless something breaks here, we wait and see what Scotland Yard turns up."

TWINS

Robert walked into his office to find Katt sitting in his chair, feet up on his horseshoe desk and wearing his forage cap backward with the peak behind her head. Her toque with the lucky moth hole was stuck on the hat rack. "Getting the feel of the place, Bob, for when I'm promoted."

"Why aren't you at school?"

"Professional day," she said. And echoing Luna: "I do believe teachers get lazier each year."

"What brings you here?"

"Public transport, Bob." Katt grinned. "Oh, do you mean motive-wise?"

"How'd you clear Security?"

"Sweet talk, Bob. Not everyone suspects I'm going to steal your stapler." She flicked the visitor's pass clipped to her chest.

"So, 'motive-wise,' to what do I owe your visit?"

"This," replied Katt, waving a book so he couldn't see the title. "Since I'm going to be a cop, I figure I should help you with the Craven case. Remember how you told me an investigation is like a book? You take it page by page, and as you finish one page, that leads to another page, and you just keep turning pages until you come to the end of the story. Correct me if I'm wrong, Bob, but what we're stalking here is your classic evil twin?"

"I see our walls have ears?"

"Or you have a booming voice."

"I'll recommend you be assigned to Special I. Mind if I sit down?"

"At ease. Fall out, Bob."

He sat in one of the minion chairs as Katt cracked the book to read. Above the title *Twins and the Double* protruded several bookmarks scrawled with notes written by her. "Interesting stuff, twins. Listen to this," she said:

"Consider what happens each time we look into a mirror. There we behold our 'twin,' the mirror-image of ourselves, seemingly a perfect likeness; yet this visual replica remains oddly, elusively different. The face in the mirror resembles our own in having identical features, but we hardly notice how these are crisscrossed, the left side of the actual face appearing on the right-hand side of the mirror-face and vice versa. In one stroke, the Twin reveals itself and tricks us, right before our eyes. We may go through our whole life without realizing that the face we see in the mirror is not the one that others see when they look directly at us.

"To see how our face actually looks, we have to place

*two square mirrors together, at right angles to each other,
and look directly at the seam . . ."*

"A photograph of our mirror-face will not overlap our
actual face," said DeClercq.

Katt read on: *"Certainly we are struck by the visual
alikeness of human twins, but this impression is mis-
leading and belies rather than exemplifies the innate structure of twinning. In a room of a hundred people it would
not take long to pick out the identical twin sisters, but the
remaining ninety-eight people could be forty-nine sets of
nonidentical twins and you would not be able to detect
them."*

Katt closed the book. "Twins are tricky, Bob. You
were raised Catholic. You recall Jacob and Esau."

"Do I?" said Robert. "Refresh my memory."

"The Old Testament, Bob. Genesis Three. Esau and
Jacob were twin brothers who rivaled in the womb. First
born, Esau was 'red and hairy.' 'Smooth' Jacob followed
'with his hand grasping Esau's heel' to pull him back.
Firstborn son got the father's blessing, so to receive it
in Esau's place, Jacob covered his arms with fleece so
he would feel hairy. The old man, eighty and nearly
blind, got sucked in.

"Rivalry, Bob. That's the key to the dynamics of
twins. You're a historian. You know all about Romulus
and Remus."

"Do I?" said Robert. "Refresh my memory."

"You're playing dumb."

"Perhaps," he replied. "You left out Castor and Pollux, the Gemini Twins. The reason many cultures hold
twins taboo is they're seen as the workings of a supernatural force to be feared. The One and the Other, with
the Other as a gate to the Other World. Castor was
mortal, but Pollux was the son of Zeus. Light and darkness figure as the ultimate set of twins in mythology.
Horus and Set, the embattled twins of Egypt. Balder and
Hodus in Scandinavia. Combine light and darkness, and
you get *twi*light."

Katt got up and paced the room, bouncing ideas off
the father she had never had. "Look what evil Hyde did
to poor Jekyll. Look what cruel Dorian Gray did to his
portrait. Look what the pinned voodoo doll does to its
human double. The ultimate curse of twinning is the

scapegoat, Bob. The sacrificial double who suffers or
dies in place of the twin. The ideal scapegoat must itself
be free of guilt. That's what I think is happening here."

"So?" said DeClercq.

"So we find the twin."

"How do we do that?"

"Start at the start."

"Starting where?"

"Conception, Bob." Katt sat on his knee like a kid
with Santa Claus. "Know a geneticist?"

"Cool," said Katt, taking in the clinical order of Biology
Section's Examination Room at the RCMP Forensic
Lab.

"Colin Wood. Cool Katt," DeClercq introduced them.

"Katt DeClercq," Katt said, shaking Wood's hand.

That shook DeClercq. This imp was a Rubik's Cube.
"We have the makings of a future Member here. She
wants to know—"

"I want to know how twins are conceived."

"I'm backup," said DeClercq. "She's the pointma . . .
pointperson today."

Wood cupped his chin in his hand and gave Katt his
attention. "You've studied biology?"

"In science," she replied. "Biology biology I take
next year."

"DNA—you've been taught—is the master chemical
directing all processes of life and death. Twinning is
what DNA is all about, for it's made up of two threads
twisted like *twine*. Working with it is RNA—DNA's *twin*
acid—which replicates the genetic code by copying it.
Messenger RNA carries the copy out of the cell nucleus
to twin the cell. All life is replication. Of twinning are
we born."

"I'm with you," said Katt, scribbling notes like a cop.

"In a normal single birth, an egg from the mother is
fertilized by a sperm from the father to create the zygote, the human embryo. This slides down the oviduct
and lodges in the womb, where the single cell develops
into a baby.

"Twin births come from two variations.

"Identical twins also evolve from one egg and one
sperm, but early in a pregnancy the zygote unnaturally

splits in two. Because they develop from one fertilized egg, such *monozygotic* twins gestate side by side in the same placenta, and later in life look alike since they share the same DNA. Siamese twins result where a zygote fails to split completely. Identical and Siamese twins are always the same sex."

Wood fetched a text from a shelf on the wall, then thumbed pages to find a photograph of identical twins. Next to it was a black-and-white shot of Chang and Eng, *the* original Siamese twins joined at the waist. Born of Chinese parents in 1811, the twins were discovered by a British merchant as they were about to be put to death as taboo by the King of Siam, and acquired later by the circus magnate P.T. Barnum, who used them for years in his sideshow of freaks.

"Fraternal twins develop if *two* eggs are released from a mother's ovaries around the same time, and these are fertilized by *different* sperms. Two zygotes produce *dizygotic* twins, each in its own placenta and each with different DNA. Fraternal twins may both be boys, girls, or one of each, and may look no more alike than family siblings who aren't twins."

Wood flipped the page to a photograph of fraternal twins.

"Wow!" exclaimed Katt. "What happened there?" She tapped the picture beside the photo of normal fraternal twins.

"Nothing in science is ever black and white," said Wood.

The text above this photo read:

These twins were the subject of an unprecedented legal wrangle in 1978. The mother, a West German woman, launched a double paternity suit on the grounds she had ovulated twice in one day, having made love to a white German and a black American soldier within hours. There are similar cases recorded in Britain, Denmark, and the USA.

The photo below showed twin boys.
One white.
The other black.

BLACK COIF

"Blood!" shrieked Lyndon Wilde QC, pointing a fat finger at the cuff of Nick's Red Serge. *"Blood!"* echoed The Hatchet, pointing a bony finger at her Assize Court robes. *"Blood!"* cried the jury, pointing twelve fingers at Mom's corpse on the floor. Behind the dock in which he stood, *"Blood!"* barked the gallery, fingers pointing at him.

Hatchett wore the wig of an Old Bailey judge. Atop it, the court clerk placed a piece of black fabric. The black coif. That grim sentencing relic which symbolized death.

"Nicholas Craven, after due deliberation by a jury of your peers, you have been found guilty of this foul matricide. Look not for pardon in this world, for yours is the most disgusting case I have ever tried, and it remains only for me to pass upon you the terrible and just sentence of the law: that you be taken immediately to a place of execution, and there be hanged by the neck until you are dead. And may God have mercy on your soul."

A gallows pole had been erected in court. Nick was dragged up the steps to the scaffold platform. Here the hooded hangman bound his hands and feet, then tightened the noose about his neck. The hood the executioner wore was the last thing Nick saw before the trapdoor sprung and he dropped.

The hood was black.

Each time the hangman breathed in, it sucked tight to his face.

The face was Nick's.

The hanged man awoke in a sweat.

ZIMBABWE

March came in like a lion hunting spring lamb. The wind had teeth, and a roar that scattered fleecy clouds east to clear the hungry sky. Outside, sunrise bloodied wool in a fresh kill.

DeClercq was leaving Special X for the start of Nick's trial in New Westminster Supreme Court when Zinc Chandler caught him at his car. "Look what just came in from Scotland Yard."

Clipped to a photophone picture in the inspector's hand was a London Met Police fax:

Zinc—
   My sergeant found this in an old Colonial Office file. It's from the preindependence Salisbury/Harare *Herald.* Whether he's the Nigel Hammond who "went missing in Rhodesia in 1966, when ZANU guerrillas launched an attack on government forces at Chinhoyi on Chimurenga Day" is anybody's guess. That quote is from a contemporary BSAP report on file here. The Zimbabwe Police Force has no file on Hammond. That doesn't surprise me. On independence in 1980, the British South Africa Police of colonial Rhodesia became the Zimbabwe Police. As the new force was to be staffed with former ZANU guerrillas, the old white guard burned many files before going out the door. Needless to say, the new black guard burned more coming in. For some reason, all trace of Hammond went up in smoke. No birth record. No death record. Just this photo.
Hilary
p.s. The ruins in the background are Great Zimbabwe.

*   *   *

The "Lost City" of Great Zimbabwe is the stuff of myth. *Zimbabwe,* a Shona word, means "Houses of Stone." In 1497, Vasco da Gama sailed to Mozambique. Portuguese traders who followed heard Swahili rumors of a "City of Gold" inland. An early report to Europe said it was the "fortress of the King of Monomotapa, which he is making of stone without mortar." Soon hearsay grew to fantasy of biblical dimensions. Monomotapa became the custodian of King Solomon's mines and the mythic land of Ophir (I Kings 10:11). Brother Joas dos Boas wrote "these houses were in olden times the trading depots of the Queen of Sheba, and from these depots they used to bring her much gold."

The glint of gold was a lure that hooked soldiers of fortune. The first white to gaze upon the Lost City was German hunter Adam Render in 1871. He showed the ruins to geologist Carl Mauch, who promptly declared "the fortress on the hill [is] a copy of King Solomon's Temple." In 1885, H. Rider Haggard wrote *King Solomon's Mines,* which both DeClercq and Chandler had read as boys.

The struggle for Great Zimbabwe was the struggle for Africa. The mysterious ruins near Masvingo (site of Fort Victoria, Rhodesia's first white settlement) are the most significant man-made relics south of the Pyramids. On a continent dotted with buildings of wood, grass, and mud, massive dry-stone walls fashioned into labyrinths of corridors and chambers stood unique. If the White Man's Burden was to "civilize" black Africa—the pious spit shining the jackboots of colonial armies—how do you explain the complex social development inherent in such ruins? Obviously, wrote Theodore Bent, an amateur antiquarian hired in 1893 by Cecil Rhodes to solve the "Mystery of Zimbabwe," an "ancient Mediterranean race" built the Lost City. His candidates were Phoenicians, Arabs, Romans, Persians, Egyptians, Hebrews, or "the mythical Pelasgi who inhabited the shores of Greece." In other words, *anyone* but black Africans.

Reclaiming the ruins' black heritage was a hundred years' war. In 1905, archaeologist David Randall-McIver concluded the relics were medieval and African-built. Journalist R.N. Hall, reflecting white outrage, blasted "McIver's hazarded hypothesis of the natural and unaided evolution of the negroid." During the War Years that followed white Rhodesia's Unilateral Declaration of Independence from Britain in 1965, black liberation guerrillas coalesced their ideology around freeing Great Zimbabwe. By 1970, government censorship decreed no guidebook, textbook, newspaper, broadcast, or film could state the relics were an African creation. With black-majority Independence in 1980, Rhodesia became Zimbabwe, and birdlike totems found in the ruins became the national symbol.

The Hill Enclosure is the oldest part. It resembles an acropolis in Ancient Greece or a Dark Ages castle atop a mount. This brooding, alien rubble probably housed the king and a spirit medium who communed with the shades. The photophone picture in Chandler's hand showed two men—white and black—posing in front of the ruins. Clipped from a sixties paper, the grainy image was reproduced with tiny clustered dots. Except for his bush beard, the white mirrored Stewart Granger as Allan Quatermain in *King Solomon's Mines*. Near thirty, he wore a safari hat with leopard-skin band, a khaki bush shirt and khaki shorts with a belted knife. Draped over his palm was a limp and bloody snake: a yard long with pale scales edged in black. The Mozambique spitting cobra, or M'fezi, lurks among Great Zimbabwe's ancient stones. If riled, a blunt head rises to spread a broad hood, then it spits a stream of venom at wide-open eyes. Causing flesh necrosis and instant agony, a 40mg squirt is fatal to humans.

The black resembled Wesley Snipes updating Granger's role. He, too, was near thirty and wore khakis like the white, but opted for the woolen cap of a British commando. Looped around two fingers spread in a V, a rubber sling was pulled back to re-create the stoning of the snake. A wicked ivory grin curled beneath aviator shades.

The cutline under the photo read: *British South Africa Police seek Nigel Hammond (left) and Clive Moon to help with their inquiries into Wankie ivory poaching and black market trafficking in kaffir artifacts.*

The man on the left was the black.

PART III

THIN RED LINE

Then it's Tommy this, an' Tommy that,
   an' "Tommy, 'ow's yer soul?"
But it's "Thin red line of 'eroes" when the
   drums begin to roll.

—KIPLING

ZAMBEZI

From its source in the Zambian highlands near the border with Zaire, the Zambezi flows south to join the Chobe midcontinent where Zambia, Namibia, Botswana, and Zimbabwe meet, then turns east to mark the border between the last two Zs, plummeting over Victoria Falls along the way, pausing to top up man-made Lake Kariba behind the dam, before snaking the final part of its S-curve under British Airways Flight 53 descending Zinc into Harare, entering Mozambique to complete its 1,230-mile course at the Indian Ocean.

Dr. Livingstone ("I presume") watched the Money Man pass Devil's Cataract to tread the path along the lip of First Zambezi Gorge, closing on Danger Point to meet the Gray by the Falls.

Two million years before Livingstone (the man, not this statue in a Foreign Legion hat) "discovered" the falls November 16, 1855, Stone Age humans chipped tools around the precipice. Fleeing from conquest by Shaka's Zulu *impi*, Makololo refugees early last century swept north from Natal. This *mfecane*—"forced migration"—ended here, where they subjugated local tribes. The Makololo named the falls *Mosi-oa-Tunya*, "Smoke That Thunders," and later brought Livingstone in a dugout canoe. Sanctimonious, selfish, pigheaded, and presumptuous, the Scotsman renamed them Victoria Falls for his queen. Even black independence couldn't shed the Colonial name.

Most spectacular now with the river in full spate, the Falls—a mile wide and 300 feet sheer—thundered millions of gallons of green-white water a minute into the chasm below, billowing clouds of sun-dazzled spray alive with ethereal rainbows. Glazed pink at dawn and metallic blue at dusk, the slow-moving Zambezi beyond flowed around palm tree islands like stepping-stones approaching the Falls, the lip islands of which were sacred sites where headmen once worshiped spirits. Drenched by deluges, the Money Man walked the precipice to Danger Point, the full force of ambush showers jumping him opposite Main Falls where the path broke unprotected. The vertiginous drop to his left was unfenced, with just an occasional thornbush as a barrier.

In his journal, Livingstone gushed: *On sights as beautiful as this, Angels in their flight must have gazed.*

Devils, too, for on the Point waited the Terrible Ones.

Common to southern Africa, the garbage line spider is easily overlooked. Reversing a pair of binoculars as a bush microscope reveals this tiny predator lurking in its web. Legs extended forward and back or hunched for camouflage, it waits in the center of its garbage line. Four main guy lines suspending it in place, the radial web is strung in a bush or tree. Stretched across the meshed hub is the stabilimentum: the garbage line. Hung along this like garbage bags are the silk-wrapped corpses of prey and empty egg sachets. Insects see in ultraviolet, so the UV-reflective garbage line shines like a landing strip. A happenstance of nature, the markings on back of the abdomen of the garbage line spider form a human skull.

That skull was tattooed on the palms of the Black and the White.

On their killing hands.

The Gray was the joint code name under which they worked, a secret whispered mouth to ear along the seedy garbage line of mercenary bars. Who they were and where they came from was best ignored, for the Gray—Black & White—was reputed to be the coldest killing team for hire. Where the Black couldn't go, the White could. And where the White stood out, the Black moved easily. Gray mixes Black & White to mask their true colors, or lack of color, truth be known.

In 1951, the Land Husbandry Act advanced Rhodesian apartheid, dividing "Native Reserves" to make space for thousands evicted from white-designated lands. The farm settled by the White's father was worked by "kaffirs" bossed by the Black's dad. One night, while the youths camped "on safari" in the bush, African Voice marauders burned the farm and hanged both men from a baobab tree. Next day, the sons took a blood oath to exact revenge. Hunting, castrating, and lynching six, the Garbage Line Spiders fled to the hinterland.

Alias "Nigel Hammond" and "Clive Moon," the color-blind pair came of age as soldiers of fortune. Elephant poaching for ivory earned them cash, followed by travel around the globe in 1956 to recover artifacts sacred to African tribes stolen last century by Victorian Imperialists. Bartered for hundreds of elephant tusks poached by tribal blacks, the pair returned the relics to their rightful owners. The next eight years saw them killing crocs in Bechuanaland, harvesting 13,000 from what is now the Okavango Delta of Botswana, exporting the hides to Europe for handbags, belts, and shoes.

In 1959, Rhodesia's African National Congress was banned. The ANC had organized urban boycotts and rural resistance. A state of emergency was declared, 500 members were jailed, and legislation was introduced to crush black demands. Black protest turned violent, so white troops shot blacks, killing eighteen and wounding hundreds. Inciting sabotage and the torching of white farms, Robert Mugabe (now President of Zimbabwe) formed the Zimbabwe African National Union (ZANU). When Rhodesia broke from Britain two years later with UDI—the Unilateral Declaration of Independence announced by Prime Minister Ian Smith—ZANU responded with the Second Chimurenga, the "liberation war" commencing April 28, 1966, when seven freedom fighters engaged white Rhodesian forces at Chinoyi.

The ZANU guns were supplied by the White through the Black.

Strictly business.

By mercenaries.

The Rhodesian War Years (1966–80) saw the pair in Zambia, formerly Northern Rhodesia. "Clive Moon" and "Nigel Hammond" were wanted for "Wankie ivory poaching and black market trafficking in kaffir artifacts" by the BSAP: British South Africa Police. When the Great Zimbabwe photo of them appeared in *The Herald,* the pair shed those aliases and assumed two new ones.

The guns they sold to ZANU rebels were bought by Prosper Vumba. Vumba coined their code names the White, the Black, and the Gray. In the final years of the Rhodesian Bush War, when the white government hired 10,000 mercenaries, Vumba hired the White through the Black to assassinate whites, a white mercenary moving through white mercenaries the ideal cover.

White, black, meant nothing to the Gray.

Only can you pay.

The end of this war in 1980 turned white Southern Rhodesia into black Zimbabwe. ZANU candidates swept the election. Far to the west, however, another black/white war raged.

A leftist coup in Lisbon in 1974 resulted in withdrawal from the Portuguese African colonies of Angola and Mozambique. White South Africa found itself flanked by Marxist black republics chaotic from civil war, with South-West Africa (now Namibia) as a buffer zone on the Atlantic side. Three black factions—the FNLA, UNITA, and MPLA—fought for control of Angola. Aided by Cuban and Soviet troops, the MPLA won. Communist-supplied and based in Angola, South-West African People's Organization terrorists (SWAPO) raided the buffer zone, intent on freeing it from South African rule. In July 1975, South African Defence Forces (SADF) entered Angola to destroy SWAPO bases. Such counterinsurgent sweeps continued for more than a decade.

The most secret and controversial unit in the SADF was 32 Battalion. Trained for reconnaissance and search and destroy missions, 32 saw more action in Angola than any other unit. When the MPLA routed the FNLA and UNITA, a joke was the FNLA acronym didn't mean National Front for the Liberation of Angola in Portuguese, but Fuck Now we Leave Angola, ha ha. Then someone in SADF Special Forces got an idea. From the losers he fashioned a vicious boomerang.

Drilled by Recce Commandos and titled Bravo Group, black FNLA troops were taught guerrilla tactics refined from those U.S. Special Forces used in Vietnam. Wearing uniforms camouflaged in Portuguese pattern, armed with Russian AK–47 assault rifles and RPK/RPD light machine guns, Bravo Group was returned to Angola for

Operation Savannah. There, teamed with Alpha Group recruited from Bushmen, this "Zulu Force" was turned loose for revenge on MPLA and SWAPO bases. Under white SADF command, which turned a blind eye, patrols were led from the front in Angola by contract NCOs.

By mercenaries.

Like the Black & White.

The White blacking-up in the bush with "black is beautiful" skin paint.

Operations in Angola lasted up to six weeks. Dropped by helicopter or trekking in on foot, 32 Battalion tracked SWAPO spoor to water holes where enemy troops converged to replenish supplies. After a fast, furious, bloody firefight, they tortured survivors to pinpoint SWAPO bases. With orders given in Portuguese, 32 was isolated from the SADF, so it had its own Reconnaissance (Recce) Wing. The Wing was how the Black & White earned their reputation. SWAPO and MPLA troops called them "The Terrible Ones."

Village to village and hut to hut, the Gray squeezed information. Men staked spread-eagled on the ground with toxic thorn wood fires lit on their bellies were left to scream long after they'd spilled what they knew. Lips cut from mothers were fried in a pan, then force-fed to their children if a village wouldn't talk. The Black & White vied to see who'd collect the most SWAPO ears, just the left ones, slung from their belts. Troops captured close to pickup time were hauled 2,000 feet up in a chopper, then kicked out one by one till someone fingered their base. For sweeps, the Gray drove Ratel–90s. SWAPO wounded were buried up to their necks in sand, then leveled with a bulldozer blade. Tongues ratted freely as heads lopped off. Driving home from a bush operation, the Terrible Ones lashed naked dead to the bull bars of the Ratels, shredding flesh and baring bones as they crashed through thorn thickets, the flayed horrors warning others "Don't fuck with us."

Bag after bag hung on the garbage line.

When UN Resolution 435 stopped the Angolan Border War in 1989, 32 Battalion was withdrawn from South-West Africa. In 1990, it was sent to Natal to quell clashes between the Zulu Inkatha and Mandela's ANC. There 32 fostered so much ANC hatred that it was or-

dered broken up and disbanded for the period leading
to this April's election.

The Black & White were looking for work. . . .

The Money Man approached Danger Point with trepidation, the sweat of fear mixing with sweat trickled by
heat and humidity. He was an accountant. They were
cold killers.

Victoria Falls results from a geological fault, into
which tumbles the mile-wide river, churning as the Boil-
ing Pot around Danger Point. No rail fenced the wet
promontory, for Africa doesn't worry about liability.
Spray obscured the depths of the abyss on both sides,
lifting now and then to expose the dizzying drop. The
Falls roared like a lion heard for miles. The Black &
White sat on the rocks tipping Danger Point.

In their late fifties, both men were turning gray. Khaki
bush shirts and shorts clung to muscled frames, sweat
darkening their armpits and blotching their black hearts.
The White wore a safari hat shading his tanned face,
hard eyes glinting from the shadow like a leopard at
night. A soggy cigarette smoldered in one corner of his
mouth. Two or three days' stubble prickled his jaw. The
hatless Black wore spattered shades, lenses so dark he
could be blind. His kinky hair resembled steel wool,
parted by a pink knife scar. One hand squeezed a rubber
ball, clenching and loosening rhythmically. Fresh from
the bush, both men stank.

"The money?" said the Black.

"In the bank."

"Zurich?" asked the White.

"Like you said."

"Two million?" asked the Black.

"U.S.?" the White added.

"Yes, not to be released till the job is done."

"Released how?" asked the Black, tossing the ball to
his other hand. The Money Man saw what looked like
a skull tattooed on his palm.

"Don't worry. You'll be paid. I'll see to that."

"The worry will be *yours,* mate, if we're not." The
White pulled a Polaroid from his shirt pocket. "Fuck us
over and this will be you."

Too early for tourists, the three had the Point to themselves. Whitewater rafts would soon dot the rapids below, and *Flight of the Angels* flights would circle above, but now the Falls were how they were before man evolved.

Gawking wide-eyed at the Polaroid, the Money Man shivered. "You'll be paid," he repeated, voice breaking as he spoke.

"Good," said the White. His lips eked a smile. The smile had all the warmth of a crocodile's.

The man in the photo was crucified to the ground, wooden tent pegs hammered through both hands and feet. Piercing his ears were barbed hooks used for tiger-fish, cinched to tight lines tied around his toes. Tension in the wires raised and bent his head, angling it to stare the length of his naked body. Eyelids removed to ensure he'd see, his abdomen was slit and peeled, exposing his insides. The sea of blood around him said he bled to death.

Ready to retire on the money they had cached, the mercenaries had hired a London investment broker. Within a year the crucified man had lost their savings in a Docklands scam, so that's why the Gray was back on the garbage line.

For one last hit.

Who funded the Money Man was irrelevant. Were they Afrikaner whites? The "third force" in the government? The ANC? Rival Zulus? Or foreign meddlers? The color of their money was all that mattered to the Gray.

Though neither man liked women, the two had gorged on sex. They'd gang-raped the wife or daughter of every Angolan chief, joking they were "egg satchets" on the garbage line. Known as "Slim," Africa is home to AIDS. Twenty percent of the populace harbors the virus. HIV positive, the Black & White were living on borrowed time.

Two million dollars.

The good life.

Precious days.

So they *would* kill the Zulu king.

And anyone in their way.

BLUDGEON

New Westminster

Pursuant to Hatchett's edict, Staff Sergeant Bill Tipple was dressed in Red Serge. As second last witness for the Crown, he was called to blow a reverse wind on the sails of the defense. The head of Coquitlam GIS and Kidd's boss, it was to him Knight had sent the photo of the trophy box. So, before calling Colin Wood to the stand, Wilde used Tipple to prove the picture of the Zulu club so the jury would have it as evidence of the means by which Nick killed his mom. That was the theory of the Crown in opening statement, and that would be the Crown's theory in Wilde's address.

His testimony over, Tipple spent this afternoon in the gallery of the court, watching Knight cross-examine Wood. Seated around him were other witnesses called by Wilde: Nosy Parker, Rachel Kidd, Gill Macbeth, Dermott Toop, and Ident techs. The jury had motive: the Mother letter. The jury had means: the Zulu club. The jury had opportunity: the birthday party at Mom's. If Wood stood fast under questioning by Knight, the jury would have Dora's blood on Nick's cuff, and the Crown would have a strong circumstantial case.

Strong enough to force Nick into the witness box.

One-on-one with Wilde.

Broompole *v.* Craven.

The problem Knight faced was the visual impact of five autorads. Here was graphic evidence going into the jury room by which the jury could *see* Dora's blood on Nick's tunic. Had there been faults in the matches—such as band shifts or faint bands—Knight would have attacked the autorads directly. Here, where the matches were clear, that would only solidify the Crown's case, so he was forced to go behind the visual evidence in an attempt to refute it by exposing the testing procedures as scientifically invalid or the tests as not properly performed.

"Concerning the control genomic DNA present on the gels and the phenotype for each locus, were they *all* in agreement with expected values derived from previous experiments . . . ?"

"You agree that without the use of a monomorphic marker of known size, the accuracy of the results would be suspect. . . ."

"The way in which VNTR alleles are classified and the approach to genotype interpretation of VNTR phenotypes is complex. . . ."

Here Knight's strategy was to overwhelm the jurors with complexities of DNA chemistry and biology, methods of analysis, population genetics, and statistics. His goal was to portray DNA matching as a new and unproven jeopardy prone to false inclusions and exaggerated statistics. The most impressive attribute of DNA evidence was the strength of statistical association. The sheer magnitude of the chances of a false inclusion—here one in one hundred billion—made it hard to avoid the conclusion "positive identification."

"How can you arrive at figures of one in one hundred billion when there are only five billion people on Earth and you have tested just seven hundred?"

But Vic Knight was tangling with the RCMP Forensic Lab, a national facility with rigid standards, not some local affair on a frolic of its own. And Colin Wood was a tough geneticist.

In the end, smoke swirled and mirrors confused the jury.

But the autorads remained true.

"Mr. Wood," Hatchett said, "you may step down. Mr. Wilde?"

Wilde flipped open his pocket watch, confirmed the time, and snapped it shut. "That, My Lady, is the case for the Crown."

"Mr. Knight, will you be calling evidence?"

"Yes, and given the hour perhaps—"

"Let's get on with it," Hatchett pressed. "Open to the jury."

The gallery was filling quickly as word spread out through the courts, but crime waits for no man and Bill

Tipple had other crimes to solve, so though the defense was about to answer their case, he had an FBI Agent to meet in Coquitlam at four. Inching against the tide of lawyers and laymen surging in, the staff sergeant made for the exit as Knight began.

The lawyer plucked a book from the counsel table and approached the jury.

"The year is 1935. In the House of Lords. The case is *Woolmington* versus *The Director of Public Prosecutions*. The Law Lord about to speak is Viscount Sankey. What he is about to say"—Knight opened the book—"has yet to be said better."

Tipple left the Heritage Court as Knight began to read, *"Throughout the web of the English Criminal Law one golden thread is always to be seen,"* eloquent words following him along the hall toward the largest picture of the Queen in the Commonwealth, *"that it is the duty of the prosecution to prove the prisoner's guilt,"* down the stairs to the Great Hall beamed with sunshine, *"If, at the end of and on the whole of the case, there is a reasonable doubt, created by the evidence given by either the prosecution or the prisoner,"* words dying as he gazed out over Begbie Square, *"the prosecution has not made out the case and the prisoner is entitled to an acquittal. . . ."*

Pushing the door so heavy it could cause a hernia, Tipple stepped out into the square, guarded by the statue of the Hanging Judge, then turned right to face the Fraser River. Down steps to Carnarvon Street, he turned right again, maple trees budding leaves along the walk, then right again to reach the door to the Law Courts' underground lot. Mounted on the wall above was a statue of Themis, but unlike the Goddess of Justice in Vancouver with her silly scroll, this woman wielded the sword of power. Engraved below in Latin: FIAT JUSTITIA, RUAT COELUM. "Let Justice Be Done, Though the Heavens Should Fall." Across which, some malcontent had scrawled BLOW ME, BITCH.

The sign on the door read PARKING.

Through this, and down steps, then through a metal door, Tipple entered a lot that barely cleared his hat, forcing him to remove it as he walked ahead to his van, parked deep in the side of the hill in the last spot on the right. Down here, the bowels of the courts rumbled. The ceiling was blasted with what looked like asbestos, but in this home of lawsuits was cellulose insulation. To the left where cars in or out passed the attendant's booth, a ventilator noisily sucked air. The pipes above gurgled. By row upon row of parked cars hidden from the booth by a concrete central support, Tipple approached his van. The single fluorescent tubes turned dark into murk, but the one by stall 40 was burnt out. He fumbled with his keys by the glow of a red EXIT sign, as unseen eyes peered through a tiny window in the door that led up to an out-only exit into Begbie Square. The concrete angle beside the van throbbed from the elevator mechanism within.

Tipple unlocked and pulled open the rear doors of the van.

Evil Eye opened the stairwell door and skulked up behind.

The Mountie stored his briefcase in back.

The ceiling too low for a downward smash, Evil Eye whirled the club from the side.

The bludgeoning caved in Tipple's skull and hurled him half into the van.

Crawling in to haul the convulsing man inside, the killer pulled the doors shut from within.

Isiko.

WITCH DOCTOR

Harare, Zimbabwe
Friday, March 4, 1994

Chief Neharawa: The One Who Doesn't Sleep. Ancient ruler of the site where this city grew.

Fort Salisbury: named for Britain's Prime Minister (the Marquis of Salisbury) by businessman Cecil Rhodes, when his private army, the Pioneer Column, marched in and took over in 1890.

"My bones will rise!" the Spirit Medium of Nehanda prophesied on the scaffold as she was hanged after the First Chimurenga ("liberation war") of 1896 was crushed by whites.

Harare: named for Chief Neharawa in 1980 when the Second Chimurenga gave control of Rhodesia's Salisbury to blacks.

The wheel goes around.

The African heart of Harare is Mbare Market. Last century when whites usurped Kopje Hill, blacks were relocated south, first to an area white supervised with a nine o'clock curfew, then to prime real estate near the abattoir, cemetery, and sewage drop. Today Mbare is the lively part of the city, with crowds of people walking the roads, cramming run-down blocks of flats, bartering in the *musika*. When Harare was Salisbury, this was Harare Township. Mbare was a chief who once held court on Kopje Hill.

The wheel goes around.

Yesterday, to kill time, Zinc had strolled through the *musika*. Except for the faces being black instead of Asian, it was Canton's Qingping Market in the Cutthroat case. A huge, sprawling complex with hundreds of small stalls, this decades-old trading center at the hub of converging roads is where Africans bring their produce in from the country to sell. Zinc's preconceptions of Zimbabwe were wrong. He expected bloat-bellied kids and litter everywhere. Poverty there was, but not the desperate kind. Shoeless children grinned, and didn't beg. Zimbabwe is litter-free because *everything* is recycled. The secondhand section of the maze was piled high with old clothes, plastic bottles, packed-paper fuel, footwear cut from worn tires, and other cobbled inventions. Lose something in Harare today and you'll find it here tomorrow. Teens sat on the ground pounding jit jive and marimba from pail drums. Perfectly stacked pyramids of oranges, greens, and bananas stocked produce wagons. Throngs sipped *chibuku* at rowdy beer stalls as porters with wheelbarrows followed the laden for a tip. Poultry cackled.

The night of the L.A. riots, Zinc was in New York, the only diner in a restaurant usually packed, the chef glaring at him from the kitchen door: *Beat it, fool, so I can run home and be safe,* while gangs in the subway chanted "Riot patrol." Here he was in "Rhodesia," which should be rife with hate, the only white face adrift in a maze of blacks, just fourteen years between now and a bloody race war, yet no squints of anger.

How did that make sense?

N'angas—witch doctors—worked throughout Mbare. Government sanctioned, their stalls were hodgepodges of skins and pods, dried plants and cowrie shells, gemsbok tails and horrid things in bottles. Snake spines strung above acted as charms. The stall that stopped Zinc dead in his tracks had two *n'angas.* The male cured ills of the flesh with bush drugs. The female spirit medium—blind, with open milky eyes—gazed on the realm of the shades.

Pollock and the Porroh Man. Lukundoo, he thought.

Now, like yesterday morning after he arrived, Zinc sat in a cab passing the High Courts, with their stern black judges in red robes and white wigs, to head north on Fourth Street. Traffic drove on the left. The cabbie thrummed the wheel to the jit jive of the Bhundu Boys on the radio as they zipped around red-and-white drums marking road construction. The car was an oven. The cabbie was cool. And Zinc would soon be a puddle on the sweaty seat. Past Livingstone Avenue, they turned right on Josiah Chinamano Avenue.

At Seventh Street, a traffic cop signaled them to halt. Beyond Josiah Tongogara Avenue a block to their left, Seventh became Chancellor Avenue, residence of Comrade Robert Mugabe, President of the Republic of Zimbabwe. A ZANU guerrilla in the Bush War, and target of several assassin runs in the 1980 election, Mugabe knows the dangers of African politics. From six P.M. to six A.M. Chancellor is closed, and those testing the order are shot on sight. Along Seventh came an embassy motorcade, each black Mercedes flapping a tiny flag on the left front fender, Big Spears leading, with Canada far behind.

Once it passed, the cop motioned them on.

Jacaranda trees lined Josiah Chinamano Avenue. To the right was Greenwood Park. Facing the park between Seventh and Eighth was a white Spanish-style building with a red-tiled roof. This was Police General Headquarters of the ZRP.

Late last century, Cecil Rhodes (of Rhodes scholar fame) recruited 500 men as the British South Africa Police. The early days of the force were spent quelling black resistance to his British invasion. The symbol of BSAP authority was the *sjambok* whip, which lashed until the Second Chimurenga of recent years. With independence, the BSAP became the Zimbabwe Republic Police. The ZANU blacks who took over promptly adopted BSAP traditions.

Passing Police General Headquarters, the cab drove further along the avenue to cross Tenth Street to a T wall. There Zinc paid the fare and stepped out into the sun.

The Training Depot at the T end was a walled camp. The red-brick guardhouse was flanked by two high blue-metal peaked gates, In to the left, Out to the right. On the cream-and-brown wall beside the In gate was the badge of the ZRP: a lion with a Zimbabwe bird in police colors of blue and old gold. Through the gates stood a red-brick building with round windows. IDing Zinc from yesterday, the guard waved him in.

Inside, the road forked left and right. Left was the armory for "musketry" drill, hospital, canteen, officers' mess, and sports club with bar and billiards tables.

Zinc turned right.

Past a row of pines stood three buildings, one on the left behind a hedge, two on the right in the open. The two were the forensic lab and police chapel, the latter—for no reason Zinc could see—barb-wired. The single-story structure behind the hedge was shaped like a horseshoe with a corrugated iron roof. The flags in front were bugled up and down at dawn and dusk. Beyond were the old stables and sergeants mess. Vehicles were parked in the inverted U. The sign above the walkway read CID HEADQUARTERS.

Zinc turned in.

If Zimbabwe follows West Africa, Zambia, and other former British colonies, the infrastructure will crumble in thirty years. Currently fourteen years into such decline, CID HQ was run-down and poorly maintained. The office of Chief Inspector Prosper Vumba baked

Zinc pink at 90 degrees F. The punkah-punkah fan over-head merely guided the flies. President Mugabe grinned on the wall behind the Victorian desk, the large yellow mark around him left by an earlier portrait of the queen or PM Ian Smith.

"Ah, Zzzinc," Vumba said, rising from the desk and switching on his smile, swirling the name in his mouth like a wine taster before spitting it out. "Not still bristling from yesterday?"

"You gave me time to sightsee the city," Chandler said dryly.

"All you expected?"

"What I expected, Prosper, was tit for tat. Before I left Canada, I faxed Interpol. Interpol—I checked—sent you my request. If it was you asking us, we'd have wired the picture to every cop in Canada, so when you arrived on a *loooong* flight there would be results. But I arrive to find the picture buried on your desk. Meanwhile, someone else could be killed. Quite frankly, I'm pissed."

The temperature rose a degree.

The fan droned on.

While Zinc craved the wind chill of a Saskatchewan winter.

Except for the Criminal Investigation Department, ZRP cops, brass included, wear khaki bush shirts, caps, and shorts. Top to bottom, the CID is plainclothed, so Vumba filled a charcoal suit the color of his skin, as Zinc melted in an ice-cream suit as wrinkled as an elephant's ear. Face to face, they were chess pieces vying for the same square.

"Are you spooks in your country?" Vumba asked.

The Canadian blinked.

"What street conveyed you here?"

"Fourth," Zinc said.

"At Fourth and Central, by the Catholic Cathedral, you passed a red-brick square bearing the sign TREASURY COMPUTER BUREAU. The top four floors are the Central Intelligence Organization. Until the War, that was the Security Branch of the BSAP. The white spooks fed spies into our camps. We 'gooks'—the Rhodies stole the term from Yanks in Vietnam—were sometimes so well-known to them that they could put a name to one of our captured guns. Interrogating us, they'd ask, 'How's

Joe in camp?' The Bureau had files on everyone: ZANU, poachers, mercenaries. Many files survived. The CIO is controlled directly by the Prime Minister's Office. Cops no longer run it, but I have contacts there."

Across the desk, Vumba pushed *The Herald* clipping of Nigel Hammond and Clive Moon at the Great Zimbabwe ruins. "After our heated meeting yesterday, I called a contact at the CIO." Vumba placed an airline ticket on the clipping. "Nigel Hammond or Clive Moon will see you there."

Zinc opened the ticket to check the destination. "How'd you find him?"

"Sifting and shifting, Zzzinc."

The African bush breeds disease: malaria, typhoid, tetanus, yellow fever, sleeping sickness, typhus, AIDS, meningitis, diptheria, bilharzia, myiasis, dysentery, rabies, giardia, cholera . . . and ebola, for those seeking the exotic. Africans show scars from bouts in the past, so the whites of Vumba's eyes were yellow and flecked with blood.

One evil eye winked.

"Tight lines, mate."

Given his ZANU rank during the Bush War, had Vumba desired, he would be a subcommissioner or chief superintendent by now. Administration, however, was not his style. He stayed where the action was. And the serious money.

The Gray had sold Vumba weapons during the War. It was Vumba who'd hired the Gray to assassinate whites. As he knew how to cure what ailed the country, his code name then was the Witch Doctor. The Gray had paid him well to watch their backs ever since, so no sooner had Zinc left his office yesterday morning than Vumba was on the phone to the Black.

Witch Doctor: "The Horseman just left. He wants the picture of you two wired around Zimbabwe. South Africa, too."

The Black: "That's the last thing we want. How did you leave it?"

Witch Doctor: "He's angry the photo isn't out. If it's not wired by the time he returns tomorrow, he'll approach the brass."

Assassinating someone is easy to do, assuming the police aren't looking for you. Escaping after, that's the difficult part. Dangerous anytime, but suicidal if the police are *already* hunting you. Armed with a picture of your face.

Two million dollars US.

To kill the Zulu king.

The clock ticking.

AIDS in their veins.

The Horseman in the way.

He must be taken out.

In a way that won't mobilize other cops.

Somewhere he won't be found.

Where death's a way of life.

The Black: "Here's what you do. . . ."

ETHICS

New Westminster

So high was Nick's level of protective custody the Law Courts sheriffs locked him in the female cells for his trial. Cells one, two, three, and four in this block, and Cell three was his. Released from it by a deputy for escort down a spick-and-span hall painted beige and brown, close to the colors of the Brownie's uniform, Nick went past the cellblock for male accused, from which someone shouted, "Yer gonna git juked, Horseman," then angled right from the booking desk near the loading bay to arrive at 371 INTERVIEW.

Knight was waiting.

Like a caged cat, the lawyer paced the eight-foot-square room, soles squeaking across the linoleum floor, shadow from fluorescent lights moving around the cream-colored walls and chocolate-colored door. Nick sat down on one of two chairs flanking a table while the deputy locked them in. The only window was a foot-square pane in the door.

"You look pumped," said Nick.

"What a piece of work that woman is. One thing for sure, Hatchett didn't *sleep* her way to the top."

"No adjournment?"

"She threw me out of chambers. Come ten o'clock, I put you on the stand."

"What happened?"

"The court clerk ushered Wilde, me, and the court reporter in. Hatchett asked why I was troubled over the Mountie found dead in the lot last night. I said Tipple was bludgeoned and gutted like your mom and MacDougall. So? she said. So if this killer murdered your mom, you were innocent. Wilde said Tipple's killing made no difference. We know MacDougall wasn't killed by you, so it was obvious someone else was cop-killing Mounties, with the Crown's theory being—like it was all along—that you used that killer as a smokescreen. Hatchett accused me of stalling, and that was it."

"What now?" asked Craven.

"The fight goes on. You know what John Paul Jones told the British. Which means the time has come for The Talk."

"The Talk?" said the Mountie.

"The Talk," repeated the lawyer. "I talk while you sit and listen carefully."

On the table lay a carrying bag for a suit, which Nick assumed held the barrister's gown. Knight took the seat opposite and leaned over the bag, eyes so firm and voice so compelling he might be plotting to assassinate the queen.

Which in a way he was.

"Here's where we stand. The Crown's circumstantial case against you is: motive, the Mother letter; opportunity, being at her home; means, the club evidenced by your mom's blood on your sleeve. By proving that, Wilde has forced you to take the stand.

"Our defense has two prongs: Schreck and the twin. The twin—proved by what you remember and Alex saw in the files—answers motive, the Mother letter. The cat breaching the back door to let Schreck in, or your mom opening the door to her other child, spread opportunity to our suspects. Schreck clubbed, then gutted your mom because he's psycho. The twin clubbed, then gutted your mom, MacDougall, and Tipple because he's zombie of the shades.

"Which leaves means, the blood."

Knight leaned closer and lowered his voice.

"Your mom's blood on your tunic can be defended in three ways:

"One, between the time Kidd seized the tunic from your home and the time Wood did his tests, other bloody exhibits tainted the cuff. You heard the evidence. Kidd to Toop to Wood, I couldn't break the chain of continuity. So that defense is gone.

"Two, Wood's DNA lab tests were faulty. One in one hundred billion, and I couldn't shake him in cross-examination. The jury has the autorads. So that defense is gone.

"Three, between the time you picked your tunic up from the cleaners and the time you left your mom's home for the dinner, somehow you innocently got her blood on your cuff.

"That's the *only* defense left.

"So what I'm saying—listen hard—is you have *no* defense if you can't explain those bloodstains on your cuff.

"Here's how Hatchett will screw you.

"The standard charge to a jury on reasonable doubt is: *You will note that the Crown must establish the accused's guilt beyond a 'reasonable doubt,' not beyond 'any doubt.' A reasonable doubt is exactly what it says— a doubt based on reason—on the logical processes of the mind. It is not a fanciful or speculative doubt, nor is it a doubt based upon sympathy or prejudice. It is the sort of doubt which, if you ask yourself 'why do I doubt?'—you can assign a logical reason by way of an answer. A logical reason in this context means a reason connected to the evidence. . . .*

"So where's the evidence that raises doubt about the blood?

"There is none. Unless *you* give it.

"When we met that first time to discuss your case, you said, 'You haven't asked if I did it.' My reply was 'I don't care. My only ethical restraint is I *knowingly* can't offer false evidence or lying witnesses. I don't "know" what you don't tell me, so keep what happened to yourself unless I specifically ask. What will this jury believe is what concerns me.' "

Leaning closer, the barrister lowered his voice to a whisper.

"Every lawyer's nightmare is standing in front of a jury without a case to make. Obviously, I can't tell you what to say on the stand. That would be suborning perjury. But as the trial sits now, logically I see two explanations for the blood:

"One, the tunic was clean when you arrived at your mom's, and her blood stained your cuff when you hit her with the club; or

"Two, the tunic was clean when you arrived at your mom's, and her blood stained your cuff when she grabbed your wrist after cutting her finger dicing vegetables for her meal.

"All I can ethically do is put you on the stand to tell the truth. If what you say doesn't explain how the blood got on your cuff, you'll spend a minimum of ten years in jail. But if what you say does explain how the blood got on your cuff, so there is a reasonable doubt based on the evidence, then leave it to me and you'll walk out of court a free man. You grasp what I'm saying in this little Talk?"

"Yes," said Nick.

"Let's be sure you understand *precisely* what's at stake. If you're found guilty because the blood on your cuff's not explained, the appeal will be heard by three judges picked by Cutter. He'll be one and the other two will be of his ilk. Hatchett admitting your tunic will be upheld. If the Supreme Court of Canada grants leave to appeal—the chance of which is slim—not only must the Court decide the Charter was infringed, but we must establish admitting the tunic brings the administration of justice into disrepute. This isn't America. There's no doctrine like Fruit of the Poisoned Tree to help us out. Your agent—the Filipina maid—did give Kidd the tunic.

"Lose here and you're fucked."

Knight glanced at his watch.

"Wilde's downstairs with a bone in his pants, and that hard-on's for you. Your Achilles' heel is blood from your mom. I want Hatchett, and I want Wilde. Don't leave me facing this jury without that blood explained.

What's really at stake here isn't your life." The Vulture winked. "It's my reputation."

Now Nick understood why every scumbag charged with murder *always* had a defense.

As he watched, the lawyer unzipped the suit bag on the table. Inside—boots, breeches, hat, and all—was a corporal's Red Serge. "DeClercq brought this to my office yesterday. He said it's your size."

Pinned to the tunic was a note:

> "Even were a VC to be sentenced to be hanged for murder, he should be allowed to wear the VC on the scaffold." (King George V).
> Good luck on the stand.
> DeClercq.

NEXT ON THE GARBAGE LINE

Africa

Zimbabwe is the lightning rod of the world. People are zapped and trees are zotted in the rainy season of November to mid-March. Outside the window of the plane, Air Zimbabwe Flight UM 224 to Victoria Falls, lightning flashed blue in vicious forks.

The plane jumped.

Zinc white-knuckled his seat.

The man across the aisle cursed in Afrikaans.

Unlike any other airline Zinc had flown, Air Zimbabwe pilots keep the cockpit door open. Too hot? Showing off? Hinges broken? Whatever the reason, it worried him to watch a hand adjust a dial, only to have another correct the setting seconds later.

"TAB," the South African said, noting his discomfort.

"TAB?"

"That's Africa, baby."

　　　　　　　　　*　　*　　*

Zinc had left Vancouver at 8:00 P.M. Tuesday night to fly for nine hours to London, arriving at 1:15 P.M. Wednesday without a wink of sleep. Stretched across a makeshift cot of four chairs at Heathrow, he'd tried to doze until the Harare flight at 10:00 P.M., but airport hubbub sabotaged sleep. His constitution such he never slept on planes, he'd endured another ten hours to Zimbabwe, landing at 8:50 A.M. Thursday morning to enjoy a brand-new day. Biorhythms confused, last night's sleep was fitful.

Exhausted, sweaty, and brain throbbing, Zinc was in a cynical, cranky mood.

Victoria Falls

In May 1904, the Cape to Cairo railway reached the Falls. Within a month the first hotel was open for business, a simple structure of wood and corrugated iron raised from the ground for ventilation and protection from pests.

The elegant hotel of today was built in 1914. The train from Cape Town would stop at Victoria Falls Station, lordly Edwardian in High British Empire style, shaded by fragrant frangipanis and flame-flowered flamboyants. A colonnade of trees led to this hotel, where blacks in starched white uniforms and gloves catered to London whims. The teatime terrace overlooked the green hills of Africa through the Falls' spray, across Second Gorge and the railway bridge. Top hat gents and primped ladies found the short walk to the Falls a strain, so a trolley carried them down to the Big Splash, then black trolley boys pushed them back up and smiled for photographs.

Zinc arrived to find no room at the inn.

Bag in hand, he stood in reception by the porter's lodge, head pounding as Commonwealth bigwigs scowled at him, some sort of CHOGM pooh-bah retreat, with too many women too young and too sexy to be delegates or wives, how many people were starving back home to gorge each entourage?

Bwana fantasies.

Black as lordly as white.

Zinc checked his bag, left word at the desk, then

poked around. He crossed the courtyard into the lounge and turned right. Crocodile tail with béarnaise sauce was on the menu for dinner in the Livingstone Room. The cocktail bar—The "I Presume"—buzzed with chortling honchos sipping G-and-Ts or zombies. Across the terrace and down steps, he rounded the south hammerhead wing to the pool (no mixed swimming for years after a maharajah refused to bathe in the view of ladies). Nearby was the African Spectacular kraal: nightly shows by Shangaan and Makishi dancers driven by fire-heated drums and an eerie kudu horn. An old man near the door weaved spirit masks while Zinc examined photos of the rituals inside. The Shangaans—a Zulu offshoot—danced with shields and knobkerries.

Baboons romped by the path in front of the hotel, and climbed rainspouts to ransack rooms with open windows. Zinc went down the gentle slope toward the Falls, until he spied the horde of hawkers about to latch like leeches. Years back, touring Egypt with Elvis Presley's plumber, he was besieged by hands seeking "Baksheesh!" A Christmas card came from Memphis that December: Mary and baby Jesus on a donkey led by Joseph, serene faced with halos around their hair, lunging at whom the plumber had drawn a smiling Arab in Arafat headdress with hand outstretched, the cartoon bubble from his mouth the word "Baksheesh!"

Zinc turned back.

The desk clerk hailed him as he entered reception. "Mr. Chandler, this was left for you." She passed him a sealed envelope.

"By whom?" Zinc asked.

"A boy paid a Zim or two to drop it here."

The Mountie tore open the envelope and withdrew a printed note: *Get your bag, walk out the door, and drop this in the car park. Yellow Hertz, bird shit on the boot, key inside, map on the seat. Eight A.M. tomorrow, I'll call.*

He got his bag, walked out the door, dropped the note, and found the car with bird shit on its trunk. The parking lot was a focus of comings and goings: *Flight of the Angels,* Snake Park, Crocodile Ranch, Big Tree, Craft Village, booze cruise, bungee-jumping, and whitewater rafting.

Zinc drove off.

The White picked up the note.

The sun in his eyes, Zinc drove west along Kazungula Road, thirty-odd miles of dry bush through Zambezi National Park to the Botswana border. The Upper Zambezi to the north being one of the longest safe stretches of water between Lake Victoria in East Africa and the Vaal Dam, not long ago Imperial Airways (forerunner of British Airways) landed Solent flying boats here at "Jungle Junction" on its London to South Africa route. Herds of sable antelope grazed by the road, both sexes with two-and-a-half-foot swept-back horns, while a spotty giraffe watched Zinc pass from above the trees. Hard to believe that tall neck had the same number of vertebrae as his own.

At Kazungula, Zinc crossed the border.

The area reminded him of an Indian Reserve, as if this lifestyle was foreign to the people. On the other side of the border, the road degenerated, potholes and bumps rocking the car. The customs shed had a stop sign and kudu head on the wall, with an elephant tusk behind the thatched roof. An election poster papered the door: CHOOSE YOUR LEADERS above photos and party banners. The desks inside were remnants from Bechuanaland Colonial days, with no computers, no typewriters, all entries by hand. To counter hoof-and-mouth disease, Zinc drove the car through a trough of disinfectant, then got out and stomped on a pair of shorts soaked with the chemical. A far cry from Heathrow two days ago!

Driving toward the Chobe River, it began to rain. Sudden dark clouds tore open overhead, pouring water by the gallon down on him. Just as suddenly it stopped and the earth began to steam, images appearing in the malarial mist. *Daga* huts, reed huts, teepeelike tents. Donkey carts, ox carts, goats in the way. Shacks ramshackle as if ready to fall.

Africa as he expected.

Then the unexpected.

As blue as the sky now pushing back the clouds, as blue as any tropical blue Zinc had ever seen, the northern border of Botswana—the Chobe River—appeared. The floodplains by the water were a mix of vegetation, thickets of bush, open grassland, and islands of packed reeds. Glancing right whenever he could as he followed the riverfront, Zinc glimpsed buffalo, waterbuck, roan, and hippo by the dozen. The rain gone, flowers by the road came into bloom. The mist clearing, rainbows arced the Chobe. The flatland beyond was Namibia: the Caprivi Strip.

After Kasane, Zinc entered Chobe National Park, a raw and primal wilderness packed with game.

Barely in, he braked to a halt.

Crossing the road was a herd of elephants.

. . . twelve, thirteen, fourteen . . .

He wondered if he should honk?

Elephants in the wild seem much bigger than in the zoo: eleven feet high at the shoulder with tusks up to eight feet long, each tusk a hundred pounds driven by a body of seven tons. The ground shook as the herd passed in front of him, amazingly graceful as they lowered each well-placed padded foot . . . *eighteen, nineteen, twenty* . . . then an old bull stopped.

Few frights are more compelling than an elephant charge, how that enormous wrinkly gray face comes pounding at you, wide ears flapping to warn you've come too close, high-pitched trumpeting getting the point across admirably, huge eyeball closing in like King Kong at the window of the Empire State Building. Bushmen say an elephant's ashamed of killing a human, so it covers the remains with sticks and grass. Some consolation. Zinc watched the mammoth beast lead with its left tusk—*Are elephants left- or right-tusked?* his scared-witless mind wondered—imagining that ivory spear smashing through the glass, pinning him to the driver's seat like an entomologist's bug, the trunk then wrapping around his neck to wrench him out through the shards, twirling him over that creased brow like a human bola, before throwing him down with contempt to be trampled by the herd.

Almost soiling his shorts, he decided not to honk.

The elephant stopped, then backed away, teaching Zinc the difference between a real and mock charge.

He was a lawman.

The law was different here.

The Law of the Jungle: *Ele has the right of way.*

Afternoon's the favored time for elephant herds to congregate at the river. The Chobe elephant population exceeds 50,000. Zinc hoped he wouldn't have to wait for *all* of them to pass. Branches cracking as trunks stripped them of leaves, saplings uprooted by digging tusks, trees trembling as giant heads butted them, slowly the procession moved from left to right. Those by the water completely abandoned themselves, rolling and frolicking like slapstick comedians, some using their trunks as snorkels to swim and submerge. Mothers lined the river with their trunks in a row, like a dance troupe leaning on canes, while calves suckled from the pair of breasts between their front legs.

The last elephant passed.

Zinc drove on.

To a yellow sign with white letters: THE EDEN GAME LODGE.

Alone in Room 406, Zinc got ready for bed. Weariness washed over him as he brushed his teeth, a fatigue so strong even jet lag couldn't keep him from sleep. He sprayed the room with Doom against malarial mosquitoes, then stepped out onto the dark veranda until the chemical mist settled.

The southern sky.

Double? triple? the stars in the north.

Hippos snorting in the river through the dead of night.

Then he heard it.

Nearby.

A chilling lion roar.

The Caprivi Strip, Namibia

Like a finger poking east to prod Zambia and Zimbabwe, Namibia's Caprivi Strip is wedged between Angola and Botswana. The Strip remains from a swap in Colonial times when Britain acquired Zanzibar and Germany netted this corridor named after Chancellor Count von Caprivi. German South-West Africa envisaged an east-west railway like Britain's Cape to Cairo route. Without sufficient colonies, they only got this far.

In the Rhodesian Bush War, guerrillas hid here. In the Angolan Border War, the Strip provided a focus for battles between SWAPO and South African forces. Buffalo in the Caprivi Strip was headquarters for 32 Battalion. Warnings by their camp read: IS THERE LIFE AFTER DEATH? TRESPASS AND YOU'LL FIND OUT. The Eden Game Lodge had to close for several years. The war made the Strip home to the Gray, to the Black & White, to the Garbage Line Spiders.

Tonight, they had returned.

Across the river from the lodge, SADF night vision binoculars watched Zinc stretch on the deck, his green-hued yawn inducing the White to stifle a yawn himself. "Him," he said, passing the field glasses to the Black, who removed his specs and pocketed them, then refocused both lenses on Zinc.

"Kill him quick or kill him slow?" the Black asked the White.

"The man has jeopardized our cash. Kill him quick and he gets off light."

The Black nodded. "Kill him slow."

"Good shoulders. Good chest. He's packing seasoned meat."

"Hang him naked above the jaws."

"Meat hook through each palm should get the point across."

"Teach the fucker to fuck with us."

"Piece by piece."

"Let him scream."

"No one to hear."

"Let him squirm."

"Piece by piece."

"Fed alive to crocs."

PERJURY

New Westminster

"Order in Court! All rise!" the sheriff barked as Chief Justice Morgan Hatchett climbed the four steps to the bench, appearing from behind the sashed red velvet curtain to assume her throne. From on high, she gazed down on the rabble: robed barristers facing her at the counsel table, and beyond in the prisoner's dock backed by the great unwashed in the public gallery. . . .

"Mr. Knight, what is the meaning of this?"

The tall, gaunt man rose from the counsel table. He turned to glance at the dock, then at the jury. "While cross-examining Corporal Kidd, I asked 'Why are you in Red Serge?' She replied 'I was told to wear it.' When I asked 'Why?', you interrupted to chastise me. 'The Red Serge is my order. This is my Court and I determine the rules. Now get on with it, and leave the dress code to me.' If your order is Red Serge for Force witnesses, so be it, Judge. The defense calls Corporal Craven. Shall we get on with it?"

The Hatchet's face turned the color of her scarlet robes. Several jurors wanted to laugh, but feared wrath from the bench. Stetson in hand, Nick stepped down from the dock to cross to the witness stand. His spur caught the oak as he stepped in. "Take the Bible in your right hand," said the clerk. "Do you swear that the evidence you shall give shall be the truth, the whole truth, and nothing but the truth, so help you God?"

"I do."

"State your full name for the record."

"Nicholas John Craven."

"Sit down," Hatchett said.

"I prefer to stand."

Knight strode to the podium beside the jury box. A hush fell over the public gallery. Nick swept the faces row by row, picking out Alex Hunt and Rachel Kidd, but missing from the spectators were Gill and the chief. He almost jumped when Knight dropped his thick trial brief onto the podium, the crash focusing every eye in court on the lawyer, then straight off the bat came the all-important question.

"Corporal Craven, can you tell the judge and jury how your mother's blood came to stain the cuff of your Red Serge tunic?"

Like spectators at a tennis match, all eyes turned to Nick.

At five P.M. on December seventh, 1993, as I was about to leave Mom's house for the Red Serge Dinner, she cut herself while dicing vegetables for her meal. On seeing the blood, I reached out to check the wound, and that's when she grabbed my wrist and said, "It's just a nick." She closed the slice by wrapping a Band-Aid around her finger, and I left Mom alive when I departed from her home.

That's what Knight wanted him to say.

And that was a lie.

Mom wasn't cut while he was there.

That would be perjury.

"Do you swear that the evidence you shall give shall be the truth, the whole truth, and nothing but the truth, so help you God?"

"I do."

In how many cases had he cursed scumbags who lied under oath to save their skins, decrying the fact that few had ethics anymore?

Engraved in French on the insignia he now wore was the Force motto "Maintain the Right."

The day he asked the chief for help, Nick had told DeClercq about the blood, "How that got on my cuff I don't know."

As if by telepathy, no sooner had he recalled that truth than the doors to the court gallery opened and in came DeClercq.

The courtroom stirred as seconds ticked by with no answer from Nick.

"Corporal, did you hear the question?"

Ten years in jail or freedom? warned the lawyer's eyes. *Don't be a fool. You're a cop. Someone will knife you in jail. What's a lie these days, when lying is the norm?*

"I repeat, can you tell the judge and jury how your mother's blood came to stain the cuff of your Red Serge tunic?"

ZIGZAG

Robert DeClercq was awakened by the ringing of the phone.

This was eight hours ago.

"DeClercq," he mumbled, coming out of sleep.

"Robert, it's Eric. Wake up and drive to New West. Bill Tipple was clubbed and gutted in the lot under the Courts. His heart was cut out."

"I'm wide awake," DeClercq said, throwing back the covers. "When was he killed?"

"Late yesterday afternoon. Near as we can tell. He was to meet an FBI Agent in Coquitlam at four. The Yank canceled so it was assumed Bill stayed to watch Nick's trial. Then went home."

"When was he found?"

"An hour ago. New West Police just called."

"The body lay in the lot for"—checking the alarm clock—"ten hours without being seen?"

"Bill's van was parked in a dark stall. He was hit as he opened the back, judging from blood spattered on the roof. The body was hauled into and butchered in the van. The killer probably drove away in another vehicle. The parking lot emptied as courts adjourned, except for cars connected to a rape trial waiting for a jury. When there was no verdict by midnight, the judge sequestered the jurors, and that's when the security guard made his lockup rounds. His flashlight caught the pool of blood seeping from the van."

"I'm on my way," said DeClercq.

Gillian Macbeth was awakened by the ringing of the phone.

This was six hours ago.

"Uuggh," she mumbled, from a dream about Nick.

"It's Robert DeClercq. Bill Tipple's dead. Meet me at Royal Columbian morgue as soon as possible. And keep your fingers crossed."

On double doors between the morgue and chill night air, a handwritten sign in red felt pen warned FUNERAL DIRECTOR, PLEASE MAKE SURE YOU HAVE THE RIGHT BODY. Once burned, twice shy. A body scale attached to a huge hook and chain dangled from the ceiling just inside the doors. Rows of refrigerated crypts lined one wall, with "limbs only" and "stillbirths only" in separate vaults. A typed note taped to one crypt told the staff to clean up messes. Crypt twenty-five across the hall took overflow, with bodies under white sheets visible through a glass-paned door. Another room displayed a gurney beneath a draped window, the anteroom beyond where bereaved peered in to identify their loved ones. A brown couch caught those overcome with grief. Taped to the wall of an office was a *Far Side* cartoon, with *When a body meets a body going through the rye* captioning bodies on gurneys passing in a field.

Polished riding boots with spurs and blue breeches with yellow stripes protruded from a crisp white sheet, as the morgue attendant wheeled a gurney from Crypt twenty-five. He pushed it across the faint red line on the floor dividing the realm of the living from the theater of the dead. From the ghetto blaster came Mozart's *Concerto for Flute, Harp, and Orchestra.* Never again would Robert relish its peaceful strains.

The morgue attendant removed the uniform from Tipple's body. He covered the hole in the chest where the heart was cut out and the disemboweled intestines with plastic, then helped by DeClercq and the New West cops, flipped the pale, bloody corpse facedown on the autopsy table.

In hospital greens, plastic apron, gum boots, and visor, Gill bent over the caved-in skull. Two pairs of gloves with soap between to ease removal later covered her hands. To ensure it didn't come off with the gloves, a ring Nick gave her last summer hung on a chain around her neck.

With a scalpel, Gill shaved the hair from the back of the head.

"Well?" said DeClercq.

"Hard to tell. That look like a zigzag to you?"

Bob George—Ghost Keeper—was awakened by the ringing of the phone.

This was four hours ago.

"George," he said, instantly alert.

"It's Robert DeClercq. Bill Tipple's dead. We need your help. There may or may not be a zigzag impression on his scalp."

"Where's the body?"

"Royal Columbian morgue."

*   *   *

Before heading RFISS ("Ree-fiss" to the Mounties), Ghost Keeper was a Hairs and Fibers tech. Before that, he was a Special Constable under the 3(b) Program on the Duck Lake Reserve. There his uncanny ability in hunting fugitives down earned him the nickname The Tracker and brought him to the attention of the RCMP Forensic (then Crime Detection) Lab. His work with Hairs and Fibers saddled him with the title The Human Vacuum Cleaner, for when he finished with a scene it was "*all* in the bag." Now—as if he didn't have enough appellations—George was The Member Who Took Down Schreck.

RFISS—the Regional Forensic Identification Support Service—provides state-of-the-art backup to cops in the field. Gone are the days of Sherlock Holmes solving cases by triumphs of logic, and plodding Jack Webb seeking "Just the facts, ma'am." The magnifying glass gave way to fingerprint lasers used in conjunction with cyanoacrylate and vacuum metal deposits, to scanning electron microscopes that magnify particles hundreds of thousands of times, to gas chromatographs or mass spectrometers that separate complex compounds into their components, and to DNA analysis. With anthropologists, entomologists, odontologists, and blood spatter physicists on call, scientists often outnumber cops around a corpse. Bob George was the Mountie who marshaled such expertise.

And so it was three hours ago that Bob reached the morgue, having marshaled himself to photograph Tipple's scalp. After selecting the most crucial plane, he used an ABFO Ruler to bracket the shot. This was an L-shaped angle with two eight-centimeter arms, three circles on which became ellipses if the perspective was wrong. The camera was loaded with Tmax 400 ASA film. Mounted on a tripod, he aimed the lens down at a vertical of ninety degrees, then after fine-focusing on the bruise and the ruler, screwed on an 18A ultraviolet filter. The filter was so black he could not see through. Donning goggles to protect his eyes, George swept a Metz 45 electronic flash around the bruise, bombarding it obliquely with ultraviolet rays. The shots snapped would enhance any marks not visible to the naked eye. That done, he asked Gill to cut away the scalp so he could backlight it for shine-through shots.

Packing up, Bob secured the equipment in his Jeep, then joined rush-hour traffic into Vancouver to process the film in Photography Section at the Lab.

Every trial has a point of epiphany, that juncture where the fate of the accused is sealed, and Wilde knew by killer instinct this was it.

"Corporal Craven, can you tell the judge and jury how your mother's blood came to stain the cuff of your Red Serge tunic?" asked Knight.

The courtroom stirred as seconds ticked by with no answer from Nick.

Forked, Wilde thought. *You don't know what to do. Either way, you lose a major piece on the board. Relate the truth and there goes the game. But you've got moral qualms about perjury. No matter what your answer, I've got you. The jury sees guilt written all over your face.*

Nick's eyes flicked to the rear of the court.

Wilde turned and saw DeClercq at the door.

"Corporal, did you hear the question?" Knight said tensely. "I repeat, can you tell the judge and jury how your mother's blood came to stain the cuff of your Red Serge tunic?"

The Mountie took a deep breath and turned to face the jury. Tongue licking his dry lips, Nick exhaled and said, "I—"

"With your indulgence, My Lady, might I have a moment with Mr. Wilde?"

The Crown counsel whirled with venom in his glare, wondering who the hell was to blame for this sabotage, knowing every millisecond counted here, the accused was coming off the ropes toward the knockout punch, and now some asshole was asking the judge . . .

The asshole was Del Van Eaton, the Regional Crown Counsel for the Fraser Region.

The man who hired Wilde.

Wilde turned to Hatchett. "Order him to answer the question, My Lady."

Knight sensed Wilde's jugular was exposed. "Don't answer!" he snapped.

"My Lady?" said Van Eaton.

"Mr. Wilde, it may be important to your case. One minute. No more," Hatchett said.

The portly lawyer strode like a rampaging elephant to the rail separating the court from the gallery. Near the swing gate stood DeClercq, Van Eaton, Ghost Keeper, and Macbeth. Before Wilde could speak, DeClercq held up two photos. "The zigzag in the color print was left on Dora's scalp. It was impressed by the club that bludgeoned her. The zigzag in the black-and-white print was left on Tipple's scalp. You'll note by the rulers, both are the same scale. Compare the zigzags and there's no doubt Tipple was bludgeoned with the same club while Craven was in jail."

Ignoring DeClercq, Wilde turned to Van Eaton, who could shut down the trial. "Those letters Hunt says she saw don't exist, Del. Craven saved her on Deadman's Island, so she's paying him back. The book she's writing will sell bigger if he's acquitted because of her. I've got him, Del. Craven must have hired someone to use the club on Tipple. It's a trick. Don't fall for it." Wilde held a close-together thumb and forefinger up in front of his eye. "I'm a cunt's hair away from taking Craven down."

DeClercq was rarely a violent cop, but enough was enough. He grabbed Lyndon Wilde QC by the lapels of his silky robes and wrenched him around to face him man-to-man. "This isn't *You versus Del*. Nor *You versus Craven*. You've turned this into *You versus Me*. Nobody railroads one of my men. The letters Hunt says she saw are fact. She didn't stab her palm, slash her back, and hurl herself down an elevator shaft to sell books. You don't have the machine that typed the Mother letter, and you told this jury in opening the zigzag club was means. These photos put that club in another hand, and that means your case just collapsed. So either you step aside gracefully, or I take the stand in Craven's defense and expose you for the malicious prosecutor you are."

Hesitant whether to push it, Hatchett's left hand twitched near the panic button under her desk. Buzz and the least that would happen is sheriff's deputies would rush into court, the most a full-scale ERT assault if prearranged. Her quandary stemmed from who was involved in verbal fisticuffs: on one side, her champion,

Lyndon Wilde QC; and on the other, this senior Mountie and the Regional Crown.

"Mr. Wilde? Mr. Van Eaton? Do we have a problem in court?"

"No, My Lady," replied Wilde's boss. The dismay on his face was that of Victor Frankenstein on seeing what he'd created. "You've spent too long in the arena," Van Eaton told Wilde. "Step aside, and get your priorities straight."

Opening the gate, Van Eaton usurped Wilde's place at the counsel table. "I hereby direct the clerk of the court to enter a stay of proceedings."

Blood pressure climbing to redden his face, Lyndon "Broompole" Wilde QC shot a look of pure malevolence at DeClercq as he subconsciously withdrew his pocket watch from his vest.

"The time is later than you think," said the chief superintendent.

The baleful look turned on Macbeth.

Gill didn't flinch.

"Checkmate," she said.

In the mid-1860s, what was the largest city north of San Francisco and west of Chicago? Raise your hands, all those who guessed Barkerville, the lure of American miners to central B.C., later known as Begbie's Hanging Ground.

The statue of the Hanging Judge in Begbie Square looked south across the plaza of the New Westminster Courts, over the roofs of the buildings along Columbia Street at the muddy Fraser River flowing left to right toward the sea. The media requested Nick pose with him, so as cameras clicked and camcorders whirled, he stood beside Begbie with his porkpie hat. When tabloids asked him to hold the end of a rope noosed around the judge's neck, he declined.

Like a receiving line, Members and court watchers approached to congratulate Nick. Only after that hubbub died did Gill join him. "Before he left, what'd Knight say?" she asked.

" 'Now you can afford all the illusions you want.' "

"He was worth the money."

"But *you* saved me, Gill."

"No, DeClercq saved you. The Last Honest Man. I've booked a victory lunch at The Teahouse for noon, with a bottle of Dom I plan to watch you guzzle by yourself. I asked DeClercq and Alex to joi . . . Well, well, look who's coming."

Nick turned to see Rachel Kidd crossing the square from the Law Courts.

"I'll meet you by the parking lot," said Gill.

The women passed without speaking.

"Corporal Craven, may I have a word?"

The Mounties met by the legs of the Hanging Judge, who lorded over them on a pedestal like an orator on a Hyde Park soapbox.

"I thought you were guilty, and I was wrong. Never could I understand how a lawyer could defend someone he knew was guilty. Now I know. Because you *never* know. If it's any consolation, the price I'll pay for my mistake is being frozen out. Congratulations on your acquittal. I'm sorry. Forgive me?"

She held out her hand.

"I'll think about it," Nick said, turning his back on her and walking away.

SAFARIMAN

Africa
Saturday, March 5, 1994

A knock on the door of Room 406 awoke Zinc at just after five in the morning.

"Game drive, Mr. Chandler," a soft voice announced outside.

"Thanks. I'm up," Zinc called back, struggling out of bed.

He showered, shaved, got dressed, and popped a cap of Dilantin, then sweater around his shoulders made his way through predawn gray to the reception hall. While other guests sipped coffee with biscuits and talked in foreign tongues, he checked the chalkboard to the right of the entrance arch. Last night when the activity coordinator asked him what he wished to do today, he told her, "See big cats if I'll be back by eight." The board said January would take him out alone.

Professional guide he may be, but January reminded Zinc of a New Orleans bluesman. His thinning hair was kinked with gray, as was the mottled beard on his pudgy chin, while he moved his bulky body with the fluid flow of a man who hears music in his mind.

"Mr. Chandler? January." Hearty shake of the hand.

"Call me Zinc."

"Mr. Zinc. Ready to go?"

"Lead on, Mr. January."

Until you see dawn in Africa you haven't seen dawn at all. As the open four-wheel drive ventured into the wild, the east began to blush like a virgin groom. Rays of primrose backed the dark horizon, as star after star snuffed for the day. Banished, the pewter moon waxed wan. Soon bronze bars caged the blazing sky, from which the fiery face of Medusa glared, halo flames writhing about her head like snakes, one direct look sufficient to stone you blind.

"First safari?" January asked.

"Yep," said Zinc.

As he drove, January leaned out of the 4WD, eyes sweeping the ground for telltale spoor. Entering a thicket of mopane woods, the guide braked the Land Rover to a halt. "Leopard," he said, pointing near the wheel. Zinc saw cat's paws in the dust, and a drag mark to one side.

"The leopard hunts in darkness, so spotting it is rare. Nocturnal, it spends the day in its lair, often a branch high above the ground. This one dragged its prey there, away from other scavengers that might contest the kill."

"We follow it on foot?"

January grinned. "The first rule of game drives is stay in your seat. Bigger than the carnivores, we'll be left alone. Game walks have different rules. It's rare, but the leopard will eat man."

From the woods, they bounced across a grassy plain of dust where rainy season gullies were baked bone dry by the sun. Grunts and grumbles rumbled from the billow to Zinc's left. A pair of eyes, then hundreds more, peered from the cloud, until he discerned the curved horns of Cape buffalo.

"Don't be fooled by how docile they look. Buffalo and hippo are the most dangerous pair in Africa. Rogue bulls and females with calves are aggressive. The horns of the male join atop the head. Eight hundred kilograms of ornery buffalo thundering at you should not be taken lightly."

January wheeled toward a water-hole pan. Everywhere Zinc glanced, game caught his eye. With white beards, shaggy manes, and clumsy gaits, a herd of wildebeests romped at the hole, snorting loudly, bucking, tossing and shaking their heads, running around in circles and rolling in the dirt. Zebra by the dozen joined the wildebeests. "Like fingerprints, no two zebras are alike." Led by a male with lyre-shaped horns, a harem of impalas crossed the pan, nearing the water hole as January tapped Zinc's arm.

"Cheetah," he said, pointing.

The Mountie focused binoculars on the outcrop. The cat used the high point as a lookout post. Spotted head with black "tear streaks" held high, sleek, streamlined body frozen motionless, it watched intently for cues of alertness from its prey. One impala saw the silhouette, and a moment later the entire herd turned. This staring contest lasted five minutes, until the impalas relaxed and the cheetah disappeared, Zinc disappointed: cheetah cheated.

January's eyes scanned the grass, his senses honed sharp as those on the hunt. Zinc saw nothing. Where was the cat? Then the impalas jumped ten feet into the air, exploding in all directions as they cried out in alarm, and he caught the blur—for a blur it was—that burst across the pan.

Everything about this cat was designed for speed. The rakish, loose-limbed body with a sway-backed racing frame. The small head, deep chest, and elastic backbone slung like a hammock between haunches. Standstill to seventy mph in seconds, the cheetah is the fastest animal on Earth. Impalas are swift and can leap thirty feet, but this cat closed the gap in a blink, covering the ground with amazing bounds, hind legs in front of forepaws for

the all-out sprint, long tail used as counterbalance to
zigzag with its prey, closing, closing, closing for the kill,
hot on the heels of a darting impala, lashing out with a
flick of the paw to trip its quarry in a tumble of flying
hooves. Jaws not strong enough for a crushing bite, the
cheetah bit the antelope's throat, twisting the head to
suffocate it.

"Whew," Zinc said.

Slowly, January drove toward the kill, braking the
4WD twenty feet shy.

The cat turned sphinxlike, its spotted bib red.

The impala twitched.

The killer began to eat.

"The cheetah's fast, but tires quickly," January said.
"It can't sustain that speed for more than a few hundred
meters. The catch is consumed immediately with no return to the kill. It eats on the run. Unlike other cats, the
cheetah can't fully retract its claws, which are blunt and
doglike for traction during a chase. Such claws are useless in a fight. Lacking the strength of a lion, the ferocity
of a leopard, the bite of hyenas, a cheetah can't defend
its hard-won meal against other predators. Watch."

Agate eyes burning, the cheetah sat erect.

Zinc followed the stare and saw three approaching
lions.

The cheetah moaned.

The lions growled.

Then sulking, the cheetah gave up its kill without a
fight.

"Lion takes from leopard. Lion takes from cheetah.
Lion takes from wild dog," January said. "Leopard takes
from cheetah. Leopard takes from wild dog. Wild dog
takes from cheetah. So cheetah eats on the run. Hyenas
take from a lioness, but not a male lion. That's why the
lion is . . ."

"King of the Beasts," said Zinc.

Tingling ran up and down the Mountie's spine. His
pulse quickened as the lions neared the kill. The male
was nine feet from nose to tail, muscles rippling under
the sleek tawny hide, body color an exact match for dry
grass, shaggy mane so dark it was almost black, framing
the face, covering the neck, extending down the belly,
long and flowing below, balding on top. The grizzled,

battle-scarred face was frightening to behold, muzzle broad, jaw strong, mouth slack to reveal fearsome lower canines. Lordly swagger. One eye gone. Land Rover open. A mere leap for him. Them without a gun. Sardines in an open can.

Already black-backed jackals lurked nearby, while hooded vultures darkened the sky.

The large eyes of a lioness assessed Zinc's meaty shoulder. She licked her chops as sweat trickled under his arms.

"Are we safe?"

"Nervous?"

"Let's say it's a new experience, sitting here in the open with lions twenty feet away."

"Thirty years I've been a guide and never had vehicle trouble. But don't be tempted to step out around lions. Loud noise or sudden movement disturbs them. If you encounter a lion—especially a lioness—while on foot, whatever you do, don't turn and flee. Running triggers the impulse to give chase. Act like prey and you'll be treated like prey."

The pride of lions began to feed. *Safaris aren't for vegetarians,* thought Zinc. First the cats lapped up all the blood, some with such relish that hair was rubbed off in patches. The carcass was opened at the flank where thigh met belly, then the intestines were neatly pulled out.

"After disemboweling," January said, "they eat the liver, kidneys, heart, and internal organs. The stomach is spared and actually or symbolically buried. They eat the haunches, flanks, and breast next, devouring them in big chunks including skin. The bones of the brisket, ends of the ribs, and nose bones are eaten, too. Bigger bones aren't crushed or cracked. The head is stripped last, and often carried away."

Watching the lions disembowel the kill, Zinc wondered if lion hunters in ancient Zululand adopted this animality as a death ritual?

Was this the origin of *umnyama?*

The call came through exactly on time. A baboon on the veranda of Room 406 peered in the window as Zinc grabbed the phone.

"Chandler?"

"Yes."

"The meet is on. Nigel will see you on his ground on his terms. Listen hard. Check out and have the lodge pack you food for two days. Then boat downstream about a mile. Watch the right bank for the buffalo grave-yard. Have the boatman put you ashore. No tricks. Just you. I'll be watching. No phones where you're going. Nine-thirty sharp."

The line went dead.

Zinc subtracted ten hours from his watch. *Ten P.M. Friday night in Vancouver,* he thought. Dialing Special X, he reached DeClercq in his office.

"Working late?"

"Tipple's dead. Clubbed and disemboweled. Whoever did it cut out his heart. Murdered in the parking lot under Nick's trial."

"When?"

"Yesterday. During court. Parking attendant found him late last night. Zigzag on his skull matched Nick's mom. Nick's acquitted."

"Serial cop killer?"

"How does Dora fit? Cop killer, yes. But something else."

"Nick's twin?"

"Got to be. Only jigsaw piece."

"Reason I called is I'm meeting Hammond."

"When and where?"

"Don't know. Probably in the bush. Very cloak and dagger. Still poaching, I guess."

"Feel safe?"

"Safe enough. Just witnessed a cheetah kill, so I feel *very* alive. If Hammond's the key, someone's got to meet him. Can't have his kid kill another Member, or go for Alex again."

"Be careful."

"If I don't call by Tuesday—Monday, your time—send the cavalry."

Africa.

Fantasy and reality.

Zinc Chandler in his teens had read Conrad's *Heart of Darkness.* He had sailed with Marlow up a *mighty big*

*river . . . resembling an immense snake uncoiled, with its
head in the sea, its body at rest curving afar over a vast
country, and its tail lost in the depths of the land . . .
Going up that river was like traveling back to the earliest
beginnings of the world, when vegetation rioted on the
earth and the big trees were kings . . . The reaches opened
before us and closed behind, as if the forest had stepped
leisurely across the water to bar the way for our return.
We penetrated deeper and deeper into the heart of
darkness. . . .*

This was nothing like that.

The *Mosi-oa-Tunya* was docked by the bank, left and
down from the game lodge pool. It once plied the waters
of the Zambezi above the Falls, and looked enough like
the *African Queen* that Zinc could imagine Bogart and
Hepburn onboard. Lined beside the barge were several
metal boats, flat-bottomed with outboards astern. The
boatman who took him downriver was a black youth
with so much cool he would probably thrive on the
streets of New York.

Down the lazy river by the old game lodge . . . Zinc
suppressed the urge to break into song. The flood plain
of the Caprivi Strip with its sunny grasslands induced in
him the same sense of freedom as the vast prairie of his
youth. Clouds flat-bottomed like the boat drifted across
the sky, trailing shadows and reflections on the blue,
blue water. Basking on the sandy banks were monitor
lizards and crocodiles.

Down the lazy river . . .

A school of forty hippos lolled on a river island, huge
fat animals, some nearly three tons, with balloonlike
bodies, puff-cheeked heads, and short stubby legs. To
Zinc, these giant pigs adapted to aquatic life were clones
of Alfred Hitchcock. Despite their girth, those on land
trotted smoothly, two feet on the ground, two feet off.
Those wallowing in mud yawned wide to bare an armory
of crooked yellow tusks. The nostrils, eyes, and ears of
those submerged in the river were all that Zinc could
see, as rumps shat fertilizer dispersed by swishy tails.
Every bull's gray hide was crisscrossed with pink scars
from endless quarrels over who should hump the cows.

"The most dangerous animal for us," the boatman
said.

"So I hear."

"Most accidents occur when hippos surface beneath boats. Canoeing down the Zambezi below the dam, a guide on safari recently dangled his foot in the water. Angry at being displaced in his school, a rogue bull chomped the boat and took his leg."

Down the lazy river . . .

"There," said the boatman, pointing.

The buffalo graveyard marred the right bank, bones bleaching and flesh mummifying under the merciless sun. "A few months back," the boatman said, "lions stampeded a herd to take out stragglers. Those buffalos in front mired onshore, while those behind trampled on them to reach the river." As he listened, Zinc imagined the wild melee, massive hulks thundering here in panic and confusion, clouds of dust billowing up to obscure the sun, air reeking of mud, dung, and the sweaty press of bodies, fear tensing the grunting herd into a chorus of bellows, lost calves bleating for separated mothers, flies buzzing in black clusters around rolling eyes and flared nostrils, the blue river churned brown by broken legs and thrashing hooves, the heads and limbs of dying and dead protruding from the quagmire, as crocs slipped from sandbars to feed on the turmoil, nosing in with arrow-ripples trailing grim snouts, cold eyes diving as they dragged victims under, jaws locked while swirling tails spun their bodies to tear chunks of living flesh from skeletons.

"Put me ashore," said Zinc.

The bow turned in.

Bag with clothes in one hand, bag with food in the other, Zinc watched the boat motor back upstream toward the lodge. Trudging up the grisly bank he was amazed by how the dead had rotted. All were desiccated, but most retained their form, each buffalo face preserving its moment of death, heads turned, terrified or pleading to be spared, front halves mummified, back halves bones, shrunken lips baring blunt teeth, hairy hides streaked white where vultures had crouched to rip out eyes, eat tongues, shred sphincters, desperately trying to get at the putrid goodies inside. Now the sun beat down on dry carrion, around the horns of which buzzed halos of flies.

Shimmering in the heat-haze, a figure walked down from the road.

When Zinc first viewed *The Herald* clipping with De-Clercq, he'd thought the white mirrored Stewart Granger as Allan Quatermain in *King Solomon's Mines*. There was gray in the bush beard now and the khaki shirt and shorts were rumpled as if he'd slept in them, for this was the same "Clive Moon" in the photo with thirty years added, but up close he was far from the Great White Hunter, heroic, good, and strong. Strong sure, for muscles corded his shoulders, chest, and arms, not a hint of fat on his powerful frame, but there was malice in his pagan eyes, cruelty in his hard mouth, sadism in his weathered squint, and a skull tattooed on the palm gripping Zinc's hand.

"Chandler?"

"Uh-huh."

"The name's White."

Africa.

Fantasy and reality.

But then perhaps fantasy and reality did meld, for face to face with "Mr. White," here was Conrad's Kurtz: *His was an impenetrable darkness. I looked at him as you peer down at a man who is lying at the bottom of a precipice where the sun never shines.* Zinc could almost hear White whisper, *"I am lying here in the dark waiting for death."* A cry that was no more than a breath—*"The horror! The horror!"* What brutal life had this man led to warp him so mean?

"Why do you seek Nigel?"

"That's between Hammond and me."

"What brings a Mounted Policeman all the way to Africa?"

"Why you? Why not Hammond here himself?"

"Guess."

"Poaching?"

"Poachers are shot on sight."

"You poached, too."

"Who says?"

Zinc flashed *The Herald* clipping.

"Why should I help you if you won't talk with me?"

"I'm told you know where Hammond is. If you won't help me, I'll go a different route. This photo will be shown to every cop in Africa. If you're still poaching, that could be a drag."

"If you want Nigel, you must go to him. Just you. No guns. Understand? I search you and your kit before you get on the plane."

"Agreed. Where am I going?"

"On safari."

REVENGE

North Vancouver

As each bone hit the table, the evil eye carved on it winked at Evil Eye. The smell in the windowless room at the heart of the Lions Den was overpowering. Wreaths of greasy smoke swirled up from the *isiko* roasting on a hibachi, Tipple's heart an offer of *ukuhlabela amadlozi* "slaughter for the shades" so Evil Eye and Black Ghost could commune. The juju room in the cabin perched high on Grouse Mountain was lit by the oil lamp that danced Evil Eye's shadow like a black ghost over the Redcoat pictures spiked to the logs. The pictures came to life . . . Fripp's "The Last Stand of the 24th at Isandlwana" transformed into a macabre aftermath, the green grass red with running blood, the veld slippery with the entrails of the slain, the corpses of white and black mixed up together with the carcasses of horses, oxen, and mules, decapitated heads placed in a ring, the "poor little drummer boys"—the British Army would never again take boys on campaign—hung up with butcher's hooks jabbed under their chins so they could be "opened like sheep" . . . Photographs of Ted Craven in the "Four Circle" and "Wagon Wheel" formations of the RCMP Musical Ride, his face X'd with crisscrossed thin red lines of blood, thrown from the saddle of his bucking charger . . . The shot of Nick Craven, also defaced, in a Color Guard to salute the Queen, crumpling in a faint under the blazing African sun at Her Majesty's unamused feet. . . .

Lady Butler's "The Defense of Rorke's Drift" . . .

In the picture, Chard and Bromhead shared a bottle of beer. The other Redcoats drank a tot of rum. Slowly, Black Ghost appeared among the whites, necromancy noted by none but Evil Eye. The screams from the picture were unnerving, a symphony of agony from spectral images too vague to discern, but through the smoky forms of which wandered Black Ghost, beckoning Evil Eye in to commune. The black ghost lamplight cast across the picture moved rhythmically to the beat of drums deep in the psycho's mind as Evil Eye entered the picture like Alice through the Looking Glass.

The world in here was a negative of the world out there. The yard of Rorke's Drift in the painting faded into haze, while the spectral images once too vague to discern materialized. Evil Eye stood in the gate of the shades' *ikhanda,* the opening facing east like an Indian sweat lodge. The dome-shaped thatch huts to either side circled around the parade ground of this military kraal ringed outside by a stout stockade, until the horns met opposite at the *Induna*'s hut. Seven hundred Zulu shades shambled about, their black skins white and the whites of their rolled-back eyes black, the only color in this kraal the red wound that killed or mortally struck down each at Rorke's Drift. The screaming came from the hill beyond.

He was trained by Shaka.

This *Induna Enkulu.*

Ferocity was important, so Zulus could have no sex until they "washed their spears," and those defeated in battle were put to death. Discipline was important, so shield-bearers shading the king from the sun who allowed rays through were put to death. Respect was important, so those who sneezed when the king was eating or failed to grieve when his mother died were put to death.

Death by *ukujoja.*

Death by impalement.

Impalement with a long stake driven up the anus so it pierced the lungs.

Impalement with several stakes rammed at different angles through the abdomen.

Impalement with a split stake that branched inside the body.

Ukujoja.

Impalement like this.

A hundred and fifty-two pairs of stakes spiked the Hill of Execution beyond the *Induna*'s hut, one pair for each defender of Rorke's Drift. The screaming from the nineteen washed already impaled shrilled like a top end to the driving bass of the drums. One stake entered the left boot of each Redcoat to pass through his body, then up his raised right arm to exit from his hand. With the other stake skewed right to left, each impaled formed a red X on the hill, white face black and Red Serge tunic as red as the X's defacing the photos of Ted and Nick Craven.

Seventeen washed from Rorke's Drift.

Plus MacDougall and Tipple.

Writhing and shrieking eternally here in the Realm of the Shades.

152 - 19 = 133 Redcoats to come.

The witch doctor walked Evil Eye out of the kraal and up the hill and through the forest of stakes. Blood ran red under their feet from the crooked crucified, as white vultures circled, circled overhead, and the kraal below faded back to haze. "Revenge!" said the *Induna* as they passed each barren pair of stakes, waiting for one of the Redcoats who escaped from Rorke's Drift, of whom King Cetshwayo said, "An assegai has been plunged into the belly of the Zulu Nation." "Revenge!" commanded the *Induna* as they crested the hill, pointing down to where the shades' kraal had disappeared, and where instead of Rorke's Drift around the killing ground, Evil Eye gazed down on "E" Division Headquarters of the Royal Canadian Mounted Police.

Redcoats.

Revenge!

KAMIKAZE

Cloverdale

The Suicide Club had met for the next to last time tonight. The final meeting tomorrow would be aboard the cruise ship *Good Luck City* at the Red Serge Ball, where each conspirator's bowels would be packed with two and a half pounds of plastic explosives.

Wayne Tarr sat slumped in a chair, swilling Scotch straight from the bottle. Spread across the table under his propped-up feet were two tickets to the RCMP dance, a high-colonic enema kit to clean out his bowels, tubes of K-Y jelly to grease the deadly snake, and components to make him a kamikaze bomb. The snake was an elongated tube crammed with two and a half pounds of moldable C4, an RDX-based commercial explosive easier to obtain than PETN military DM12, cyclotrimethylenetrinitramine putty stuffed into gray synthetic skin by a butcher's sausage machine. Beside it lay a detonator, powered by hearing-aid batteries, trailing an aerial tail.

Missing was the single radio control that would set off both human bombs.

So the blasts would trigger together, that was with Evil Eye.

HINTERLAND

Africa

It was a short dusty ride from the buffalo graveyard to Kasane Airport. The terminal was small, modern, clean, and deserted. DEPARTURES—BA BA BOLOLANG read a sign above a door to the right, surmounted by a picture of Dr. Q.K.J. Masire, the President of Botswana. Seated on a bench inside, Zinc sipped a pop while White tossed his bags: shirts, pants, underwear, socks, medical kit, including disposable needles in case he required a jab, you don't trust African hypodermics with HIV infecting 20 percent, suit, shoes, tie, and belt with the old man's hunting knife. The taste of Sparletta conjured up memories.

When he was a kid on the prairies, all cream soda was red . . . till Pop took him and his brother Tom to the Calgary Stampede.

Calgary Cream Soda was crystal clear.

Like 7UP with vanilla taste.

In New York City, cream soda was brown.

Here in Africa, Sparletta cream soda was green.

Inconsistent world, Zinc thought as White unsheathed Pop's knife, holding it out like King Arthur with Excalibur, thumbing the edge to compare it with his own Ka-Bar.

"You said no guns. That's a knife."

White tossed it back in the bag unsheathed. "Now you," he said.

They entered the men's room off the Kasane Airport lounge. For security, there are searches and there are Searches. Till now, the best pat-down Zinc had endured was at the Old Bailey, when he was Special X liaison in London before the Ghoul case. The IRA was on a bombing run, so Zinc was stopped at the top of the stairs to the court galleries. "A moment of your time, sir. Hands out from your sides."

The man in blue was past retirement, guarding the Realm no doubt while Zinc was still in diapers, stiff not the word, rigid more like it. Deft fingers ruffled his hair, then slipped behind his ears, then probed the seams of his shirt and his underarms, chest, back, pockets, belly button, then down both legs into his shoes and up the inside—where the guy fudged inches from his groin. Most military men are homophobes, so if you're going to pack it, pack it there. Mr. White had no compunctions. The way he cupped Zinc's balls you'd think he owned them.

Which he thought he did.

"A safe flight," White said. "And give my best to Nigel."

Zinc left by the door marked DEPARTURES—BA BA BOLOLANG.

The single-engine Cessna had seen better days. So had the pilot. The plane, a Stationair 206, was a dirty rattle-trap with scorch marks on the nose cone and Band-Aids on the wings, several decades of undisturbed dust griming the instrument panel. The pilot was Danish with wild blond hair, tufts sticking here and there as if to mock combs, pale stubble on his chin, the only feature about him dark the bags beneath his eyes. "Five hundred dollars up front," he said between bites into a mango. "US, not Zim."

Zinc paid him.

"That puts you in and brings me out. How long you staying?"

"Say tomorrow afternoon, to be safe."

"Another five hundred'll bring me in to take you out. In advance."

Zinc grinned. "Credit equals trust. Two-fifty now, the rest when you pick me up. I'll be there. Two-fifty says so will you."

The pilot grinned. "Deal," he said.

It took the Dane six tries to start the propeller, which coughed, sputtered, and belched smoke before it whirled. *The things I do for Canada,* Chandler thought, as they taxied out to take off. The shrill drone of an engine cranked to the max, brakes off, bumps, shudders, and they were in the air. Whenever Zinc flew in a one-crew plane, he wondered what you did if the captain had a heart attack?

They bush-drifted west.

The Chobe River to the right changed name upstream to the Itenge, then to the Linyanti, then to the Kwando as it veered north toward Angola. Gazing down as if the ground was his only map, the Dane flew with the ease of a bush veteran, adjusting knobs and tapping dials while munching from the mango. "Firebreak," he said when Zinc indicated parallels akin to train tracks. Forty minutes of flying saw them across Chobe National Park, over the Savuti Channel dry for many years, over the Gubatsaa Hills and Magwikhwe Sand Ridge into the wilds. The size of France but populated by only 1.3 million huddled in the south, Botswana equates with raw wilderness. One of the last virgin landscapes on this shrinking globe, the vast seemingly endless expanse beneath the plane exuded the aura Africa of Old.

On they flew. On they flew. The land below wet and wetter.

"Okavango," said the Dane.

Rivers rise inland and empty into the sea, forming deltas on the coast. The Okavango River is the reverse, rising in the rain-soaked mountains of Atlantic Angola to flow southeast for 1,000 miles to form its delta in the hinterland. Called "the river that never finds the sea," it crosses the Caprivi Strip and enters Botswana from the north as a wide "Panhandle," then fans fingers south across sands of the Kalahari Desert as one of the seven natural wonders of the world: the 9,000-square-mile Okavango Delta.

This "Jewel of the Kalahari," this land that time forgot, swept a shimmering oasis under the plane. Water lilies flowered on oxbow lagoons, and serpentine channels wound through papyrus reeds, interlocking islands crowned with palms. Water, water everywhere, as far as the eye could see, creeping downstream in convolutions that forked again and again, a labyrinth of swamps and thickets by the hundreds, a tranquil maze teeming with exotic birds and game, an ever-changing tapestry of ebb and flow, Africa's third longest river spreading slowly south, fanning, evaporating, and seeping into the sand, the only way in by plane or punting boat, until it died far from here in a sandy trickle where wasteland began, the deadly Kalahari Desert, last remaining home of San Bushmen.

Descending into the central reaches of this Last Eden, Zinc searching in vain for a landing strip, the Cessna skimmed dazzling lagoons at treetop level, then bump, bump, bump, bounced across bumpy earth, clouds of dust rising behind.

The engine gagged, the prop stopped, and both men got out.

The sun was now at broiling height so it was sweltering hot. Under a flawless sky that arced horizon to horizon, heat waves warped the Delta into a mirage. The silence was so intense it was threatening, as if Nature itself had died. Merely unloading his bags drenched the Mountie in sweat.

"Where are we?" Zinc asked.

"The End of the Earth."

"Why stop here?"

"The camp you want is through those trees."

"Now what?"

"You're on your own as far as I'm concerned." Foot up and hand in the cockpit under the overhead wing, the Dane climbed back into the plane.

"You *will* return tomorrow?"

The pilot grinned. "Credit equals trust," he said, slamming the door.

Dust billowing behind, the Cessna took off. Engine noise filled the eerie green hell. In banking east, the plane buzzed Zinc on the ground, perhaps the only human meat in a hundred miles. Tomorrow the Dane would return as promised, not for the other two-fifty from Zinc, but to testify he was nowhere to be found. In one pocket of the pilot's shorts were the hundreds from the Canadian. But in the other pocket of those shorts were *thousands* from the White.

Fleeing the scorch and glare of the landing strip, Zinc entered the stifling shade of dense trees. At home he knew the name and use of every plant, but here among rain trees that dripped insect spit, and strangler figs that slowly garroted their hosts, and fever berries the bark of which cures malaria, and buffalo thorns said to be an aphrodisiac, and tambotie that blinds if its sap hits the eyes or poisons if its wood is burned to cook, Inspector Zinc Chandler was a babe in the woods.

Pain stabbed his arm.

Twice the size of a housefly and utterly silent in flight, iridescent black wings now crossed scissorlike on his pale skin, the tsetse fly bit into Zinc like the sting of an enraged wasp. Was it true that tsetse flies swarmed from the trees in clouds to blacken your hands, face, hair, and every inch of bare skin to sting you in a mindless fury of needle-sharp bites, leaving sleeping sickness behind in your blood? Slap! Slap! Slap! Three more flies.

Then he saw what looked like a flag strung between two trees, a pair of deep blue stripes flanking a patch of black. The tsetse fly control was the first sign of man Zinc had seen in the Delta. Flies drawn to the blue bit into the black, coated with poison.

He pressed on.

From the leafy canopy filtering the sun, something crashed down into the bush. The hair on his forearms as stiff as could be, Zinc thought *Leopard* and froze where he stood. Pop's hunting knife still packed in his bag, he searched the ground for a club of any kind, spotting a broken branch yards away. *Inch for it or make a dash?* he wondered, hearing a tense ripple of breath inflating nearby lungs, then a furious bark erupted, the foliage parted, and a baboon bounded by.

Club held like Babe Ruth out to bash the Big One, Zinc made it to the hidden camp near a lazy stream. The camp was a canvas tent 10 × 10, tall enough for a man to stand, with a sleeping bag under mosquito netting. No food. No supplies. No one home.

A bush path from the tent led to the stream, where a *mokoro* was beached onshore. Hewn from the trunk of a sausage tree, the dugout canoe had a rounded hull that rolled when Zinc stepped in. If he sat, it swayed wildly every time he moved. Hollowed from wood heavier than water, it would sink if tipped while floating. Bushmen pole them standing up like Venetian gondoliers, a skill requiring years to perfect, balancing them from the hip like walking a tightrope stretched across water. *Mekoro* leak, so they're lined with straw.

Nothing to do but wait, Zinc sat by the stream and

used Pop's knife to whittle the branch club into a *voya-geur*'s paddle.

Hours later, he heard the drone of an approaching plane, but when he hiked back to the landing strip to meet Nigel Hammond, the drone was gone with no aircraft in sight.

Apprehension tickled.

Bushmen don't eat crocodile meat. The poison found in crocodile brain kills in five days. Bushmen eat puff adder meat. The fat under the skin is used to cook the snake, textured like crayfish and tasting like chicken. Bushmen eat larvae from termite mounds, grains of rice like unsalted caviar. Zinc had no idea what to eat, and might as well be Adam in the Last Eden, blazing the way hit-and-miss for gourmets to follow, if he was stranded here for days . . . months . . . years!

Puff adders like to sun themselves to sleep, and don't like tenderfeet kicking them awake, especially fools without an antivenin kit. Eyes down to watch for snakes on the path, Zinc turned to leave the runway for camp, then—the second time today—froze rigid in his tracks.

Dust on the landing strip bore the imprint of his shoe, made earlier when he was dropped off by the Dane. He didn't see it, didn't smell it, didn't sense its presence, but over the imprint of his shoe, a lion had superimposed its paw.

The sun went down into a sea of blood, vultures on the highest branch of the tallest tree starkly outlined against the bleeding sky, all ruffled feathers and long scraggy necks and beaks that strip antelope to the bone in half an hour. An ominous omen?

With the dark came mosquito hordes, *buzz . . . buzz . . . buzz*ing to drink from him. Their incessant dive-bombing drove him into the tent, and when that brought little respite, under the mosquito net.

Flying British Airways from London to Harare, Zinc had tracked the plane's route over Africa in *Highlife,* the inflight magazine. Under the map of Africa was an ad for Paludrine antimalaria pills, a downer unexpected in a corporate rag. Zinc took that to mean the subject was important.

Damn right.

Every African he'd met slyly slipped a question in about prophylaxis, then spooked him with vampire tales about malaria. Caused by a blood parasite in anopheles spit (in Mosquitoland, females are the aggressors) it hits in waves with fever, shivering, and hallucinations at night. Some strains have slipped the yoke of modern drugs and *plasmodium falciparum* is fatal if not treated at once.

A billion mosquitos and he was the only soda fountain in miles.

Buzzzz . . . buzzzz . . . buzzzz . . .

Bushmen say it's possible in the still of an ink-black night to hear the stars in song. What Zinc heard through the buzzing was the shrill of frogs, crickets, bats, and baboons competing with one another for center stage, and beyond that, a hungry lion's roar. The roar began with a deep-throated challenge to those who might want to hunt (him?) in the Delta tonight, rumbling down to a warning, then a rebuke. The roar died as a series of irritable grunts, one according to Bushmen for each year of the lion's life.

Zinc counted twelve.

Like many white boys who misspent their youth in the fifties, Zinc grew up on Tarzan and Jungle Jim. The weekend meant a drive into Rosetown with Mom for that pagan ritual: the Saturday Matinee. The local theater—The Hitching Post—was crammed with kinetic kids, here to watch classic cinema at its best, a Gene Autry movie kicking off the show, followed by a fest of *Tom & Jerry* cartoons, and the 1940s serial *Flash Gordon's Trip to Mars,* Zinc wiggling in his seat pocked with chewing gum, feet tapping a floor sticky with spilled pop, Pez dispenser in one hand, peashooter in the other, waiting on pins and needles for the second feature.

When Johnny Weissmuller—*the* Tarzan—spoiled his loincloth physique with lard, a bush jacket turned him into Jungle Jim. In that darkened theater, imagination unleashed, Zinc thrilled to *The Lost Tribe, Pygmy Island, Jungle Jim in the Forbidden Land, Voodoo Tiger* (a tiger in Africa?), *Valley of the Headhunters, Killer Ape, Cannibal Attack,* and *Devil Goddess,* promising himself, *One day I'm going there.*

Alone with the Law of the Jungle . . . and just Pop's knife.

He'd come a long way from The Hitching Post.

STAND FAST

West Vancouver
Saturday, March 5, 1994

The last thing DeClercq wanted this case—or any case for that matter—to center on was race. Draw race into a case and logic went out the door, leaving behind bias and resentment to work it out. A friend of his was in L.A. at the time of the last riots, and being a good journalist, thought he should phone an eyewitness piece to his station. Close enough to see the smoke and catch the sirens, but far enough away not to nose in, he made the call and was promptly told to hold on for a cross-Canada hookup. So there he stood, in the street, public phone to his ear, holding on . . . holding on . . . until three youths cornered him. The youths were black, armed with pipes, and hate brimmed in their eyes. The journalist dropped the phone and held up his hands. He showed the youths his Canadian ID, told them he was from up North reporting a balanced story, and then—logically enough—said whatever was troubling them wasn't his doing. "You white," one youth replied, and struck him with the pipe, breaking his jaw and dropping him to the sidewalk for a stomping, which might have been fatal had a black cabbie not chased them off with a bat. Draw race into a case and logic went vamoose, so race was the last thing DeClercq wanted this to be about.

"It's about race," he said.

"These days everything's about race," said Chan. "Speaking of which, between you and me, the Public Complaints Commission has cleared Tarr in the ERT shooting tragedy. Expect backlash when the announcement is made on Monday."

"Does Tarr know?"

Eric shook his head. "I hear he's drinking heavily and may have loose lips. The race angle's volatile. The Mad Dog'll tell him on Monday."

"Glad we live here and not somewhere waiting for a riot to blow."

"That's for sure," said Chan.

Sunbeams through the glass roof and walls ignited the roses Robert hybridized. Wearing his chef's hat and apron, Katt entered the Greenhouse with breakfast on a tray. Plates of huevos rancheros, fruit, and a steaming coffeepot. "Looks good," Eric said. "This gourmet fare has a name?"

"Katt food," Katt said. With a tip of the hat, she left the Mounties to talk.

"Wild Katt," Eric punned.

"Not you, too?"

"I hear Katt's mom is your date to the Red Serge Ball?"

"Who's the fink?"

"My wife," said Chan. "Corrine phoned Sally to get the lowdown on what to wear."

"You married a snitch."

"Why the big secret?"

"To quell speculation by whimsical romantics like you."

"Sally booked a limousine to drive us to the boat. It's all arranged. We're picking you up. Nothing like a moonlight cruise—"

"That's what we have to discuss. It might be wise, Eric, to cancel tonight's Ball."

The fork with huevos rancheros stopped halfway to Chan's mouth. The fork returned to his plate. "Why do I feel indigestion coming on? More secrets you're keeping from me?"

" 'You keep race at bay your way, I'll keep it back in mine.' Those were your words when we disagreed over Kidd seizing Nick's Red Serge. 'Nick's case isn't about race,' I said. Then you said, like you said just now, 'These days everything's about race.' I fear you were right and I was blind. And by denying the issue, I cost Bill his life."

Chan sat back. "Out with it," he said.

"The Craven family history is draped in Red Serge. John Craven fought the French on the Plains of Abraham, and fired on American Colonists in the Boston Massacre. William Craven faced Napoleon. Rex Craven won the Victoria Cross defending Rorke's Drift, where he collected relics for a trophy box. Both Ted and Nick Craven stand for the family tradition this century."

Lifting a file from the floor beside the La-Z-Boy, De-Clercq opened it in his lap. "This picture of the box appeared in the London *Times* in January 1956." From the file he handed Chan the UBC copy. "An agent for African interests saw the photo and wrote to Ted as heir to the trophy box, saying he'd be in Canada the first week of March, and would drop by to discuss purchasing the Zulu bones." He passed Chan the photofax from Scotland Yard of the black and white at Great Zimbabwe ruins. "That's when Nigel Hammond"—he indicated the handsome black—"knocked on the door while Ted was away on a manhunt up North."

Chan studied the African.

"Nine months later, Dora gave birth to twins. What happened that night, I'm convinced, is the key to solving not only Dora's murder, but Jack MacDougall's and Bill Tipple's as well."

He handed Chan a copy of the white-and-black twins from Colin Wood's text. "Three people were present for the double birth: Dora, Ted, and Eleanor, Ted's younger sister. Sometime that evening Ted took a bullet to the head from his service revolver. No record survives from the inquest, but Medicine Hat Detachment finally found its closed file."

He passed Chan the rest of the folder.

"Ted was a bully and a bad cop. His service record has black marks and he was disciplined twice. Medicine Hat uncovered sexual abuse of Eleanor. Not only incest with her brother, but Ted once wagered his sister in a poker game. Ted's father—a Member-turned-rancher and a bully, too—was convinced the girl wasn't his, so he turned a blind eye to her complaints. Eleanor was sent away to Sacred Heart, and Ted remained the apple of his proud father's eye.

"Dora married Ted when she was sixteen. Later that year, her parents died in a car crash, and she was an only child. Ted was her savior, but soon he beat her instead. Dora and Eleanor, both abused, had much in common. Eleanor was training as a midwife in Medicine Hat, so Dora went to stay with her for the twin births. Ted arrived from Lethbridge for the blessed events. Out came his son Nick, white as the falling snow, then out came Hammond's child, black as the night beyond. So how would Ted react to a shock like that? Sulk away with a bottle and shoot himself?"

"He went berserk?" said Chan.

"Dora was bruised. A note in the inquest file."

"Forcing one of the girls to shoot him in self-defense?"

"Here we have two farm girls still in their teens, with a black baby and a dead Mountie on the floor. It's the 1950s, on the Canadian prairies, where everything's white except Indians and *Amos and Andy* on TV. And where a murder charge ends with a noose.

"Only the two of them knew about the twins. So the white stayed with Dora and the black went with Eleanor to be placed through Sacred Heart where she was sent as a girl. The Hammond twin was shipped somewhere unknown, and both conspirators swore a single birth was followed by suicide. When the investigation exposed Ted for what he was, the suicide verdict kept the Force untarnished in court. Dora brought Nick here and thirty-some years passed."

Chan had programmed the Headhunter hunt in 1982. Chan developed the Violent Crimes Analysis Section, and Chan introduced Criminal Profiling from Crime Scene Analysis to the Force. There was no need for DeClercq to suggest placement abuse warped a psycho killer.

"For years the Hammond twin had fantasized about revenge. On the December seventh birthday shared with Nick, the psycho rapped on Dora's door and was let in. That's when she made the fatal mistake of producing the trophy box—"

"And the black twin's psychosis coalesced with the African fetish," said Chan.

"Like Pandora's box in the Greek myth, Zulu shades were released to seek revenge. The twin became a zombie of reprisal for them, and because the Force is the last vestige of the British Colonial Army, our Red Serge is a stand-in for the defenders of Rorke's Drift. The twin was rejected because it wasn't Ted's offspring, and all its mother love went to Nick instead, so our Red Serge is also a symbol for family revenge. Not only does the killer get even with Dora, Ted, and Nick, but conquest is symbolically wreaked on all Imperial Redcoats in the Craven family past, whose racist Colonial 'White Man's Burden' enslaved the soul of Africa: its black family's past."

"Why didn't you tell me this before?" said Chan.

"It's too politically incorrect for a 'sensitive' soul like you."

Chan glowered.

"That's a joke, Eric. Only with Tipple's death did I have proof the killings are all tied to the box. Even that's stretching it, since we can't see if a zigzag is on the club. Zinc's in Africa closing in on Hammond in Botswana. My hope was through the father we'd have the twin by now. Meanwhile, the Ball is tonight and there's a Red Serge psycho loose."

"You know who it is!"

"I don't have proof."

"Suspicion will do."

"Nick picked his Red Serge up from the cleaners, and swears his mother's blood didn't stain the tunic while he wore it. That means the cuff was blooded after it was seized. Kidd gave Nick's tunic to Dermott Toop, who had a sample of Dora's blood from the autopsy in the Lab."

"Toop *framed* Nick?"

"Either him or Kidd. Kidd was around Dora's blood at the murder scene. Fraternal twins can be either sex. Toop and Kidd have tickets to the Ball tonight. Killing Tipple was so blatant I fear the zombie's psychosis is out of control. If the twin's a Red Serge psycho, Nick and hundreds of other Members will be in danger on the cruise ship."

"Would you cancel?"

"It's your call, Eric."

"For over a hundred and twenty years, the Mounted Police have stood fast. The Force will not retreat with me the one holding the line."

ALL ABOARD

At Canada Place Berth Two, the cruise ship *Good Luck City* was ready to sail. "Good Luck City" is Hong Kong's name for Vancouver, as more Colony astronauts live here than anywhere else. An astronaut's a business immigrant who purchased Canadian citizenship for himself and his family, but still commutes to Hong Kong to wheel, deal, and avoid Canadian taxes. The *Good Luck City* was owned by a Colony billionaire gradually relocating his ships before China got Hong Kong in 1997. Last May, the Force had saved his son from kidnapping for ransom by Triad thugs, so providing the boat and catering the Ball was his way of showing gratitude. Tonight the ship would sail north up Georgia Strait, rounding Vancouver Island to cruise the Pacific south, returning by Juan de Fuca Strait to dock tomorrow morning.

Five hundred forty feet in length and 18,000 gross tons, twin screws powered by four seven-cylinder Burmeister & Wain-Hitachi geared diesels, the *Good Luck City* pampered 740 passengers and 300 crew. The Marco Polo Ballroom fronted the Silk Road Deck, its walls and dance floor gilded gold under crystal chandeliers. The tables for eight were set with white linen, red flowers, gilt cutlery, and gold candelabras. The stage displayed the instruments of the RCMP Band: not the hearty oom-pah-pah of military brass, but the let's-dance-lure of electric guitars, two keyboards, wind and brass, percussion, and a marimba. Mounted behind the CO's chair was a massive horned buffalo head flanked by RCMP flags and red-and-blue banners. Each banner bore the Force crest above a mounted Member. Stored in the ship's walk-in freezer to keep it from melting was an ice sculpture of a Horseman with a lance.

Everyone hoped the party would be a blast.

West Vancouver

"How do I look?" asked DeClercq, modeling his mess kit: a waist jacket of Red Serge over a ruffled white shirt with black bow tie, blue trousers and black half-Wellington boots with box spurs, gold crowns representing his rank on the epaulets, gold regimental crests sparkling on his lapels.

"Dashing," said Katt. "You'll wow Mom. She'll fall in love. You two will get married. And I'll live happily ever after with my new family."

"Too many trashy romances. Broaden your reading a bit. Take good care of Napoleon. Don't feed him Cheezies tonight."

Katt waved *TV Guide* in the air. "Dog and me are gonna watch *White Zombie* on the tube."

"Dog and I . . ." corrected DeClercq.

Coquitlam

Rachel Kidd examined her reflection in the mirror, eyes rising from long blue skirt to Red Serge tunic to troubled black face. The Ball would be an ordeal, but she had to go. Like falling off a horse, you must climb back on, or time will eat at your nerves till you can't face your fear.

A knock on the door.

Dermott Toop.

Vancouver

Brittany Starr had bleached her hair blond for the Ball, donning a sheer scoop-necked gown that clung to every curve, lips and nails painted the same tint as Red Serge.

Brittany Starr had never been to a formal dance, having quit school at fifteen to turn Lolita tricks. Now one of her johns saw her as Cinderella in *Pretty Woman*, treating her to a similar whirlwind shopping spree, repeatedly assuring her she'd turn every head at the Ball.

Brittany Starr hefted her breasts to get the cleavage right.

A knock on the door.

Her Red Serge date.

* * *

Struggling with crutches and a full-length dress, Alex half hobbled, half crawled into Nick's car. "Every guy aboard will envy me," he said, while Gill positioned Hunt's cast along the back seat.

"Whose tunic?" Alex asked.

"Mine," Nick replied. He held up his sleeve so she could see the dime-size patch cut from its cuff by the Lab. "Knight got it released from court."

"I hope there's a polka," Alex said. "I'm in the mood to dance."

The limousine crested Lions Gate Bridge on its way to fetch DeClercq. "You're quiet, Eric," Sally Chan said in back.

"Am I? Sorry," her husband said. "Something on my mind."

"Forget work," his wife chided. "Tonight we relax with friends."

His bowels were packed with two and a half pounds of plastic explosives. Wayne Tarr had reserved a hotel suite above Canada Place, from the balcony of which he could watch the *Good Luck City,* sleek and white against the dark chop of the harbor below. Here, he had flushed his bowels with the enema kit, a gurgling high-colonic bloat that bulged him like a pregnant male. Next he had squeezed the C4 tube every few inches, until it resembled a chain of sausage links. Naked in the bathroom, a hand mirror on the floor, he had straddled the image of his butt like the Colossus of Rhodes. Lubricating the first link with K-Y jelly, he'd squatted in the stance of a sumo wrestler to push the bulb of C4 plastic into his anus. Then link had followed link like a train into a tunnel, snaking this way and that within his abdomen. Tucked into the last link was the radio detonator. Now only the aerial stuck from his ass like an obscene tail.

Wayne Tarr felt the urge to take the mother of all shits.

Threading the receiver wire up between his buttocks, the rogue cop taped the aerial along his spine. Then he waddled out to dress.

Keep a clear head, he warned his reflection in the bedroom mirror, buttoning his Red Serge tunic down the front.

But it was hard to keep his eyes off the bottle of Scotch.

North Vancouver

The stench from Tipple's burned heart lingered in the juju room of the Lions Den high on Grouse Mountain, while in the harbor far below the *Good Luck City* set sail.

The club, the bayonet, and the pouch of bones were gone from the Rorke's Drift box.

Evil Eye had taken them to the Red Serge Ball.

THE TERRIBLE ONES

Africa
Sunday, March 6, 1994

The Garbage Line Spiders were coming for Zinc.

Though in their late fifties, the Gray were tough men. Three-two Battalion had seen to that. Recce Wing was led from the front, so NCOs had to pass muster with their grunts, a grueling ordeal designed to flush limp boys from hard men. Preselection phase: a 15-mile march in full gear in six hours carrying a rifle with a 66-pound sandbag; a 4-mile run in 45 minutes with rifle and kit; 40 push-ups, 8 chin-ups, 68 sit-ups in a set time; 40 seven-yard 90-second shuttle runs; then a clocked 45-yard swim. Selection phase: three days of ration/water/sleep deprived survival in the bush; endurance and body building through speed marches 10 miles in full kit and around the parade yard holding a 55-pound marble weight above the head; free-fall and HALO (high altitude, low opening) parachute jumps; rappelling, diving, and commando training. Crunch phase: a forced march of 18 miles with food and ice-cold drinks offered as incentive to stop; rations waiting at the end inedible from contamination by diesel fuel; then a surprise order for an additional 14-mile march, again with food enticements to give up; capped by being taken "prisoner" by terrorists and forced to solve mind-boggling puzzles without sleep and meals. The Gray—though age now claimed its toll—had passed.

Three or four times a week Zinc worked out at the gym: a few weights, a few laps, a basketball game, then a l-o-n-g steam to sweat away the sweat, not the man he used to be, but then who is? Working the farm as a teen for Pop had developed his physique, but the shot in the head in the Cutthroat case and knife in the back in the Ripper case had set him back.

Tough tag team versus tattered loner.

The White wore night vision goggles and his Ka-Bar knife, in one hand a .458 Winchester Magnum Browning A-Bolt fed Barnes Super-Solid Monoliths, enough rifle to drop an elephant, in his other hand a Walther P38 9mm semiautomatic with a sound suppressor, eight rounds in the magazine and one in the chamber, backup mags in the skeleton webbing over his chest, enough pistol to Swiss cheese Zinc. The Black had the same goggles, knife, and Walther, but instead of a rifle carried two roped meat hooks and "The Croc."

Ferocious firepower versus Pop's knife.

The Garbage Line Spiders were coming for Zinc.

The plane Zinc heard yesterday afternoon was the Dane landing the Gray on an island upstream. Experience from years of hunting Delta crocs evident in how they balanced the boats, from there the two had poled *mekoro* through the swamp, camping three sandbars away until dark. Now they beached the boats on the far side of the island with Zinc's camp, and stalked across the landing strip toward his tent.

The Horseman poking his unwelcome nose into their affairs had forced the Gray to pull the assassination forward. Killing the Zulu king the day before the April election would be ideal, but now was as good a time as any for bloody civil war. In Africa, hacking machetes and headless bodies in the river lurk behind volatile tribal rivalries. All it takes is a well-timed tinder spark.

Today Zinc.

Tomorrow the Zulu king.

How the Mountie died had to buy time. Killing him in Harare, Vic Falls, or Chobe would alert the cops in force, might as well let him show their picture around. That's why the White had warned Zinc: "No phones where you're going," so he'd phone home to say he was venturing into the bush, bush which in Africa means watch for claws and fangs. Death here is natural, not suspicious. Death here is the Law of the Jungle.

Time would pass before the Canadian was overdue. Time would pass while they inquired where he went. Time would pass while they dogged his trail. Time would pass while they determined what happened here. And that was more than time enough to kill the Zulu king. In the end, even if they spoke to "Nigel Hammond," Chandler's death would be attributed to crocodiles.

The Croc would see to that.

The surefire way to kill Zinc was creep up on the tent, then on the silent count of three, *pfffft pfffft pfffft* . . . fire both Walthers. Slugs would rip the canvas in two lines, one from the White's spray, the other the Black's. Each man would reload before they yanked back the flap, and entered, *pfffft pfffft,* for the *coups de grâce.*

But that meant bullet holes.

Instead, they would haul Zinc half asleep from the tent to greet his last dawn, and string him up stripped of clothes by hooks through both palms, hanging from a tree branch feet just off the ground on the riverbank, scream, mate, scream, howl as much as you want, lots to scream about with each bite of The Croc, teeth clamping his genitals and tearing them off, teeth ripping chunks of meat from his body, bite, twist, tear, bleed, tossed in the river, The Croc feeding crocs drawn by blood to the island.

The Croc was a weapon that had served the Gray well, resembling a pair of pliers two feet long, the size and shape of gardening shears. The jaws of a real crocodile lined the vise grip, yawning or snapping as the handles moved, so real croc teeth clamped, tore, and left their mark. When Zinc's remains were found by cops flown here by the Dane (the Gray's boot marks broom brushed away), what they'd recover was what remained of a reptile feed.

By then the Zulu king would be dead.

And the Gray, retired, would have $2,000,000 US to spend.

Seen through night vision goggles, the terrain was green. Green dust puffed about green boots crossing the landing strip, by Zinc's green footprint stomped with a green lion's paw, green gloves parting greenery black without the goggles. The Gray knew the swamp from their croc years, and how to pole *mekoro* through the reeds. Zinc was alone at the End of the Earth with nowhere to go, the only boat a Bushman's boat that took years to learn how to pole. Stand astern and he'd overturn in seconds.

The first hue of dawn pinked the sky to the east.

There was the camp.

There was the tent.

There was the path to the river.

Guns aimed, the Terrible Ones flanked the zippered flap behind which the Canadian Mountie had bedded down for the night.

African bushmen versus mapless tenderfoot.

The Garbage Line Spiders were coming for Zinc.

RED SERGE BALL

Georgia Strait

A chill wind blew from the west, slave-driving the sea, lashing the hunched backs of the waves while flapping the flags of the ship. The *Good Luck City* sailed into the teeth of the gale, under Lions Gate Bridge joining the mountains to Stanley Park, from Vancouver's inner harbor into English Bay. There it swung starboard past Bowen Island and along the Sunshine Coast, heading northwest up Georgia Strait between Vancouver Island and the Mainland to the right.

The darkening sky was a chessboard of star patches and clouds, scudding in crosshatched pattern across the pockmarked moon. Each time the lunar face donned a different veil, the silver haze encircling it foretold oncoming death.

One death.

Two deaths.

Three deaths.

Four . . .

Brittany Starr laughed so hard Gill Macbeth feared her eye-popping breasts would burst free from her plunging gown. Mad Dog Rabidowski, hand on the hooker's thigh, winked at Alex when her gaze dropped to the jiggling caused by his joke.

"What's so funny?" Gill asked.

"You don't want to know," the Mad Dog said between sips of single malt. "I was telling Brit about our last baseball game. A bitch in the Force complained ours was an all-male team—Hell, we been playing ball together for eight years—and demanded we sexists let her cover first base. I balked, so she recruited a Dickless Tracy team."

"What possible reason could you have for not letting her play?" Gill frowned at Alex, still awed by Brittany's grand canyon.

"Principle," the Mad Dog said. "She *told* me what to do."

"No one makes Eddie jump hoops," Brittany giggled, "except bare puss in garters with a cat-o'-nine-tails in hand."

"Hussy," snarled the Mad Dog, plying her with more champagne.

"The joke?" Gill pressed.

"You don't want to know."

"I'm a big girl. *I'll* decide that. So, yes, I do."

"You heard the lady," Rabidowski said to the rest of the table. "Against better judgment, she won't leave it alone."

At the next table, Colin Wood aborted a joke while the decanter of port passed from hand to hand, Mounted tradition being the bottle can't touch the table until every glass is full. Rachel Kidd—as she'd predicted—was shunned by those in Red Serge, the fate of Mounties who botch an attempt to turn on one of their own, caste

as an untouchable no matter what color your skin. She
and Toop were sitting with civilian techs from the Lab,
unaware Special 0 had secret eyes on them. Loyal Toasts
to the Queen and to the Force completed, Wood drained
his port and asked, "Where was I?"

"A zebra died and went to Heaven," Rachel said.

"Right," the DNA expert nodded. "This joke's worth
a glass."

Toop passed him the decanter, which Wood emptied
to its dregs.

"Zebra, says Saint Peter, who mans the Pearly Gates,
you look like a beast with trouble in mind. Saint Peter,
says the zebra, I'm puzzled by a question. Am I white
with black stripes, or black with white? Whoa, says Saint
Peter. That's a touchy issue. If you want an answer, the
Big Guy's around the corner. So off trots the zebra to
speak to God.

"Rounding the bend, he sees a burning bush. God,
asks the zebra, approaching head bowed, am I white
with black stripes, or black with white? A voice booms
from the bush, You are what you are.

"Back at the Pearly Gates, Saint Peter asks, Did you
get a satisfactory answer? Yes, says the zebra. White
with black stripes. Whoa, says Saint Peter. That can't be.
The Big Guy's wisdom always cuts both ways. What exactly did he say?

"You are what you are, the zebra replies.

"How does that tell you you're white with black
stripes?

"Because"—Wood locked knowing eyes with Toop—
"if I was black with white stripes, he'd have said, You
is what you is."

Prick, Rachel thought.

Across the sea of Red Serge under swirls of smoke,
Chan sat beside DeClercq at the head table. "Toop and
Kidd look miffed," he whispered, leaning close. "Think
Wood said something off-color to them?"

"We'll know soon when Special 0 reports. Pass wind
at that table and it feeds hungry ears."

"I wish I'd brought binoculars," Chan said with a
sigh. "Rabidowski's date could breathe new life into
three-D."

"Three-D?" DeClercq said. "Forty-three D's more like it."

Sally Chan had switched seats to chat with Corrine Baxter. Switching back, she nudged her laughing husband in the ribs. "What's so hush-hush, Eric? Why the tête-à-tête?"

"Sorry, dear," Chan said. "This tit-a-tit's for CO eyes only."

The RCMP Band was founded in 1874, a pair of tent pegs thumping a large tin dish on the Great March West to crush Fort Whoop-Up. Added to morning "Reveille" and "Lights Out" ending the day, every change in Force routine had its bugle call. The first "organized" band was struck at Swan River Barracks in 1876, debuting on May 24, for Queen Victoria's Birthday. The "official" band was established in 1938, premiering at the Royal Visit of King George VI. Growing to forty-six Members in two ensembles—the Concert Band of big band sound and the eight-piece Bison—it performed 300 gigs a year until funding ran out. Recently disbanded, tonight marked the last waltz of West Coast players, amid ugly rumors the Musical Ride was next. When the band launched "Corrine, Corrina," the Big Joe Turner/Phil Spector/Ray Peterson hit, Sally Chan spurred DeClercq, "That's your cue to dance."

Meanwhile, at the table drawing sideways glances, Rabidowski, arm around Brit, puffed a phallic cigar. "I told her, women don't have what it takes to play ball like men."

"Bullshit," Gill said.

"Her reply exactly. Said she'd make me eat those words, and challenged us guys to a may-the-best-sex-win game."

"*Better* sex," Gill said. "Unless you know something I don't."

"Whatever." The Mad Dog shrugged, tapping ash on the floor.

"Need I ask who won?"

"We did," Ed replied. "To show grace in victory, I sent a box of donuts to the girls' changing room. We always top a game off with donuts and beer."

Alex caught a peek of nipple when Brittany howled, marveling again at the science-fiction dimensions of her bust.

"What's so funny?" Gill asked, back where she started.

"Before sending the donuts, I snapped a Polaroid. Like I said, women don't have what it takes to play ball like men. Satisfaction is, she ate *my* words."

"Gave her the sweat off his balls," Brittany added lightly.

From his tunic, Rabidowski withdrew a photo. In it a team of naked men kneeled behind a bench, each penis poked through one of a dozen donut holes lining the bench like wheels.

"You showed her the photo!" Gill choked.

" 'Course not," the Mad Dog scoffed. "Never give a humorless bitch grounds for a sex harassment suit. Hey, babe"—he squeezed Brit—"let's make the two-backed beast."

The sergeant, steroid muscles straining the fabric of his tunic, and Brit, no panty line to spoil the cling of her gown, bumped their way to the dance floor, to do what . . . The Dog?

"That man has a raw, unrefined, retrograde charm," Gill said dryly. "He's the sort who thinks 'harass' is two words."

"Assure me that isn't Brit. It's silicone," Alex begged.

"If so, that's the best tit-job I've ever seen. Oh no," Gill groaned. "Her gown's slit to her waist."

"Gosh, such a fine, formal affair with historic pageantry, and what's got us clucking? Brit and her boobs."

"You'd rather talk about the cost of Medicare? The South African election? What *The New York Times* thinks of Trudeau's *Memoirs*? Sharon Stone sheds her panties, and instantly she's a star. Madonna makes headlines off her breathless voice? Nothing gets highbrows, lowbrows, and brows in-between tittering quite like someone baring her taboo."

"Birth of two Barbie dolls."

"You wish, Alex. It's because we're *not* built like Barbie and she is, that Brit's got us ogling like wean-bruised men."

"Speak for yourself," Alex said, puffing out her chest.

"Not even close," Gill said sadly, cracking up her new friend.

*   *   *

In one of the cabins below deck, Wayne Tarr (without a date) drank Scotch straight from the bottle. He was counting the minutes he had left to live. At 9:30, both walking bombs would meet by the dance floor, where Evil Eye would press the button to blow the Mounted to hell and gone.

Serves you fuckers right for blackballing me, Tarr thought.

Since no search was done of Members going aboard—paranoia like that would surely mean canceling the Ball—there was no need for the rectal pack. Tarr, however, was a martyr out to make a statement, so stuffing his butt with C4 was his symbolic act of mooning the entire Force in its smug face.

The rectal pack was Evil Eye's idea.

Stealth and mobility were essential to any suicide run.

Befuddled by drink and muddled by chronic depression, not once had Tarr seriously questioned his coconspirator's motive.

Big mistake.

The world is full of deception.

9:21 . . .

9:22 . . .

9:23 . . .

JET LAG

Africa

The harder the old man hit the bottle, the harder Zinc had to study. Not school study, but study that big well-thumbed anthology of English poems to survive "the gauntlet of the bards." Pop and Zinc were locked in an unhealthy battle of father/son one-upmanship, which Zinc planned to win.

The midnight oil burned.

He lost himself in the poems.

And to this day his favorite remained Wordsworth's "The Prelude":

> One summer evening (led by her) I found
> A little boat tied to a willow tree
> Within a rocky cave, its usual home.
> Straight I unloosed her chain, and stepping in
> Pushed from the shore. It was an act of stealth
> And troubled pleasure, nor without the voice
> Of mountain echoes did my boat move on;
> Leaving behind her still, on either side,
> Small circles glittering idly in the moon,
> Until they melted all into one track
> Of sparkling light . . .

Jet lag held Zinc in its sleepless grasp, internal clock so screwed up it might never tell time again, one good night's rest at Chobe only a brief respite, so now he lay awake in the tent, hands joined behind his head, reciting the words of Wordsworth in his mind, boat out there, stars out there, primal river waiting, the Jewel of the Kalahari, the End of the Earth, here in the Last Eden, going, going, gone, away from the city with its sirens in the night, far from the crap that passed as meaningful life, the boat, the stars, the river calling him, not another human for what? a hundred miles? alone with the deep boom of Pel's fishing owls, punctuated by piping from a zillion reed frogs, hyenas giggling while they burrowed into a kill, nightjars and Peter's fruit bats thrumming air, hippos grunting and snorting in the pool upstream, and roaring from a far-off rogue lion on the hunt.

Zinc threw back the mosquito net and climbed from damp sheets. He unzipped the tent and stepped out into the night.

No moon, the track to the boat was lit by stars, silver pinpricks twinkling on the glassy river, parting for the prow as he pushed off. Against the diamonds of celestial wealth, ilala palms, and knob thorns, and rain trees were black.

> I dipped my oars into the silent lake,
> And, as I rose upon the stroke, my boat
> Went heaving through the water like a swan . . .

*   *   *

Not a man-made light around to spoil the view, the
Mountie lay back in the boat and gazed up in awe at
the stellar display. Twice as many first magnitude stars
in the Southern Hemisphere compared to home, he
could see the Milky Way spilled across the vault, The
Centaur and Southern Cross bright in front, Alpha Centauri, nearest star to us, aligned with Beta Centauri and
The Crux, Magellanic Clouds floating away.

Now as the first hue of dawn pinked the sky to the
east, Zinc sat up, gripped the paddle he'd carved from
the branch, and dipped it into the river.

He thought:

> With trembling oars I turned,
> And through the silent water stole my way
> Back to the covert of the willow tree . . .

Dipping the paddle . . .
Dipping the paddle . . .
Dip . . . He froze midstroke.

Ahead was the camp, ahead was the tent, ahead was
the shore to beach the boat, but flanking the tent were
men with guns in their hands, one black, one white, the
pair from *The Herald* clipping, the black aiming at the
flap the white unzipped, the white covered by the black
as he stepped inside, the white exiting quickly as both
men went on the hunt, searching the bush, searching the
shore, scanning the stretch of river . . . "There he is!" the
black shouted as Zinc turned the *mokoro* downstream to
paddle for his life.

The Gray opened fire.

LAST DANCE

"I wonder what Zinc's doing?" Alex Hunt said.

"Time in Africa?" Gill asked.

"Seven-thirty tomorrow morning. **Ten** hours ahead."

"He's awaking after a night of sweet dreams about you, lulled to sleep by the grunting of hippos humping under the stars."

"Zinc's a country boy," Alex said. "Hope he isn't humping a hippo in substitute for me."

"Don't worry," Gill said. "He'll come home. No matter how good a hump she is, few hippos look as good as you."

"You're a bawdy woman."

"No," Gill said, watching Brit dance. "She's the body woman."

"Excuse me, ladies," Nick said, rising from the table. He'd been conversing with Katherine Spann, his immediate superior at Special X. "I'll be gone a dance or two. Fence to mend."

"Dance with Brit," Gill said, "and you won't live the night."

The band was playing The Drifters' "Save The Last Dance For Me" as Nick crossed the room, weaving between tables of Mounties drinking, flirting, and kibitzing as they have at Red Serge Balls for 121 years. Rachel Kidd and Dermott Toop danced cheek to cheek, while Special 0 cops waltzed around them. "Sorry to cut in," Nick said, tapping Toop's shoulder. "The way this sea is rolling, it may be my last chance. The rest of the cruise will be spent hanging over the side."

"I'll be at the bar," Toop said, relinquishing his date.

"I thought about it," Craven said, taking Rachel's hand. "If I were you, I'd have charged me, too. Apology accepted. Accept mine?"

"The hatchet's buried," Kidd said as Brit and Ed whirled by. "Why does a knife-wielding psycho threaten me less than that chick's chest?"

"Trust the Mad Dog to bring a hooker. Regimental formals would be stuffy without him."

Rachel tugged the tight collar of her tunic. "Bet it's not stuffy in her air-conditioned gown."

Nick grinned. "She looks stuffed in to me."

Craven and Kidd, both in Red Serge with corporals' hooks on their sleeves, him in blue yellow-stripe trousers tucked into box spur boots, her in a matching blue floor-length skirt, made a handsome duo on the crowded floor. Discounting Special 0, however, all eyes were on Brit, the minds behind them hoping or fearing her gown was going to pop.

Brittany Starr had the best body the Mad Dog had ever fucked. He'd balled a lot of hookers, and she was the queen. Come off an ERT assault with his nerves hot wires, it took a hell of a woman to level that adrenaline out. He could count on Brittany to go all night or day.

The Mad Dog was the horniest stud Brittany'd ever fucked. She'd milked so many johns she thought she'd forgotten how to come, until that day the Mad Dog paid her after an ERT assault, rattling her bones until he had her begging for a truce. Truth be known, he was the one man she'd fuck for free.

"Y'ever thought of settling down?" Brittany asked, making sure he danced with his leg slid between her thighs.

"Y'ever thought of savin' it for me?" the Mad Dog asked, gazing down her gully all the way to China.

"Y'ever thought of comin' home to crotchless panties, Hap-penis, musk oil, and—"

"Hold the thought, Brit."

Wayne Tarr, without a partner, stumbled onto the dance floor, the look in his eyes what you'd expect from a man facing the gallows. "Where ya been?" the Mad Dog said, collaring him. "I been huntin' for you. Let's talk outside."

Arm around the unsteady drunk, Ed steered him to the door, ignoring Tarr's protests he had to meet some-one inside. The exit off the dance floor led out to the bow. On deck, moonlight shone and dimmed with each passing cloud, wind from the west flapping their cuffs and whipping their hair, the sea below rising, falling, rising, falling again, each plunge hurling spray up over the rail.

"Pull yourself together, Wayne," Rabidowski said. "Don't disgrace the tunic and don't disgrace the team. Word is the Complaints Commission ruled against undue force. A split-second decision with guns firing all around, you called it as you saw it in a dark room. The report goes out Monday."

A look of boozy disbelief loosened Tarr's squint, turning to oh-my-god horror when he noticed the boat alongside. With so many Members aboard, detachments and sections had skeleton crews, so a 580 Hurricane launch equipped with a ninety-horsepower Johnson outboard was rigged to the stern, in case an emergency called someone ashore for chopper pickup. That boat was now in the water, with Evil Eye in control, riding down and up the valleys between the waves, visible, then invisible as clouds smothered the moon, tracking the *Good Luck City* to keep in radio range.

Nine thirty-one, by Wayne Tarr's watch.

In his mind's eye, the suddenly sober dupe of the Suicide Club envisioned his coconspirator pushing the radio-control button.

"I'm wired!" Tarr shouted. "My ass is crammed with plastique! It's a setup! I'm going to blow! I'm the only bomb!"

Any other Mountie might hesitate, cold-bloodedness fighting with humanity. But not the Mad Dog. All his strength powered the punch that snapped back Tarr's head, then he heaved the unconscious turncoat over the bow rail.

Gunning the Hurricane away from the cruise ship, out on the water Evil Eye pressed the deadly button, beaming the radio signal as Tarr plunged into the heaving sea.

Of no effect underwater, the signal failed to blow the detonator.

The ship's prow plowed the Pacific like a farmer's field, cleaving the ocean to suck the bow swell under the hull, sweeping the flotsam and jetsam of Wayne Tarr toward the stern. Flanking the rudder and powered by the geared diesels in the engine room, twin four-bladed screws churned the passing brine, driving the ship forward through the waves. The port propeller sliced Tarr like fine salami.

Strike a detonator and it will explode.

Chunk, chunk, chunk, head to foot the brass blades cut, till *ping!* one pounded the detonator and set it off, hurling the plastic bomb starboard toward the rudder.

BOOOOOMMMMPHH! Like a depth charge, the C4 blew underwater.

Jerking the rudder.

Jamming it.

Veering the ship toward the reef called Neptune's Trident.

MOKORO

Africa

Except for the Stampede and canoeing in the woods, Zinc felt his father was never there for him. But had the gauntlet of the bards not led him to Wordsworth, would he have been cruising when the Gray attacked? If not for Pop, would the knife be sheathed at his waist, and would he know how to handle a canoe? Pop may not have been there for him in life, but in death he was here for him now.

Ironic if Zinc resolved his feelings on the day *he* died.

Pfffft! pfffft! pfffft! Walther shots zipped by.

Sound suppressors attached to both barrels spoiled the Gray's aim, also hindered by distance and diffused light. The slugs splashed water at Zinc like miniature depth charges, one tearing splinters from the bow above the waterline. Profile to the camp, he paddled paddled paddled.

The White stuck the Walther into his belt to brace the Browning A-Bolt against his beefy shoulder.

There were *coureurs de bois* and *voyageurs* in the Chandler past. Knees spread wide to balance the *mo-*

koro, body hunched low to shrink him as a target, shoulders eking every inch of push from the oar, Zinc propelled the boat toward a clump of reeds. Glancing left, he saw the White aim the rifle.

Master eye aligning both sights with Zinc's head, body angled forty-five degrees right of the target, feet firmly planted shoulder width apart, forestock hand advancing the muzzle so the Mountie rowed into the shot, the mercenary drew a breath, exhaled half, held the rest, then squeezed the trigger.

The .458 Magnum blast erupted like a bomb, driving birds from the treetops in flocks.

Sensing he was on a collision course with death, a few yards short of the reeds Zinc shifted weight, leaning back to raise the bow and sink the paddle deep, the boat zigging right a moment before the bullet spit from the barrel, the whine of the Winchester hollow point an inch from his ear, before he zagged back on course into the reeds.

The White worked the bolt to eject the spent cartridge, then slammed a live round into the chamber. His master eye sighted on the reeds, tracking tassels swaying as the prow parted stalks.

Again the Magnum boomed.

No sooner did the *mokoro* slip into the shelter of green, cliffs of reeds, rushes, and papyrus soaring ten feet up above him, rising dense from the water to reach fine brushlike tips in the air, narrowing the sky to a thin swath parallel to the boat, than Zinc fell forward into the canoe, arms stretching the oar in front of the bow to whip it back and forth against oncoming stalks, trembling tassels six feet ahead as if they were bumped by the prow.

Sucked in, the White sighted too far forward. The bullet whizzed by where Zinc should be, snapping stalks like a scythe. The Mountie dipped his hand in the water to brake the boat. *Bwam! Bwam! Bwam!* Three more shots. All off target where the phantom *mokoro* was thought to be. Zinc heard crashing through the bush away from the camp. Was their boat beached on the far side of the island?

In here, the Okavango seemed to be an impenetrable jungle of grass. Zinc sat up to paddle on. For half an hour he tunneled through interwoven mats, walled in and shadowed by papyrus fronds and the long slashing blades of delta reeds. Stalks parted in V's before the wedged snout of the boat, then sprang back as soft whips that slapped his face. Suddenly, like pickets around an open park, Zinc broke through the green dike onto a dazzling lagoon. The heat was searing. A sun the color of watermelon blazed to the east, hurling rays bounced off the water at his dizzy eyes, silvering lily leaves floating on the surface, their flowers blooming saffron, violet, and rose. To cross the lake he paddled as hard and fast as he could in case the gunmen chanced on him. Emerald-green flashes arrowed across the bow as malachite kingfishers flitted by. Wherever Zinc squinted, there were birds: fish eagles perched high on sentry posts; Pel's fishing owls with extra long claws to catch river bream up to five pounds; water-level trotters with stretched-out toes darting across lily leaves as if on a ballroom floor; lilac-breasted rollers with hues so vivid a king reserved the feathers for his throne. Narrowing in, the lake became a serpentine channel, twisting then turning forward and back through dense swamp growths, first the sun full in his face then burning the nape of his neck, the stream a limpid flow of bronze or white or amethyst according to the light, snaking under a mangosteen hung with sleeping bats, past ugly snuffling warthogs eyeing him hatefully and dragonlike monitor lizards mating on the bank, male straddling female as both flicked their tongues. A mauve heron soaring low just above his head, Zinc rowed through an archer's quiver of wild bamboo to traverse another lake flashing like a mirror. The sun a giant magnifying glass burning him into dust, and sweat pouring from his pores faster than he could replace it with scoops from the river, the Mountie's head throbbed at the Cutthroat wound, the Mountie's muscles knotted where the Ripper stabbed his back, while on and on he paddled into the swamp, past iridescent dragonflies and multicolored frogs, popping two Dilantin against an epileptic fit, channel, lagoon, channel, lagoon, sun to shade to sun, lost in a complex maze akin to Snakes and Ladders, waterways circling in on themselves as loops, some rejoining main river streams, others choked to dead ends by papyrus thatch, time lost backtracking to the last fork, direction overpowered by instinct to survive, senses totally immersed in sounds and colors with nothing to do, yet everything to do with him as a man, devolving into the African creature from which we all sprang, till hours of heat broiled everything into a seemless solar blur.

A Walther shot.

Zinc glanced over his shoulder to find the Black close behind, sound suppressor missing from the barrel of his gun. The Black stood upright in the long narrow hull, hips swaying rhythmically as he poled the dugout south in a race to overtake him. Three more shots, all off target. The Black wore glasses fogged with sweat, a hindrance hard to overcome with just two hands. *Thank God for age,* Zinc thought, muscles straining with every do-or-die stroke.

Hunter and hunted had crossed paths on one of the main streams. The gondolier used it because he knew the land. The *voyageur* chanced upon it when he paddled from a winding canal tangled with bullrushes. An archipelago of islands humped ahead, like a sea serpent swimming in the Okavango. Those an inch or two above the waterline would only be visible in dry times like now, before the floodwaters of the Panhandle crept down. The bow-shaped island directly in Zinc's path forked the river permanently, ilala palms waving above giant umbrella thorns. The string side of the bow ran straight downstream for hundreds of yards, a shooting gallery if Chandler chose that route. Any doubt was settled when the White poled from marsh grass further left to block that fork and cut him off. To the right the island curved like a cutlass blade, the arc of the bow hiding the course of this fork beyond the bulge.

Zinc branched right.

The sides of the *mokoro* cleared the river by three inches, the white sands of the Kalahari just three feet under the hull. So translucent was the water that every detail below, every sunken leaf and frond, was as crisp and vivid as if it floated on the surface. The equinox approaching, the sun was at his back, so Zinc's shadow matched him stroke for stroke, skimming over the sandy bottom patched with submerged reeds, vibrant green with touches of dull red. Under waxy lilies white, pink,

and blue, this was still wild Africa. A baby crocodile
nipped the oar, lips curled over tiny white teeth.

Zinc looked back.

The Black was gaining, *mekoro* designed for poles
not paddles.

Zinc looked down.

The bottom was retreating, the channel deeper with
every stroke.

Zinc looked forward.

The bulge was nearing, the island bowing out into
the stream.

Life-or-death questions vexed his aching mind. Was
the White poling parallel to him down the straight fork
beyond the island to his left, soon to round the point
where the channels met, boxing him in a cross fire with
the Black? Did the bottom of this fork sink deeper and
deeper around the bow, until the Black's pole would no
longer reach, unleashing him to cross the channel where
hopefully a side canal would take him to a safer part of
the Delta?

As if reading his mind, the Black opened fire. Two
shots whined by both Zinc's ears, stereo whistles, one a
second delayed. The next shot blew splinters from the
paddle blade, almost wrenching the oar from his hands.
Around the island bow a screen of reeds knifed from
the water, so Zinc cut close to the bulge for cover. Beyond the curve the back channel deepened into a pool,
before narrowing where the forks joined at the island's
tail. Standing resolute against the blue sky, feathered
palms to the right backed the glassy depths.

The White poled around the island into the narrows
ahead.

The Black behind fired shots through the screen of
reeds.

Beach on the island and Zinc was trapped.

Cornered, he paddled right to traverse the pool, a
spread of open water where the guns could pick him off,
knowing the odds were slim he'd make it to the far side
without taking lead, then . . .

I'm dead, he thought, oaring in reverse.

Directly ahead, the glass of the pool rippled and
broke, two nostrils and a pair of ears rising from the
depths like a sub's periscope. Both ears began to flutter,

a sign of trouble indeed, then a fierce *whooosh* of breath expelled from the nostrils, water swirling about the cavernous yawn that bellowed at Zinc, a gaping pink maw with jutting ivory teeth, before the pool erupted with balloonlike girth, and the angry larded gray hippo attacked.

TITANIC

Georgia Strait

Gill Macbeth was below deck fetching Gravol from her cabin when the ship hit. The force of the collision threw her across the stateroom where she struck her head. Blood oozing down her temple, she passed out between the beds flanking the porthole.

Of all navigation hazards in Georgia Strait, none sinks more ships than Neptune's Trident. The West Coast of British Columbia is nature's most rugged: thousands of islands, inlets, straits, sounds, capes, and hull-tearing reefs along hundreds of miles. Submerged midchannel in Georgia Strait, Neptune's Trident has three rocky tines around which the sea glows with eerie phosphorescence. Sailors say this glow's the ghosts of all the lives claimed, and charts warn captains to give the Trident a wide berth.

Rudder jammed at twenty knots from Tarr exploding, the bow of the *Good Luck City* swung two points (twenty-two degrees) to starboard. The ship sheered the savage sea with misguided momentum, veering uncontrollably toward the barbed tines. Faced with such an obstacle, a vessel should present her stem, not her broadside. Unfortunately Tarr not the captain set this course, so underwater a spear of rock jabbed the hull behind the reinforced collision bulkhead of the bow, gouging, then piercing, then crumpling the weaker broadside plates like tin foil. In ten seconds, the jagged spar ripped a 300-foot gash along the belly, crunching it like chains being jangled down the side, peeling the starboard open with a tortured squeal, gutting that flank before it disappeared astern.

No need to sound the ship.

Nothing could save her soul.

Already listing, the wounded *Good Luck City* was going down.

Nick was in the men's room when the ship hit. The force of the collision hurled him from the sink. Those at the urinals spun like whirling sprinklers spraying a summer lawn. Cubicles popped to eject the bewildered with pants around their ankles. Heavy vibrations shook the boat: the grating of a giant steel knife against a grindstone.

Amidships, down below, the engine room made water fast from the tear in the hull. Foaming green sea spray exploded through the hole a few feet above the floor plates where the starboard flank was sheared the full length of the room. Spewing in as geysers to hiss like serpents, it splashed the hot machinery and turned to steam, while ruptured pipes and exhaust ducts filled the cavern with oil and poisonous black fumes. Big-jointed connecting rods jerking like skeletal limbs, colossal pumping engines throbbed menacingly. Insistent alarm bells rang above watertight doors that closed in a futile attempt at sea containment. The fore-and-aft transverse bulkheads were torn where the breach extended into the abutting compartments. Rushing or seeping, attacking or exploring, water invaded the forepeak and water besieged the stern. Lights flashed as sparks flew and oil spills ignited *foom! foom! foom!* In a desperate attempt to reach escape ladders, terrified men waded waist-deep through the fiery lake churning around the power plant. Burning engineers wailed like wicker men, until the ocean claimed the room and rose to the deck above.

Alex Hunt was thrown from her chair when the ship hit. Her good ankle sprained. The ashtray on the table crashed to the deck and smashed. Those who were dancing sprawled left and right. Masked by the band playing "In the Mood," Tarr exploding was a muffled *whuuu-ump!* from the stern, raising eyebrows but not concern. Veering to starboard was common enough, and hardly noticed in the rough sea. But like the din of a thousand

men hammering on sheet iron, the shriek of steel against
rock booming in from outside as sparks shot skyward
like fireworks, and the clatter within akin to trash cans
rolling down stairs seized attention. Instruments tumbling, the band was replaced by the cymbal crash of
trays, pots, pans, plates, knives, forks, and glasses. Service doors from the kitchen swung open to belch a cacophony of toppling cauldrons and boilers, then the
high-pitched scream of a chef scalded by slop from the
Mounties' traditional steamed pudding. Portholes and
windows vomited glass. Every nail and rivet squeaked
from strain. Chandeliers overhead swung like hypnotists'
watches. Tables overturned, breaking bones. The buffalo
head fell from the wall to gore Chan's back. Brit's spaghetti straps snapped, freeing her breasts. The ballroom
smell of tobacco smoke, whisky, leather, and salt air was
overpowered by the sour sweat of fear.

The Mad Dog was almost tossed overboard when the
ship hit. Only powerful muscles kept him clinging to the
rail. Pandemonium was rife when he forced his way back
into the ballroom, swimming against the human tide
wanting out. The Force was trained for military order,
but not its dates.

Bare-breasted Brit had looped her arm about Hunt's
waist, supporting crippled Alex as her other hand held
the ripped bodice to her bountiful chest. A scene off the
cover of a cheap romance, the Mad Dog tore the Red
Serge from his beefcake torso and gallantly draped it
over Brit's shoulders to hide her modesty. If they survived, it would be an earthshaking fuck.

"Where's Gill?" Nick asked, grabbing Hunt's arm.
He'd searched in vain for her since leaving the men's
room. Worry etched his face.

"Down below!" Alex said, realization dawning. "She
felt queasy and went for Gravol in her cabin."

"Christ!" cursed Nick. "That's *two* decks down."

As he angled upslope toward the amidships stairs, the
list of the ship chaotically tumbled a set of drums with
cymbals clanging across the room. A table had tipped
onto the head of a steward thrown to the floor, who
thrashed convulsively, then was still. The ballroom was
a shambles, debris an obstacle course: smashed bottles,
lumps of food, guttering candles, broken chairs, aban-

doned handbags, dropped cigars. Dangling from a wire, a chandelier tore loose, crashing to scatter prisms like sledgehammered ice. "We're going down! Going down!" freaked a woman whose panicked face was pale as a death mask. Nick descended the stairs as she was slapped to shut her up.

"Ed," DeClercq shouted, collaring the Mad Dog. "We may have trouble with the port-side boats. Take charge starboard and see that order's maintained. Any problem, do what's necessary."

There was panic when the *Titanic* sank. Same with the *Lusitania* and *Andrea Doria*. Every saga of sinking has more tales of feet in faces than of heroics. Ideally, the line would hold, but Mounted recruits are now college grads who fill out too many forms. Only a few will ever draw their guns. The test of backbone is to stare death in the face. Allocating lifeboats was too important for ordeal by water. Caution urged DeClercq to police the police. Rank is for peacetime. Muscle quells panic. Unleashed, the Mad Dog yanked Brit and Alex toward the door.

"Ahhh!" Hunt cried, leg buckling beneath her.

"What's wrong?" Ed snapped.

"I hurt my good ankle."

"Then hang on," he growled, heaving Alex over his broad shoulder like a sailor's duffel bag. "Guard her cast, Brit."

The horned bison head was a mammoth trophy dating from the days of the North-West Mounted Police. That it had gored Chan's lung was ironic indeed. Comforted by Sally as Corrine bandaged him, slashing the tablecloth with a knife for dressings, Eric wheezed shallowly as blood bubbled in his chest. Man and ship were metaphors for each other.

"Kathy," called DeClercq, summoning Spann as he assumed command. "Find a stretcher, or make one, and carry him outside."

The ship was heeling quickly—no less than twenty degrees—by the time DeClercq clambered up to the portside doors. The peril was as he foresaw. Suspended from davits and lowered by winches, lifeboats operate with gravity. Standard procedure is winch the boats to deck level so castaways can board before sending them down to the sea. Here the ship's tilt made that impossible. The severe cant angled the davits up, wedging the boats in over the deck. Cranking the winches wouldn't slide them down, and manpower was too weak to shoulder them uphill. Did the starboard boats have enough room for everyone aboard?

DeClercq traversed the ship to find the reverse of the problem. Here the boats swung too far out from the deck, with manpower too weak to reel them in with ropes so castaways could board. First the boats had to be lowered to the sea, then passengers had to descend by ropes or ladders, and cross a watery gap to reach the further-out boats. And no, there wasn't enough room for everyone aboard.

Far below, whitecaps slapped the rent hull, undercurrents surging in through the submerged gash. As the weight of floodwaters filled her bowels, the *Good Luck City* listed more with every wave . . . twenty-two . . . twenty-three . . . twenty-four degrees. Bustling about the davits, crewmen launched the lifeboats with canvas tarpaulins in place so the heaving sea wouldn't swamp the unmanned shells. The Mad Dog kept the crowd back from the rail, enforcing the no-man's-land with his raised fist. Blood on his knuckles showed he had decked a queue-jumper or two. Some of the davit pulleys were sticky with fresh paint, so those boats went down jerkily, first the bow, then the stern. Cranks turning and ropes creaking from strain, one by one the lifeboats were lowered away, the last about to pass below deck.

Suddenly the ship's whistle let out a shriek, then shrieked and shrieked and shrieked and shrieked, shredding human nerves. Lights still on meant the generator room was watertight, but somewhere the sea was cross-circuiting wires.

High overhead, red flares sizzled.

As suddenly as the whistle, a civilian snapped. He broke from the crowd and dashed screaming for the rail. Scaling it, black tux against black horizon, he tried to swan dive across to the last boat, hands clawing the canvas-covered gunnel before he plunged to the waiting sea.

DeClercq joined the Mad Dog, backing muscle with rank. "Members of the ERT team, step forward," he said. "One to a rope, rappel down and prepare the boats. Any trouble loading, do what's necessary."

With not enough boats to save everyone aboard, it fell to DeClercq as Acting CO to choose who lived and who died.

He would face death.

That he knew.

He'd made the first choice.

Crewmen threw ropes, ladders, and inflated rubber rafts over the side. Others fetched the protective net that covered the swimming pool, lashing it to the starboard rail to form a descending web. It fell short of the ocean, but closed the leaping distance.

Twenty-five . . . twenty-six degrees . . .

For most women, staying in place on the upslant of the deck was a herculean task. As they kicked off high heels, nylons slipped on oil slicks. Those gowned in silk and satin slid if they sat down. First Brit, then others pulled off panty hose, hiking up their skirts oblivious to what they flashed. When that didn't work, most removed their panties and tossed them aside. Only those who sat bare-bottomed defeated the tilt.

Funny the things that pass through your mind at a time like this. In days gone by, the rule was *Women and children first.* Now the rule is *Treat women equally.* Given the choice between death or recanting what's been gained, how many avowed feminists would die for that principle?

"Male and female civilians first," said DeClercq.

Twenty-seven . . . twenty-eight degrees . . .

Down human chains formed to cope with the slanted deck, an orderly stampede to the rail ensued: faces contorted, fearful, and confused. Dread filled the eyes of those without life jackets, jealousy in the looks cast at those who'd found and strapped themselves into bright orange life preservers. Wave after human wave crawled over the rail, women ripping formal gowns to free their legs, men shedding jackets, bow ties, and shoes. Spidermen all, down they went, as portholes rose like ascending balloons.

Through one, Tarr's Scotch bottle rolled about.

Through another, Gill lay unconscious between two beds.

Without warning, the chain locker released, hurling the starboard anchor into the sea. A man on a rope above the foremost boat got caught up in the huge links that twisted around his body like an iron python, yanking him, crying for help, down into the dark depths of Davy Jones's locker. Cleaved by the anchor, the boat blew apart, tossing those scrambling aboard back into the brine.

DeClercq peered over the rail at the chaos below. The last civilians were halfway down, burning the flesh of their palms as ropes slid awkwardly through clenched hands. Frantic swimmers thrashed the sea beneath them, struggling to reach the lifeboats tethered to the ship by snarled umbilical cords, one motionless woman tugged through the water by her hair. Wind and waves chucked the boats about as ERT team Members hauled half-drowned bodies out of the drink. A drunk descending a ladder, life jacket on backward, lost his grip and tumbled into the sea. Kept afloat by the Mae West while wailing he couldn't swim, waves propelled him into the darkness beyond the stern.

"Members aiding the injured, help, carry, or sling them down," said DeClercq.

As the lifeboats filled, the ship's crew panicked. Seized by herd instinct, over they went, those behind diving past those on the ropes and net, devil take the hindmost, survival of the fittest. Lifeboats oared away to keep from being swamped.

Twenty-nine . . . thirty degrees . . .

Funny the things that pass through your mind at a time like this. Those left on deck all wore Red Serge. With 16,000 Members, promotion is slow. Many constables retire with that rank. After tonight, the thin red line would be much thinner. Would the consequent chances for promotion galvanize the Force?

"We're all in the same boat. Literally," said DeClercq. "It's every Member against the sea. Uphold our tradition. *Maintiens le Droit.* Strong swimmers help the injured and weak. Constables first, over the rail. Then corporals and higher ranks inversed up to me. Swim 300 yards out or risk being sucked down with the ship. Okay, let's go."

Thirty-one . . . thirty-two degrees . . .

*   *   *

. . . going down! Going down!" freaked a woman whose panicked face was pale as a death mask. Nick descended the stairs as she was slapped to shut her up.

The amidships stairs from the ballroom to the deck below faced the stern. The Chrysanthemum Deck housed a pizzeria, wine and caviar bar, pâtisserie, beauty center, health club, and ritzy shops. An anorexic mannequin had crashed through the window of Chic & Fancy at the foot of the stairs. Broken glass crackled under Nick's boots as he reversed direction to descend lower. Activated by the shock of hitting the spar, fire sprinklers showered the bowels of the ship. The odd angle of the list threw him off balance. Down one flight of steps he leaned forward and right; down the next back and left. Behind him someone shouted, "All up on deck, unless you want to drown."

The lower Nick descended, the more surreal it got. Gill's stateroom was on the Willow Deck. Here damage to the infrastructure pulled walls out of line and jammed cabin doors. Nick was Conrad Veidt in *The Cabinet of Doctor Caligari*. Spray from the sprinklers slicked the floor. Smoke seeping from below watered his eyes. Fire alarms shrilled along the hall. Nick lost equilibrium, stumbling to the deck, and slid to the low side of the corridor. Runoff from the sprinklers guttered under his knees. A metal door marked CREW ONLY burst open ahead. Gagging smoke billowed into the hall, followed by four oil, brine, and blood-soaked men. A voice trailing them beseeched, "Don't leave me!" Footsteps echoed down the hall as the fugitives climbed the amidships stairs. The tinkle of glass breaking sounded below. "No!" the voice implored. "Not my hand!" The *clang!* of an ax head striking metal made Nick wince. A shriek of pain howled from below. *445. 447. 449.* Cabin numbers passed as he groped along the hall toward the door belching smoke above the wailing man. Boots scaled a ladder. The howl ascended. Then a bloody stump lunged from the smoke, jabbing at Nick like a hookless Captain Hook. Tourniquet cinched around his arm, the groaning wretch appeared, face and clothes sprayed with gore from his hand being chopped off. Someone behind—the ax man?—propelled him into the hall. *451. 453. 455 . . .*

The door to Stateroom 457 was locked, blocked, or jammed.

Nick struggled frantically with the brass knob but it wouldn't give.

Again and again like a battering ram, he threw his shoulder against the wood.

The door held fast.

The ax, he thought.

Smoke so thick he couldn't see three feet in front of his eyes, hacking like a consumptive coughing up his lungs, Nick clawed his way back to the CREW ONLY door. Unable to breathe, he slumped to the floor and tugged off his boots, wrenching the box spurs from both heels. Then he removed his socks, soaked them in the gutter, and pulled his boots back on.

One sock in his pocket, the other masking his nose and mouth and gripped in his teeth, Nick slid down the crew ladder hand under hand. Here above the engine room was a hell of a frightful noise, metal banging metal amid shrill shouts of steam from punctured pipes, sucking, grinding, rumbling, and the distant poom-boom of a giant war drum. His boots hit plating hot beneath their soles. Smoke-blind, he lurched his way along the slant, toe poking here and there hunting for the ax. Spasmodic shudders shook the hull. The starboard tilt increased with each convulsive heave. Ballast pumps below fought a lost battle. The sea surged in faster than they could pump it out. Brine slopped over the bulkheads yet to be breached, sloshing in like an overflowing bathtub. On hands and knees, Nick crawled along the V where the slope met the lower wall. Fingers searching instead of his toe, he touched something wedged in the crack of an almost shut watertight door. Squinting, his eyes caught the raw stump and white bones of a severed hand. By the hacked wrist lay a bloody fire ax.

Water gurgled through the crack as Nick scrambled back to the ladder. Water oozed through the floor plates as he began to climb. Foaming water followed him like a predator at his heels, while faulty electrical circuits buzzed like flies in his ears. Wet, sweaty, oily hands slipped from the bloody rungs, but the tilt of the ship kept him from falling so he could grasp again. Back on the Willow Deck, he slammed and secured the CREW ONLY door.

Swinging the ax sideways, Nick cleaved the stateroom door. Splintering a hand hole, he reached in to turn the knob, but a wardrobe within had wrenched free from its bolts, falling the width of the cabin to barricade him out.

Again he wielded the ax.

Hinges hacked and lock smashed, finally the door gave out.

Nick clambered over the wardrobe to reach Gill between the beds. The tilt of the cabin had moved the sea closer to the porthole than when he'd last looked out. Outside, people were drowning. Face forward so he could mask her mouth with his other sock, Nick hauled Gill over his shoulder like the Mad Dog had Hunt.

Trudging uphill against a thirty-five-degree list, Nick hefted Gill over the wardrobe to regain the hall, panting from overexertion but afraid to pause. One foot on deck, the other on the wall, he lumbered toward the amidships stairs, the only human sound aboard the thudding of his boots. Three times the incline thwarted his attempts to reach the exit, then fingers gripping the banister to stay on his feet, Nick heaved Gill step by laborious step up to the Chrysanthemum Deck. Forced to stop between levels to catch his breath, he pressed on up to the Marco Polo Ballroom.

Like two kids on a playground slide, dragging Gill he slid down the dance floor to the starboard doors and across the deck outside to the rail.

Nick glanced down.

The lifeboats had oared away to keep from being swamped, abandoning hundreds to the hungry sea. Off the bow was *The Queen of the North,* awaiting the return of boats launched to save the drowning. Relieved from her route between Port Hardy and Prince Rupert, the ferry was sailing south to a refit at Deas Dock when the SOS was heard. To avoid being sucked down with the sinking ship, her lifeboats were racing time, fishing Redcoats from the sea like a salmon run . . . one, two, three, four, away all boats.

Too late for Nick to catch the last boat.

The deck beneath his feet lurched another degree.

The black water below beckoned him.

Dragging Gill by one arm, he struggled toward the stern.

There he kicked off his boots and ripped her skirt seam.

Climbing over the rail, he pulled Gill with him.

Burdened, he took the plunge.

CROCODILE

Africa

Even at two and a half tons, the African hippo can outrun a man, and doesn't much care what stands in its way. In water, crocodiles know to stay clear, what Zinc was desperately trying to do by rowing in reverse. The stern of the dugout brushed the offshore reeds, fifteen feet from the sandy bank at his back. The Black closing from the right fed his Walther another clip, then, pole planted to steady his aim, straight-armed the muzzle to sight on Zinc. The White hugged the island as he poled in on the left, a hundred feet, ninety feet, narrowing the gap. The hippo lifted its huge angry bulk from the pool, froglike eyes furious at Zinc. It shook its head in rage and slashed the air between them with its ivory teeth. The river parted in rolling waves as the dreadnought plowed at Zinc, blunt head blitzing like a rhino charge. The surging tide swept the *mokoro* sideways, and water slopped in to drench the rolling hull. Shot after shot plumped into its lard as the snorting hippo rammed the stern, hurling Zinc into the reeds twelve feet from shore. Its tiny brain wrestling with how to escape, the water here too shallow to submerge, the wallowing beast abandoned the river to pound up the bank and crash into the bush, tall trees whipping apart moments after it vanished, followed by a shudder as if from a quake. The hippo began to squeal and squeal and squeal like a stuck pig.

"I got him!" the Black shouted to the White.

Zinc's *mokoro* rocked upside down in the reeds, air trapped in the hollow keeping it afloat.

Or so the Black thought.

Legs apart for balance and one hand gripping the pole, he drifted cautiously into the reeds to find the Horseman's body, Walther sweeping back and forth across the shallows, eyes probing the murk the hippo disturbed for any sign of the kill.

Downstream between here and the approaching White, what looked like a log slipped from the shore into the Okavango.

His back against the white sands of the Kalahari, reeds caressing his cheeks like the arms of an octopus, Zinc held his breath and stared up into the overturned canoe, submerged gunnels rocked by his hands. The left fist also grasped Pop's knife.

The rivers of the tropics are rife with parasites, like the *loa loa* worm that burrows in between the toes and wriggles up to thrive and grow in the fluid of your eyeballs. Zinc was so frightened he wanted to piss his pants, but was more frightened of what might happen if he did . . . Like the *candiru*—the toothpick fish—which, spiny gills outstretched like barbed needles, scoots up the urethra of any fool who urinates in the wrong tropical stream. . . .

Gun aimed down to blast whatever moved, the Black poled closer to the overturned boat. . . .

The rivers of Africa are rife with parasites, like bilharzia spread by waterborne flukes that relinquish their snail hosts to worm into us, traveling along the bloodstream to veins in the bladder or intestine walls, where they mate, lay eggs, and multiply, ruptured blood in the urine, ruptured blood in the stool . . . Like guinea worm invaders that also sneak in, growing in cysts and bursting out like that *Alien* thing, horrible worms with heads like cobras. . . .

Lukundoo, he thought.

Zinc's heart pounded like voodoo drums.

Zinc's lungs crumpled from lack of air.

The Kalahari sand settled to clear the murk, about to expose him to eyes above.

Three feet, two feet, one foot from the overturned

canoe, the Black extended the pole to joust the *mokoro* aside.

The tip tapped the bottom.

Anybody home?

Now! thought the Mountie, shoving the hull forward like a battering ram, clipping the snout of the Black's *mokoro* to roll it like a log, dumping the African into the river as Zinc kicked out his foot, shoe connecting with the gunman's head, the Mountie thrashing around to lash out his arm, right hand gripping something, the other man's jaw, muscles contracting to reel him in and hammerlock his head, left hand arcing across his neck, knife tip jutting toward his spine. *"Whatever the job, this will see it done,"* Pop said, then the razor-sharp edge ripped left to slit the mercenary's throat ear to ear.

Blood reddened the river as Zinc broke through the surface for air.

Twenty feet away, the White took aim.

Then like a Polaris missile launched from the sea, a crocodile exploded from the shallow reeds, jaws open wide so Zinc gazed down its gullet.

CASTAWAY

Georgia Strait

He fell for what seemed an interminable distance, then Nick hit the ocean feet first and seemed to sink forever, the shock of the dive knocking the breath out of him. The water was cold, so cold it was painful, its bite, as he plunged deep, quick and sharp as a shark's. Lungs compressed by the frigid slap, he fiercely fought the impulse to inhale salt water. One arm locked around Gill covering her mouth and nose, he thrashed with the other and kicked upward against the undertow, racing to surface before his muscles cramped. Bump, his head hit rubber, pushing him down. Nick swam sideways, surfaced, and coughed bitter brine from his throat. Gasping, he hooked his arm into the rubber raft. Gill pulled free, sputtered, and gulped for air. Nick struggled onto the raft and hauled her in.

Cast adrift by someone rescued by a boat, the raft had bobbed along the hull toward the ship's stern. Nick had spotted it from the starboard rail, towing Gill by the arm to track it back, before jumping into the ocean to intercept it here. With Gill centered to balance the raft until she gathered herself, Nick grabbed the only oar and paddled paddled paddled.

A sinking ship forms a whirlpool that sucks like a drain, pulling surface objects into the watery grave. The list of the *Good Luck City* said she was going down. Unless they got away fast, the suction would take them, too.

Globs of coagulated oil fouled the waves astern. The props churning the sea white in their wake had stopped. Through rents in the dome of cloud and smoke hiding the peekaboo moon, starlight sheened the rising, falling, rising, falling sea. Paddling south behind the stern to clear the lee of the ship, Nick turned east so the wind was at his back, hoping to surf the whitecaps away from the wreck.

Up, down, up, down, Gill paddle-wheeling her hand as Nick oared at the helm, the inflated raft rowed into the night.

Behind, the ship turned on her center of gravity, suddenly plunging forward as a groan rang out over the sea. Waves moved in quickly to engulf the bow, rolling swells pounding the bridge and splaying back along both sides of the deck. Bow down, the stern rose out of the water, exposing the jammed rudder and twin screws. The din from within was a muffled roar mixed with rumbling booms, like standing under a railway bridge as a train passes. Fatally seasick, the ship threw up innards that somersaulted into the bow, wrenching the engine room apart as heavy turbines, dynamos, generators, and pumps tore loose from their mounts. Deep in the hull of the vessel, something blew. Millions of sparks belched from the funnel rocketed into the sky. Fanning as it soared, the red spurt showered a fountain of fire. Lesser bombs followed, dull and heavy below the waterline. Forward movement ceased while the keel pivoted, the floundering stern continuing to rise. Soon the ship stood perpendicular and motionless, then she began a slow corkscrew into the sea. In a searing flash, all the lights aboard snapped on. Lights lit the portholes. Lights lined the decks. Lights blazed in the submerged bow of the ship, suffusing the sea with soft green radiance. The lights doused in unison, out forever, the hull now silhouetted like a huge black finger flipped at fate. Swallowed by Neptune, down went the ship, the lifeboats on the port side finally breaking free, spinning wildly within the whirlpool eddied by the sinking, sucked down into the maelstrom never to surface again, the pull of the vortex widening, widening, like a black hole.

"Heave!" Nick shouted. "The suction's yanking us back!"

Both hands in the water, Gill churned sprays from the sea.

Back they surged, farther still, drawn toward the drain, fighting a reverse current too strong for human will, then *whooosh!* the raft shot forward like a flying carpet, riding the mammoth white wake born from the closing womb, a tidal wave, a wall of water, a burp from the deep, propelling them atop its crest as Nick and Gill leaned this way and that to keep the raft trim, their peril changing to shoot the tube and ride the pipeline, dudes, once the torrent began to curl for its downward crash.

The raft flipped, throwing them clear, in the barrel of the wave. The swell curled like a sausage roll and took them under. Nick thrashed, air bubbling from his lips, as the sea embraced him. Lungs aching, salt water seeped into his mouth. He surfaced, choking, and looked for Gill.

No raft.

No Gill.

A triangle burst from the foam.

Shark! he thought. *Great White! They prowl here!* The shock of meeting a shark alone in the dark shook him. *Too early. Too cold. Ship's debris . . .*

Another wave swamped him. The tow tugged him down. Brine burned his eyes. Salt stung his lungs. The ocean threw its weight at him in wave after wave, each roller breaking above with a ghostly glow on its crest, before toppling in a downrush to push him under, holding him there till the next drowning swell moved into place. It was a battle to tread himself clear for every breath. *Gill . . . Gill . . .* but just as Canute couldn't command the tide, so it was only a matter of time till Nick stayed down.

Tears blended with the brine that splashed across his face. Blows from the deep rolled over him in a series of slow punches. The cold clear light of the moon shone between two clouds, rainbowing the slick of oil sliming the sea. Exhaustion from venturing below deck, carrying Gill, swimming, and paddling undermined him. Another heavy wave washed over Nick. No choice but to let the tide take him where it wanted, he uprose, sank, uprose, sank, nauseatingly. Cold cramped his muscles so they refused to move. A weariness stronger than dread overwhelmed him. Down he went like a knight clubbed on the field of battle, slipping under the waves to let the sea clean his bones. . . .

His feet struck bottom.

Barnacles ripped his soles.

A wave knocked him forward.

Shells cut his palms.

Arms too tired to hold him up, he collapsed on his chin.

Robinson Crusoe, he bled onshore.

Where he was, Nick had no idea.

Time and space had lost all meaning.

Rocked by the sea, arm outstretched, he panted between waves.

Seconds? Minutes? Hours passed?

A shadow moved across him.

Gill!

A human form.

As he pulled his outstretched arm in to roll onto his side, the twenty-two-inch socket bayonet of the British Colonial Army rammed through his palm.

A voice behind his ear joined Nick's cry.

"Hello, brother."

NAKED PREY

Africa

The Nile crocodile deserves its killer reputation. Staring down triangular jaws edged with tear-along-the-dotted-line teeth, Zinc time-traveled back 200 million years to the age of dinosaurs. Twenty-one feet long and 2,200 pounds, the dark, cold-blooded monster with darker crossbands on the tail snapped its conical canines into quivering human flesh, sharp-cutting edges impaling the arm while short blunt molars crushed the bones. Shocked gasps escaped from Zinc as the armor-plated reptile did its notorious "death roll," spinning round and round in the water flashing its lighter-colored belly until the Black's arm tore from the corpse still locked in Zinc's grip. Long, slender snout without a forehead, round eyeball with a vertical pupil slit, mouth leaking water as it rose from the stream, largest tooth the fifth one in the upper jaw, the notch beside it for a canine in the lower jaw, five webbed toes on each front foot: dread burned every detail into Zinc's mind as the croc raised its snout high to juggle the Black's arm into position, then tossed back its head so the chunk still gripping the Walther literally fell down its gullet. Inside the mouth was orange.

With teeth no good for chewing and jaws that don't move sideways, crocs gulp their prey whole and rely on a dual stomach with strong acids to dissolve even the bones. Zinc released the corpse as the reptile snapped again, curved fangs clamping the Black's torso to jerk the body from the river and heave it in the air. A meal too big to be consumed intact, the croc began to thrash the Black into swallow-size chunks by violently shaking its bloodstained snout. The neck slit to the spine gave first, hurling the African's head like a bowling ball, followed by the remaining arm, both flailing legs, then strewn khaki clothes. Some crocs go two years between meals, so this voracious horror gulped the Black with mouth-smacking relish.

Standing in his *mokoro* twenty feet away, the White held his fire convinced the croc would finish Zinc off, then as the Mountie broke from the kill to splash from the shallows, realized a shot was needed after all. By the time he squeezed the trigger, waves rippling from the feeding frenzy rocked the boat.

Bam! Bam! Slugs smacked or ricocheted off the bony button osteoderms of the reptile's armor.

Bam! Bam! The Walther wavered this way and that to hurl lead at the sky.

Bam! Bam! Bam! Click! Wild shots hit the shore and threw up puffs of sand.

Like the Queen's Own Rifles beaching at Normandy, Zinc stormed from the green reeds awash with warm blood and dashed across the fiery sand that burned the soles of his shoes, spurts of water then sand then clay then dust spewing about him, the air so charged with heat it felt electrified, once shot in the head, then knifed in the back, so truly amazed none of the shots fired today had hit him, wondering if his luck was fate, or God, or the odds, and then he was into the dense bush cemented together with shadows, heading for the hippo squealing like a stuck pig.

In 1964, Cornel Wilde filmed *The Naked Prey*. The year is 1840 and a white safari attracts disaster when British Colonials humiliate a local native chief. Naked and unarmed, Wilde is given a spear's throw head start and ends up fleeing through Africa with a band of angry lion hunters dogging his heels, determined to kill him with their assegais. On a date with Jackie, the love of his teens, Zinc caught the movie at the Bison Drive-In, but hand sneaking under her bra as Jackie tongued his throat, he had missed the climax of that black on white chase. Now, scrambling through the jungle of Crocodile Island, Zinc atoned for his oversight by *living* Wilde's terror.

One stark difference.

This was White on white.

Close behind to Zinc's right, the White leapt from the

mokoro into the shallows, loading a fresh magazine as he waded ashore, firing six shots at random into the bush.

Camel thorns, spike thorns, knob thorns, umbrella thorns snagged Zinc's clothes and scratched his skin. A brood of hooting baboons rattled the palms above as the fugitive kicked and crushed an ape skull on the ground. Egrets took flight from the highest branches. Rain tree and leadwood and jackalberry and ebony encaged him in a shrubby tangle of green on green. Like Tarzan vines in Darkest Africa, the serpentine coils of a strangler fig webbed saprophytically around a host tree. How long ago it was set was anybody's guess, but the squealing hippo was caught in a deadly Bushman's trap, having snapped a trip wire stretched across the ground, releasing a spear weighted with rocks suspended above, plunging a gravity harpoon into its own back. No time to pause and finish it off, Zinc zigzagged around as *plump! plump!* two more shots perforated the lard.

On the run, the White yanked another magazine from his skeleton chest-webbing. Through the trees he caught glimpses of Zinc crashing ahead, crossing the island to reach the bank of the far fork down which the White had poled. A smile creased his jaw. The Horseman was in for a jolt.

Zinc heard the African angling in to intercept him from behind to the right. Blinding blue flashed between the trees in front of his eyes. Head turning to compute if he should veer up-island to the left, Zinc witnessed a six-foot demon trailing him, a nightmare so horrid he feared he was psychotic.

Adrenaline fuel-injecting his heart, the cop burst from the bush and stumbled down glaring sand in a last-ditch effort to ford the stream, but a moment later was churning back in retreat.

Crocodile Island took its name from this bask of crocs, sunning up and down the beach with eyes shut and jaws open so adroit little birds could pick their teeth clean, or slowly cruising the Okavango with S-sweeps of their eel-like tails. The sudden approach of fresh meat galvanized them. Bodies twisting side to side as limbs rowed sand, some belly-crawled off the bank to wait for Zinc in the stream, ready to drag him under the instant he waded in. One gave the shore a resounding smack with its tail, hurled itself in the air and looped into the river, then shot vertically out of the water to walk on the end of its tail. The less patient launched peremptory attacks. Crocs onshore rose long and lean on squat reptilian legs, high walking bellies and tails off the sand, snouts snapping hungrily as they came. Crocs offshore lunged onto the bank, fearsome bursts of speed in pursuit of Zinc, propelled many body-lengths by thrashing tails and leaping hind legs, webbed toes digging in for push, trying to topple Zinc with sledgehammer blows from their jaws.

Eaten alive or shot through the heart, Zinc made a choice.

Scrambling back and framed by bushes bordering the beach, he formed a perfect target outlined against the sky.

Eight shots fired at point-blank range.

GAUNTLET

Georgia Strait

Evil Eye clamped a handcuff around Craven's wrist, yanking the bayonet from Nick's palm to wrench his hand behind his back and lock both arms. "Wonder how I found you?" the psycho asked, leather gripping the Mountie's hair to haul him from the ground, the other glove tearing a button from the cuff of his Red Serge. "Special 0 transmitter hidden in this button. Backup plan to track you in case you beat the frame. Twins we are in birth, but I'm smarter than you. No matter how fate plays it, you're destined to pay."

The Hurricane from the *Good Luck City* was beached downwind. The wash of the tide and brine in Nick's ears had hushed its approach. Dressed, masked, and gloved in black, the psycho looming over him was dark against the moon. Madness and hate burned in the eyes behind slits in the balaclava. As if possessed by the beat of silent African drums, the snakeskin pouch around the killer's

neck swayed hypnotically. Dropping the lunger so its
blade wedged in a fissure, Evil Eye grabbed Nick with
both hands and shoved him toward the boat, drop-kick-
ing him in the ribs when he stumbled and fell.

"Uungh!"

Kick.

"Uungh!"

Kick.

"Uungh!"

Kick.

"Uungh!"

Evil Eye a striker, Nick the soccer ball, the pair moved
along the shore to the Hurricane. "Mom confessed how
we were conceived." Heard through water, the voice
seemed to rise from the bottom of the sea. "Nigel came
to Lethbridge while Ted was up North. Ted was an asshole who treated her bad. Nigel was a hunk from exotic
Africa. March seventh, Ted returned while Mom had
Nigel in bed. Hammond escaped bare-assed out the bedroom window. Naked, Mom intercepted Ted in the hall.
He was so randy he fucked her over the living-room
couch. One man gened me. The other gened you."

Curled up in a fetal ball near the Hurricane, Nick
vomited into our primal womb. From a bag in the boat,
Evil Eye withdrew the Zulu knobkerrie. The first blow
bounced off Nick's skull, cracking his clavicle. The
Mountie yelped with agony as blood gushed across his
face.

"Touch a knife to someone's eye and truth spills out.
Before she fell down the stairs, Eleanor recounted the
night we were born. Ted was drunk and shouting the
twins weren't his when Mom was in labor at his sister's
home. Mom assumed a neighbor had seen Nigel escape,
but it was merely Ted's insecurity, same as *his* dad
doubted Eleanor. Mom confessed, cowed by labor pain,
and Ted began hitting her during my birth. That's when
Eleanor shot him with his thirty-eight, saving Mom while
avenging incest rape in her youth."

Three blows in succession rained down on Nick's
head, causing him to dry heave as the psycho kicked
him again.

"Two dads. Two babies. Too much hate. You born
perfect. Me with outcast skin. Would Mom have rejected

me if I were her only child? Thanks to you, brother, I got sloughed off. Mom didn't want me. Nor did Eleanor. Sacred Heart couldn't place me because of my skin. So I spent *years* in that Newfoundland hell!

"Every night the Brothers would creep through the dorm, selecting four or five of us to drag to bed. Cock up my ass or down my throat, crying for the Mom who put me there. Only revenge keeps you sane.

"Took me years to find her but I never gave up. It was hate that won me all those scholarships. Then someone blew the whistle on the orphanage, and my placement surfaced in the investigation. Sister Superior, Eleanor, and Mom paid . . .

"That leaves you, brother."

The eyes above Nick pinned and dilated. "Hear them screaming? The Redcoats on the Hill? Twinning every man whose shade escaped Rorke's Drift? One stake bare . . . saved for you. . . ."

Glove gripping Red Serge, Evil Eye dragged Nick to his knees. Crabs scuttled around them, fleeing for the sea. "I hate you, brother. You owe me a lifetime of love. Pay up!" the psycho cried, raising the knobkerrie high against the moon, shouting "He's yours!" to Black Ghost as the club came down.

BLACK MAMBA

Africa

Southern Africa squirms with seventy-six species of snake. The largest—the python—like bush and mole and green water snakes is harmless to us. Others are lethal. The bite of the fat flat bloated gaboon viper says bye-bye. Egyptian, spitting, rinkal, and forest cobras get their share. The Great Zimbabwe M'fezi in *The Herald* photo of the Gray squirts a spray of venom at the eyes. The puff adder, *boomslang,* vine snake . . . the list goes on. But deadliest of all is the black mamba.

The White first saw a mamba moving across a mealie field, back when both he and the Black were boys on his father's farm. Head six feet in the air and tail on the ground, the snake passed left to right while he gawked, top unjarred like a tank cannon mounted on a gyro, the lower eight of fourteen feet slithering fast. Never had he seen a more fearsome sight.

Fleeing through the jungle with the White closing in, Zinc had glanced left to compute if he should veer up-island, and that's when he saw the serpent stalking him. Adrenaline hit the Mountie's heart like a vampire stake.

For decades the White had survived in the bush, an eye on the lookout for predators. Minutes ago, however, his "brother" was killed, the only man alive who meant a damn to him, so now every sense focused on taking the Horseman down, boxing him between the crocs and muzzle of the gun. Zinc vanished through the blue hole in the bush, then reappeared when he scrambled back from the jaws, so sharp a silhouette the African couldn't miss, and that's when the White heard a hollow *hisssss* to his left. He turned as the sleek coffin-shaped head zoomed in, mamba reputed to be the fastest snake known, twice as fast as any North American species, able to lash out forty percent of its length, narrow hood wide and mouth agape to bare the black lining, tongue flicking rapidly from side to side, then both fangs sank deep into the African's neck.

Zinc saw the snake strike again and again, filling the White with enough venom to kill ten men, while *bam! bam! bam! bam!* . . . the man emptied his gun, blasting the dark gunmetal gray serpent in Eden in half, eight shots followed by a *click!*

Gasping, the African stumbled two steps before his knees buckled, slumping against a termite mound curved like a rhino horn in which the dead snake had made its home.

The gun was out of ammo. The webbing held no more clips. The White clawed his throat, choking for breath. Zinc crossed the distance between them to kick away the Walther and yank the Ka-Bar from his belt, tossing the blade out among the crocs. Right arm pinning the White to the mound, he pricked Pop's knife against the wildly beating heart.

"It's over," Zinc said.

Heat off the sand overflowed into the shade, sucking sweat from the face-to-face men. The quickest mamba kill recorded is twelve minutes. Neuro and cardiotoxic, mamba venom inhibits breathing and the vagus nerve that controls the heart, slowly shutting down both lungs and pulse. Strangled, the White would stay conscious as his muscles paralyzed, then locked in a rigid body, would die claustrophobic.

"Do it," begged the African, eyes on Pop's knife. "Please," he added.

"For three answers," the Canadian replied.

LUNGER

Georgia Strait

They say you see a flash of white light when you die, beckoning you across to the Realm of the Shades. On his knees, head back, sheened by the moon, moonlight shining silver along this pooled shore, the shadow of Death over him with that falling club in its hand, Nick saw the flash of light burst from Death's chest, white on black.

The club stopped in midair, then tumbled into the surf.

The streak of light withdrew into the black heart.

Evil Eye crumpled in front of Nick.

Only then did he see Gill behind with the bayonet in her hand.

"He's dead," she said, shivering, without bothering to check. The pathologist knew exactly where to stick the blade.

"You made it," Nick said, his features etched with relief and pain.

"Women have more fat to survive cold. Match endurance, not strength, and we're Nature's pet. Let's see how bad you're hurt."

Squatting, hair and torn dress plastered skintight by the sea, Gill gave Nick a moonlight physical head to toe. "Fractured clavicle. Punctured hand. Bruised gut. Battered noggin. Prognosis is you'll live."

"Check his pockets, then the boat for the handcuff key."

"Who?" Gill asked, reaching down to peel the black hood from Evil Eye's face.

"Dermott Toop," Nick said. "Mom's blood was in the Lab from the autopsy. He used it to stain my Red Serge for the DNA test."

JUNGLE JUSTICE

Africa

"Why kill me?" Zinc asked the White.

"Nothing personal," the dying man choked. "You got in the way of a business deal. We didn't want our photo flashed around."

"How do I get back to camp?" Zinc had a flight to catch.

"Main stream. Keep left where it forks."

"Alberta in the fifties didn't welcome blacks. Why did Nigel go for the bones instead of you?"

A don't-you-get-it look furrowed the White's brow. "Nigel Hammond and Clive Moon were aliases. Just two of many we used. *The Herald* mistakenly stuck the label "left" on the wrong man. Don't believe everything you read in the papers."

Suddenly Zinc saw it in the bones of his face. The White had shaved off his beard for the Zulu hit, baring features passed on to Nick.

"I'm Nigel Hammond," the mercenary said.

COLOR-BLIND

Georgia Strait

Throat, to chin, to nose, to eyes, then clear of hair and head, Gill peeled the balaclava from Evil Eye's face. At first Nick thought his mind was playing tricks, but gradually pieces fell into place in his battered brain.

The motive wasn't race, a black/white thing.

The motive was Oedipus, with a twist.

Unresolved desire for the love of Mom, and hate of Redcoat Dad who turned Mom against him.

On the ground lay Ted Craven's son. Did he have a physical trait revealing that link? Is that why Mom and Eleanor rejected him? He was the spawn of the brute who sexually abused them both?

If so, Nick wondered, *who's my dad?*

The man dead on the shore had *"outcast skin."* The fifties. The Prairies. Conform with God. And witch hunt outsiders and mutants. Did the purple birthmark obsess him with genetics? Why me? Why favor my *"perfect"* twin? The Lab was heaven-sent for the frame. Mom's blood. Him in charge. And Toop brought him the swatch from Nick's tunic. First he stained the cuff cut-out with Mom's blood from the autopsy, then he tested the Red Serge for her DNA. Who showed DeClercq the photo of the black-and-white twins?

Black . . .

White . . .

Color-blind . . .

Evil Eye was Colin Wood.

AUTHOR'S NOTE

This is a work of fiction. The plot and characters are a product of the author's imagination. Where real persons, places, or institutions are incorporated to create the illusion of authenticity, they are used fictitiously. Inspiration was drawn from the following nonfiction sources:

The Advocate: Harris, L. "Judge Sir Matthew Baillie Begbie" (1971, vol. 29); Pettit, S.G. "Judge Matthew Baillie Begbie" (1948, vol. 6); Watts, A. "The Honourable Sir Matthew Baillie Begbie" (1966, vol. 24); Williams, D.R. "Begbie & Duff J.J." (1985, vol. 43).

Bancroft, James W. *Rorke's Drift.* Tunbridge Wells: Spellmount, 1988.

Berglund, Axel-Ivar. *Zulu Thought-Patterns and Symbolism.* Cape Town: Philip, 1976.

Bull, Peter. *The Teddy Bear Book.* New York: Random House, 1969.

Chayko, G.M. and E.D. Gulliver and D.V. Macdougall. *Forensic Evidence in Canada.* Aurora: Canada Law Book, 1991.

Creeweel, John. *A Brief History of the Victoria Falls Hotel.* Harare: Zimbabwe Sun Hotels, 1984.

Davis, Chuck (editor). *The Vancouver Book.* North Vancouver: J.J. Douglas, 1976.

Duncan, John and John Walton. *Heroes for Victoria.* Tunbridge Wells: Spellmount, 1991.

Guggisberg, C.A.W. *Wild Cats of the World.* New York: Taplinger, 1975.

Hart, Bernard. *The Psychology of Insanity.* Cambridge University Press, 1957.

Heitman, Helmoed-Romer. *Modern African Wars 3: South-West Africa.* London: Osprey, 1991.

Hoffer, William. *Saved! The Story of the* Andrea Doria—*the Greatest Sea Rescue in History.* New York: Summit, 1979.

Holt, Simma. *The Devil's Butler.* Toronto: McClelland & Stewart, 1972.

Horn, Richard. *Fifties Style: Then and Now.* Philadelphia: Courage, 1988.

Horrall, S.W. *The Pictorial History of the Royal Canadian Mounted Police.* Toronto: McGraw-Hill, 1973.

Knight, Ian. *Nothing Remains but to Fight: The Defense of Rorke's Drift, 1879.* London: Greenhill, 1993.

Knight, Ian. *Zulu: Isandlwana and Rorke's Drift: 22nd-23rd January 1879.* London: Windrow & Greene, 1992.

Lash, John. *Twins and the Double.* London: Thames and Hudson, 1993.

Luard, Nicholas. *The Last Wilderness: A Journey Across the Great Kalahari Desert.* New York: Simon & Schuster, 1981.

McBride, Angus. *The Zulu War.* London: Osprey, 1976.

McCrea, Barbara and Tony Pinchuck. *The Rough Guide to Zimbabwe and Botswana.* London: Rough Guides, 1993.

Morris, James. *Heaven's Command: An Imperial Progress.* London: Penguin, 1979.

Morris, James. *Pax Britannica: The Climax of an Empire.* London: Penguin, 1979.

Pitta, Robert and Jeff Fannell. *South African Special Forces.* London: Osprey, 1993.

Ross, Charles A. (editor). *Crocodiles and Alligators.* New York: Facts On File, 1989.

Royal Canadian Mounted Police. *Honors and Protocol Manual.* Ottawa: RCMP, 1995.

Royal Canadian Mounted Police Fact Sheets. Ottawa: RCMP, 1992.

Shirer, William L. *The Rise and Fall of the Third Reich.* New York: Simon & Schuster, 1960.

Simpson, Colin. *Lusitania.* London: Longman, 1972.

Sisman, Adam (editor). *The World's Most Incredible Stories: The Best of Fortean Times.* New York: Avon, 1992.

Smyth, Sir John. *The Story of the Victoria Cross.* London: Muller, 1963.

Swaney, Deanna and Myra Shackley. *Zimbabwe, Botswana & Namibia: A Travel Survival Kit.* Hawthorn: Lonely Planet, 1992.

The Vancouver Sun.

Van der Post, Laurens. *The Lost World of the Kalahari.*
London: Chatto & Windus, 1988.

Wade, Wyn Craig. *The Titanic: End of a Dream.* New
York: Rawson, Wade, 1979.

Wolf, Leonard. *Horror: A Connoisseur's Guide to Liter-
ature and Film.* New York: Facts On File, 1989.

Wolf, Leonard (editor). *Wolf's Complete Book of Terror.*
New York: Potter, 1979.

Zuehlke, Mark. *The B.C. Fact Book: Everything You
Ever Wanted To Know About British Columbia.* Vancouver: Whitecap, 1995.

Slade's respect for the RCMP is earned respect. It comes
from defending over a thousand cases against the Force.
My thanks to the Commanding Officer and Members of
"E" Division (with a tip of the Stetson to the Corps
Sergeant Major in Ottawa) for answering my questions
and inviting me to the Red Serge Ball and Regimental
Dinners.

My trip to Africa was no less exciting—but much less
dangerous—than Zinc's. But there were moments: the
spitting cobra at the ruins, the croc under the canoe, the
lion's paw imprinted on my foot mark when I wandered
off alone to experience "the real Africa." All the guide
said was "Lucky she wasn't hungry." So thanks to all in
the bars and around the campfires of Harare, Masvingo,
Kariba, Vic Falls, Hwange, Chobe, and lost in the Delta
who took me in deep and brought me out alive. It *was*
a long way from the Ridge Theater in 1956. Tight
lines, mates.

The story survivors will return in the next Special X
novel.

Slade
Vancouver, B.C.

Be sure to catch
these other tales of
heart-stopping horror
by Michael Slade,
published by Signet. . . .

A killer who refused to be caught . . .

Headhunter
by Michael Slade

A killer was loose, a killer whose victims were found savagely mutilated, and no woman was safe. The police combed the sexual undergrounds of two continents in search of the fiend responsible for the trail of headless bodies. But not even Detective Robert DeClercq could prevent the madman from striking again—and again. . . .

**"A real chiller . . . the most gruesome
I have ever read!"
—Robert Bloch, author of *Psycho***

**What you don't know
can hurt you.**

Ghoul
by Michael Slade

The bodies were all the same. First they had
been stripped naked. Then the blood had been
drained from them while they were still alive.
Then their hearts had been cut out. The police
looked for a psycho-killer. The press screamed
that a vampire was loose. But they were wrong.
It was worse. . . .

**"A complex horrorfeast . . .
Ghoul sure lives down to its moniker."
—*The Philadelphia Inquirer***

**Hunting for a
savage serial killer.**

Cutthroat
by Michael Slade

From the cutting edge of psychological terror
comes this spellbinding novel that reaches from
the darkest depths of the past to today's highest
tech. . . . A bizarre series of grisly murders had
San Francisco in a death grip, the work of a
twisted serial killer somewhere between man and
monster. Behind his horrific rule lies a mystery
as old as the American West itself . . . a secret
worth protecting . . . and worth killing for.

**"Fast paced, gritty action . . . not for the
faint of heart or weak of stomach."**
—*Science Fiction Chronicle*

**Jack the Ripper
lives.**

Ripper
by Michael Slade

Who would slash the body to shreds, then rip the face off America's foremost feminist—and hang her out to die? Who would take a pair of twin hookers on a terror trip that made death seem innocent and sweet? Who would turn a secluded island gathering of bright and beautiful people into a carnival of carnage? What grim and grisly figure stood, dripping knife in hand, at the end of the most horrifying trail of death and deception Detectives Robert DeClercq and Zinc Chandler ever followed?

A lot of people were dying to find out. . . .

"Would make de Sade wince!"
—Kirkus Reviews

ONYX

BORIS STARLING
Messiah

"The killer's good...The best I've ever seen."

The first victim was found hanging from a rope. The second, beaten to death in a pool of blood. The third, decapitated. Their backgrounds were as strikingly different as the methods of their murders. But one chilling detail links all three crimes. The local police had enough evidence to believe they were witnessing a rare—and disturbing—phenomenon: the making of a serial killer...

"He'll kill again."

Investigator Red Metcalfe has made national headlines with his uncanny gift for tracking killers. Getting inside their heads. Feeling what they feel. He's interviewed the most notorious serial killers in the world. He knows what makes them tick. *But not this time.*

"Pray."

❑ 0-451-40900-0/$6.99